Praise for the novels of Michael Prescott

Last Breath

"[A] taut psychological thriller. . . . Prescott has managed to delve into the depths of the most twisted minds to produce a chilling, character-driven tale that will revitalize readers on a sleepy, snowbound night."　　　*—Publishers Weekly*

"Well written and psychologically sophisticated, filled with pulse-pounding suspense and page-turning plot. . . . Prescott's depiction of both the world of the cop and the killer is truly masterful. Scary and suspenseful, *Last Breath* will leave you breathless."　　　—Bentley Little, author of *The Return*

The Shadow Hunter

"[Weaves] brilliant elements of psychological horror into the standard hunter-and-hunted story."　　　*—Publishers Weekly*

"A thriller that gives new meaning to the word, *The Shadow Hunter* expands the parameters and adds a new dimension to the genre. . . . The fast-paced plot twists and turns like an out-of-control roller coaster, making the read irresistible, un-put-downable, and absolutely not a book you want to start late at night—not if you have to work the next morning."　　　—Crescent Blues

Comes the Dark

"Michael Prescott delivers a harrowing thriller of the first order. His characters are flesh-and-blood real, the atmosphere's intense, and the plot races along unceasingly."　　　—Jeffery Deaver, *New York Times* bestselling author

"Prescott effectively captures the pain experienced by his characters and how it leads them to terrifying acts of desperation."　　　*—Publishers Weekly*

"A first-class thriller. . . . Prescott's smooth writing propels readers through a series of flashbacks woven into ongoing events. . . . First-rate!"　　　*—The Arizona Daily Star*

ALSO BY MICHAEL PRESCOTT

Last Breath
The Shadow Hunter
Stealing Faces
Comes the Dark

Published by Signet

NEXT VICTIM

Michael Prescott

A SIGNET BOOK

SIGNET
Published by New American Library, a division of
Penguin Putnam Inc., 375 Hudson Street,
New York, New York 10014, U.S.A.
Penguin Books Ltd, 80 Strand,
London WC2R 0RL, England
Penguin Books Australia Ltd, Ringwood,
Victoria, Australia
Penguin Books Canada Ltd, 10 Alcorn Avenue,
Toronto, Ontario, Canada M4V 3B2
Penguin Books (N.Z.) Ltd, 182–190 Wairau Road,
Auckland 10, New Zealand

Penguin Books Ltd, Registered Offices:
Harmondsworth, Middlesex, England

First published by Signet, an imprint of New American Library,
a division of Penguin Putnam Inc.

First Printing, December 2002
10 9 8 7 6 5 4 3 2 1

 REGISTERED TRADEMARK—MARCA REGISTRADA

Printed in the United States of America

PUBLISHER'S NOTE

This is a work of fiction. Names, characters, places, and incidents either
are the product of the author's imagination or are used fictitiously,
and any resemblance to actual persons, living or dead, business
establishments, events, or locales is entirely coincidental.

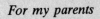

For my parents

For they have sown the wind,
and they shall reap the whirlwind.

—Hosea 8:7

PROLOGUE: 1968

The standoff was in its fourth hour.

Mason Howard, sheriff of Cibola County, stood under the noonday sun in the parking lot of a Howard Johnson's Motor Inn fifty miles west of Albuquerque. Not far away, traffic rushed past on Route 66—truckers on long hauls, locals running errands, families taking road trips. And maybe, every once in a while, somebody in flight from the law.

Somebody like the woman whose Buick Grand Sport was parked outside room 24 of the HoJo, the woman who had locked and barricaded herself in her room and was holding a gun.

Howard lifted the bullhorn in his left hand—he was keeping his right hand free in case he had to draw his sidearm in a hurry—and tried again to get through to her.

"Mrs. Beckett." His amplified voice rippled across the hot macadam. "There's no need for anyone to get hurt, ma'am. We can settle things nice and reasonable if you'll just come on out here."

The window of room 24 was open, although the drapes were drawn. Music played inside the room— the same damn song, over and over.

Above the music rose a high, quavering reply: "Leave me *alone!*"

Howard lowered the megaphone. He glanced at Deputy Trilling, standing beside him against the open door of a department cruiser. Never having been in a shoot-out, Trilling seemed to believe that the door would offer cover if the lady opened fire. He was wrong. Bullets could cut through a car door as easy as a knife through cheese.

Howard decided not to disabuse him of the notion. All he said was, "She's losing it."

Lloyd Trilling made a snorting sound, his nearest approach to laughter. "I'd say she lost it a long time ago. 'Round the time she amscrayed with the kid and went on the lam."

The kid. Right there was the nub of the problem. If Melinda Beckett had been alone in the motel room, Howard would have been content to wait her out indefinitely.

But there was the kid, Melinda's eight-year-old boy, trapped with his suicidal mom. Yesterday she'd abducted the boy from her estranged hubby, a Mr. Harrison Beckett of Casper, Wyoming, and driven six hundred miles while an APB was put out across all the western states.

At seven-thirty this morning Deputy Trilling had spotted the gold Grand Sport convertible with the flashy red stripe in the HoJo's parking lot. After confirming the license number, he'd radioed for backup. Howard had hoped to take the woman by surprise when she checked out, but one of the arriving deputies had made the mistake of driving past the window. Melinda had seen the squad car and figured out what was going on.

Now she was holed up inside with a gun and a kid

and a bunch of psychotic thoughts racing through her head. And she was playing that stupid record again and again.

"What the hell is that song, anyway?" he muttered.

"The one she's hooked on?" Trilling was a pop music buff. "It's the Surfaris, Mason. God, weren't you ever young?"

"If I was, I don't recall it now. What or who are the Safaris?"

"*Surf*aris," Trilling corrected. "Rock 'n' roll band out of California. Like the Beach Boys. You heard of *them*, haven't you?"

"I may have. You still didn't tell me the name of the song."

" 'Wipe Out.' That's what they call it."

"Great. 'Wipe Out.' That sounds mighty encouraging."

There was a pause, and then Trilling asked, "So what the hell we gonna do, Mason?" He kept his voice low so the other deputies positioned around the parking lot, eight in all, couldn't hear him address the sheriff by his first name. It was an informality Howard permitted no one else while on duty. He and Lloyd went back a ways, and besides, Lloyd had married Howard's sister.

"We keep talking," Howard said stolidly.

"I don't know. She's losing it, like you said. She might just go ahead and pop that little munchkin of hers."

"She loves the boy. That's why she snatched him."

"Love makes a woman do crazy things."

Howard couldn't argue with that. He'd been through two wives and was working on his third, and as far as he was concerned, all three had been as nutty as a pecan pie when love got hold of them.

"If she gets the idea that we're gonna take the kid away from her," Trilling went on, "she could shoot him just out of plain spite."

"Well, what do you propose we do, Lloyd?" Howard meant the question to be rhetorical or sarcastic or whatever the word was, but Trilling was ready with an answer.

"I say we go in through that open window."

"There's a lady on the other side of that window with a firearm that may be loaded."

"Here's how I see it. You talk on the bullhorn, right? She has to get near the window in order to shout back and be heard over that song. Me and Thompson and Donnigan, we're waiting, crouched down, right outside. When she yells to you, we'll know pretty much exactly where she is. We go in through the drapes, and I tackle her just like Dick Butkus bringing down Bart Starr."

"That's great, Lloyd. Then while you're rolling around on the floor with her, she snaps off a round and plugs you in the chest."

"Hell, she's a woman. I'll pin her to the mat before she can do a damn thing."

"Forget it. I'm not making Barbara a widow."

"We got to do *something*."

"We *are* doing something. We're keeping her contained. We're wearing her down."

"You might wanna think twice about that, Sheriff."

The voice belonged to Deputy Arnold, who was supposed to be minding the station house and was instead creeping up behind Howard's cruiser.

Howard reminded the deputy that he had left his post, in a tone that strongly suggested he'd better have a good reason.

He did. "Two pieces of news for you, and neither one of 'em ought to go out over the squawk box. First off, Darnell over at the *Trib* has got wind of this and he's coming over. And if Darnell's in on it, you know Lucy can't be far behind."

"Damn." Lucy Pigeon was a reporter for Albuquerque radio station KKOB, and she and Tom Darnell of the Albuquerque *Tribune* were engaged to be married. "So we'll have two reporters on the scene, one of 'em broadcasting live."

"It gets worse."

"How can it?"

"The husband of Ma Barker in there"—Arnold jerked a thumb at the motel—"called me from the Texaco in Alcomita. He's coming to the station house. Been on the road ever since the cops in Casper told him we'd located his wife and kid."

Howard shook his head. This was a pickle. The press, a radio reporter—and Harrison Beckett, the hostage's dad. The town of Alcomita was only a few miles from the sheriff's station in Grants. Mr. Beckett would be there in no time. And once Lucy began airing the story, every radio and TV station from here to Flagstaff would be sending a crew. Things would get ugly in a hurry.

"See, Mason?" Trilling blurted. "We got to make our move."

"Don't call me Mason, Deputy," Howard snapped for Arnold's benefit.

"Sorry, sir. But we can't wait her out. It'll be a circus soon. We'll lose control of the situation."

We never had control, Howard wanted to say. It was just like that mess they had going over there in Vietnam. There was the illusion of control, of a strategy, but all the time circumstances were conspiring to shoot the generals' careful plans all to shit.

He thought for a minute as a seam of sweat stitched down his cheek.

"Okay," he said. "We'll do it your way, Deputy Trilling. Get Thompson and Donnigan together and fill 'em in."

Trilling scooted away to find the other two.

"And you, Deputy Arnold—get back to the station. When Mr. Beckett shows up, stall him. Keep him the hell away from here. And if you need to reach me again, use the damn radio. I don't care who picks up the signal."

Then Arnold was gone, and Howard was alone by the side of his car. He adjusted his hat, licked his fingers so he'd have some traction if he had to draw his gun, and hoped he had made the right decision. In the distance that damn song kept playing. "Wipe Out"—he hoped it wasn't an omen.

Two minutes later he saw Trilling, Thompson, and Donnigan approach the motel door, hugging the wall. Their revolvers were out, sunlight glinting off the barrels. Thompson and Donnigan looked wary. Trilling seemed to be enjoying himself. He was a hot dog, that one. Get himself killed someday.

Howard waited until the three were in position by the window. Then he switched on the megaphone.

"Mrs. Beckett? We can wait all afternoon if you like, but I don't see how that'll accomplish much. You and your boy must be getting hungry. How about you open up and we get you both some breakfast?"

Only music from the room. Trilling glanced at Howard, who tried a second time to elicit a response.

"Even if you're not hungry, ma'am, I'll bet your boy is. They got a good restaurant here at HoJo's. What do you say I have them fry up some eggs and nice crispy bacon?"

Still nothing but the song.

"Mrs. Beckett?"

Sunlight reflected off the megaphone onto Howard's face. The heat and glare were something awful.

"Come on, Mrs. Beckett, I'm making a very reasonable offer, don't you think?" He tried a little joke. "It's not every day you get a free breakfast."

All she had to do was curse him out, tell him to go to hell, say anything that would allow the three deputies to establish her position before they climbed through the window. But she wasn't talking.

Howard figured he'd give it one more try. If it didn't work, he'd call off the forced entry and go back to his original plan, and if Lucy Pigeon made it a circus, so be it.

"I know what you're going through, Mrs. Beckett. I know how hard it can be." He thought this approach just might reach her. "Nothing's fair in this world, but—"

A sound cut him off. A faraway sound, not loud but easily recognizable. To an unpracticed ear it might have been the snap of a clothesline on a windy day or the smack of a screen door slapping shut, but Howard knew it was a gunshot, and it had come from room 24.

"Mrs. Beckett—"

A second crack of sound.

The drapes in the open window rustled in a breath of wind.

Trilling was looking at him. Howard shouted, "Go in!" and broke into a run, covering yards of hot macadam, while the deputies arrayed around the parking lot scrambled to follow.

By the time he reached the window, Trilling and the other two were already inside. The drapes had been thrust apart, and even before climbing into the room, Howard could see the sprawled shape of a woman's body on the carpet, a dark pool like an oil stain spreading around her head.

She was finished. Over the years Howard had seen enough of death to know it at a glance.

But there had been two shots, damn it.

"Where the hell's the boy?" Howard yelled over the blare from a portable phonograph as he swung both legs over the window frame.

"In here."

Trilling's voice. Low and shaky.

Howard muscled Thompson and Donnigan out of his way and entered the bathroom. Deputy Trilling stood over the tub. Howard moved closer and saw soapy water sloshing against the porcelain sides, water dyed pink with slow spirals of blood.

The boy lay faceup in the bath, nude, a toy submarine floating near him.

"God damn," Howard said.

"Like I told you." Trilling barely whispered the words. "Just out of plain spite."

Howard marshaled his professionalism. "Get the boy out of there. Check for a pulse. Try mouth-to-mouth and chest compression."

It was hopeless, but procedures had to be followed. Howard left Trilling with his arms in the bloody water and returned to the main room. Donnigan was nearest the phone.

"Call for an ambulance," Howard ordered.

Donnigan blinked. "Is the boy . . . ?"

"Just do it."

He looked at the record player, resting near the window. One of the deputies, scrambling in, must have jostled the machine and scratched the disk. The stylus was stuck in one groove, repeating the same sound over and over—someone's giggly falsetto saying, "Wipe out . . . !"

His radio crackled with Deputy Arnold's voice. "Sheriff?"

"Wipe out . . . !"

Howard thumbed the transmit button. "I copy, over."

"He's here, sir. Mr. Beckett is here."

"Wipe out . . . !"

"Turn off that fucking thing," Howard said to the nearest deputy.

A screech as the stylus was yanked across the platter.

"Sheriff?" Arnold again. "You read me?"

"I read you, Deputy."

"What should I tell him, sir? What do I tell Mr. Beckett about his wife and boy?"

Mason Howard stared out the window and wished he knew the answer to that.

PART ONE

PART ONE

1

She was running hard down an alley with her Sig Sauer 9mm in her hand, her shout echoing off the high brick walls.

"Stop, FBI!"

The suspect did not stop or even turn to look at her. His shoes slapped the asphalt. He was pulling away, blending into the nocturnal shadows. Soon he would be only another shadow himself.

She put on some speed. There was no point in shouting again. She would only waste her breath.

Yards ahead the alley opened on a street streaming with traffic. She saw the suspect as a silhouette, his figure limned by rushing headlights.

If he reached the street and made a dash through the traffic, he would lose her.

But she wouldn't let that happen.

With a rush of adrenaline she lengthened her strides, closing the gap until finally she reached out with her left hand and grabbed his shirt collar.

She gave it a hard yank and jerked him off balance like a dog surprised by a sudden tug on its chain— and like a dog, he snarled as he whipped around, and she saw a flash of teeth.

Not teeth. Steel.

A knife.

The blade drove at her. She spun clear and almost fired at him, but she was afraid that a shot at point-blank range would kill him, and she didn't want him dead.

Instead she chopped his wrist with the side of her hand, splaying his fingers. The knife fell, and before he could retrieve it, she'd taken a step back and fixed him in the pistol's sights.

"Don't move; you are under arrest."

She still thought he might try something, and she was ready to try for a nonlethal shot, in violation of her academy training, in which the advisability of always taking the kill shot had been emphasized.

But he surprised her by raising his hands in submission. Then she heard footsteps behind her, approaching at a run. She didn't want to take her eyes off the suspect, and especially the suspect's hands, the two danger points, so without looking back she called out, "Who's coming?"

"LAPD," a male voice answered.

Must be the uniformed cop she'd seen on Melrose. It didn't escape her notice that it was a patrol officer, not the two special agents sharing surveillance duty with her in the van, who'd come to her aid.

"I'm FBI," she said, still watching the suspect. He remained in silhouette. A lanky figure, medium tall, with close-cropped hair and wiry arms. She could not judge his age or ethnicity. If he was a white male around forty years old, she would be very happy.

The patrolman trotted up beside her and gave his name—Payton.

"Tess McCallum," she said.

"What the hell happened? I saw you jump out of a parked minivan and take off after this guy."

"He was already running. That's why I chased him."

"Come again?"

"He was about to go into Aspen." Aspen was a club on Melrose Avenue, near the entrance to the alley. "Then he caught sight of you and turned away. As soon as you weren't looking, he broke into a run."

"Scared of cops, is he? Now why would that be?"

Payton snapped on his flashlight to get a look at the suspect, and Tess was instantly disappointed.

He was a white male. That much was good. But he wasn't any older than twenty-five.

He was not the man she'd hoped for.

"I don't know him," Payton said. "He put up any resistance?"

"Tried to cut me." She bobbed her head at the knife on the asphalt. The flashlight beam swung over to it, revealing it as a cheap switchblade.

"That wasn't so smart, asshole. Up against the trash bin. Come on, move it."

Payton handcuffed the suspect, then made him spread his legs as he patted him down. In the pocket of the young man's pants he found a bag of white powder.

"Coke," the patrolman said. "He was probably going into the bar to make a sale. Saw a uniform and freaked."

Tess had put her gun back into the special compartment in her purse now that Payton was in command of the situation. "Well, it's your bust. Local crime."

"Unless you want to make it assault on a federal officer," Payton said, obviously hoping for a bigger collar.

"I'll let it ride. The knife probably just slipped a little in my direction. Isn't that right, sir?"

The suspect, who hadn't said one word so far, looked at her and muttered, "Suck me off, bitch."

Payton told him that was no way to address a lady. Tess just laughed.

"LA's one hell of a town, isn't it?" Payton said wearily.

"I wouldn't know. I'm just visiting."

"Lucky you."

"You didn't really think it was him, did you?"

Tess looked at Special Agent Collins as she climbed back into the van. "You never know," she answered. "He was the right height, right build, and he ran from a cop. Thanks for backing me up, by the way."

Collins shrugged. Diaz, wearing headphones as he listened to the sounds in the bar, was more conciliatory. "We had to keep an eye on Barber." Julie Barber was the agent stationed inside Aspen, whose job was to fend off come-ons from patrons who didn't match the profile, while encouraging anyone who looked like a possible suspect.

"Anything happen inside?" Tess asked.

"Not a thing," Collins said. "Like last night, and the night before that, and the night—"

"Point taken." Tess refused to be ruffled. "We're not the only ones pulling this detail. Maybe one of the other squads will get lucky."

"Maybe pigs will fly. Face it, this son of a bitch is too smart to return to this neighborhood. He'll show up someplace else next time. Santa Barbara, San Diego. Anywhere but here."

Tess was inclined to agree. Trouble was, they couldn't watch every bar on the southern California coast. They had to make a stand somewhere.

She was about to point this out when her purse began to chirp. Her cell phone was ringing.

She answered it. "McCallum."

"You'd better get over to the field office," said a voice she recognized as belonging to Peter Larkin.

She disliked Larkin. And she didn't intend to let

him order her around. "I'm working surveillance, remember?"

"I remember. Let Collins and Diaz handle it. You got your own vehicle there?"

"Yes, but—"

"Stop wasting time, Agent McCallum. Just haul ass over here."

"What's going on, Peter?" she asked in a more cautious voice.

"Nothing much. It's just that we may have got him, that's all. I really hope you can find time to join us."

He clicked off, and she was left staring at the silent phone in her hand.

2

We may have got him.

The words chased Tess McCallum like ghosts as she guided the bureau sedan west on Wilshire Boulevard, past the shops and palm trees of Beverly Hills. The sunset had faded out hours ago, and somewhere above the smog, the stars were shining.

She powered through an intersection as the stoplight cycled from yellow to red, ignoring a horn that blared at her. She would not be stopped by traffic lights.

She had to see him. Had to look at his face.

Could they really have caught him—finally, after two years? There was no way to be sure. But she wouldn't have been pulled away from the undercover detail on Melrose if all they had was another "possible," like that one last week, the salesman who had turned out to be only a run-of-the-mill adulterer.

The streets were busy, as always, and she had to swing from lane to lane, passing slower cars. The bureau car—or "bucar" in the ridiculous terminology of the FBI—was a blue Crown Victoria, only two years old, with good acceleration and smooth handling. It invited her to take risks. She only hoped a cop didn't pull her over. The FBI badge in her wallet would probably save her from a ticket, but a traffic stop would slow her down.

She reached the intersection of Wilshire and Santa Monica. Not far from Westwood now. The dashboard clock read 9:58.

She wondered if Andrus had been called. If he had been, then they must be really sure. It was March 29— Friday on Easter weekend—and although she didn't think of Andrus as particularly religious, she knew they wouldn't disturb an assistant director on Good Friday without cause.

On impulse she removed her cell phone from her purse and speed-dialed the field office's switchboard, then asked for Larkin. "This is McCallum again," she said when Larkin came on. "I'm five, ten minutes out. What's going on?"

"Nothing that can't wait till you get here." As always, Larkin treated her with supercilious disrespect. It wasn't possible to hear a man smirk over the phone, but Tess could swear she heard it anyway.

"Just give me the rundown," she said.

He sighed, perturbed at this misuse of his time. "The guy's name, address, DL, and SSN all check out. No priors. They haven't read him his rights yet." It was legal to obtain preliminary information on a suspect without a Miranda warning. "Right now we've got him cooling his heels."

This was standard procedure. Some suspects lost their nerve after as little as ten minutes alone in the bare institutional setting of the interrogation room. Then the Stockholm syndrome would kick in, and they would cooperate with their interrogators, sometimes even confess. The downside was that often these confessions were false.

"Are Gaines and Michaelson there?" she asked. Gaines was a profiler working the case. Michaelson was the squad supervisor, experienced at interrogation.

"Gaines just arrived. We're expecting Michaelson any second."

"Who made the bust?"

"Tyler, Hart, and DiFranco. They're in the surveillance room. Michaelson and Gaines may want Tyler in on the questioning at some point."

"And me? Do they want me in?"

"I don't think that's such a good idea."

She hadn't asked for his opinion. "We'll talk about it. How about Andrus?"

"He's here."

So they *had* called him. "I guess he looks good for it, this guy?" she said, holding her voice steady.

"It's still preliminary."

Obviously Larkin would tell her only the bare minimum. She ought to be angry, but all she felt was nervous tension. "Try to hold off the interview till I get there."

"Michaelson's the case agent. He's the one in charge."

Tess knew that. "Just take your time briefing him, okay?" She clicked off without waiting for an answer and dumped the phone back into her handbag.

She hated talking to Larkin. Hated talking to any of them, really, except Andrus. The others treated her with a mixture of pity and scorn. Pity for what had happened in Denver. Scorn because they liked to think they would have handled it better. They were men, after all. They didn't let things get to them. But she was a woman—and women, well, they got emotional about these things.

Of course, they didn't know the whole story. Only Andrus knew, and she had prevailed on him not to share it with the others. It was irrelevant to the case.

It was her private life. She had given enough of her life to the bureau—more than enough. There were some things she meant to keep to herself.

She was in Westwood now, coursing down the wide corridor between rows of high-rise apartment buildings. Ahead, on her right, was Westwood Village, a cluster of movie theaters and T-shirt shops crowded with UCLA students.

Her destination lay to her left, at the southwest corner of Wilshire and Veteran—the twenty-story Federal Building that housed the Los Angeles field office of the FBI.

On most homicide investigations, local law enforcement authorities had jurisdiction and took the lead, and the bureau was brought in, if at all, only to provide consultation and analysis. But not this one. This was a federal case, and had been ever since the night of February 12, two years ago.

February 12.

The key in the lock. The key, turning. The key . . .

But she couldn't think about that now.

She pulled into the large, open parking lot adjacent to the building. Ordinarily it would be almost empty at night, but on weekends the lot was used by visitors to the Village. Even so, she found an available slot after less than a minute of searching.

She killed the Crown Victoria's engine and hurried inside, where she stabbed the elevator button and waited, shifting her weight restlessly.

The key in her hand, key in the lock, turning, no resistance . . .

Reliving the event was a symptom of posttraumatic stress. Her therapist had explained it to her. A traumatic event triggered stress hormones; the more hormones were pumped out, the more intensely the memory would be burned into the amygdala, a bundle of neurons in the brain. Whenever the experience was relived, new stress hormones were produced, further reinforcing the memory.

To break the cycle, it was necessary to brush aside the memories. Think about something else.

Something else. But there was nothing else. There was only the key in the lock, forever turning. . . .

Turning, and the door opening as she stepped into the house . . .

The elevator arrived, chiming faintly. The sound startled her into the present.

When the doors slid apart, she saw two men in suits.

Cops, not feds. She knew instantly. They had to be cops because she saw the faint outlines of their firearms under their jackets. But they weren't FBI, because their suits weren't stylish enough. Elitist but true.

She got in, pressing the button for the seventeenth floor.

"Going up?" one man asked. "So are we."

"We are?" the other cop asked with a lifted eyebrow.

"We are now," the first man said.

She looked at him. He was about forty, trim and self-possessed, but with a vaguely disreputable air. It was nothing she could pinpoint, just a suggestion of cunning that she disliked and distrusted.

"Didn't you just come down?" she asked.

"From eighteen." The elevator began to rise. "We were meeting with Tom Danner. Know him?"

"No." Distantly she remembered that Danner was a profiling consultant, like Gaines. Profilers often acted as liaisons with the local police. "If you've just seen him, why are you heading back up?"

He smiled. "No special reason. It's just a nice night for a ride."

Just what she needed. Don Juan in a cheap suit.

She looked at the numbers above the doors, not wanting to continue the conversation.

"I'm Jim Dodge," the cop said. "West LA Homicide. This is my partner, Al Bradley." Bradley was a big, broad-shouldered man with sleepy eyes.

"Nice to meet you," Tess said, turning away.

Dodge wasn't deterred. "And you are . . . ?"

"In a hurry."

"Hey, this is LA. Everybody's in a hurry. But you've got to slow down sometime. Stop and smell the flowers."

"I haven't had a lot of flowers in my life lately." The words came out fast, and instantly she regretted them. He would take the statement as a flirtation.

"You must have a name," he pressed. "It comes standard issue with the birth certificate."

"Tess McCallum." It was easier to tell him than to argue.

"You're new to this field office."

"Temporary assignment."

"Not too temporary, I hope."

Dodge was looking her over without a hint of self-consciousness. She found herself wondering if she looked all right in her gray suit and white blouse and Western-style string tie. The thought irritated her.

"Where you from?" he asked.

She wished the elevator would move faster. "Denver."

"Nice town. Enjoying LA?"

"I'm not here for enjoyment. I'm working."

"You can't work all the time."

"Look, Detective—"

"Jim."

"I'm involved with a case right now."

"So am I. Whole bunch of cases. How many open cases we got, Al?"

"More than I can count, Jimbo." Al Bradley spoke in an exhausted baritone.

"More than he can count," Dodge said, "and that's using his fingers *and* toes. We catch one bad guy, another pops up to replace him. The job never ends. To stay sane, you've got to loosen up a little. Not everything is life-and-death."

"That's a funny attitude for a homicide detective to take."

"I'm just saying you can't let a case take over your life."

"I already have."

"Oh, I get it. This time it's personal."

He wanted to be funny, but the joke hurt her like a slap.

"Extremely personal," she said.

The doors opened, and she stepped out. Behind her, Dodge said, "Hey." He was holding a business card. "In case you get lonely."

"No, thanks."

"Take it. It's good for a free dinner."

Because she didn't have time to debate the issue, she took the card and stuffed it in the side pocket of her jacket without even giving it a look.

"That's my cell number. You can reach me anytime." He smiled. "It's my snitch card. You know, the one I give out—"

"To informants. I'm glad to join such elevated company."

She walked away, not looking back, and heard Al Bradley ask his partner, "What the hell was that all about?"

The elevator doors slid shut before she heard Detective Dodge's answer.

She had been rude to him, but—oh, hell, it didn't matter.

Larkin buzzed her into suite 1700 and greeted her in the reception room. "You must've exceeded a few posted speed limits," he said.

"All in a good cause. Which room is he in?"

"Whoa, not so fast. Andrus wants to brief you first."

"Can't you handle that?"

"You know, Agent McCallum, most people wouldn't turn up their nose at a meeting with the AD."

"I guess my instinct for personal advancement isn't as refined as it could be."

"I'd say that's obvious." Larkin opened the door to the interior corridor with a card key and led Tess out of the reception area.

Tess waited almost a full minute before allowing him to know that he'd gotten to her. "What made you say that?" she asked as they strode down a carpeted corridor past rows of squad room doors.

Larkin didn't bother to glance back at her. "Say what?"

"Don't play around. It's boring."

"You mean my comment about your career advancement? All I meant was that you're still stuck in the Denver office, when by now you probably could've been—should've been—a SAC or at least an ASAC somewhere."

"By now. After Black Tiger, you mean."

"You got everybody's attention with that bust, but you didn't know how to use it. So now you're taking orders from guys like Michaelson—and taking a lot of shit from people like me."

She couldn't argue. By his own petty logic Larkin

was right. She had been on the fast track, and if her career had stalled, it was no one's fault but her own.

"Speaking of Michaelson, did I beat him here?" she asked.

"Got here a few minutes ago."

"Damn."

"Don't get your knickers in a twist. You haven't missed much."

"How would you know?"

"The interrogation is just under way. They're probably still working up the nerve to Mirandize the guy."

This was likely to be true. The recitation of the Miranda warnings was a tricky business that had to be approached with care. Handle it wrong, and the suspect would insist on seeing his lawyer, ending the interview before it began. The trick was to lead up casually to the warnings, then deliver them in a perfunctory tone that minimized the importance of the ritual. If the suspect thought the reading was a formality, he would usually waive his rights.

"I still wish you'd waited," she said irritably.

"Point taken and duly noted."

"Who is he? What's his name?"

"The AD will tell you everything you need to know."

"Right." *You officious little prick.* "How long has Andrus been here?"

He looked at her, a thin, ambiguous smile riding on his lips. "Little while now."

She didn't see what was so funny. She continued the walk in silence.

With its carpeted floors, fluorescent lighting fixtures, and utilitarian furnishings, suite 1700 could have passed for the headquarters of any bland corporate enterprise, and in fact much of the work done here was decidedly white-collar—investigations of check-fraud rings, telemarketing scams, Ponzi schemes, and assorted nonviolent activities. That was the more genteel part of the operation. Then there was the stuff that made the news—bank robberies, star stalkings, drug busts, an occasional high-profile abduction, and terrorism, the bureau's new focus, the crime of the new millennium.

The LA field division was one of the bureau's largest, employing six hundred agents and covering a vast metropolitan sprawl. For these reasons, and because LA was a nexus of media coverage, the office was run by an assistant director, rather than a special agent in charge. Andrus had been on the job for two years, and no doubt would be promoted before long to a stint at bureau headquarters in DC. Unlike Tess, the AD's instinct for career advancement had never been in need of any honing.

She and Larkin reached a corner of the suite, where the media office and the office of the assistant director were arranged catercorner in evident acknowledgment of the importance of public relations in the AD's job profile.

Andrus's voice—thin, reedy, with carefully cultivated enunciation—was audible through his open door.

"What do you mean, deteriorated?"

A beat of silence as an answer was given. Andrus was on the phone.

"Hard target? You mean she's on to you, for Christ's sake? . . . Damn it, Tennant, you can't afford to screw this up."

Tennant. The name was familiar to Tess, but she couldn't place it.

"All right, all right. Let me know as soon as you've got them in custody."

The conversation was over. Tess wondered what it

had been about. But she dismissed the question. It didn't matter.

Whoever Tennant was and whatever he was involved in, it had nothing to do with her.

3

Amanda Pierce had hoped to lose her pursuers nearly six hours ago, when she had driven through Sacramento.

She'd left Interstate 5 at the outskirts of the city limits, then had taken the surface streets through the center of town. The time had been four P.M., the start of rush hour on a Friday afternoon, and traffic had been heavy.

At first, watching her rearview mirror, she had seen no one obviously tailing her. She'd allowed herself to believe that she was safe. She'd been misinformed. Her contact was paranoid, probably, like most of the people in his line of work. The ones who were still alive, anyway.

Pierce was still congratulating herself on her good fortune when she glimpsed a white van behind her. There were two occupants, and both appeared to be Caucasian males, a not uncommon profile for employees of the FBI. The van was sticking close, as was necessary for clandestine pursuit in dense urban traffic.

Damn, damn, damn.

It could be just an ordinary van, but she knew better. She'd seen it on I-5, a hundred miles north of Sacramento. The same two men inside.

So her contact wasn't crazy, after all. The fucking feds really were on to her.

Briefly she considered aborting the mission. But of course it was too late. If they knew enough to shadow her, they knew enough to put her in a federal prison. And she could expect no leniency from any judge or jury—not when they learned what she was carrying in the suitcase on her Sunbird's backseat.

They would put her away forever. Maximum security. Lesbian guards, dangerous showers, broom-handle rapes—shit, her life would be a goddamn made-for-cable movie.

The chilly feeling at the back of her neck was dread. She honestly hadn't expected to be caught. She'd thought she was playing the game so adroitly, staying three steps ahead of any possible threat.

Now the threat was right behind her, in the form of a white van with two pale white men inside.

The van was the command vehicle, the one in direct visual contact with the target—the target, in this case, being Pierce herself. There would be other vehicles, most likely a total of four or five, all weaving a loose, flexible net around her, a formation known in mobile surveillance work as a "floating box." She had to identify them if she was to know what she was up against.

She guided the Sunbird through the grid of city streets. The second vehicle was easy to pinpoint. It was a station wagon puttering along ahead of her, the driver using his brakes too often. Standard surveillance technique—distract the target with intentionally poor driving. Anyway, she was fairly certain she had seen the station wagon on the interstate also.

She looked back, careful to use only the rearview mirror—the first rule in this game was never to look over one's shoulder—and saw that the van was gone. An amateur would have taken comfort in that fact. Pierce knew it was only a standard signature shift, the characteristic leapfrogging pursuit of an A-B surveillance protocol.

The vehicle now in visual contact with her was a taxicab. It had changed places with the van to make the detection of either automobile less likely.

Three of them so far. There might be one or two more. Outriders on her left and right.

To find out, she executed a quick left turn at the next intersection, not using her turn signal. The taxi continued straight through, but a coupe in the left lane peeled off and followed her.

Now the coupe was in the command position, and the other vehicles were pacing her on parallel streets. If she could ditch the coupe, she might break out of the box altogether.

She eased into the right lane, behind a slow-moving bus, forcing the coupe to motor past her to avoid being conspicuous. When it was safely ahead, she checked her rearview mirror. Still no sign of the van, the taxi, or the station wagon.

Taking advantage of a momentary break in the traffic, she flipped a U-turn, cutting off a motorcyclist in the opposite lane, who threatened her with a gloved fist.

She ignored her rearview mirror now. The driver of the coupe would not be so foolish as to attempt a high-profile maneuver like a U-turn directly behind her. Instead she watched the oncoming traffic in the other lane.

There. A panel truck was making a left turn onto a side street. As she passed the street, the truck pulled out behind her.

This was the fifth vehicle, now in the command position.

She might yet have a chance to break out. Ahead of her, a stoplight was cycling from green to yellow. She gunned the Sunbird's motor and flashed through the intersection just as the light turned red. The panel truck was stuck idling at the light. Redboarded.

Gotcha, Pierce thought with savage satisfaction.

Wait.

Ahead of her, parked at the curb—the white van. It pulled out in front of her.

And here came the taxi, cruising at her rear.

There was no way out of the box. The feds were all around her, hemming her in. And after her recent exhibition of evasive driving tactics, they now knew she was on to them. It would be harder than ever to break free.

She could not break out of the box. Not here.

Her best shot was to get back on the freeway and continue south. LA was a bigger city. It offered more possibilities for countersurveillance action. And she would have hours to sort out her options, reacquaint herself with her intel training, and determine her next move.

They hadn't beaten her yet. They had her in a corner, but she could fight her way out of a corner if she had to.

And if they tried to take her down, she wouldn't go alone.

That had been six hours and four hundred miles earlier. Now, rigid at the wheel, fatigued after the day-long drive and the 360 miles covered on Thursday, operating on no sleep and almost no food, Amanda Pierce drove into Los Angeles.

She took the 405 freeway when it branched off from I-5. It carried her through the San Fernando Valley, over the mountains toward West LA.

In the darkness she could no longer see the vehicles in pursuit, but she knew they were behind her and ahead of her and probably pacing her in other lanes. She'd made no effort to lose them after leaving Sacramento. By now, her friends from the FBI might have been lulled into thinking that her evasive actions had been merely a precautionary measure. They might believe that she actually had no idea she was being followed.

She hoped so. Their complacency might give her an edge. An edge she desperately needed, since soon she would have her last chance to break free.

The dashboard clock read 10:15. She was expected to be at the hotel by eleven. It would be tight. Would her contact wait for her if she was delayed?

"He'd better, God damn it," Pierce muttered, her voice raw from the tension stiffening her vocal cords.

She had risked everything for this meeting. And now that she was exposed, her cover blown, she needed it more than ever.

The freeway crested the low range of the Santa Monica Mountains and descended. The basin of Los Angeles slid into view, a huge bowl of light cupped by the black fingers of hills and desert and sea.

Pierce thought she'd come a long way from Hermiston, Oregon.

And whatever happened tonight, however things worked out, she wasn't going back.

4

The assistant director's office was tidy and almost sterile, not unlike its occupant. His desk was uncluttered, the walls all but bare. There were none of the usual accoutrements of power—plaques and certificates, photos of the agent shaking hands with the president or receiving a commendation. In the bureau this sort of display was known cynically as an I-love-me wall. Nearly every office had one. But not this office.

"Evening, Tess," Andrus said as she and Larkin entered. "I suppose you heard some of that phone call."

"The tail end," Tess admitted, before Larkin could deny it.

"Typical bureau infighting. This guy flies in from outside the division and wants to do everything his own way. I have to ride him hard just to get him to check in with me. It's just one of many hassles you'll have to deal with when they make you an SAC one day."

He said this without focusing his gaze on either of them in particular, but Tess felt sure the comment had been intended for her. Then again, maybe Larkin felt the same way, and maybe Andrus had meant to keep them guessing. He enjoyed little power plays of that sort.

"Anyway," Andrus added, "I'm glad you're here, Tess. I just hope this isn't a false alarm."

She felt her optimism fizzle just a little. "You think it is?"

"It's thin."

"There must be something to it, if Agent Larkin called you in."

"Actually I never left. Working late. If I'd been gone, I doubt Peter would have buzzed me."

"Not on something this preliminary," Larkin said. Tess looked at him, and he pasted a smile on his face. "I'm sorry, Agent McCallum. Didn't I make myself clear?"

He'd been playing her, she realized. It had amused him to build up her hopes.

"Have a seat," Andrus said, oblivious to the interplay.

Tess felt too restless to sit, but in the long run it was always quicker to do things Andrus's way. That was a lesson she had learned in Denver, when for three years Gerald Andrus had been the special agent in charge, supervising her on a daily basis, before moving on to bigger things.

She sat across from the AD, hunching forward, while he leaned back behind his desk. Larkin settled into a chair in a corner.

"So," Andrus said, "you want the long or short version?"

"Just the basics."

He nodded. For a moment he said nothing, and she knew he was organizing the relevant facts in order to present them with maximum efficiency. Everything about Andrus suggested a spare, abstemious discipline, from his gaunt physique and erect posture to the steel-framed glasses riding on his pinched nose. He was unmarried, a workaholic in his early forties, a man sketched in shades of gray—ash-gray eyes, silver-gray hair, and a pale, unlined face.

"They picked him up at the safe house at nine-thirty," Andrus said finally. "He was carrying a roll of duct tape. Tried to use it on Tyler."

"Same brand of tape as before?"

"No."

"How about the knife?"

"Either he didn't have one, or he ditched it. I have two people scouring the safe house now."

This sounded less and less promising. Wrong brand of tape, no knife . . .

"Does he fit the profile?" she asked, looking for a reason to be hopeful.

Andrus waved off the question. "Profile. You know how much confidence I have in that psychobabble crap. I'll trust my gut instinct every time."

Tess did her best not to smile. If there was one thing Assistant Director Andrus lacked, it was gut instinct.

He had never been much of a street agent. His skills were managerial, bureaucratic. He was a paper pusher, a desk jockey. He knew how to cut overhead, allocate resources, do more with less. These talents had made him popular with his superiors on Ninth Street— bureau-speak for FBI headquarters—but had done nothing to endear him to agents in the field.

Then there was the family connection. Andrus's father had been a top man under Hoover, part of the inner circle of those days. It was generally assumed that if his daddy hadn't been a bureau man, Andrus would be pushing papers for a blue-chip corporation, not working for Uncle Sam. Tess found it admirable, in a blanched, joyless sort of way, that Andrus had devoted himself to law enforcement when he might have been happier and wealthier pursuing other goals. Other agents merely resented him for the fast career track that came with being a privileged son.

"Well," she said evenly, "sometimes Behavioral Sciences gets it right. Does he fit the profile or not?"

"He fits," Andrus conceded. "Of course, we hardly need a profiler to tell us the more obvious things—residence in Denver at the time of the last murders, above-average intelligence, knowledge of mathematical concepts."

"This man is from Denver?"

"Colorado Springs," Larkin said, wanting to join the conversation. "And he's a civil engineer."

Tess looked at them both. "An engineer."

Andrus nodded. "Worked on the Metro Red Line, the subway system, or so he says. But before you get excited, let me reiterate what I said earlier—it's thin."

"Because of the tape and the knife?"

"Yes. And the assault on Tyler. It was clumsy, tentative. Not what we would expect from Mobius."

Mobius.

Even now, Tess hated to hear that name spoken aloud. The three syllables seemed to hang in the office's recirculated air like a death rattle.

"Nothing about this case," she said softly, "is what we would expect. Not in a rational world."

Andrus shook his head with paternal benevolence. "Who ever said it was a rational world, Tess?"

Larkin allowed himself a little laugh.

Tess didn't answer. Andrus was right. Yet there had been a time, not so long ago, when she had thought the world made sense. Part of her still wanted to believe it.

Another part of her, the dominant part, could not forget the evening of February 12.

The key in the lock . . . the door opening . . . and in the kitchen, the water running in the sink . . .

Briskly, Andrus reviewed the details of the bust. The suspect was William Hayde, forty-two, never married. His age, his Colorado background, his solitary lifestyle, his job as a civil engineer—it all fit.

"And even so," Andrus finished, rising, "I still say

Hayde is a red herring. I'll bet you lunch at Giuseppe's on that."

Tess smiled. "Giuseppe's?"

"Great restaurant. You've got to try it."

"I haven't had much of an appetite lately."

Andrus didn't respond. He straightened his jacket—in the years Tess had known him, she had never once seen him with his jacket off—and shrugged on a dark trench coat, just like in the movies. Tess asked where he was going.

"Home . . . where all decent self-respecting people should be on a Friday night. I have a Yorkshire terrier who needs to be fed—assuming he hasn't broken open the kitchen cabinet by now and foraged for his own dinner—and there's a stack of three-oh-twos I'm over-due about reading."

"Sounds like fun."

"I lead a full life, Tess. Call me if this clown turns out to be the real thing. Believe me, I'll be happy to pick up the tab at that restaurant." He turned to Lar-kin. "Step into the hall, Peter. I want a moment in private with Agent McCallum."

Larkin, peeved, did as he was told. Andrus shut the office door. "So, Tess . . . how are they treating you?"

She shrugged. "The way any interloper would be treated. With suspicion, aversion, and disdain."

"I can talk to them."

"Please don't. That only . . ."

"Makes it worse?"

"It's office politics. They know I worked under you in Denver. They see me as some kind of threat. At least, some of them do. The more paranoid ones."

"And the rest? How do they see you?"

"As a washout."

"You're not, you know."

"I'm not sure what I am."

"If it weren't for Mobius—and what happened that night—"

The key in the lock. Water in the sink. Her footsteps on the stairs as she climbed to the second floor . . .

"I'd be in a different place right now," she said, finishing his statement for him. "Don't I know it. But thinking 'what if' doesn't get you anywhere."

Andrus hesitated, evidently dissatisfied with this answer. "What I really want to know is . . . how are you holding up?"

"Just fine."

"You're handling this okay?"

"Don't I seem to be?"

"I didn't mean professionally. I meant . . . on an emotional level."

Up the stairs to the upper floor, the gun in her hand, no sound anywhere in the house . . .

"I'm great," she said. "Really. Never better."

"We both know that's not true."

She saw his disappointment. He wanted her to trust him enough to level with him.

"Okay," she admitted, "I've been better. I've also been worse. Working other cases, waiting for this one to open up again—that was harder."

"At least now you're back in it."

"Right. And I'm hanging in there."

"Aren't we all." He hesitated. "Maybe I shouldn't have brought you in."

"You had to. And I have to be here. I have to be involved."

"Then I hope it brings you some closure."

Closure. God, how she hated that word, with all its smug psychoanalytic neatness. As if there could ever be closure. As if grief were a room in a house, and she could just shut the door and seal it away.

On the upper floor, moving down the hall toward

the bedroom, the door ajar, her heart beating loud against her ears . . .

"Thanks," she answered. "I hope so too."

There was a short silence as both of them tried to think of something more to say.

"If you need to talk . . ." Andrus managed.

"You're available. I know."

"Please keep it in mind."

She wouldn't, though. Andrus was not a man she would feel comfortable confiding in. He was too coldly analytical, too fussy and well organized. Besides, he knew too much already. She could preserve her privacy only if she kept her feelings to herself. Because her feelings were the only private part of her she had left.

But she couldn't tell him any of this, so all she said was "I will. 'Night, Gerry."

" 'Night, Tess."

She joined Larkin in the hall. They headed deeper into the maze of squad rooms and offices.

"Despite what the AD thinks," Tess said, "Mr. Hayde sounds promising to me."

Larkin grunted. "Mr. Hayde. You know, that name's almost like 'Mr. Hyde.' Only with an A."

"So?"

"Think it's an omen, maybe?"

She looked at him and saw that goddamned smirk. More games.

"Have we got a warrant for his house?" she asked.

"No probable cause. They checked his car, though. Without a warrant."

"I guess that's why Andrus didn't mention it."

"Probably. Anyway, they gave it a quick once-over—no forensics, just a visual. Didn't find anything."

"Anything else the AD neglected to tell me?"

"Only that Hayde's a cold fish. Didn't even break a sweat when we left him alone in the interrogation room for twenty minutes."

"If he's our guy, he'd have to be cold."

"Yeah. *If.*"

He must be, she thought. He had to be.

They turned a corner and came upon two closed doors. The one on the left had a sign on it reading, DO NOT DISTURB—INTERVIEW IN PROGRESS.

Behind that door was Mr. William Hayde, who might or might not be the only man Tess hated on this earth.

Larkin reached for the other door, then turned to her. "I know this case has cost you, Tess."

She wanted to say that he had no idea how much it had cost her, but she held back, because he had addressed her without irony for the first time.

"I met him once, you know. Paul Voorhees."

Her voice caught. "Did you?"

"In New Orleans. I was working a multiple rapist, and Paul came in to consult. Helped us a lot. We snagged the guy. Eddie Mullen—they called him the Devil, because he wore a Mardi Gras devil mask. Paul must've told you."

"I don't think he did." She wondered how many other cases he had left undiscussed.

"Well, anyway, Paul was a good guy. And I know it's tough—losing any colleague, let alone your partner."

Let alone someone who was more than a partner, she thought, but Larkin didn't know about that part of it, and didn't have to know.

"You've been through a lot." Larkin looked away. "I hope tonight ends it. For everybody's sake . . . but most of all for yours."

"Thank you," she said with a quick, faltering smile that her mouth couldn't quite hold.

"Okay, then." Larkin clapped his hands, signaling an end to whatever sort of moment they had shared. "Let's settle in for some Q and A."

He pulled open the door and gestured for her to enter the observation room, where agents Tyler, Hart, and DiFranco stood before a bank of TV monitors watching the suspect from several angles.

From this distance Tess couldn't see his face on the multiple screens. She wondered what he would look like. She wondered if he would match the face that visited her in nightmares.

Larkin was waiting for her to enter. She brushed past him, trembling just a little as she stepped inside the room.

5

At 10:45, Amanda Pierce drove into the short-term parking lot of Los Angeles International Airport. She ditched her Sunbird at the curb, grabbing her small suitcase out of the backseat, and disappeared into the concourse.

She had chosen the airport because it was large and brightly lit and would be crowded on the first night of a holiday weekend. Also, she didn't know if the feds realized that LA was her final destination. There was a chance she could convince them she was taking a flight to another city.

LAX offered an additional asset, one that might prove critical—the ready availability of taxicabs. Not many places in this city were so accommodating.

But the taxis would be of use to her only if she could shake free of the people who had trailed her for a thousand miles, all the way from northeastern Oregon to southern California. The first step was to force them out of their cars so she could get a look at them and see how many there were.

The terminal was enormous, and despite the late hour, plenty of shops and eateries were still open. The place was like a garish shopping mall, crowded with stores and bars and luridly decorated restaurants.

Palm trees were planted along the concourse under skylights and before wide windows. The floor shone beneath the bright overhead lights.

Toting her suitcase, Pierce entered a store selling magazines and souvenirs, then feigned interest in a selection of Dodgers T-shirts while watching the store entrance from the corner of her eye.

A man entered, glancing at her in a way that was not quite casual. He seemed to mutter something to himself, but she knew he was actually speaking into a throat microphone, reporting his reacquisition of the target.

She called him Alpha, using standard law enforcement code. Alpha lingered near the entrance. But there was another way of leaving the store, a second exit at the far end. Pierce wandered in that direction. Alpha did not follow. Some other agent must be covering that exit.

She got close enough to see a second man studying a rack of magazines a few steps inside the entryway. Call him Bravo.

Pierce left the store, knowing that Bravo would not be so conspicuous as to follow immediately. Another person would pick up her trail.

When she paused by the shop window just outside the exit, pretending to study a display of leather luggage, she caught the reflection of the third man, Charlie. He had started walking and stopped when she did.

Clumsy, Charlie. Poor technique. Time for you to take a refresher course at Quantico.

She entered a coffee shop and ordered a burger and Coke, her first food other than a couple of granola bars she'd consumed in the car. She sat at a small table with a view of the concourse and ate her meal, barely tasting it, knowing only that she needed nourishment to stay alert.

When she left, she took care to wad up her paper napkin and leave it on her chair.

In the concourse she paused to fiddle with her suitcase, a maneuver that afforded her the chance to see yet another man—Delta—approach her table and retrieve the napkin. There was nothing written on it or hidden in it, but her pursuers couldn't know that. Observing what might have been a dead drop, they had to check it out.

A similar ruse revealed the fifth agent, Echo, who peeled off to follow an innocent traveler after Pierce bumped into him near the escalators. This could have been a brush pass, the surreptitious transfer of an item in a seemingly accidental moment of contact.

Pierce was pleased with herself. Not only had she forced Echo to reveal himself, but she'd sent him on a diversion, improving the odds.

Perhaps she could lose another one. She picked out a man at random and asked him the way to the taxi stand. This was information she did not need, having checked the airport's layout in her road atlas while driving. The man snapped off an answer and bustled away.

Another bystander took off after him. The sixth agent. Foxtrot.

Pierce kept walking. She saw a woman break into stride just ahead of her, obviously having been posted there in an advance position.

Number seven.

She hadn't expected to have to count that high. How many of them were there, for Christ's sake?

A custodian was cleaning out a trash can. She caught the hint of a wire threaded from his ear to his collar. Stand-alone body rig. He was number eight.

There couldn't be more. But watching her from an

alcove near a candy machine, a man wearing a priest's collar. Nine.

Was that all of them? She took out her compact. In the mirror she glimpsed a male figure watching her from an upper level of the concourse. He was an older man with the close-cropped gray hair of a military officer, and she had a feeling he was the one in charge, looking down from a high vantage point on his operatives, who had spread throughout the terminal while Pierce was eating her burger.

He made ten. And she had no reason to think she'd spotted them all.

She scanned the area and noted security cameras installed in the ceilings. By now, someone would be watching her on the monitors.

She had underestimated the bureau. They'd pulled out all the stops for her. Multiple redundant modes of surveillance. She was caught in a box inside another box inside yet another. . . .

Even so, she wasn't out of options. Not by a long shot.

She entered a ladies' room, where two women were chatting at a row of sinks before a large mirror. One of them had flamboyant red hair that looked artificial. The other was dark-haired like Pierce herself.

Pierce nodded. They would do.

Taking a stall, she shut the door without latching it, then placed her suitcase on the toilet tank and stood on the lid. No one looking at the space under the door could tell that the stall was occupied.

She reached down to her belt buckle and opened the secret compartment that held the knife.

It was a switchblade, small enough to be folded inside the oversize buckle. The blade was two and a half inches long, a tiny tool, but she knew how to use it.

She opened the knife, then held it in her right hand and waited.

The two women left. The rest room was empty now. Pierce knew the feds would get curious after a while. They would send someone to check on her.

Footsteps.

Through the narrow opening in the stall door, she saw a woman enter the rest room—the same female agent she'd seen earlier. Number seven. Blond, young, her eyes wide and alert as she studied the room. A slight bulge in her belly—concealed weapon? No, something else. Something better.

Pierce waited until the woman had moved directly outside the stall, then pushed the door open and grabbed her from behind, pressing the knife against her neck.

"Shhh," she whispered, her voice nearly inaudible. The woman would be wearing a throat microphone sensitive enough to pick up almost any sound.

Slowly she lowered her free hand and ran her palm over the smooth, slightly rounded contour of the woman's belly.

Pregnant, as she'd thought. That was helpful.

She lowered the knife to the bitch's abdomen. "Do what I say"—her words barely spoken aloud by lips pressed against the woman's ear—"or your baby dies."

She felt, rather than heard, the female agent's sharp intake of breath, and she knew she had found the point of maximum emotional vulnerability she needed.

Softly: "Tell them you've lost the target. The bathroom is empty." The woman hesitated. Pierce teased the round belly with the knife's edge. "Tell them."

"This is Kidder," the woman said in a low, husky voice directed at her throat microphone. "Have not acquired target. Rest room empty, target gone, repeat, target gone."

Pierce plucked the earpiece from Agent Kidder's left ear and heard a gruff male voice initiating a lost-command drill. There was a flurry of responses from other agents, but Pierce wasn't listening anymore. She was applying sudden strong pressure to Kidder's carotid arteries, shutting off the blood flow to the brain.

The woman slumped. Pierce lowered her onto the toilet and quickly removed her own jacket, then peeled off the agent's brown blazer and shrugged it on. She slipped out of her skirt and donned Kidder's slacks. She fitted the earpiece in her own ear and secured the microphone to her jacket collar and the small transmitter to her blouse.

The other agents had not yet thought to check on Kidder. They were preoccupied with finding the target. From the confused transmissions coming in over her earpiece, it was clear that they assumed she had left the rest room almost immediately after entering, disguised as one of the two women who had been gabbing at the washstand—one woman dark-haired like Pierce, the other possibly wearing a wig. Either of them could have been the target in disguise.

The women had not been followed, and the full resources of the surveillance operation were now focused on reacquiring them. No one was watching the rest room.

Pierce spoke into her lapel. "This is Kidder." Her voice, a throaty whisper, was indistinguishable from any other female voice. "Am in command of the target."

The gruff voice snapped, "Location?"

"Central exit doors. Lower level at arrival area B. Target has left the building, is proceeding toward taxis at curbside."

"All squads, central exit ground level. *Move.*"

While her pursuers converged on the taxi area on the ground floor, Pierce left the rest room, deposited the communication rig in the nearest trash can, and rode the escalator upstairs to the departure level. She took the first exit. Outside in the warm night, she saw a cab drop off a passenger and immediately hailed it, climbing into the backseat.

· As the taxi pulled away, she permitted herself a rearward glance and saw no one following.

"Where to?" the driver asked.

She gave the name of a hotel—the new meeting place arranged last night—then sat in the backseat of the cab with the suitcase on her lap, fingering the soft leather, caressing the bag like a baby.

It was all she had left in the world now. She had given up her job, her home, her identity. She could never go back. Could never undo what she'd done. And she didn't want to.

She would meet the man at the hotel, give him what he wanted, and earn what she was due.

Then she would be on her way to another country, a new life, and anything that happened afterward would not be her concern.

She just had to keep saying that to herself. She was selling information, that was all. If the purchaser wanted to . . . *do* something with that information—well, she couldn't be responsible for other people's actions.

She had herself to look out for. Now more than ever. Now, when she was committed and there was no return.

6

The observation room was dimly lit. Like the room next door, it was soundproofed with acoustic tile, but the voices from the interrogation room were clearly audible over digital speakers attached to the TV monitors.

Tess stopped just inside the doorway, listening.

"So you've been in LA how long?"

"Two years."

"You like it here?"

"It's all right."

"Me, too. Before this, I was stationed in Salt Lake City. Pretty hot there in the summer, and colder than hell all winter long."

"I'll bet."

"That's one thing about LA. Can't beat the climate."

"I prefer a four-season climate, myself."

"Do you? Guess you miss Colorado then."

"Sometimes."

"What brought you to LA?"

"Work."

"Well, you have to go where the work takes you. Same with Ed and me."

The voice asking questions belonged to Michaelson.

The Ed he'd referred to was Ed Gaines, one of the profiling coordinators assigned to the LA office. A profiling coordinator consulted with police and drew up psychological profiles of suspects. Gaines was one of the more experienced profilers, not only trained at Quantico but an occasional lecturer there.

Agents Hart, DiFranco, and Tyler stood around watching the monitors. A young man whose name Tess didn't know sat in a swivel chair, using a keyboard and mouse to input data into a desktop computer. She looked closer and saw sine wave patterns hurrying along the computer screen, their ups and downs reflected in the lenses of his eyeglasses.

He was running a CVSA—computerized voice-stress analysis. The lines on the screen were an enhanced record of the microtremors of the vocal cords' striated muscles. Vibration at the rate of eight to ten cycles per second was normal; a higher frequency indicated stress, which was often correlated with efforts at deceit.

The sine wave pattern presently on display seemed to be within nonstressed parameters. The computer operator would be looking for a sharp break in the sequence, especially the so-called "square-block" pattern of modulation cycles.

Officially the bureau eschewed voice-stress analysis, deeming it unreliable. The results could not be used in court, which was probably just as well, since the technology was new and quite possibly flawed. Many agents regarded it as an outright scam, akin to tarot cards and palmistry—or polygraphs, for that matter.

But Michaelson believed in CVSA. He always used it behind the scenes, despite its inconvenience and expense. This was just one of the many little quirks that no doubt made him lovable to his mother, if to no one else.

"So you're a civil engineer," Michaelson was saying. "I guess it was construction work that brought you here."

"The Metro project. The Red Line."

"I've ridden the subway a few times. You guys did a great job."

A grunt of acknowledgment.

"You moved here two years ago, right?"

"I already told you so."

"Thing is, the Red Line was nearly done by then, wasn't it? So you couldn't have worked on it very long."

"Four months."

"Hardly seems worth uprooting yourself for a four-month stint."

From the drift of the conversation, Tess knew that Hayde had already been Mirandized. Michaelson was getting down to business, trying to undermine Hayde's explanation for why he moved out of Colorado.

"I didn't think it would be only four months," Hayde said. "They were still talking about extending MOS Three."

"MO-what?"

"MOS. Minimum Operable Segment. The Red Line is divided into three self-contained sections. MOS Three was finished last. Originally, it was supposed to extend farther east and west. The contractor fed me a line of bull, told me they had a shot at getting the additional funding to proceed with the extension."

Tess moved toward the bank of TV sets. Linda Tyler looked up and acknowledged her with a smile. Tyler had been civil, even friendly, from the start. Maybe it was the camaraderie of being two females in an organization still dominated by men. Women made up only fifteen percent of the bureau's 11,500 agents, and many of the female agents had been relegated to the least glamorous squads, offering the lowest profiles and the smallest chance of advancement.

Hart and DiFranco barely noted her arrival. To them, she was the outsider, the intruder on their turf, and they didn't seem as convinced as Larkin that her skills at office politics were no threat to their own careers.

The two men kept their gazes fixed on the monitors. An array of cameras with miniature lenses, concealed in the walls and ceiling of the interrogation room, provided comprehensive surveillance without being as obvious as the traditional two-way mirror. The entire interrogation was being digitally videotaped and audiotaped.

"You must've been pretty pissed," Michaelson said. "To come all this way for a new job and have it disappear after four months."

"I thought about going back to Colorado. But I was able to find work here."

"So I guess you've learned to like LA?"

"I told you, it's okay."

"This time of year, you can't beat it. Easter weekend and it's eighty degrees."

"Nice weather."

"And that breeze off the ocean—man, we even get it here, and we're four miles inland."

"It's terrific. I thought you were with the FBI."

"I am, Bill. I showed you my ID. We both did."

"I know that. But I was starting to wonder."

"Were you?"

"Yeah. I thought you might be with the chamber of commerce, what with all this crap about the weather."

DiFranco stifled a laugh. William Hayde wasn't buying Michaelson's just-getting-to-know-you routine. And it looked like he hadn't Stockholmed, either.

Tess allowed herself to study the image in the nearest monitor.

The interrogation room looked as it always did, a drab, spartan chamber with no clock on the wall and no windows. A steel table, gunmetal gray. Four straight-backed steel chairs, deliberately uncomfortable.

Two of the chairs were occupied by Michaelson and Gaines, a third by William Hayde. Gaines was seated next to the suspect, while Michaelson sat on the diagonal. This was standard procedure. Never sit directly across the table from the person you're interrogating. You need to be able to lean close and invade his space, then back off if he starts to confess. Like the room itself, the techniques of interrogation were designed to put the suspect at the greatest possible psychological disadvantage.

Michaelson wore a dark gray suit and a blue tie, and he was leaning forward, his hand on the table near a tape recorder that was ostentatiously recording the interview. The tape recorder was for show. The real recording was done by the audio equipment in the surveillance room.

"You're right, Bill," Michaelson said. "We're not here to talk about the weather. We've got a little problem, you see."

"Looks like you think I'm the one with the problem," Hayde answered, unperturbed.

Tess stared at his face on the screen. A smug, unlined face. Thin lips, sharp cheekbones, eyes that squinted without humor. He was clean-shaven, his cheeks ragged with a hint of stubble. His hair was cut short, blondish on top, darker at the sides. He had no obvious scars, moles, or birthmarks. There was nothing distinctive about him at all.

Was it Mobius's face? Could he be this ordinary, this forgettable?

There was no way to know. Dozens of people had

seen Mobius in Denver, and a few had seen him in LA, but no two of them ever seemed to see the same man.

All that could be said about Mobius was that he was Caucasian and at least five-foot-ten, with a lean but wiry build. All the bartenders and witnesses agreed on these details. That he was white was no surprise; for some reason, nearly all ritualistic sex murders were committed by white men. That he was physically strong was no surprise, either—it would take a strong man to hold down a struggling woman while duct-taping her to a bed.

Nothing else was known about him. Sometimes his hair was brown, sometimes blond, sometimes thick and long, sometimes thin and close-cropped. He wore glasses occasionally but most often did not. Beards and mustaches came and went on his face, changing as frequently as his style of dress—casual one night, stylish the next.

People remembered him as anywhere from thirty to fifty. He was a young professional or a middle-aged working man. He reminded some people of a plumber or electrician, while others had him pegged as a college professor or business executive.

He had never used valet parking, and no one had ever seen his car. He wore a condom and left no semen for the forensic analysts to find. And he was careful to present them with no other clues—no fingerprints, no telltale fibers. He routinely cleaned and disinfected every surface at the crime scene before departing.

He was cunning and obsessed, and he gave his enemies nothing to work with.

After the second killing, the Denver media had nicknamed him the Pickup Artist. Although the case had been widely publicized, there had been no decline in the number of people frequenting singles' bars. Evidently the element of danger injected into the dating milieu had served as a turn-on. No one in LA was paying attention, either—but the media had not yet connected Angie Callahan's death with the Denver story from two years ago.

Eventually the details would come out, but most likely curiosity and a pleasurable thrill of passing interest would be the only public reaction. Tess ought to have been happy about that. It made her job easier. But she couldn't help wondering if passive acceptance of a phenomenon like Mobius was not, in the long run, a greater threat than Mobius himself.

She noticed that the computer operator was sneaking glances at her. She returned his stare, and he smiled, embarrassed. "You're Tess McCallum, right? The Black Tiger case."

Black Tiger again. People always wanted to talk about that.

"Yes," she said with a shrug.

"We, uh, we studied it at the academy."

This made her feel old. "Thanks."

"That was some amazing work you did."

"It was a long time ago."

"Not so long. Seven, eight years, right?"

She turned away, ending the conversation. "Seems longer."

Seems like a lifetime, she thought.

"Well," Michaelson was saying, "why don't we see if you can help us with our problem, Bill. I want to talk about what happened tonight."

"Nothing happened tonight," Hayde said.

"Nothing?"

"Nothing important. Hell, I thought LA was supposed to be laid-back. Live and let live, isn't that the local philosophy?"

He seemed calm. Tess wasn't certain if this was a good or bad sign. Most innocent people, accused of a crime, would protest noisily. But there were exceptions—people so sure of their innocence that they figured it was all a misunderstanding, easily worked out. Or people who simply didn't allow themselves to be flustered, people who needed to be in control.

Of course, a sociopath wouldn't be flustered either.

Tess wondered which kind of man William Hayde was.

"It's the land of casual sex and sunny hedonism," Hayde said. "At least, that's the subliminal message in all the brochures, not to mention every TV show of the last thirty years. So where did I go wrong, Officer?"

"I'm not a police officer," Michaelson said. "I'm a special agent of the FBI."

"Like Mulder and Scully, right?"

"I don't watch cop shows. I take it you do."

"That's a mark of criminal tendencies, isn't it? Exhibiting an unhealthy interest in fictional presentations of law enforcement? Part of the profile, maybe?"

"How do you know about profiles?"

"TV. Everything I know, I learned from TV. It's our great national educator."

Tess frowned. His coyness was maddening. He behaved like a guest at a cocktail party, not a suspect under interrogation.

Mobius might be this smooth, this unflappable. But would he be reckless enough to show it?

She looked at his hands—large hands, the prominent knuckles tufted with pale hairs.

A killer's hands?

One of those hands was manacled to a leg of the table. The other was free to gesticulate. Hayde was doing a lot of gesturing, but his hand movements were lazy, almost insolent. He wore flashy cuff links, black pearls set in silver borders. The cuff link on his free hand flashed, catching the light. It seemed to be winking at her.

"Anyway," Hayde said, "whenever I watch a cop show, I root for the good guys. I'm a big fan of the boys in blue—and that includes blue suits, you'll be happy to hear." This with a nod at Gaines, who wore a suit of that color. "Now, are you going to tell me what this is all about, or am I going to have to invoke my right to an attorney and get all legalistic and tight-assed?"

He was smiling as he said it. Tess knew he was smart. Of course she would expect an engineer to be of above-average intelligence. His vocabulary only confirmed that presumption—words like *legalistic*, *hedonism*, *subliminal*. Two-dollar words, as her father would say.

Mobius was intelligent also. They had known that from the beginning. He would have to be intelligent, even charming, to be successful in the bar pickup scene. Anyway, serial killers classified as the organized type—methodical, obsessive, cunning—were often of above-average IQ.

"Let's talk about what went on with Agent Tyler at the apartment," Michaelson said.

"Hey, hold it. That's the end of the story. You have to start at the club."

"Where you picked her up."

"If you ask me, she's the one who picked *me* up."

"Does that happen to you often? Women pick you up?"

"No, I'm a virgin, Officer. Sorry, I mean, Special Agent. I've never been with a girl before. Is it true they don't have a wee-wee like boys do?"

"I'm just asking—"

"If I think I'm a stud? Not really. But in this town, on a Friday night, action isn't hard to come by. Lots of times it'll come looking for you. How about you, Officer Friendly? I'll bet that genuine FBI badge gets you a piece of tail now and then, doesn't it?"

"We're not talking about me, Bill."

"Gosh, I'm Bill now. That's real nice, how we're such good pals all of a sudden. What was your name again?"

"Richard."

"Dick. Okay, Dick. What else did you want to know about picking up babes, Dick?"

Tess glanced at another monitor, covering Michaelson and Gaines, and saw irritation flicker across Michaelson's face. She knew he hated being called Dick. She also knew he would have no luck getting William Hayde to open up to him.

DiFranco reached the same conclusion. "This creep isn't gonna fall for the good-buddy act, no matter how they play it."

"You're right," Tess said. "He's too smart."

"Smart like our guy, you think?"

She glanced at DiFranco and noticed that the others were watching her as well. "I want it to be him," she said carefully. "But . . . he's sarcastic. Childish, in a way."

"So?"

"Mobius is a lot of things, but childish isn't one of them."

"I don't know. There are those postcards."

"He has a sense of humor. But not like this." She heard the inadequacy of her own explanation and tried to elaborate. "I can't define it precisely—but I have a sense of what he's like. Of his manner, his . . . mien."

"Mien?" DiFranco sounded dubious, or maybe he was just unfamiliar with the word.

"What it's like to be around him when he's just being himself."

"Not a good place to be. Around him, I mean."

"No," she said. "Not if you want to live."

There was no more discussion. Tess knew they were all thinking of Angie Callahan.

Angie Callahan had been a systems analyst for a defense contractor in Marina del Rey. She drove a Porsche, she had 150 channels on her satellite TV system, and she'd recently broken up with a marketing executive based in San Francisco who flew down to LA every Tuesday and Friday on a corporate jet.

Eleven days ago, Angie had gone to a bar on Melrose Avenue populated by an upscale thirtysomething crowd. It was a meat rack, but an exceptionally high-class meat rack. According to the eyewitness accounts of the bartender and several bar patrons, the man she'd left with had been well built, with thick brown hair and strong features behind his mustache and beard. No one had heard him say his name, and he paid in cash, leaving a tip that was neither large nor small enough to cause comment.

When Angie failed to arrive at work the next morning, her colleagues tried to reach her. Phone calls to her condo went unanswered. Messages to her pager were not returned. By late afternoon, her friends had prevailed on the president of the condo association to unlock Angie's door.

They found Angie in the bedroom, her wrists duct-taped to the headboard of her bed, her throat cut.

It was a police investigation for a few hours, until

Robbery-Homicide's nationwide database search for crimes with a similar MO turned up the Denver case code-named RAVENKILL—in reference to a bar called Raven's Roost, where the first victim had been acquired. Then the police brought in the FBI.

Tess learned about the killing at ten o'clock, as she was turning down the bedcovers and debating which of three books to read. The phone rang, and it was Assistant Director Gerald Andrus in LA. Except for the obligatory Christmas cards, he hadn't been in touch with her since he was transferred out of Denver a year and a half earlier.

"It's starting again," Andrus said without preamble.

For a moment she hadn't trusted herself to speak. Then she'd asked Andrus why he was calling her.

"I've arranged for a loan-out. You're coming to LA to be part of the task force."

"You've cleared it with Cooper?" SAC Cooper was Andrus's replacement at the Denver field office.

"I've cleared it with the people who will clear it with Cooper. I have friends in high places, Tess."

Of course he did. He might very well have called the director himself.

"It's a violation of policy," she said for no reason except that her mind had lost the ability to focus on anything that mattered. "I mean, I have a personal connection with the case."

"I'm well aware of that. I want you here anyway. Be on a plane tomorrow."

"I can leave tonight."

"No, get your rest. You'll need it."

But she'd gotten no rest that night, and in the ten days since, she'd slept only when her body gave out from sheer exhaustion. Even then there was no rest. There were dreams. Dreams of the night of February 12, the bedroom door—and what lay beyond it.

She wondered, at times, what kept her going. Was it simple inertia, the inability of a body in motion to cease its forward progress even when there was nowhere to go? Or was it revenge—and if so, was that an honorable motive for someone sworn to uphold impartial justice?

Tess knew she could never be impartial in this case. She could not seek justice in its sterile, socially acceptable incarnation. Justice was the blindfolded lady with the balanced scales. She could never be that lady again. She had lost all sense of balance, and no blindfold could shut out the things she saw with her eyes closed.

Whatever drove her, she had used it as fuel to stay awake and alert and on the move, twenty hours a day, as the task force was assembled and deployed.

All the obvious avenues of investigation had been followed. Angie Callahan's coworkers had been questioned. The bar had been staked out on the chance that the killer would return. Undercover ops were carried out in a variety of bars and nightclubs on Melrose Avenue. Linda Tyler had been the bait at one nightspot tonight. Tess, with agents Collins and Diaz, had been backing up another female agent working undercover at a different bar. So far none of the operations had yielded results—unless Hayde was their man.

Physical evidence retrieved from the victim's body had established that Mobius had engaged in antemortem intercourse—probably consensual, as there was no sign of rape. The murder weapon had been taken, and since none of Angie's cutlery was missing, it was believed to be a pocketknife carried by the killer. The width of the wound channel matched the cuts inflicted on the Denver victims, suggesting that Mobius was using the same knife he'd employed before.

The wound itself, like the earlier ones, said a great

deal about Mobius's mind-set. He had slit Angie Callahan's throat with care, avoiding the carotid arteries, so that the blood trickled out, bringing on death by slow degrees.

And what had Mobius done during that long interval when Angie had felt her life bleeding away? Had he spoken to her or kissed her, or had he simply watched?

Tess turned back to face the monitors. Michaelson was asking about William Hayde's movements throughout the evening, and Hayde was answering in his bored, contemptuous voice, his free hand tracing slow circles in the air, the pearl-and-silver cuff link still winking as if it knew a secret it would not share.

Tess wanted him to be Mobius. She wanted it so much.

Please, God, she thought. *Please let this man be a monster.*

Was that so much to ask?

7

"Do we tell the AD?" Jarvis asked.

"Not yet."

"I thought he wanted to be informed—"

"We'll inform Andrus later. Right now we've got higher priorities."

Nobody contradicted him, which was just as well. Jack Tennant wasn't used to being contradicted.

Tennant was sixty years old, three years past the bureau's ostensibly mandatory retirement age. He was tall and thick-muscled and bull-necked, and with his buzz-cut gray hair he looked like an aging drill instructor. In point of fact, he had been a drill instructor in the Marines during the Vietnam War, preparing the troops on Parris Island, and he still knew how to fire off an order in his gruff bulldog bark.

Restlessly he paced an office in the FBI's resident agency at LA International Airport. Seven faces were arrayed before him—two agents he'd brought with him from DC, and five more who were among the twenty supplied by the field office in Portland, most of whom were out canvassing all hotels within a two-mile radius of LAX.

Last night, when Amanda Pierce had stopped at a

motel in Salem, Oregon, after four hours on the road, she had received a call on her cell phone. The phone was a black-market model equipped with powerful encryption features, and the signal could not be tapped. But a long-range microphone aimed at Pierce's motel room had picked up scattered words of her end of the conversation. It appeared that her contact in LA had called to change the details of their scheduled rendezvous. The microphone had caught Pierce saying, ". . . meet you at the hotel . . ."

The next words had been lost in the drone of ambient noise from freeway traffic and buzzing air conditioners. There was no way to know what hotel it was, but possibly it was near the airport.

The squad members from Portland were on the telephone, using either their secure cell phones or the office landlines, talking quietly and rapidly and taking notes. Five taxi companies handled nearly all pickup and delivery of passengers at LAX—America's Best, Checker Cab, South Bay, United Independent, and Yellow Cab. The squad was putting in calls to all of them, requesting information on a pickup of a Caucasian female, thirty-eight years old, from the departures area thirty minutes earlier.

The remaining two agents, Tennant's own men, were consulting blueprints of the LAX terminal and comparing them with single-frame images captured from airport security tapes.

But every one of them was looking at Tennant either directly or surreptitiously, and every one of them wanted to know what the hell Tennant was going to do now.

Tennant wished he knew.

His cell phone buzzed. It was Kidder, checking in from the hospital. Her preliminary examination

showed no sign of injury, but she would be held over-
night for observation—"just in case I was, you know,
exposed," she said.

"You'd have experienced symptoms by now."

"Not if I had only cutaneous contact. In that case,
symptoms can take hours to develop. And there's no
telling what that bitch might have done while I was
unconscious. How are things at your end?"

"We've got everything under control." *Bullshit we
do,* he thought. But there was no point in worrying a
pregnant woman who'd been held at knifepoint only
half an hour earlier.

Laura Kidder was the only other agent from DC
that Tennant had brought with him. He'd thought the
woman's condition might be an asset—a pregnant lady
was less likely to be pegged as part of a surveillance
op. Great thinking on his part. He'd nearly gotten
Kidder and her baby killed.

"Hey," Tennant said, "we didn't have much time
to talk earlier. You were in direct contact with Pierce.
Give me a seat-of-the-pants psych evaluation."

"Hostile. Desperate." Kidder thought for a moment. "Ruthless. It's all about survival for her now.
She knows she's been made, and there's no going
back."

"Kill or be killed."

"That's my impression."

"Okay, Laura. Take care of yourself and that baby
of yours."

He ended the call and turned to Kidder's colleagues
from the DC office, Jarvis and Bickerstaff, or J&B, as
they were called. "You map out her route?"

Jarvis looked up from the blueprints and security
camera freeze-frames. "She went straight to this
exit"—he tapped a spot on the blueprints—"on the
departures level and caught the taxi."

"Which, by the way, is against airport regs," Bickerstaff added in a voice like a sigh. The voice matched the agent's rumpled suit and his still more rumpled face, a face that sagged with the impress of every frown it had ever known. "Passengers aren't supposed to be picked up on that level. It's for drop-offs only." He nodded toward the Portland agents working the phones. "So even if we do get through to the cab company, we may not be able to get them to admit they took the fare."

"We'll threaten to subpoena their records. They'll talk." Tennant looked more closely at the freeze-frames. He knew the camera wasn't sharp enough to show the license plate, but at least they ought to be able to tell what kind of cab it was. "You can't see the taxi logo at all?"

"Camera coverage is spotty outside," Bickerstaff said. "We can only see the wheels. Rest of the vehicle is out of frame."

"Another angle—"

"There are no other angles, sir. Spotty coverage, like we said."

"Okay." Tennant wagged a finger at them. "Come with me."

He led J&B onto the concourse, where they could have a private conversation. The agents requisitioned from Portland knew only the bare minimum about the case—that Pierce was a security officer with a government contractor, that she'd gone rogue, and that tonight she was planning to meet in LA with a representative of a black-market arms dealer.

That was all they had been told. They knew nothing about the purpose of the meeting—or the contents of Pierce's suitcase.

J&B knew. Tennant could speak freely with them.

"This never should've happened," he began, though of course they already knew that.

"It's not your fault," Jarvis said.

"Like hell it isn't. I'm the one who fucked this up. I should've snatched her out of the motel in Salem last night. I was too concerned about catching her with the contact, getting a two-for-one deal. I should have prioritized differently."

The last words out of his mouth irritated him. Prioritized differently—had he really said that? After thirty years with the bureau, had he finally learned the jargon that every SAC used to cover his ass?

Bickerstaff tried to be optimistic. "We've got her credit card companies ready to red-flag transactions on any of her plastic in real time, under her real name or her alias. The minute they get a hit, we'll know her whereabouts."

Tennant would not be cheered up. "Suppose she uses cash. Or suppose she's got an extra set of ID and plastic we don't know about."

"We only need to reacquire her before she completes the transaction, and we're golden."

"And if we don't reacquire her," Tennant said sourly, "we're shit. Hell, she might be completing the deal right now."

"Even if she does move the merchandise," Bickerstaff said, "there's no immediate threat. She's a salesman dealing with a middleman. It's not like either one of them is gonna actually use the stuff."

Tennant sighed. "We don't know what Pierce might do if she's feeling"—what was the word Kidder had used?—"desperate."

"That kind of raises an issue." Jarvis looked at Tennant. "I know you want to hold off on telling the AD, but, uh, don't you think it might be time to bring the local recruits up to speed? They don't understand the urgency."

"They understand their orders."

"Yes, sir." Jarvis didn't sound convinced.

Tennant hated to explain himself. He saw it as a sign of weakness, just as old John Wayne had once said. *Never apologize and never explain*—that was the Duke's motto. But sometimes explanations were necessary to keep the troops on his side.

"Look," he said, "we have to keep this contained. Right now, no one on this coast knows anything, other than the Portland SAC, the AD here, and the four of us from the District. And I guess the doctor who's treating Kidder. That's it. That's as far as it goes— and we're keeping it that way. Because if the media gets hold of this thing, they'll start asking questions we don't want answered."

"Like where Pierce got the stuff," Bickerstaff said. "And what exactly her job was."

Tennant nodded. "Questions with foreign policy implications. International fallout. Not to mention the consequences for this city if the public overreacts."

"All right," Jarvis said. "But if we get in a showdown with her and she decides to uncork it—"

"Then it doesn't matter what the guys from Oregon know or don't know." Tennant looked down the concourse. "Nothing will matter, at that point."

8

"Let's run through it again."

"I've told you what happened three times already. It doesn't get any more interesting the fourth time around."

"Humor us. We're trying to see how it happened, Bill. We're really trying to understand."

Tess watched the bank of monitors, where William Hayde's image flickered in the semidarkness of the surveillance room. Above the TV screens, the digital clock on the wall read exactly 2400. Midnight.

Hayde's background had been established. His movements and actions throughout the evening had been reported. Specific facts had been elicited, facts that could be checked and confirmed.

That was part of the strategy, she knew. Get him to commit to verifiable details.

Michaelson had done most of the talking. Now and then, when Hayde began to lose patience with him, Gaines eased himself into the conversation. It was nothing as simplistic as good cop/bad cop. The two interviewers complemented each other in a subtler way. Michaelson was genial and laid-back. Gaines was more businesslike.

"Okay." Hayde sighed. "Here goes. I was at this club on Melrose. It's early—nine o'clock. I'm on my first drink when I see *her* eyeing me."

He nodded at the chair now occupied by Special Agent Linda Tyler. Tyler had been added to the mix twenty minutes ago, after her pager buzzed in the observation room, showing the message *10-88*. This was police code for "Request backup," and it meant that Michaelson and Gaines wanted her in there with them.

She sat across the table from Hayde, saying nothing, watching him. The intent was probably to rattle the suspect, but it wasn't working.

Nothing was working.

"I check her out," Hayde said, "and she checks me out, and I think we've got a little thing going. So I buy her a drink, try to make myself sound interesting. She keeps asking me where I'm from, what I do for a living. More I tell her, the more she wants to know. She's real fascinated by Colorado Springs, says she's always wanted to live in that part of the country. Likes the mountains, blah blah blah. And she loves the idea that I'm a civil engineer, it's like a turn-on for her. I'm thinking this is almost too easy. So I say this place is gonna be a zoo pretty soon, and she says maybe we could have a drink at her place. Sounds good to me, so we walk over there—it's right down the street." He paused in his narrative. "I assume that's not her real digs."

"Just a furnished apartment," Gaines said.

"All part of the act, huh? Well, she lets me in, fixes me a drink, asks if I want the guided tour. Next thing I know we're in the bedroom and I'm sneaking a kiss. How about that kiss, Linda? Pretty tasty, wasn't it?"

Tyler was silent. Michaelson said, "We're not here to rate your proficiency at seduction."

"You might learn a few things. Anyhow, I kiss her, she seems okay with it, I figure it's all systems go. Why wouldn't I?"

"And that," Michaelson said, "is when you tried to tape her wrists."

"Well, yeah."

"You carry a roll of duct tape with you."

"A small roll. Fits in my pocket."

"And you decided it would be a good idea to use the tape on this woman you'd just picked up."

"Oh, hell. I told you already, *she* picked *me* up. And as for the S and M—hey, it's not like I didn't warn her. I mean, not explicitly, not in so many words, but I'd been dropping hints since we started to talk. You know, jokes about how I like it rough, she looks like she's been a bad girl, maybe she needs a spanking . . . She didn't pull back when I said that shit. She was eating it up. She wanted to hear more, like she was into it."

Tess knew why Agent Tyler hadn't objected. A fascination with sadomasochism was part of Mobius's psychological profile.

According to the experts in Behavioral Sciences Section, Mobius had started with a routine S&M fetish. He would have frequented the Denver leather bars, engaging in consensual sadomasochistic liaisons, always acting as the dominant partner. Dominance was important to this man. He would need to be in control, with the woman tied or duct-taped—helpless.

One night he must have gone too far. Carried away, he'd ignored the safety word or signal they had arranged. He'd killed his partner. It would have been partly an accident, partly an act of sheer recklessness.

Realizing what he'd done, he would have tried to cover up the crime. Still, he probably spent several anxious weeks waiting for the rap on his door. But the arrest never came. He had gotten away with murder. The ultimate act of dominance, of control—a rush unlike any other.

He liked it. And so he proceeded to do it again, this time in a more methodical fashion. He improved his technique, using disguises, false names, avoiding the S&M bars because he knew the police might be watching those venues in the wake of the first killing. Most likely he engaged in regular sex, marked only by his domineering style. Afterward, he restrained and gagged the victim, then cut her throat.

As he continued to elude apprehension, he became arrogant, his narcissism escalating to full-blown grandiosity. By now, he must think that no one could stop him.

Maybe he was right.

"So you grabbed her from behind . . ." Michaelson was saying.

Hayde shook his head. "It's not like I *grabbed* her"—he made air quotes around the verb with his free hand—"in a violent way. It's just that it, you know, gets me hot. She sees me peel the tape off the roll, and I'm saying, 'This won't hurt a bit,' which is just part of the act. Then all of a sudden there's a gun in her hand and she's yelling for backup."

"You attacked her," Gaines said, his voice flat.

"It was foreplay."

"Foreplay."

Hayde glanced at Gaines, then let his gaze drop to the bulging manila folder on the table, just out of his reach.

At some point in the interview, Gaines had left the room for a minute and returned with the folder, which he'd set down with a hard thump. Tess had no idea what was in it—the thick sheaf of papers might be Mrs. Gaines's recipes, for all she knew—but the folder was meant to convey the idea that the feds had compiled a mass of evidence and William Hayde was in serious trouble.

Hayde's stress level hadn't risen measurably, however. And he did not seem unduly curious about the folder.

"Look," Hayde said, looking only slightly embarrassed, "I don't know what gets your rocks off, but this is what does it for me. And I didn't think it was any big deal. Like I said, this is La-La-land, everybody to his brand of perversion, no questions asked. At least that's what I thought. I'm starting to feel like I never left Colorado Springs."

Michaelson picked up on that. "Or Denver, maybe."

"Denver?"

"It's pretty close to Colorado Springs."

"You spend a lot of time in Denver when you were in Colorado?" Gaines asked.

"Yeah, I went to Denver now and again. On weekends or whatever. I like going to a city, getting some action."

"Action like tonight?" Gaines pressed.

"You the sex police or something? What's your problem? Not getting enough at home? You two guys, you ought to shack up together. You make a cute couple."

Neither man reacted. One of the cardinal rules of interrogating a suspect was to avoid a personality conflict.

"I guess you thought you and Agent Tyler would make a nice couple," Gaines said.

"Not exactly. I thought we'd make some nice coupling, if you see the distinction."

"When she picked you up," Michaelson said, "did you think she was a whore?"

"A hooker? The thought crossed my mind. But she never mentioned money."

"I didn't mean a hooker. I meant, did you think she was a tramp, a slut?"

"What?"

"That's what I would think," Gaines said, "if some woman came up to me out of nowhere and started hitting on me. I'm not saying I wouldn't be flattered . . . but I'd have to figure she's pretty loose, if you know what I mean."

"Lots of loose women in LA," Michaelson said. "Town's full of them. They'll fuck anybody that's got a dick. They use their bodies like a welcome mat."

Gaines nodded. "You act like a welcome mat, you've got to expect someone's going to walk all over you. It's just human nature."

This kind of talk was a tactical move. Blame the victim. Imply that she'd had it coming. Sometimes a suspect would open up if he thought his interrogators were on his moral wavelength.

"You two for real?" Hayde looked genuinely amused. "Slut, loose woman—did I go through a time warp when I came in here? Is this 1954 or something? Or are you guys charter members of the Joe Friday fan club?"

Tess glanced at the computer. Voice stress remained low.

Michaelson leaned forward, abandoning informality, and hardened his voice. "Let me be straight with you, Mr. Hayde."

He had switched to addressing the suspect by his last name. It was a signal to Gaines to try the direct approach.

"What we're looking at is not just this one case," Michaelson said. "It's a pattern. Your actions tonight are part of that pattern. Your actions eleven days ago fit the same pattern."

"Eleven days ago? What are you talking about?"

On the computer screen, the sine waves had broken up, indicating increased stress but not necessarily deception.

"Monday night, March twentieth. Angie Callahan. Ring a bell?"

"No."

The sine waves were smoothing out. The technology said he wasn't lying.

Tess studied Hayde's face on the nearest monitor. She saw no darting eye movements, no defensive body language. Hayde was not looking toward his upper right, as he might if he were unconsciously accessing the creative centers of the right cerebral hemisphere.

"Sure it does. You picked her up—or maybe she picked you up. It doesn't matter. You went back to her condo. Your memory clearing up, Mr. Hayde?"

"I've never heard of anybody named Angie Callahan."

"You knew her. And you killed her."

"Say again?"

"You taped her wrists to the headboard of her bed, and you slit her throat, didn't you?"

"You think I'm a murderer?"

"We know you are. We've nailed you. It's over. We've got all the evidence we need."

To punctuate his partner's statement, Gaines held up the bulging folder.

Tess thought they were laying it on a little thick. But they had to get a reaction, had to rattle the unflappable Bill Hayde, who just sat there shaking his head in amazed derision.

"You think I'm a friggin' serial killer, for Christ's sake?"

"Who said anything about a serial killer, Mr. Hayde?"

"You just said it's a pattern. And you're asking me about Denver. I'm not as dumb as I look, gentlemen. I can put two and two together and usually get four. You're after the Pickup Artist, right?" He sounded more intrigued than alarmed.

"What if we are?"

"He killed, what, three people in Denver a couple years ago?"

"Four," Gaines said, and Tess mouthed the same word, thinking of the fourth victim.

"Yeah, that's right, four. Last one was a feeb like you guys, as I recall." Hayde was smiling, and Tess had never hated anyone as much as she hated him in that moment, for that smile. "And now you're trying to pin all that on me? Just because I tried to pork Agent Starling here?"

"Agent Tyler," Michaelson corrected, seeming confused, as if he didn't get the reference.

Hayde ignored him and leaned back as far as the straight-backed chair would allow. "Man, you folks must be desperate. I mean, if a little S-and-M action is enough to get me pulled in, you've got to be scraping bottom."

Tess checked the computer. Smooth sine waves. The agent manning the console caught her glance. "Stress is low," he said.

"Fucking sociopaths can beat those machines," Di-Franco muttered.

"They can beat a polygraph." This was Larkin. "Not a CVSA."

"They can beat anything," DiFranco persisted. "Voice stress is bullshit, anyway. Even if it wasn't, these guys are so crazy, they don't even know when they're lying."

"Does he strike you as crazy?" Tess asked quietly.

They all looked at her. No one spoke for a moment. Then Hart said, "Sometimes they can pass for normal. It doesn't prove anything."

"Maybe not," she conceded. "But I know what would." She took a breath. "Let me see him. Face-to-face."

9

Jim Dodge slid into the corner booth at Lucy J's and ordered a seltzer water.

"Drinking the hard stuff?" Myron Levine said with a cocked eyebrow. When Levine did that, he looked a lot like the guy who played Dr. McCoy on the old *Star Trek* show.

"I'm on duty," Dodge said.

"On a Friday night? What's cooking?"

"I'm catching calls all weekend. Tonight there was a gangbang on Robertson." Nearly all violent crime in the West LA district took place along a short strip of Robertson Boulevard. "Two assholes got into it at a video store. One of them was stabbed. I'm supposed to be on my way over right now."

"Is the kid dead?"

"Critical."

"White?"

"Black."

"Huh." Levine shrugged, losing interest as Dodge had known he would. A wounded black banger wasn't news—not TV news, at any rate. And Levine was a crime reporter for KPTI-TV. Except he didn't call it crime reporting. To hear Levine tell it, he was the Channel Eight JusticeWatch correspondent.

The job title was bullshit. TV news was bullshit. Truth be told, most of the actual facts reported in the news were bullshit, too. Fucking reporters either got the facts wrong or just plain made them up.

Dodge wasn't judgmental about any of that. He didn't blame Myron Levine and his associates for peddling a load of crap to an ignorant public. Hell, it was a living.

He knew Levine wanted to get right to the point, which was why he decided to make him wait a minute or two. "You were in Denver for a while, right?"

"Couple years at Channel Three. Why?"

"Ever hear of an FBI agent name of Tess McCallum?"

Levine nodded. "Black Tiger."

"Black Tiger? What the fuck is that? Some kind of secret code?"

"A case she worked."

"In Denver?"

"In Miami, as I recall. But it was news everywhere for a while. I even tried to set up an interview with McCallum when she transferred to Denver, but she wouldn't talk to me."

Dodge wasn't surprised. "She's not too talkative. I noticed that myself."

Levine was getting antsy. "So what does Tess McCallum have to do with the price of beer in China?"

"Not a fucking thing. Just a matter of personal curiosity."

"You called me out here to satisfy your curiosity?"

"No, that was just a side issue. I've got something for you. Something you'll like."

"I hope so. I mean, don't get me wrong, I'm always grateful for a heads-up, but I've got a lot on my plate right now."

Dodge didn't give a shit about Levine's plate. "How interested are you in the Grandy case?" he asked.

That cocked eyebrow again. "What is this, an IQ test? I'm interested. Obviously I'm interested. Everybody's interested. We ran with it as our lead story on the ten o'clock show tonight."

"I said, *how* interested?"

Levine considered the question. "A thousand."

"What I have is more interesting than that."

"Fifteen hundred."

"Cheap doesn't look good on you, Myron."

"Give me some idea of what you've got, and we'll talk."

Dodge shrugged. "Fair enough. I can tell you what Mr. Delbert Grandy, upstanding citizen and innocent motorist, was overheard saying not long after a nine-millimeter soft-point round pulverized his clavicle."

"Overheard by who?"

"It's *whom*, Myron. Correct grammar is *whom*. Don't they teach you TV dipshits basic English?"

Levine ignored this. "Who the fuck heard it?"

"Me, for one. My partner, for another. You know that Bradley and me were in the neighborhood, so we were early on the scene. Got there before the EMTs, even."

"Yeah, I know that. I also know that you wouldn't give me anything that can be linked that closely to you or to Al Bradley."

"Of course I wouldn't. I'm not a moron, Myron." Dodge smiled. "Hey, you ever notice how much those two words sound alike? Moron. Myron. It's like your parents had a, what d'you call it, premonition."

"Fuck you, Dodge."

"Touchy." He sipped his seltzer. "Anyway, Mr. Grandy's words are now known by all members of the grand jury, not to mention miscellaneous other individuals present in the courtroom today, not least of whom is the lady bystander who testified about it. So nothing can be linked to me. That's why I'm giving it to you."

"*Selling* it to me."

"Your formulation is more accurate. The information is indeed for sale. What's it worth?"

"Two thousand. That's my limit."

Dodge pretended to think it over, though he had already known Levine would max out at two thousand and that he would take it. This was the way it always worked, and the haggling was only a game they played to show each other how smart they were.

Levine had been buying information from Dodge, and no doubt from other people, ever since his arrival in LA last year. Most journalists, whether out of ethical considerations or simple impecuniousness, refused to pay their sources. Levine was different. He was graspingly ambitious, desperate to rise to the heights of TV news stardom, probably gunning for an anchor spot on *60 Minutes* someday.

He was also a pretty goddamned homely son of a bitch with limited investigative skills. To get ahead, he had to pay his own way. Since he pulled down more than three hundred grand a year for his current gig at KPTI, he wasn't exactly hurting for cash. And as long as he kept getting the goods, his producers weren't likely to inquire too closely into his methods.

By now, Dodge figured he'd made Levine wait long enough. "Okay, Myron, I'll cut you a break. It's a deal."

"So give."

"You know my policy. Cash in advance."

"I came directly from the station. I don't have that much on me."

"There's an ATM down the street. I'll wait."

Levine blew out a heavy breath. "Fuck it." He opened his wallet and passed a small stack of bills under the table. Dodge pocketed the money without counting it.

"All right. Mr. Grandy, the innocent African-American motorist gunned down by racist West LA cops, was screaming, and I quote, 'I'm gonna kill you, motherfucker. I'm gonna fucking kill you.' End of quote."

"He was saying it to the cop who shot him?"

"He was saying it to the world in general, but I think we can safely assume his rage was primarily directed at lily-white Officer Perkins."

Levine contemplated this, probably wondering if he'd gotten his money's worth. "Screaming threats," he said finally.

"Righty-o."

"Interesting."

"Like I told you. Suddenly Mr. Grandy's not the victimized father of three who lives in Baldwin Hills and is pulled over for Driving While Black. Suddenly he's not Mr. Rising African-American Middle Class. Instead he's just another ornery, angry, fucked-up, probably drugged-up nigger asshole who probably had it coming."

Levine waved this off. "Jim . . ."

Dodge knew Levine was uncomfortable with overt displays of racism. Levine was a liberal, and as such, he had a certain romanticized self-image to uphold. No doubt he shared all the thoughts and opinions Dodge so colorfully expressed, but he kept them secret. In his eyes, this made him a better person. To Dodge, it just meant he was a priss and a coward, in addition to being an all-around asswipe.

"Forgive my politically incorrect characterization of the facts," Dodge said. "I'll leave the sociopolitical interpretations to intellectuals like yourself."

Levine wasn't listening. He seemed perturbed. After a moment he said, "You wouldn't be spinning me, would you, Jim?"

It was Dodge's turn to cock an eyebrow. "I never thought of myself as a PR flack."

"It just seems as if this particular testimony might be helpful to the LAPD."

"For the reasons I just stated."

"Yes. For those reasons."

"What makes you think I give a fuck about helping the LAPD?"

Shrug. "I'm just looking at all the angles. This evidence bolsters Perkins's claim that he was shooting in self-defense."

"Grandy said it *after* he was shot, not before."

Another shrug. "Even so."

Dodge was amazed. This goddamn self-important little prick seemed to actually think he was an investigative reporter, when all he did was read copy off a TelePrompTer to fill time between the comedy weatherman and the comedy sports guy. Still, Levine would have to be massaged to keep things friendly.

"I can see how you might view it that way," Dodge said. "But you'd be wrong. I don't take sides. I hand out whatever information it's safe for me to reveal. And to prove it, I'll give you another little tidbit that's definitely not helpful to my brothers in blue."

Levine sighed theatrically. "How much is this one gonna cost?"

"Pay for my drink. That'll cover it."

A skeptical squint. "You're in a generous mood."

"I value our friendship, Myron. I want it to continue." This sort of comment was another part of the game. Both men knew that whatever the nature of their relationship, *friendship* was not the word for it.

Levine waited as Dodge removed a slip of paper and unfolded it. He slid it across the table, holding the corner between two fingers. Levine took a long look.

"This is from Grandy's medical file," Levine said.

"That's right. Bullet trajectory analysis. Want me to translate the medicalese into plain language?"

"I can read it." Levine spent another minute poring over the document. "They're saying the bullet passed through the fleshy part of his left hand before entering his collarbone. So what?"

"Look at the entrance and exit wounds on the hand."

Levine looked. He got it. "His palm was facing out." He glanced up at Dodge and pantomimed raising both hands in front of him, palms forward.

"Not exactly an offensive posture, is it?" Dodge said.

"He was holding up his hands when Perkins capped him."

"Bingo. Still think I'm spinning?"

"No, I don't." Levine started to pull the paper toward him. Dodge yanked it back.

"Sorry, Myron. You can look, but you can't have."

"Why not? Is this the original?"

"It's a Xerox I ran off when nobody was looking. But if anybody finds this on you, it'll be traced back to me, and my ass is grass. In case you've forgotten, leaking grand jury info is still considered a criminal act. We're talking contempt of court, mandatory prison term, good-bye career, good-bye pension."

"They'll never find it on me. I won't burn you, Jim."

"I know you won't, Myron. Because I won't give you the chance." Dodge folded the paper and stuck it in his pocket. "Anyway, you don't need the paper.

You know what it says. Now go home and write up a story. Make it a good one. Maybe this is the year you'll cop that Golden Mike."

He waved over the waitress and ordered a slice of apple pie.

Levine stood up. "I'd better get out of here. Hey, didn't you say you have a crime scene to go to?"

"I'll get there when I get there. What the fuck, Bradley's probably on the scene by now. He'll handle the preliminaries. He's good at that routine interview bullshit. Makes him feel like a real cop."

He saw the question that flickered in Levine's eyes: *When was the last time you felt that way?*

But all Levine said was, "Take care of yourself, Jim."

Dodge smiled and patted the side pocket of his windbreaker, where the money was. "What do you think I'm doing?"

Dodge finished his pie and left a nice chunk of change for the waitress, a pretty little thing with a Jennifer Lopez ass. He glanced around as he rose from his seat, pleased to see that no one was looking at him.

He wasn't really worried about being recognized. The coffee shop was in the heart of Hollywood, far afield from West LA Division, and even the Hollywood cops didn't come here, preferring dives with more atmosphere and a less seedy clientele.

A low profile was critical in his dealings with Levine. If word ever got out that he was selling police secrets, he would be in very deep shit.

The legal consequences were the least of it. Most likely he wouldn't live long enough to stand trial. He would be fucking crucified by his fellow officers—and *crucified* was not necessarily a figure of speech. Dodge had once seen a suspect handcuffed to the bars of a holding cell with his arms above his head, almost exactly in the pose of the crucified Jesus. The asshole had been left that way till his shoulders separated and he passed out from the pain. Dodge never did learn what exactly the guy had done, but it was pretty clear he'd pissed off the boys in uniform.

He was taking a hell of a risk for a couple of grand here and there. Except that the money added up, especially since none of it was reported to the government. At the rate he was going, he could retire in five years on a full pension and have a tidy nest egg on the side. No second career as a security consultant, no part-time work to raise extra cash, no money worries at all. Maybe he would even relocate to an island somewhere—the Bahamas, Cozumel, whatever. Someplace tropical, with lots of jiggly island women who'd be impressed by an ex-cop from LA with money to throw around.

He left the coffee shop. Outside, a stream of traffic was cruising past on Hollywood Boulevard. Rap and hip-hop blared from every second or third passing car. It was a Friday night—well, early Saturday by now—and everybody was out having fun.

Except him. It pissed him off that he was stuck catching calls on a weekend. Especially now that he and Bradley were stuck with a piece-of-shit stabbing case. Some nigger with a knife in his gut—nobody was going to lose sleep over that, except maybe the punk's mother, who was probably a fat whore living on blow jobs and AFDC money.

The Robertson cases were the downside of working West LA. Nothing that happened in that neighborhood was important. None of it was worth selling. It was strictly spade versus spade, or spic against spic.

Not even worth a mention on the local news, unless a baby got hit, in which case Levine might be able to milk it for a little sentimental appeal.

But let some guns go off a mile or two to the west—in Westwood Village, say—and let a college kid get caught in the cross fire, and bam, it was the lead story on every newscast. Levine would pay good money for info on a story like that.

See, the victim had to be "affluent." That was the magic word. A gang shootout on Robertson Boulevard, or in Inglewood or South Central or Watts, wasn't news. At most it was an interesting statistic—"This weekend, a record fourteen homicides were recorded in Los Angeles County. Now here's Phil with the weather."

On the other hand, a shooting in an "affluent" neighborhood was gold. And most of West LA was affluent as hell, at least by the conveniently elastic standards of the news media. Dodge had seen TV reporters who pulled down two hundred Gs a year doing live remotes in Culver City, in a cul-de-sac where people had their cars up on blocks in their driveways, and talking about the shock of crime in this "affluent, exclusive" neighborhood.

What a crock. But they got away with it, either because the public was too fucking dumb to see they were getting yanked, or because they just didn't give a shit. And why should they? It was only entertainment, after all—something to watch in the dead zone between *Oprah* and *Dateline*.

Dodge shook his head, wearied by the stupidity and pointlessness of the world.

He headed down a dark side street toward his car, parked at the curb alongside a yellow no-parking stripe. As he neared the car, he saw movement in the shadows near the driver's-side door.

It looked like he might have a situation here. Someone trying to boost his car. Not even his personal car—this was his department wheels, a black-and-white Caprice. A new policy required most detective vehicles to be painted like patrol cars.

Dodge kept walking, not altering his stride, while he drew his Smith & Wesson 9mm from its shoulder holster. He passed the car, then pivoted and stepped into the street, training the gun on a teenager who knelt by the door, working the lock with a pick.

"Hey," Dodge said. "Pancho."

The punk looked up and saw the gun. He was some Mexican kid. Well, maybe Guatemalan or El Salvadoran, but to Dodge they were all Mexicans, and they were all named Pancho.

"That car's the property of the motherfucking LAPD," Dodge informed him. "Didn't you see the goddamned DARE sticker, for Christ's sake?"

Pancho stared up at him from his crouch and said something in Spanish. Dodge knew a little Spanish, but he didn't feel like getting into a conversation with some amateur car thief. Didn't feel like booking him either. For one thing, it was a bullshit collar. Pancho would get only a reprimand or, at most, some time in a juvey camp. The paperwork and the court appearance would be more trouble than the bust was worth. Besides, Dodge didn't want to advertise his presence in Hollywood. He didn't want people asking what he'd been doing here when he should have been working with his partner at the crime scene.

Goddamn wetback needed to be taught a lesson, though.

Dodge gestured with his gun. "Get up."

Pancho stood, his slight body trembling even while his pockmarked face remained impassive.

"The thing is, Pancho," Dodge said, "I'm a little overprotective when it comes to my vehicle."

He punctuated this point by delivering a kick to Pancho's crotch. The kid doubled over, and instantly Dodge was behind him, snapping a handcuff over his left wrist, then quickly patting him down. He was clean.

"Crawl," Dodge said, jerking him by the cuff.

Pancho tried to resist. Dodge jerked him harder.

"Come on, you're an animal, you should be good at crawling."

On his knees and elbows the punk crawled around to the rear of the car, where Dodge secured the other cuff to the underside of the chassis.

"Stay there," he said, while Pancho sank to his knees, holding his nuts.

Dodge unlocked the car and started the engine. He thought about just taking off, dragging Pancho behind him for a block or two, but that would be cruel. Worse, it would lead to inquiries and repercussions, two things Dodge disliked.

He left the car idling and walked around to the rear again, then grabbed Pancho by the hair and shoved his face against the muzzle of the exhaust pipe.

"Suck on it. Suck hard."

Pancho's eyes, rolling, were too big for his face. There was a stain on his pants where he'd pissed himself.

He closed his mouth over the pipe and kissed it for a good half minute, obviously struggling not to breathe. The swirl of fumes got to him anyway. He started to choke, tried to pull his face away. Dodge tapped the nape of his neck with the gun.

"More."

Pancho again clamped his teeth on the pipe.

"That's it, amigo. Work it good. This is excellent practice for you. You'll be real popular in county lockup, which is where you'll be going one of these days."

Pancho began to make retching noises. His face was sweaty and pale.

Dodge reached over with his free hand and pinched Pancho's nostrils shut, simultaneously leaning on him from behind, forcing the pipe deeper into his throat.

"Breathe deep, piece of shit."

Pancho struggled, tugging at the handcuff, shaking his shoulders. Dodge held on. He had wrestled bigger punks than this one.

He didn't let go until he was sure the wetback had taken a nice big hit of carbon monoxide, enough to make him good and sick. Then he stepped away and allowed Pancho to jerk clear of the pipe. The kid fell over on his side, wheezing and shuddering, and Dodge unlocked the handcuffs and pocketed them.

"Still want the car?" Dodge asked.

Pancho just lay there as a dribble of vomit pooled on the asphalt beside his open mouth.

Dodge smiled. "I didn't think so."

He slid behind the wheel and drove off, leaving the kid on the street like so much trash.

10

"You and him," Larkin said, "face-to-face?"

"It's the only way," Tess answered evenly.

"Might work." DiFranco sounded intrigued. "Could get a reaction out of him, at any rate."

Tess nodded. "If it doesn't, nothing will."

"I don't know." Larkin was shaking his head. "He's probably expecting to see you."

"Is he? Why? As far as we know, he's not even aware that I'm in LA. If I walk in unannounced, he may betray something. In his eyes, or"—she nodded at the computer—"in his voice."

DiFranco and Hart exchanged a glance. On the TV monitors, the interrogation continued, Michaelson and Gaines pressing, Hayde unfazed.

"We've gotta clear it with Michaelson," DiFranco said finally.

Tess shrugged. "Buzz him."

Larkin looked peeved, but he sent a signal to Michaelson's pager. A moment later Michaelson touched the vest pocket of his jacket, feeling the pager's vibration. He excused himself, leaving Tyler and Gaines with the suspect.

A moment later he entered the surveillance room. He was a thin man with a hawklike proboscis that had earned him the nickname of the Nose. His slightly nasal voice may have contributed to the appellation. Tess had seen one of her squadmates create hand shadows on the wall of his cubicle to produce a passable likeness of Michaelson's profile. "Watch yourselves, everybody," the agent had warned in a stage whisper. "Never let down your guard. Remember . . . the Nose knows."

Tess found herself staring at that nose as she told Michaelson what she wanted to do. He listened impatiently, then looked past her and asked, "Nothing on the stress analysis?" He was always looking past her, or through her, or around her. She was an obstacle in his life, nothing more.

"No significant deviations from sine wave baseline," the agent at the computer said.

"Hell." The Nose stared at Hayde's multiple images on the TV screens. Tess waited. She knew it was Michaelson's call. "All right," he said finally. "Let me go back in there and resume the interrogation. Give it five minutes. Then send in McCallum."

Referring to Tess in the third person even when she was three feet away was another of Michaelson's winning personality traits. She didn't bother to thank him. He wouldn't have heard her, anyway.

He left the observation room. Tess stared after him, thinking that she had won a small victory. She ought to feel pleased. Instead what she felt was a sudden tremor, subtle at first, working its way through her body.

She needed a moment to pinpoint its meaning. Then she knew: It was fear.

Five minutes, and she would be in the same room with the man who might be Mobius.

In the same room.

Michaelson was seated at the steel table again. Tess

turned to Larkin. Holding her voice steady, she said, "I'll be back in a minute."

"Where the hell are you going?"

"Ladies' room."

She walked out without further discussion. She knew the others would think it was a sign of weakness that she had to find some privacy, compose herself. She didn't care.

All she really wanted was a few moments alone. At least that was what she told herself. But when she entered the rest room, a stronger urge overcame her. She opened the nearest stall and leaned over the commode and vomited up her dinner.

When she was through, she flushed the toilet, then flushed it again. The gurgling water soothed her somehow. She walked to the counter and ran her hands under a stream of hot water, splashing her face. Then she turned on the cold and rinsed out her mouth. She looked at herself in the mirror and saw dark crescents of fatigue underscoring her gray eyes. Her face was pale, fringed in strawberry blond curls. A scattering of freckles stood out on her forehead and cheeks. People had told her that she looked young for her age, but tonight exhaustion made her look older than thirty-four.

She dried her face, took a breath, and checked her watch—12:25. It occurred to her it was no longer Good Friday. Good Friday, the day innocence had died.

For her, innocence had died on February 12, two years ago.

She resisted the pull of that thought. She tried to focus on better things, on her life before Mobius. In those years she had never missed a Good Friday mass. The candles would be extinguished one by one until

only the paschal candle was left. That last flame was
carried out of the church, leaving the congregation
in darkness.

Tenebrae, it was called. The Service of Shadows.

Those same words, she thought, could describe her
life, her job. She and Andrus and their colleagues—
all of them, Michaelson and Gaines, Collins and Diaz,
even a supercilious little prick like Larkin—all had
devoted their lives to the darkness. They lived for the
night, when the predators prowled. They fought the
shadows, and in time they became little more than
shadows themselves.

And if they were shadows, what then was Paul
Voorhees? Less than a shadow now . . . only a shadow's memory, fading out.

The key in the lock . . .

She didn't want to think about it. But she couldn't
help herself.

The key turning, the lock yielding without resistance . . .

The door had been left unlatched.

In that moment she knew something was wrong.
Paul would never leave the front door unsecured.

There was a miniature flashlight on her key chain.
She switched it on and aimed the penlight beam at
the lock. In the dim red glow, she made out scratch
marks on the metal—marks left by a tension bar and
a pick. The lock had been opened without a key, by
someone using burglar's tools.

Someone.

Mobius?

She dismissed the idea. Of course it wasn't Mobius.
Mobius had no way of knowing where she lived. And
nothing in his modus operandi suggested a facility with
lock-picking tools.

But he was full of surprises. And the psych experts had warned her that he might try to make physical contact.

She reached inside the special compartment of her handbag and withdrew her Sig Sauer 9mm, then slowly opened the door and looked inside.

She and Paul lived in a modest split-level in Englewood, a suburb of Denver. The house was a rental. It was her place, but Paul—unknown to their colleagues—spent most of his nights here and had his own key.

The front door opened on a small living room, minimally furnished, with a cramped kitchen adjoining it. Track lighting threw a wash of yellow light on the bare white walls. Tess had been meaning to buy some paintings for those walls, but she'd never seemed to get around to it.

Now she wished she'd had the foresight to buy a mirror. Leaning in the doorway, she could see only half the room. A mirror would have shown her the other half.

She listened. No sound. That troubled her. When Paul was around, there was always some electronic background noise. He was addicted to talk radio and cable news.

She knew he was here. His car, a Hoover-blue bureau Crown Victoria like hers, was parked in the carport.

She almost called out his name. Although it would be stupid to announce her presence if an intruder was here, she couldn't stand the ambiguity of the situation, couldn't stand not knowing if she ought to be terrified or merely annoyed at him for frightening her like this. And she wanted to hear his voice.

But she stayed silent. She was a professional, and in moments of danger she reverted almost instinctively to her training.

Since she couldn't scope out the entire living room,

she made a quick entrance, ducking through the door-way and instantly pivoting toward the unseen side of the room as she dropped into a half crouch to make a smaller target.

That part of the room was empty also.

She crossed the living room fast, the 9mm held close to her body, not extended in two straight arms as it often was in movies and TV dramas. The greatest risk in drawing a firearm was that it could be taken away and used against you by your assailant. Holding the gun close made it easier to maintain control.

There was no one in the kitchen, either. But from the tap dribbled a thin stream of water. There were dishes in the sink, the remains of a microwaved dinner floating in a film of detergent bubbles.

Paul had eaten alone. Not an unusual circumstance when Tess was held up at the office, as she frequently was on the Mobius case. He had been washing the dishes. He always cleaned up after himself—one of the small considerate acts that meant so much to her—and in the middle of the chore, he had simply stopped. Stopped and left the room, with the water running.

She reached out to turn off the faucet, then decided not to. Someone else in the house might notice if the hiss of water in the pipes suddenly stopped.

Of course that other person might have heard her pull up in her sedan. Might have heard the slam of her car door. Might be waiting for her right now.

No ordinary burglar would wait for the homeowner to find him. But if it was Mobius . . .

If it was Mobius, she knew where he would be.

The bedroom. That was always his killing ground.

She stepped out of the kitchen and took a long look at the stairs.

Stairs were dangerous. She would be exposed, with-out cover or concealment.

The smart thing to do was call for help, get some backup in here, but she knew she wouldn't do the smart thing.

She took the steps fast but quietly, grateful for her soft-soled shoes that made no noise and the firm treads that did not squeak. Then she was on the second floor, in the hallway near the laundry nook, smelling the aroma of fabric softener as she tried to look in both directions at once.

To her left was the guest bedroom, made up as a den. Lamplight glimmered from inside, but it signified nothing. The lights in there were on a timer. Next to the den was the bathroom, dark. To her right, the master bedroom. Light spilled through a crack in the door, left a few inches ajar.

She moved toward the bedroom, taking long, sliding steps, the way they'd taught her in Hogan's Alley.

She reached the door and stood back, peering through the narrow opening. She saw the dresser and the mirror over it, reflecting only the bare white wall across the room.

Not quite bare. She saw smudges on the wall. Red smudges.

Blood.

She forgot caution, forgot her training and everything else in a spurt of fear that sent her rushing headlong into the bedroom where Paul lay in bed, fully clothed, his wrists taped to the nightstands flanking the bed, his throat opened by a knife and coated in blood.

Mobius.

His MO.

He'd learned her address, picked the lock—

She spun in a full circle, looking for Mobius, wanting him to be there, willing to let him shoot her if she could get a shot at him first.

He wasn't there. She checked the closet. Nothing.

She turned to Paul again, feeling the wound in his neck to see if the blood still flowed. A flow of blood meant a pulse, and a pulse meant life.

There was no pulse.

He was dead. She had seen death at other times in her life, and she knew the feel and smell of it.

"Why did you do this?" she whispered in a stranger's voice, a voice hoarse and raw as if from prolonged weeping. "Why did you take him? He wasn't the one you wanted. I am. I am."

Slowly she raised her head, understanding that this was true.

He had come for her. He had seen the bureau car in the carport and the lights inside the house. He might even have heard the sound of dishes being washed as he opened the front door. So he'd entered the kitchen, ready to seize her from behind—only to find a man there. A man he'd never seen.

Paul might have heard him, sensed him, or perhaps he'd never heard anything at all. Either way, he had been overpowered, knocked unconscious. He must have been, or there would have been signs of a struggle in the kitchen. And he had remained unconscious until the end. Tess was sure he had because his mouth had not been taped. There had been no need to gag him when he was out cold.

Probably he hadn't suffered much. Probably it had been quick, a blow to the head, a moment of surprise, then oblivion. Probably it hadn't been too bad, not too bad.

"Not too bad," she whispered, and then she realized how insane it was to think that anything about this was not too bad.

She touched the wound again, still hoping vaguely to find the warmth of life, but the blood on his neck was dry and tacky, as were the few blood spots spattered on the wall.

The killing had been done some time ago. An hour at least. And Mobius was gone.

But he couldn't be.

"You can't be gone!" she shouted at the stillness of the house. "Come out and face me, come on, *come on!*"

She left the bedroom at a run and bolted into the bathroom, pulling aside the shower curtain, half ripping it from its hooks. He wasn't there. She stumbled down the hall and entered the den, pushing the TV off its stand to look behind it, scattering the pillows on the sofa. Finally she fell on her knees with her hair tangled over her face and her thin arms shaking. She had lost the gun, dropped it someplace, and even if he had been here, she couldn't have shot him.

"You son of a bitch," she moaned, her face in her hands. "Piece of shit, motherfucker . . ."

But she couldn't hurt him with words. Couldn't hurt him at all.

She knelt for a long time, aware of nothing but pain, pain that was her world now, pain that was everything.

11

Her face in the mirror.

It startled her as she came back to herself. She was in the rest room of the LA field office, two years and six weeks had passed since that night, and she was about to introduce herself to a man who might have robbed her of everything that mattered.

People could tell her that they knew what she'd lost, but they didn't know that Paul Voorhees had been much more than her partner.

In dreams Tess sometimes found herself with him again, hiking an alpine trail in the Rockies. They would pause in their ascent, looking down at the path they had taken, and all the world below would be screened in white mist.

Then she would think that she and Paul had risen above the clouds, to the top of the sky.

It's not like they told us in church, she would say. *No harps. No wings.*

And Paul would laugh, and she would turn to look at him, but she couldn't see his face—it was hidden in the sudden overpowering brightness of the sun.

She always awoke then. And she could never get back to sleep.

At times Tess believed that the trail was real, and

she and Paul would climb it someday. At other times she believed in nothing but darkness and the damp earth enclosing an urn of ashes.

Bereavement leave and therapy had not healed the hurt. Nothing could heal it.

She checked her watch. Nearly ten minutes had gone by. Time to go.

Leaving the bathroom, she walked down the hall to the door with the DO NOT DISTURB sign. The door was unlocked, a violation of normal procedure, but necessary if she was to enter unannounced.

So this was it. Open the door, enter, and meet William Hayde.

It seemed like such a simple thing, yet for a moment she wasn't sure she could do it. She remembered a parachute jump years ago, the final seconds of standing in the airplane's open hatchway, waiting to leap into space.

Then, at least, she'd had a parachute.

She opened the door, entered the room.

Everything slowed down. The world grew big around her, its small details looming large in her perception. The glare on the steel tabletop, the creak of the straight-backed chairs, the handcuffs securing Hayde's right hand to the table, his head lifting, his eyes—brown eyes, ordinary eyes—locking on hers.

She met that gaze and held it, and held her breath also.

And saw . . . nothing.

A flicker of curiosity, perhaps. No surprise, no hostility, no recognition.

He did not know her. He had never seen her before.

"Agent Starling's older sister," Hayde said. "Pull up a chair, join the party."

"I'm Tess McCallum," she said.

"Bill Hayde."

Her name had drawn no reaction. He looked bemused at her arrival, her rigid stance and staring eyes.

She tried one more time, though she knew the effort was wasted. "You sent me postcards in Denver."

"I don't think so. I'm not much of a correspondent."

"Novelty postcards."

He shook his head. "Must've been some other perp."

She said nothing. She turned and left the room, shutting the door.

Larkin was in the hall. "Nothing on voice-stress," he said.

"Right."

"He didn't seem to know you."

"He doesn't know me."

"So you think . . . ?"

"He's just a jerk who likes to tie women up. That's all he is. He's not Mobius. He's not anybody."

A moment later Michaelson joined them. He looked at Larkin, ignoring Tess altogether. "I'm kicking him loose," he said.

Larkin nodded.

"There's nothing for us to hold him on. The circumstances of his sexual play with Agent Tyler are too ambiguous to permit prosecution. Mr. Hayde himself seems to have understood as much from the start."

"He's a cool customer," Larkin said.

"I'm not ruling him out yet. Not totally. I want you and DiFranco to look into his background, see if his story checks out. If it doesn't, we can set up surveillance or bring him in for more questions."

"Will do."

"If we talk to him again, we need some facts to trip him up. Another staring contest"—he still didn't look at Tess—"isn't going to get it done."

Michaelson disappeared inside. Tess leaned against a wall, worn out.

When the door opened and William Hayde emerged, she straightened up. The FBI had an image to maintain, and so did she.

"Pleasure doing business with you guys," Hayde was saying. He turned to Tess. "You seemed pretty anxious to see me—and even more anxious to get away."

"I thought you were someone else," she said, her voice flat.

He surprised her with a sympathetic look. "The Pickup Artist?"

She said nothing.

"You've been after him awhile," Hayde said.

"What makes you say so?"

"The way you stared at me when you walked into the room. Like you'd been waiting for that moment a long time."

"You're very perceptive, Mr. Hayde."

He shrugged off the comment. "You'll get him eventually."

"I'm sure we will."

"In the meantime . . . hang in there, okay?"

She actually smiled. "Considering what we put you through tonight, you seem awfully solicitous toward me."

"I have a weakness for pretty women."

Her smile vanished. "Oh."

He stepped closer, lowering his voice. "I don't suppose—"

"I'm not into tie-up games, Mr. Hayde."

"Your loss, baby."

He walked away, whistling. Michaelson and Gaines escorted him out. Tess stared after him, wishing he'd been the one.

She felt someone watching her. Turning, she saw Larkin in the doorway of the observation room.

"Anything from the other undercover ops?"

"Nothing so far."

She glanced at her wristwatch. It was one A.M. "We've missed him."

"He could be getting a late start. Or maybe he's not out there tonight."

Tess didn't answer. But she knew Larkin was wrong.

Mobius was out there.

He was always out there.

12

The agent's name was Dante, he was a young hotshot from the Portland office, and he was excited.

"Got it," Dante told Tennant as he slammed down the phone. "Driver for America's Best Cab remembers picking up Pierce at LAX. He delivered her to the Century Plaza Hotel."

"When did she get there?" Tennant snapped.

"Twelve-fifteen."

The clock on the wall read 1:05. She'd had fifty minutes to meet her contact. Too much time.

"Let's move," Tennant said, hoping for the best.

The two unmarked bureau cars were parked in a passenger loading zone outside the terminal. Tennant and J&B took the first car, accompanied by Dante and another Portland man named Wilkins. The others followed in the second sedan.

Jarvis drove, Tennant riding shotgun.

"I'm betting she's still there," Dante said from the backseat. "Probably checked in for the night, stupid bitch."

"If she's so stupid," Bickerstaff pointed out, "how come she gave us the slip?"

Tennant cut off this conversation before it could

become even more of a waste of time than it already was. "We go into the lobby and fan out, then proceed to the coffee shop, the pool area, and any other public spaces. Remember, she may still be waiting to meet someone, in which case, wherever she is, she'll be watching the door. We know she's already made some of us, so when she sees us coming, there's a good chance she'll run for it."

"Any dark-haired lady breaks into a sprint, we'll tackle her," Dante said, trying to be funny.

"I don't care if it's a dark-haired lady or a blonde or a little kid with a lollipop. Anybody does anything suspicious, we hold them for questioning. If we're lucky, we'll get her *and* her contact."

"And the suitcase," Jarvis said under his breath, his voice low enough that only Tennant could hear.

Tennant nodded. Amanda Pierce wasn't important. Even her contact would be a lower-echelon operative. The suitcase was what really mattered.

"Let's say she starts shooting," Bickerstaff said as the car sped north on Sepulveda Boulevard.

"She used a knife on Kidder." This was Wilkins. He reminded Tennant of what used to be called a preppie, complete with an Ivy League law degree. "There's no reason to think she's packing a firearm."

"No reason to think she isn't, either," Tennant said. "Maybe she just didn't want to fire off a gun in the rest room and alert the rest of us. Anyway, if her contact is with her, he'll be armed for sure."

"This turns into a shooting match, it'll get ugly." Dante, stating the obvious.

Tennant didn't hesitate. "If she or her partner draws a weapon, return fire—and go for a kill shot."

"Then we lose the chance to interrogate." Wilkins the boy lawyer.

"There are worse things to lose." Tennant hesitated,

then added, "Don't wait to see a gun. If she even opens her suitcase, light her up."

Jarvis glanced at him and nodded. They both knew what was in the suitcase, even if Wilkins and Dante did not.

Her contact still hadn't arrived, and Amanda Pierce was getting scared.

True, she'd been waiting only about an hour. But she shouldn't have had to wait at all. She was the one who'd been delayed. Her contact should have been the one waiting for her.

Unless he'd left already. In which case, she was seriously fucked.

She looked around at the hotel lobby, the high chandeliers, the arched windows framing tropical plants. Nice place to hang out, but not for her, not now.

She pressed one leg against the suitcase that rested by her own stool, holding it protectively. She had to stay upbeat. The feds hadn't been lying in ambush for her at the hotel, so evidently they didn't know where the rendezvous was scheduled to take place. Even if her contact never showed, she might still have a chance to arrange another meeting—if she could elude capture long enough.

In the meantime there was another problem, ridiculously trivial, yet one that threatened everything.

She had no money.

Nearly all of her cash had been used on taxi fare and as payment for the overpriced ginger ale she had ordered at the bar. She could not check in, because doing so would require using her credit card. The card was part of an identity kit she had put together over the past two months, under the name of Lucy Mallone. She had used the card to check into the motel last night—but with her cover blown, she couldn't rely on the card any longer. If she used it again, her whereabouts would be instantly traced.

Nor could she use her legitimate credit cards or her ATM card. Same problem. Charging a purchase to a card registered to Amanda Pierce would be like firing a signal flare to guide the feds straight to her.

Her wallet contained less than one hundred dollars in hard currency. Anyway, she couldn't pay cash for a rental car, and that was what she needed—transportation.

Amanda, God damn it, you are up a frigging creek. . . .

Wait.

A man had entered the lobby, tall, casually attired. His age was difficult to judge. Forty or a little older.

As he approached the bar, she studied him. He wore a sport jacket—useful for concealing a weapon— but no necktie, which could be used by an opponent to gain a stranglehold in a fight. His eyes were masked by dark glasses, another good sign.

Her contact might have made an appearance, after all.

There was no way to know, not yet. She had never seen him. He might be anyone, of any description.

The man reached the bar area and stopped, looking slowly around. She gave him a momentary glance before averting her eyes. If he was her contact, even this brief signal should be enough.

Movement. On the periphery of her vision he rounded the bar and slipped onto the stool beside her.

He must be the one.

The bartender appeared. The man ordered a gin and tonic. When the bartender turned away, Pierce tensed, knowing that now was the moment for him to initiate the conversation.

"Beautiful hotel, isn't it?" he said.

She looked at him. Behind the shaded lenses, his eyes were as blank as a baby's.

"Yes," she answered, hearing her own voice from a great distance. "Very beautiful."

"My name's Donald Stevenson. From Aurora, Illinois. In town on business."

"Lucy Mallone."

"From?"

"Seattle."

"Great city, Seattle. Rains a lot, but I wouldn't mind that. I like the rain."

"Me, too," she said absently, trying to decide what to do.

He was not her contact, obviously. He was just some asshole looking for a little action.

The bartender delivered the drink. "Put it on my room tab," Donald Stevenson said, opening his wallet to take out his electronic room key.

Pierce glanced inside the wallet and saw credit cards and a thick sheaf of bills.

Suddenly she was glad Donald Stevenson had chosen to sit beside her. She'd been wrong to think of him as useless. Quite the contrary.

She began to think he could be very useful indeed.

13

The two bureau cars turned east onto Pico Boulevard and rushed toward the skyline of Century City, an upscale complex of office buildings and shopping malls built on what was once the backlot of Twentieth Century Fox.

"Ever been to the Plaza?" Bickerstaff asked Tennant.

"In 'eighty-four, when Reagan was reelected. He held his victory party here."

"And you were on their invite list?"

"Fat chance. I was working out of the LA office at the time. Secret Service brought some of us in for extra manpower on election night."

He remembered that night—the tidal wave of votes crushing that wuss, Mondale. Afterward, he had shared a drink with some friends at the hotel bar. . . .

"The bar," Tennant said with a snap of his fingers. "If she's waiting to meet somebody, the bar is where she'll be. It's smack in the middle of the lobby. Gives her a way to watch the front doors without being noticed. And it offers more avenues of escape than any other part of the hotel."

"If she's in the lobby," Dante said, "she may see us as soon as we enter."

"Right. So we go in fast, and we stay alert. Got it?"

They got it. There were no more smiles from Dante, no more smart comments from attorney Wilkins.

Jarvis hooked left onto the Avenue of the Stars— only in LA did they have street names like that—and steered the sedan into the curving driveway of the Century Plaza Hotel. A parking valet approached their car as the doors flew open. Tennant badged the guy. "Official business, stay back."

Tennant told the three agents from the second car to cover the hotel's side and rear exits and monitor the tactical frequency on their Handy-Talkies. Then he led Wilkins, Dante, and J&B up the steps and into the lobby, his hand under his jacket, touching the Sig Sauer 9mm holstered to his hip.

She would have to kill him.

Amanda Pierce had never killed anyone, but she had no doubt she could do it. Survival was her imperative. Other lives were of no consequence in comparison to her own.

"You visit LA often?" she asked.

"Three or four times a year. I've got clients here. How about you?"

"First time in LA."

"Business or pleasure?"

"Pleasure trip."

Stevenson chuckled. "Well, we can all use some pleasure from time to time."

The lobby was spacious and elegant and nearly deserted at 1:15 A.M. The clerk at the reception desk gave Tennant a look that said, *May I help you?*

Tennant ignored him. The bar, identified as the Lobby Court, was straight ahead, its patrons in silhouette against the two-story windows that looked out on a spotlighted garden. Tennant led his team toward the bar, hardly daring to hope that Amanda Pierce would still be here, and then he saw her.

Dark hair, clipped in a bun. Brown blazer and slacks—the outfit she'd stolen from Agent Kidder.

She was seated at the far end of the bar, perched on a stool, a drink in her hand, chatting to a man who might be her contact or maybe some tourist trying to pick her up.

Her upper body was turned at an angle to give her full attention to the man beside her. She hadn't seen them enter.

"Approach from all sides," Tennant said. "Remember your orders. You've got a green light."

A green light to take her out. Just like James Bond—a license to kill.

"Of course," Stevenson was saying, "if you're gonna stay in LA, this is the place."

"It lives up to its reputation."

"Yeah—unlike a lot of things in this town. Hey, can I refresh your drink?"

"Sure."

"What're you having?"

"Ginger ale."

"Nothing stronger?"

"I don't drink." This was true, but even if she'd been a drinker, she needed a clear head tonight.

Wilkins and Dante veered to the right. Tennant, with J&B, headed left.

"I don't see the suitcase," Bickerstaff said under his breath.

"Could be against the bar, out of sight."

"Or she could've passed it on already."

Tennant shook his head. "If she'd made the exchange, she wouldn't hang around."

Pierce still hadn't looked their way. The man next to her might have registered their approach, but he showed no reaction. Tennant didn't think he was the contact. Most likely Pierce's contact hadn't shown yet, and she was making small talk with this guy to be less conspicuous as she waited at the bar.

Wilkins and Dante were closing in. Pierce would see them any second now.

Before she could react, Tennant reached her from behind and clamped a hand on her shoulder.

"Don't move," he said in a firm voice that brooked no argument, "you're under arrest."

A twitch of surprise from her, and she swung around on her stool. Tennant almost drew his weapon, and then he was looking at her face.

The right hair, right jacket, right figure—but not the right woman. Not Amanda Pierce. This woman was ten years older, with too much makeup.

"What the hell?" the woman said.

"Anyway," Stevenson was saying as the bartender placed a fresh glass before each of them, "you come to the Pacific coast, you want to see the Pacific, am I right? I like to sit on the balcony and breathe in the salt air. I always get a room with a Malibu view."

"Malibu view?"

"Facing north—or is it west? The coastline zigs and zags so much, I don't even know. But I like to see the lights of Malibu off in the distance."

"I'll remember that for next time."

"You've got to ask for it special. That's the thing

about the MiraMist. They take care of their longtime
guests. Treat you like family."

"That's good to know."

"I've stayed at other places. The Beverly Hills, the
Century Plaza—you ever been there?"

"The Century Plaza? Yes."

About an hour and a half ago, she added silently.
But I didn't stay long.

Tennant left the bewildered woman and her consort
without explanation. Pierce might still be here. After
meeting her contact, she could have gone to some
other part of the hotel.

He led his team to the pool area. No one was there.

"Coffee shop," he snapped.

She must be here somewhere.

"Nice ambience, the Century Plaza, but I'll still take
the MiraMist. We're, what, a half mile from the
beach? You can't beat it." Donald Stevenson leaned
back on his stool. "Who knows? Maybe I'll retire
here."

"That'd be nice."

"If I could afford it." He laughed. "Property taxes
alone would eat me alive. And then, wouldn't you
know, with my luck I'd be out here six months and
they'd have the Big One and this whole town would
slide into the fucking ocean."

"I guess you can never be completely safe anywhere," Pierce said with a smile.

No luck.

Tennant and his squad had searched every public
space in the Century Plaza Hotel. Amanda Pierce was
nowhere—unless she had checked in.

Tennant returned to the lobby and asked the desk clerk if he had seen a woman matching Pierce's description enter the hotel within the past ninety minutes. Answer: No.

Outside, the two valets stood pondering the unmarked bureau cars. Tennant asked them the same question.

One of them had seen her. A cab had dropped her off. She'd started to walk toward the hotel—then when the cab was gone, she'd retraced her steps. He'd thought it was kind of weird.

"Where'd she go?" Tennant barked.

"Nowhere. That's the thing. She got into another taxi."

Tennant closed his eyes. She had known the first cab might be traced, so she'd led her pursuit to the wrong hotel.

"Did you see what kind it was?" he asked hopelessly.

"What kind?"

"Checker Cab, Yellow Cab?"

"Sorry, sir. I didn't notice."

"Do any security cameras cover this area?"

"This is a hotel, not a jail."

Not a jail. Of course it was not a jail. The way things were going, Amanda Pierce would never get anywhere near a jail.

Tennant turned to face J&B, Wilkins, and Dante, all gathered behind him. They'd heard everything. He tried to marshal his thoughts, to think of a plan of action, some order to give, but nothing came to him.

"She could be anywhere in the city," Bickerstaff said, his voice hollow.

"We lost her," Jarvis added.

Possibly for the first time in his life, Jack Tennant felt like an old man. "We lost her," he echoed, turning away.

14

It was after one-thirty A.M. when Donald Stevenson finally asked if she would like to see the Malibu view from his room. She said yes, of course she would. He smiled, thinking he'd scored a conquest, when all he'd actually done was ensure that the Malibu view was the last sight he would ever see.

The kill would be quick and quiet, and she would leave him there to be discovered, eventually, by the housekeeping service, while she took his wallet—cash, credit cards, bank card—and the keys to his rental car. There might be other valuables in his luggage. She would take whatever she could get, then relocate to another part of the city, someplace in the broad, flat interior, far from the sea. From the safe haven of a motel, she would try to arrange a new meeting.

Her plan could be salvaged. Despite setbacks, the chance of success remained high. All that was necessary was for Donald Stevenson of Aurora, Illinois, to die tonight, and for Amanda Pierce this was no hardship at all.

They rode the elevator to the sixteenth floor. He led her to room 1625 and unlocked it with his card key. The drapes trembled in a breeze from the balcony. The room was cool, almost chilly, lit by a single bedside lamp.

Pierce stepped inside, then hesitated, reluctant to let go of her suitcase. But it would look odd if she continued to hold it. Carefully she placed it on a desk chair and joined Stevenson at the sliding door.

"You can see all the way up the coast," he said with a theatrical gesture at the panorama framed in the glass.

"You're right. It's a great view."

"You on the other side of the hotel?"

"Uh, yes."

"They stuck you with a view of the street. Next time you're in town, ask for this view specifically."

Looking away, she studied the room. She noticed a suitcase on a folding table, a coat in the closet, a ten-dollar tip already left out for the maid. She reminded herself to take the ten dollars when she departed with his wallet and keys. No point in wasting it on the help.

"Want something from the minibar?" he asked.

"No, thank you."

She touched her belt buckle, thinking she could do it now, end this goddamn game. But the open balcony door worried her. If he cried out, his scream might carry on the night air.

"It's a little cool in here," she said, hugging herself.

"Oh. Sorry."

She nearly went for him while he locked the door and fastened the drapes. But her fingers fumbled with the belt buckle—perhaps she was more nervous than she had been willing to admit—and before she could work the mechanism, he had turned to face her again.

"You're a beautiful woman," he said.

She smiled. "Every woman is beautiful at two in the morning."

"Don't say that. I'm being serious here. I mean . . . look at you . . . You're just . . . wow."

She wasn't sure what to say in response, and it

didn't matter, because suddenly he was drawing her near and pressing his mouth on hers, gently at first, then with mounting heat, and she felt a rush of pleasure in her body that was almost dizzying.

"Lucy," he said, his voice a whisper.

She hadn't planned to go all the way with this guy. Still, she was prepared to do what was necessary. She needed Donald Stevenson dead, and if she couldn't kill him now, she would have her chance once he'd gotten his rocks off.

"There a problem?" he asked, watching her, and she realized she hadn't moved or spoken.

"Not at all," she said, and with one deft hand she unbuttoned her blouse and shrugged it off, letting him see her white bra and the small hills of her breasts.

She expected him to say something stupidly sentimental, but instead he just reached out and pulled her with him onto the queen-size bed, rolling on the floral spread. Slowly he stroked the cup over her left breast. His fingers were gentle, surprisingly dexterous—long fingers, she observed, with prominent joints and clearly defined blue veins. He did not rush to unhook the bra. He let his hand trace careless circles on the underside of her breast in a slow, teasing motion that tickled and made her warm.

Finally he reached behind her and unclasped the bra, letting it fall away. Her breasts, paler than the surrounding flesh, rose and fell with her breathing.

He was stroking her breast again, then cupping his hand to lightly squeeze . . . releasing the pressure almost before she felt it . . . then again, lingering a moment longer before the next release . . . again and again, finally drawing his fingers along the smooth sides of her breast and pressing his palm against the nipple and turning his hand slowly, and now the room was turning also, the bed in motion, the ceiling rotat-

ing like the blade of a fan, and she heard a moan
tremble out of her throat, soft as a bird's call.

And still he hadn't undressed, hadn't even removed
his jacket, even as he stripped the clothes from her.
She understood that this was how he wanted it to be—
himself fully dressed, while she was naked.

He leaned closer on the bed and kissed her—not
on the mouth, as she expected, but on her right eyebrow, then on her left, then on each eyelid, the bridge
of her nose, its tip, and then lowering to her mouth
but bypassing it for her chin, her neck, the hollow of
her throat, everywhere but her lips, which wanted the
kiss now, wanted it and waited as he pressed his
mouth to her cleavage, her belly, and then he lifted
his head and gave her the kiss she needed, his lips on
hers, her mouth opening and their tongues meeting
with a shock that was almost electric.

"It's better," he said when he pulled gently free, "if
you wait for it. If I *make* you wait. Don't you think?"

Other men had never made her wait. But he was
right. It *was* better.

"The Hindus know about love," he was saying as
he moved his fingers slowly through her hair and
brought a rush of tingles to her scalp. "They wrote a
sutra on it, dedicated to Kama, the god of love. Have
you read that book?"

She shook her head no. He eased her onto the pillows, then removed her slacks, her underpants, using
one hand only, while the other hand continued to
touch her in new and unexplored places, and his voice
whispered, "They say there are sixty-four arts of love,
and a man skilled in all of them will be a leader of
other men and of women."

This was a strange way for Donald Stevenson of
Aurora, Illinois, to be talking, but she couldn't think

too much about it, not when his hands were now stroking the insides of her thighs.

"They know that love is powerful," he whispered. "Love is godlike, and gods have power. . . ."

His hands moved in close to her sex and then eased away, and she knew he was teasing her again, as he had when he touched her breasts and when he kissed her. He was making her wait, making her want it, want *him*. She ought to have resented him for this exercise of power over her, but she felt no anger, no reproach, nothing but the ripples of warm and cold energy pulsing through her body like a disturbance in the clear waters of a pond.

He lifted a finger to his lips, as if he meant to shush her, though she was making no sound. As she watched, he licked the finger, and then she felt it slide down her belly to the vee between her legs, parting the moist lips. He lingered inside her, gently testing every niche, while his other hand curved behind her and kneaded the place where her buttocks met her back.

She wanted him to go deeper, and because she wanted it, she knew he would not do it, not yet. But he surprised her, abruptly thrusting his finger into her depths, then just as quickly withdrawing. Another tease, and she should hate him for it, she really should.

"Again," she breathed.

"Beg me."

She wouldn't. It was crazy, humiliating. Who the hell was he to make her beg for anything?

"Please," she said.

Another thrust, two fingers this time, wet with her moistness, plunging in hard and fast, then pulling free.

"Please," she repeated. She had no dignity. She hated herself.

Two fingers again, probing deeply, and inside her the fingers curled, pressing the walls of her inner cavity as if sounding stops on a flute, fingers that searched for something and then found it, racking her body with a sudden terrifying plunge of pleasure that nearly stopped her heart.

"Please," she gasped, not begging, not communicating, the word meaningless.

After that, there were no more words in her mind. There was only the lightning stroke of pleasure—again—again—his hand in her, and her body shaking, writhing, wetness everywhere, his breathing and hers, a hand on her breast rubbing hard, her belly clenching, pain and joy and explosive colors flaring behind her eyelids, and at last when she couldn't stand it any longer, he pulled his hand free and said, "Now for the real thing."

A brief pause, and she realized he was putting on a condom, and then his cock was in her, and she felt its stiff curvature, its bursting pressure, and she almost screamed but his hand was on her mouth, muffling the cry, and at that same moment he released himself.

For a long time afterward, Pierce lay still, fighting for control of her breath and her thoughts. Distantly she felt him pull out of her, then roll over to lie by her side. Even now he wore his jacket. A well-dressed lover.

She didn't look at him. She stared at the ceiling and tried to remember why she was here. She'd had some purpose, a secret intention.

Oh, right.

She had to steal his stuff. And first, he had to die.

She almost regretted having to do it. The man was such a goddamn good fuck. Well, at least he would go out with a bang.

Reaching beside her, she found her discarded slacks, the belt still strung through the loops. Carefully she opened the heavy belt buckle, with no fumbling this time, and took out the knife.

She palmed it, the blade still safely retracted, and considered her options. A straight cut across the throat would be instantly fatal, but the carotid arteries would geyser. She needed a clean kill. Her best maneuver was to drive the blade into the torso below the rib cage on the left side, then angle it upward, puncturing the lung and perhaps the aorta. Even if the wound didn't kill him at once, he would be too badly weakened to put up any resistance, and she could finish him with a slash across the back of the neck.

Pierce rolled onto her side, the switchblade snapping open, and then his wrist closed over hers, wrenching hard, his fingers exerting painful pressure on the ball of her thumb until her hand opened and she released the knife.

She stared at the dropped weapon on the sheets, at Donald Stevenson, at the cold amusement in his eyes, and she knew with sudden certainty that she had made a serious mistake.

"Let me go," she said for no reason, except that the words seemed to come of their own will.

"Not a chance," he said softly.

She kicked at him and at the covers, trying to gain some traction and propel herself off the bed, but the covers merely skidded under her, bunching up at her feet, and then he was on top of her and there was a knife in his hand.

Not her knife. Not a switchblade. This was a hunting knife, seven inches of carbon steel with serrated edges, and along the ragged line of the blade she saw dark flecks of dried blood.

She parted her lips to shout for help. He slapped

her into silence with a blow that nearly knocked her unconscious.

Then there was only her hoarse breathing and a whirl of light and shadow and the pressure of tape on her mouth, sealing her lips, then more tape binding her wrists to the headboard.

She was naked, gagged, bound, more helpless than ever in her life, and it made no sense. Who the fuck was this guy? What the fuck was going on?

Maybe he was her contact, after all. Maybe he'd been instructed to kill her instead of paying her off. But that couldn't be right. She hadn't given him any information yet. And now her mouth was sealed, and she couldn't tell him anything.

It was crazy, just crazy. . . .

Crazy.

The word quivered through her like a twitch, and she understood.

Yeah, Amanda. That's just what it is.

He wasn't her contact. He was a psycho—and probably a killer.

For the past hour she'd been playing with this man, never suspecting that all the while he was playing a subtler game of his own.

"Handy little item you've got," he said with a glance at the abandoned switchblade on the bed. "You handled it with a certain professional aplomb. But it appears you miscalculated. I'm the one who'll cut . . ."

With his knife he traced a line along her left forearm, raising a thin welt.

". . . and run."

She tried to say something through the tape pasted to her mouth, but no words could get out, and she didn't know what she could tell him anyway.

He pulled on a pair of rubber gloves from his jacket, then fiddled with her knife, clicking it open and shut.

On the desk chair across the room lay her suitcase. Pierce thought with bitter irony of its contents and what she could have done with them, the awful surprise she could have had for this man.

He noted the direction of her gaze. "You seem awfully interested in your luggage. I wonder why."

Getting up, he moved toward the desk chair. She saw him smooth out his jacket, adjust his collar, zip his fly.

He opened the suitcase and groped among its contents. "Cell phone . . . toiletries . . . change of clothes . . . and this." He lifted out a sealed metal canister, ten inches long. "This is interesting."

She watched him, trying to betray nothing with her eyes.

"There's liquid in here," he said. "If it's nitro, I'm probably in imminent danger of blowing myself up." He tossed the canister lightly. "But anybody can get hold of nitro. Nitro is no big deal. This is something else, isn't it, Lucy?"

He set down the canister and rummaged in the suitcase's zippered pocket, where he found her two wallets—one containing her Lucy Mallone identification, the other her real documents.

"Huh. Looks like Lucy isn't even your name. Is it, Amanda?" He smiled. "So what have we got here? A lady traveling under an assumed name, with a professionally tricked-out belt buckle concealing a very high quality switchblade, carries a canister of liquid into the City of Angels. You know what I think you are, Amanda a.k.a. Lucy? I think you're one of those bad people our government is always warning us about. I think . . ."

Abruptly his smile winked out.

"Forgive me. I got so wrapped up in my deductions— sherlockholmesing it, in James Joyce's little neologism—

that I almost lost sight of the main event. Let's get to work, shall we?"

From a side pocket of his jacket, he removed a portable cassette player and hooked it up to the clock radio on the nightstand. He turned on the player. Faint music came from the radio's cheap speaker. He kept the volume low, inaudible from adjacent rooms, but Pierce could hear the music well enough as it played inches from her ear.

"You like surf rock?" He nodded his head to the rhythm. "It was born here, on the left coast."

He smiled.

"Welcome to California."

Pierce didn't want to look at him. Didn't want to think about what would happen next. Eyes shut, she listened to the music. She knew this song. The last song she would ever hear.

It was called "Wipe Out."

PART TWO

PART TWO

15

Tess was exhausted when she drove to her motel.

At two o'clock in the morning, the streets were not too busy, but the rush of traffic in LA never fully stopped. She took the 405 Freeway north into the San Fernando Valley, exiting at Ventura Boulevard.

Andrus had booked her into an extended-stay motel, the kind of place where relocated executives passed the time waiting for the moving company to arrive with their furniture. She couldn't complain about the accommodations, but that term "extended stay" bothered her. She wondered how long her stay would be—and how many victims Mobius would claim before he was stopped.

The room was well-appointed and quiet, and she didn't spend much time there anyway. It was lonely, of course, but she was used to that. She'd been lonely for two years and six weeks.

After Paul Voorhees had become her partner, people had occasionally asked her what he was like. "Centered," she would say. People took this to mean "focused," but what she really meant was "complete."

She wasn't sure she could describe exactly what she was getting at. Maybe that he wasn't always reaching beyond himself for some kind of external validation or acceptance. He had nothing to prove, no one to impress.

In one respect, at least, he and Andrus were alike—neither of them had an I-love-me wall in his office. Andrus didn't want the plaques and signed photos because he knew they would be seen as a sign of vanity and therefore weakness. Paul just didn't want them, period. Andrus never took off his jacket because he had an image to maintain. Paul had no image. He was unconscious of the way he appeared to others. Tess had never seen him look in a mirror except to shave.

Federal agents were supposed to be tough. But too often they were tough on other people and easy on themselves. Paul took the opposite approach. He cut himself no slack, but he gave others the benefit of every doubt. Once, she was with him at a party when he patiently absorbed the sarcasm of a minor city bureaucrat who had applied to the bureau and had been rejected. It was only too obvious that the man resented Paul for succeeding where he had failed. Later Tess had asked Paul why he hadn't just squashed the guy with a cool retort; it would have been easy, and the guy'd had it coming. Paul just shrugged and said there was already enough pain in the world. "Why add to it?"

Answers like that had earned him the nickname "Saint Paul," but people used the term with affection, and when Paul eventually found out about it, he had a good laugh. Jokes at his expense never got him angry. Nothing angered him in any visible way except the mistreatment of the helpless. She'd seen him throw an IBM ThinkPad against a wall after visiting the scene of the rape and murder of a pregnant woman. But when he helped bring in the killer, he showed no emotion other than calm satisfaction.

Most feds got jaded, but Paul always seemed surprised by evil. "What the hell was this guy thinking?" he would ask as he reviewed his case notes on another homicide or abduction. The question was more than a venting of frustration. He honestly didn't understand how people could make the conscious choice to do wrong when there was the potential for so much good.

Saint Paul. The nickname fit him, and yet it was a cop-out, really. He was just a decent man, clear-headed, with a sense of right and wrong—a "value system," in the current jargon. It seemed obvious to him that if people just followed the rules and treated each other with kindness, everyone would be better off. Why didn't more people see this? What the hell *were* they thinking?

She knew he'd been sad sometimes, worn down by the grief in the eyes of witnesses and victims, but what she preferred to remember were their hikes in the Rockies, the crisp air, the great silence, Paul's face ruddy behind a plume of frosty breath, her gloved hand in his.

At 2:25 she pulled into the motel parking lot. Before leaving the car, she removed her Sig Sauer 9mm from her purse. The purse had been specially modified to hold the pistol and two spare magazines, a solution she had chosen when every other method of carrying a concealed weapon—shoulder rig, belt holster, trench coat pocket—had proven undesirably cumbersome.

When she got out of the car, she was holding the gun close to her side, her finger applying light pressure to the trigger. There was no reason to think Mobius knew where she was staying. Most likely he thought she was still in Denver. But she was taking no chances.

The motel was a two-story L-shaped building. Her room was number 14, on the ground floor. She had noticed that there was a break in the sequence of room numbers, with unlucky number 13 omitted. No one wanted to stay in room 13, apparently. Yet of course someone was staying there. She was staying there. They could put a 14 on her door, but the room would still be the thirteenth in line.

She didn't care. She wasn't superstitious. Even so, she wished she had been given a different room.

Still holding the gun against her right hip, she walked to the door and unlocked it. Her free hand found the wall switch and flipped it, turning on twin bedside lamps. She stood in the doorway, checking out the parts of the room she could see, then studying the image in the mirror to get a look at the rest. There was no movement, no sign of intrusion, nothing out of place.

Finally she entered. She ducked into the bathroom, emerged, checked the doorway again, then circled the living space. Nobody was there. She shut the door, locked it, threw the bolt, and even fastened the useless security chain, which could be broken by one quick kick.

She hadn't checked her message machine in two days. She sat on the bed and dialed her home number. An electronic voice told her that she had seven messages.

One was her friend Donna asking where she was on Thursday night. "We were supposed to have dinner, remember?" Tess hadn't remembered. Although she carried an electronic organizer that listed all her appointments, she hadn't looked at it once since her arrival in LA. It was as if her personal life had been put on hold until this case was cleared. Or maybe it was truer to say that her life had been on hold in Denver, and now, finally, she was free to take action.

There were a few more messages from friends calling to find out where she was, then a call from a guy in her apartment building—a successful attorney, she believed—who'd been showing an interest in her. He wanted to go out for coffee. She wondered what she would have said to that offer if she'd been home. Was it time to go out again? Time to take that kind of risk?

The last message was from the manager of her building, saying there was a UPS package waiting for her in the office. Tess knew what it was—a vintage edition of *A Child's Garden of Verses* that she'd ordered from an on-line dealer in rare books. She had loved those poems once, and on impulse one night, alone and restless, she had tracked down the volume on the Internet and ordered it, perhaps hoping to rediscover the meaning they had once held for her. To rediscover her own innocence, she supposed.

But of course it was too late for that. Probably she had known it even at the time.

She erased the messages, making a mental note to return Donna's call tomorrow.

A small stack of mail had been left on the bureau by the maid. Tess had started receiving mail forwarded from her Denver address earlier this week. So far she'd been informed of an art gallery opening she'd missed, a magazine subscription that was expiring, and the amounts she owed on two credit cards. Today's mail was more of the same. Water bill, thank-you note from her niece for a recent birthday present, statement from her broker . . .

And a postcard.

She lifted the card slowly, holding it by the corner. Even before turning it over to read the message, she knew who had sent it.

The picture on the front of the card was of a bikini-clad nymph striking a cheesecake pose in the surf. The caption read, *Come on in, the water's fine!*

On the back was her address in Denver, a Los

Angeles postmark and a yellow forwarding label, and a few words neatly printed in block letters.

YOU'LL NEVER CATCH ME THAT WAY, TESS. DO YOU THINK I'M SO STUPIDLY PREDICTABLE?

Like his other cards, this one was signed *MOBIUS*.

Gently she put down the postcard, not wanting to risk further contamination. It was a useless gesture, of course. There was no chance of finding his prints on it. He would have worn gloves, and besides, the item had been handled by too many other people.

When had the card been sent? The postmark was March 22. Three days to get from LA to Denver. Four days to reach her here. It wouldn't have been forwarded at all if it hadn't borne a first-class stamp.

Had Mobius known her mail was being forwarded? Was that why he used the stamp? Possibly. She thought of the wording of his message: "You'll never catch me that way, Tess." *You*, not *they*. As if he knew she was personally involved, again on his trail.

And he knew something else as well. Her Denver address.

"He knows where I live," she heard herself whisper.

She had thought she was safe. She'd believed there was no way he could find her—and now he was casually announcing that he could have paid her a visit whenever he pleased.

She sat on the sofa opposite the bureau and thought of the first postcard he'd sent, a picture of a jackrabbit with antlers, with the caption, *The Jackelope, one of Colorado's Most Unusual Critters.*

A tacky, jokey card—like all the ones that followed. There had been a chimp on skis (*Goin' Ape for Colorado!*), a prospector on a tired mule (*Tarnation, Is My Ass Sore!*), a rock climber dangling from a cliff face

(*Hanging Out in the Rockies*), and a trio of busty ladies in an Indian casino (*Loosest Sluts in Town!*).

Five cards in all, sent to her at the Denver field office, never her home. The investigation had been handled by the Denver PD back then, with the FBI field office merely consulting on the case, but he had never shown any interest in contacting the police. He seemed to feel he deserved the attention of the FBI. Anything less than the federal government wasn't worthy of him.

His other cards had been postmarked from various ZIP codes around the Denver metropolitan area. Mobius never mailed a card from the same location twice. He left no prints except impressions of smooth gloves. He provided no handwriting samples, just carefully printed capital letters. The pen he used was a generic ballpoint. The messages were brief and cryptic. He was playing games with her.

The jackelope postcard had arrived shortly after the second murder in Denver. He'd established his bona fides with a few details of the killings that had never been publicized. Then he'd written, *I HOPE I HAVEN'T BEEN KEEPING YOU TOO BUSY*, and printed the name *MOBIUS*. That was the first time the killer had identified himself.

In subsequent postcards he'd taunted her further, his messages increasingly personal.

October 16: *I ADMIRE YOU FROM AFAR, SPECIAL AGENT.*

December 3: *DO YOU THINK ABOUT ME AT NIGHT, AGENT McCALLUM?*

January 22: *I KNOW YOU'RE AFRAID OF ME, TESS McCALLUM. YOU SHOULD BE.*

February 8: *YOU'RE GETTING IN DEEP, TESS—UP TO YOUR NECK.*

By that time, she felt sure he'd become interested in her as a potential victim. It turned him on to know that a woman was after him. Her picture had been in the media, and he surely knew what she looked like. If he had begun to fantasize about her, his thoughts would have moved inevitably toward the culmination of the encounter—the duct tape, the knife.

After the second postcard, she'd been told he might try to reach her by phone. A tap-and-trace had been installed on her home and office phone lines, and psychological profilers had given her advice on how to handle the conversation.

But she'd had no opportunity to use any of the tricks she'd learned. He had never called. And after the fifth postcard, he had not written to her again. He had killed three women by that time. And on February 12, he had struck once more. He had killed Paul.

After that, Mobius had gotten at least part of what he wanted—the complete attention of the federal government. RAVENKILL had become a federal case. The murder of a federal officer was a federal crime. The law required that the homicide be committed as a direct result of the officer's performance of official duties, a stipulation that was difficult to meet—but since Paul had provided some of his expertise as a profiler in the Mobius case, the statute's requirements were deemed to have been satisfied. Everyone knew that Paul Voorhees had not been the intended target, of course. Everyone knew it was Tess who was supposed to be dead.

Still, this legalistic sleight of hand had been enough to put the bureau front and center in the investigation. Not Tess, however. She had been placed on bereavement leave, forced to undergo counseling, and told she was too personally involved in the case to be permitted an investigatory role. For two years she had worked other cases in Denver.

And as for Mobius, he had simply . . . stopped.

No more killings. For twenty-five months he had lain dormant, like a deadly cocooned insect.

In some ways, his silence was more maddening than his communications had been. Part of her needed to know that he was still thinking of her. To have invaded his thoughts was small revenge, but better than nothing. Possibly she'd cost him a few sleepless nights.

Now he had resurfaced in LA. Maybe Denver was too small for him, and he yearned for the big time. He might have come to California for the same reason so many others did: to be a star.

There was no way to know. He had revealed nothing of himself, except a compulsion to kill women and the name he had chosen for himself.

Mobius. Possibly a reference to the so-called Möbius strip—an endless loop formed by giving a strip of paper a single twist before attaching the two ends. The result was a one-sided surface without a break. It was a concept that would be familiar to someone trained in mathematics or engineering. But what did it mean? Was it his way of saying that the murders were an unending chain, that he would go on killing indefinitely? The nickname could be a boast or a taunt. Anything was possible. His psyche was a black hole from which no light could escape.

And now he was making contact again.

She took a breath, then called Andrus. She knew he always kept his cell phone on his person or near him. He had told her to call at any hour if there was a new development in the case.

The phone on his end rang four times before a sleepy voice answered. "Andrus."

"It's Tess."

"What's happened?" He sounded instantly alert.

"Another postcard."

"Christ. Did he send it to your motel room?"

"No, my home address. It was forwarded."

"Let me get my pen. Okay, give it to me."

She repeated the message.

"I'll send a courier to pick it up," Andrus said. "We'll run it through the lab tonight."

"It won't accomplish anything. You know he wears gloves. Doesn't even lick the stamps. Uses the self-adhesive kind."

"Maybe this time he slipped up."

"Fat chance. He's not making any mistakes, Gerry. Just the opposite. You heard what he wrote. He knows we're running undercover ops. He's not falling for it."

"You got all that out of two sentences?"

"Yeah, I did. That's what he means by being stupidly predictable. He's saying he knows we're trying to bait him by laying traps on Melrose. And he's not going back there. He'll strike somewhere else next time."

"You could be right." She heard the creak of mattress springs as Andrus shifted his position in bed. "Wait a second. You said the card went to your home address."

"Right." She had moved after Paul's death. She had thought Mobius couldn't find her again. "How the hell could he track me down?"

"We both know an unlisted address doesn't mean anything these days. Anybody can obtain that info on the Web. There's no privacy anymore. No safety—for anyone." Andrus was silent for a moment, then added, "You can't go back there."

"Yes, I can."

"Not if he *knows*—"

"You don't understand, Gerry. I *can* go back—because when I do, Mobius will be in prison."

Or dead, she added to herself.

Andrus sighed. "I take your point. You know, he may also be aware that you're in LA. He might even be watching the Federal Building. He could have seen you come and go."

"We have anybody scoping out the street?"

"We will, as of tomorrow. In the meantime, you'd better change motels as a precaution."

"Let's not get paranoid."

"If he was scoping out the Federal Building and saw you leave, he could have followed you to your motel."

"I hope so. I hope he tries something. I really do, Gerry."

"I don't want you being a cowboy on this thing, Tess. Cowgirl. Whatever."

"Hey, I'm just your average civil servant doing her job. And if I happen to get the opportunity to blow this bastard's head off—well, that's one of the perks of federal employment."

"We'll talk about it in the morning. The courier will be there in twenty minutes. Once you've handed over the document, try to get some rest."

She couldn't argue with that advice. She told him good night and heard the click on the other end of the line.

Then she was alone in the room, without the illusion of companionship Andrus's voice had provided.

Really alone.

Do you think about me at night, Agent McCallum? Mobius had written.

"Yes," she whispered. "I think of you. And you think of me, don't you, you son of a bitch?"

16

Amanda Pierce had vanished, but Jack Tennant was not giving up. He intended to find the bitch.

His only lead was the words recorded in Pierce's phone conversation—"meet you at the hotel." He had to assume the meeting would take place somewhere in LA. But LA was a big town, with lots of hotels.

"So what do we do?" Dante had asked after the debacle at the Century Plaza. "Visit every hotel in the city? There's not enough shoe leather in the world for that detail."

"We don't need shoe leather," Tennant had said. "We need a fax machine."

He set up shop in a squad room at the Westwood field office, nearly deserted at this hour. The squad blast-faxed Pierce's driver's-license photo to every hotel in town, along with a bulletin alerting the recipients that the woman was armed and dangerous.

"With luck, somebody will have noticed her," Tennant said.

"We haven't been lucky so far," Bickerstaff observed with a sigh.

"That's why we're due for a break."

At three A.M. they got a call from a desk clerk at the MiraMist Hotel in Santa Monica. "Yeah, I saw her. Gets kinda boring on the night shift. I remember checking her out."

Tennant shook his head. "Doesn't sound like our suspect. She wouldn't have been checking out of the hotel. She just got into town tonight."

"No, man, you don't get it. I was, you know, checking her out. . . ." He put a lascivious emphasis on the last word.

"Oh. I see." Tennant felt old and stupid. "Where'd you spot her?"

"Sitting at the bar."

"Alone?"

"Some dude perched next to her after a little while. They got to talking."

Her contact, possibly. "Was the woman carrying a suitcase?"

"Sorry, didn't notice."

"But you're sure she's the one in the photo?"

"Pretty sure. I mean, I looked right at her."

"Is she a guest at the hotel?"

"Could be, if she checked in before I came on duty."

"When was that?"

"Eleven."

Pierce hadn't even left LAX until 11:45. She wasn't staying at the hotel. Unless . . .

"Did you see her leave?"

"No, I don't know what happened to her. I took a break around one-thirty, and when I came back, she was gone."

"The man, too?"

"Man?"

"The . . . dude on the next bar stool."

"Yeah, he was gone. I remember thinking maybe he got lucky."

"He a hotel guest?"

"Could be, but I didn't recognize him."

"The bartender would know whether they left together."

"I guess. Chris went home hours ago."

"What's his home number?"

"Hey, it's three A.M. You're gonna call him now?"

"Yes, I am."

Tennant got the number and hung up, then called the bartender. Twenty rings. No answer.

"He could be spending the night with somebody else," Wilkins suggested.

"Maybe." Tennant frowned. "Or he may have just turned off the ringer on his phone. Get his address out of the reverse directory."

Twenty minutes later, Tennant was banging on Christopher Albright's apartment door. "Mr. Albright, open up! Open up now!"

He was rewarded by the sleepy shuffling of feet. Albright answered the door wearing only a terry-cloth robe. He was a thin, sallow guy with a stubble of fuzz on his cheeks. "What the hell . . . ?"

"FBI." Tennant produced his creds. "You the bartender at the MiraMist Hotel?"

"Uh . . . yeah."

"We're looking for a woman who may have been at the bar earlier tonight. This woman." Tennant showed him the photo. "Recognize her?"

"I think so. Yeah, I do. She got there a little after midnight. No liquor, just ginger ale."

"Was a man with her?"

"A guy joined her." By now Albright had led Tennant, accompanied by Jarvis and Bickerstaff, into the mess that was his living room. Evidently he had fallen asleep on the sofa. The TV was still on, flickering in a corner, the volume low. "He was trying to pick her up."

"And did he?"

"They left together."

"And went where?"

"Didn't see, but I'd guess it was his room."

"So he's staying at the hotel?"

"Definitely. Charged the drinks to his room tab."

"Which room?"

"Hell if I remember."

"What was his name?"

"Shit . . ." Albright ran a hand through the loopy tangles of his hair. "I'm sorry, I don't know."

Bickerstaff asked, "What was he drinking?"

"Gin and tonic, twist of lime," Albright said immediately. He smiled. "Occupational hazard. I never forget a drink."

"So if we check the bar tab . . . ?" Tennant asked.

"You'll find him that way. Sure. He was there for maybe forty-five minutes. Sucked down two, maybe three gin and tonics."

"Okay. Thanks. You've been very helpful."

"What's this all about, anyway? What'd this woman do?"

"Parking tickets," Jarvis said. "A whole lot of 'em."

Tennant told Wilkins and Dante, waiting at the hotel, to review the bar tab. By the time he arrived with J&B, the hotel guest had been identified as Donald Stevenson in room 1625.

"Description?" Tennant asked Bickerstaff.

"According to his Illinois DL, he's Caucasian, blond and blue."

"Got to be a fake ID."

"Unless he's just a businessman looking to get laid, and Pierce decided to use him for cover."

"It's possible." Tennant looked at Jarvis. "His credit card number's on file from the check-in, right?"

"Sure."

"Run it. See when it was issued."

Tennant turned the office behind the registration desk into a makeshift command center. On one of the newly installed phones, he called the Santa Monica Police Department and got through to the commanding officer of the OSE, the Office of Special Enforcement, waking him at home. He summarized the situation: armed and dangerous fugitive traced to a local hotel.

"We need SWAT," Tennant said. "Yours and ours."

The captain insisted that the department squad be first in the door, with the FBI team on hand only as backup. Tennant didn't argue the point.

"SET will roll in fifteen minutes," the captain promised.

"SET?"

"Special Entry Team. That's what we call our SWAT guys. They're good, Agent Tennant. Regularly win statewide SWAT competitions. We're not a big department, but we're not yokels either."

"I believe you. Look, Captain, we need to keep this off the radio in case the suspect is monitoring."

"SMPD communications are all digital and encrypted. Scanners can't access the signals."

"It's possible she could have a stolen transceiver." Tennant wanted to cover every angle.

"Wouldn't do her any good. We assign each radio to a specific user. If it's lost or stolen, we disable it remotely. Relax, Agent Tennant. You're in good hands."

Tennant got off the phone with the SMPD captain and phoned the FBI office to arrange a SWAT callout. Then he checked with Jarvis.

"Credit card is new," Jarvis reported. "Donald Stevenson obtained it only a month ago."

"Interesting."

"There's more. I had the credit card people give me his SSN. Ran it through the database. It belongs to Donald Stevenson, all right—but he died in 1989."

Tennant felt a kick of adrenaline. "He's our guy. No question."

"So they're in the room together. Fucking like bunnies, I guess."

"That's not the way these transactions usually end." Tennant frowned. "Maybe the room's empty, and they both snuck out during the night."

"We can ring room 1625 and see if anyone answers."

"No. We can't risk alerting them that anything's up. With any luck, they're both still there."

And the suitcase is with them, he added silently. *And everybody lives happily ever after.*

A half hour later Tennant was sitting in an undercover mobile command post parked on a side street near the hotel, conferring with Lieutenant Garzarelli, commander of the Santa Monica PD Special Entry Team.

Garzarelli's men were stationed in a stairwell on the MiraMist's sixteenth floor. Members of the FBI SWAT squad were also inside the building, occupying less forward positions in deference to the locals. An engine company stood by, ready to dispatch paramedics to the scene if something went wrong.

"Evacuation's complete," Garzarelli said. "Floors fifteen, sixteen, and seventeen have been cleared of guests and staff." The lieutenant peered up at the white tower of the hotel. "You mind telling me what the hell we're dealing with?"

"You already know. Female fugitive, armed—"

"Don't give me the boilerplate. You don't pass out gas masks and oxygen canisters to the primary assault squad for a routine arrest."

Tennant met his stare. "Think of her as a courier."

"What's she carrying?"

"Let's say it's something that could do a lot of damage if she or her friend has a chance to release it."

Garzarelli was quiet for a long moment. Then he said softly, "Ebola?"

"What?"

"Is it the Ebola virus?"

Tennant almost laughed. Ebola. This guy was watching too much TV. "No, Lieutenant. It's not Ebola. It's not a virus at all, or any kind of germ. But just to play it safe, let's treat it like it is Ebola, and maybe no one will get hurt."

Garzarelli nodded, looking relieved. Tennant knew his relief would vanish if he knew what was in Amanda Pierce's suitcase.

"If everything's set on your end," Garzarelli said, "we can rock 'n' roll whenever I give the word."

"Not yet. I have to get up there."

"You?"

"Relax. I won't get in anybody's way. Your boys get to do the rough stuff, but I'll be right behind them to help secure the scene."

"They don't need any help in that department."

"Today they do. I know what to look for. They don't." Tennant walked away without further discussion, adding as he left the command post, "Give me ten minutes."

In nine minutes he had joined the SET squad and donned his tactical vest and ballistic helmet, his Nomex gauntlet-style gloves, and finally his SF-10 Avon gas mask and oxygen canister. Through his ear-

piece he heard Garzarelli check in with his team. The
element leader affirmed that they were loaded and
locked.

Tennant had seen the eight-man team strap on the
gear they carried in a rapid-mobilization diesel SUV.
They had a hand-carried battering ram to break open
the hotel room's door in the event that the electronic
lock had been disabled. Should they encounter resistance, they had flash-bang grenades to confuse and
disorient the suspects. The lead assaulters could flip
down night-vision goggles if the room was too dark
for normal eyesight—a possibility, since an observation post across the street confirmed that the drapes
remained shut.

"Clear tactical frequencies," Garzarelli ordered.
"No chatter. You men are good to go."

This was it—ass-pucker time. In a few minutes
Amanda Pierce and her contact would be either in
custody or dead. Tennant didn't care which way it
worked out, so long as the suitcase was recovered and
none of the good guys got hurt.

The risk was that Pierce and her friend might have
time for a defiant, suicidal gesture. The gas masks
were intended to provide for that contingency. But
this kind of warfare was still new to him. Hell, it was
pretty goddamn new to everybody. It was a brave new
fucking world.

Tennant followed the squad down the carpeted hallway to the door marked 1625. The scout produced a
boxy piece of electronic equipment and pressed it
against the outer wall of the room. The unit was a
RadarVision scope, which used ultra-wide-band radar
to see through concrete, wood, or plaster.

Tennant saw a luminous blob dancing on the LCD
panel.

"We have movement," the element leader whispered into a throat microphone on a breakaway strap. His LASH radio headset transmitted the words clearly to Tennant's earpiece. "Minimal but rhythmic, consistent with deep respiration." The rise and fall of the abdomen was detectable by the radar pulse. "Movement located near northeast corner, in approximate position of bed." They had studied the room's layout before suiting up.

There was no other movement, Tennant observed. Either the two suspects were sleeping so close together that the radar could not distinguish two separate respiration signatures, or one of the pair had left—possibly taking the suitcase.

But one, at least, was still there.

The scout put aside the radar scope. The element leader took out the passcard for the room's electronic lock and inserted it in the slot. Above the lock, the red LED turned green as the latch released. Silently he eased the door an inch ajar.

The two assaulters took up their positions flanking the leader, who served as point man. Their HK MP-5 9mm submachine guns were held at port arms. Night-vision goggles were perched on their foreheads, ready to be snapped down over their eyes if needed. Gas masks hid their noses and mouths.

The element leader ticked off a silent count on his fingers.

On three, they went in.

Where there had been silence, there was a sudden eruption of noise as the door was thrown wide, the SET squad rushing in to cover both sides of the doorway, the leader shouting, "Police, you're under arrest!" More shouts from squad members checking the bathroom, closet, and balcony—"Clear!" "Clear!" "Clear!"

Tennant watched from outside the doorway. When

his chest started to hurt, he realized he'd forgotten
to breathe.

Then the leader reported, "Team leader to base,
premises are secure. There is one, repeat one, occupant
of this room, a female, and she is one-eight-seven."

One-eight-seven was the section of the California
Penal Code that covered homicide.

Amanda Pierce was dead.

"You say one-eight-seven?" Garzarelli asked over
the radio, seeking confirmation.

"Affirmative, sir. She's about as one-eight-seven as
it gets."

Her contact had killed her. Tennant could think of
a dozen reasons. She had been followed from Oregon
and had inadvertently endangered them both. The
killing might be her penalty for that mistake. Or
maybe it was an insurance policy, a way to ensure that
she never talked.

Tennant didn't care about the reason. What mattered to him was that Donald Stevenson, whoever he
had been, had killed Pierce and left the room.

Which meant he must have taken the suitcase.

Slowly, Tennant stepped through the doorway into
the room and looked toward the bed, where the
breathing had come from.

Amanda Pierce was on the bed, but she wasn't
breathing.

His gaze tracked to the nightstand, where a room-
service menu flapped in the breeze of an air-
conditioning vent. A rhythmic flutter, which the scope
had read as respiration.

He looked around the rest of the room and saw the
suitcase. It lay on a desk chair, its contents scattered.
He experienced a wild moment of hope, which died
when he looked over the miscellany of items.

There was no metal canister. It was gone.

The team leader's voice, loud in his earpiece, took him by surprise. "Looks like her partner offed her," he said.

Tennant realized the SET officer was addressing him. He nodded and turned toward the body again.

Amanda Pierce's eyes stared at him, wide and somehow angry, even in death. She had been duct-taped to the headboard, her throat cut.

Duct-taped . . .

Throat cut . . .

Tennant kept up with the major investigations handled by the bureau. He remembered the maniac in Denver who had recently resurfaced in LA.

"It wasn't her partner," Tennant said slowly.

The element leader glanced at him. "Sir?"

He didn't answer. He stood staring at the bed, thinking of the missing canister and the case codenamed RAVENKILL.

Things had been bad before. But they had just gotten a whole lot worse.

17

Mobius.

His name, his mantra, coiling through his mind, a snake swallowing itself in a perpetual act of self-devouring, of unappeasable appetite.

It was a name that signified many things, but above all the loop of time coiling to intersect itself, merging past and future in an endless present, the great *now* extending forever.

He had killed before and he would kill again, but always it was the same act, the same victim, the same moment in time.

Always he saw there, the gun in her hand, the song playing like background music, the theme song of his life.

She spoke to him, and then there was the gunshot blast, the heat and pain, and the water closing over him like the petals of a flower as he sank into a humming brightness.

He tried to call to her for help, but the water got in the way, the water that flooded his mouth and filled his eyes like tears, and around him slow tendrils of blood unwound in the water, making clouds of red. . . .

And then—and then—

He was out of the water, he was strong, reanimated,

and he was holding her down, taping her wrists to the headboard of the motel bed. A knife was in his hand, and she couldn't hurt him. He was the one who would do the hurting now, and the bitch couldn't stop him. The bitch could only writhe and struggle and die.

That was how it had been tonight, in the MiraMist Hotel. That was how it was, every time, always.

Mobius had left the MiraMist at 2:45, taking the stairs to the lobby, exiting via a rear door without being seen by the hotel staff. His car was parked a short distance away. He had driven east on Wilshire Boulevard, into the Westwood district.

At 3:15 A.M. he parked on an elm-shaded side street outside the Life Sciences Center on a university campus. He put on his gloves and took the canister with him when he got out of his car.

The campus was deserted at this hour. The Life Sciences building was situated along one side of a picturesque quadrangle. He was considering the best way to break in when he noticed a light in the basement windows.

Someone was at work in a lab.

This was very convenient. Although he had intended to perform the procedure himself, he knew he would be unfamiliar with the new equipment. Now, by pure good fortune, he had found an assistant.

It took him no time at all to defeat the lock on the front door of the building with a set of tools from his glove compartment. Silently he descended the stairs. A sign with an arrow pointed to ORGANIC CHEMISTRY LAB II. The lab door had a window in it. Looking through, he saw long countertops crowded with Bunsen burners, Pyrex flasks and beakers, test tube racks, and triple-beam balances. This much he'd expected, but what surprised him was the quantity of computer gear in the lab—keyboards and monitors and boxy CPUs.

At the far end of the room stood the lab worker in the white coat, bending over a table. Mobius opened the door and entered, unheard. When he was halfway across the room, he rapped his knuckles on a counter, and the other person turned.

"What the hell? How'd you get in here?"

"The building was unlocked."

"No, it wasn't."

"It is now."

Mobius looked over his new friend. He was just a kid—early twenties at the oldest. Sandy hair, thin build, hard plastic goggles over his wide, alarmed eyes.

"What are you up to at three-thirty in the morning?" Mobius asked.

The kid took a step forward. "Get the fuck out of here."

"You're a poor host."

"I'm calling security."

"No, you're not."

The kid reached for a phone. Mobius closed the distance between them, and in a quick downward arc his knife sliced through the lab coat and incised a shallow wound in the kid's lower abdomen.

He expected shock and fear to incapacitate his victim immediately, but the kid surprised him, lunging at Mobius in a wild attempt at self-defense. Mobius stepped backward, stumbling, off balance for an instant, and the kid flailed with a looping swing that swept a row of flasks onto the floor with a shattering of glass. Then Mobius steadied himself and caught the kid a second time with the knife, slashing his thigh, and the kid collapsed, a surge of red dyeing his pants.

Mobius stared down. "Don't be a hero, asshole. It only costs you blood."

The kid touched the two wounds and gasped, shaking all over, then lifted his head to gaze up at Mobius with eyes that were now utterly cowed.

"You plan to cooperate now?"

The kid nodded.

"No more bullshit?"

"No."

"Fair enough. So tell me, son, what's your name?"

His lips worked for a moment before he answered, "Scott Maple."

"You're a student, I assume. Too young to be a teacher."

"Grad student." Another shudder worked its way through him as he looked at the widening stain on his clothes, the red pool on the floor. "Christ, it won't stop bleeding."

"Yes, it will. The first cut is barely more than a scratch. The second one's a little more serious, but you have only yourself to blame for that. You never answered my first question. What are you up to?"

"Research project. For my Ph.D. thesis."

"On Easter weekend, in the middle of the night?"

"Deadline."

"What's the nature of this all-important project?"

"Analysis of carcinogenic environmental contaminants." He spoke in a dull monotone, as if reciting a memorized lesson. "Pesticide concentrations, industrial residue, vapor discharged from burning fossil fuels. I'm using bomb calorimetry—"

"Bomb what?"

"Calorimetry."

"You make bombs?"

"Not exactly. I mean, it is a kind of bomb, but . . . Look, what the hell do you care?"

"Bombs interest me." Mobius looked Scott Maple

up and down. "So are you calmer now? Are you lucid?"

"Guess so."

"Good. Because I've got a job for you. I found this item." He held up the canister in a gloved hand. "There's liquid in it. I want to know what kind."

"Is it . . . something dangerous?"

"Probably. But you handle toxic substances all the time, don't you? Pesticides, industrial residue. You just told me so."

"I . . . yeah, that's what I told you."

"You have a gas chromatograph in here, I'm sure."

Maple jerked his head in the direction of an oven-size box hooked up to a computer. "There."

"Okay, then." Mobius tossed him the canister, and Maple caught it reflexively. "Get to work."

The kid struggled upright, holding on to a counter for support. By now the bright flush of blood on his lab coat and pants was fading. The flow had ebbed.

"You have safety masks available?" Mobius asked.

"Sure."

"Give me one. You put one on, too. And put on gloves."

Mobius donned his mask, then stood back, careful to keep his distance from the canister. Scott Maple kept talking nervously, aimlessly, as he started a software program on the computer linked to the gas chromatograph.

"Okay, okay. The chromatograph is a Hewlett-Packard 5890. The PC maintains a stable environment for the chemical separation process. Okay, so first I turn on the FID air and hydrogen. FID, that's—",

"Flame ionization detection," Mobius said.

Maple glanced up, startled. "Uh, that's right. Sensitive to zero point four five parts per million. Next we ignite the flame." He pressed the ignition button on the chromatograph. "It ought to register at least fifteen on the screen. Okay, there it is."

"Stop saying, 'Okay.' "

"Am I doing that?"

"You are."

"Okay. I mean—I'll stop. Now we just, uh, set the appropriate values." On the computer, he chose *Set Method*, then set the temperatures of the injector, oven, and detector to their defaults. "Check the status. Then we . . . we have to wait. Till it warms up, basically. Shouldn't take long."

"While you're waiting, prepare the sample."

"Right. The sample." He studied the canister. "How do I extract the contents if I don't know what I'm dealing with?"

"How would you handle the pollutants you're cataloging?"

"Use a pipette to siphon out a few drops . . ."

"There you go. And by the way, it would be a good idea to stop trembling. If this stuff is what I think it may be, you can't afford to make any stupid mistakes."

Maple drew a quick, shallow breath that pulled the face mask tight against his nostrils. His goggles were steaming up with sweat.

He opened the cannister and transferred a few drops of clear liquid into an Erlenmeyer flask. When the gas chromatograph's temperature reached 325 degrees Centigrade, he fed the sample into the injection port and initiated the run.

The details of gas chromatography had changed in the twenty years since Mobius had attended college, but the basic science was the same. The sample, heated to a gas, would travel into a column lined with silicone grease. The grease would absorb the gas molecules and release them at varying intervals, known as exit rates. Every compound had its own unique exit rate, a chemical fingerprint. When the exit rates of the molecules were registered by the flame ionization detector, the exact chemical composition of the vapor would be known.

He and Scott Maple waited until a readout appeared on the PC's screen.

"Exit rate of forty-five point three seconds," Maple said.

"What is it?"

"Not sure. Almost like a pesticide, maybe. I'm running it through the database now. We ought to— Oh, shit."

His voice had dropped an octave with the last word. Mobius took a step closer, and on the monitor he saw a long chemical name beginning with *O-ethyl-S*.

"Tell me," he said.

"It says here this is . . . this is . . ."

Maple turned toward him. Above the antiseptic mask, his eyes were wide and helpless.

"Tell me," Mobius repeated.

The kid told him.

And Mobius smiled.

When he was finished at the lab, Mobius visited Tess.

He knew where she was staying, of course. He had even sat in the motel parking lot and watched her enter and leave on a few occasions. It had occurred to him that it would not be difficult to kill her whenever he wished. So far he had felt no particular urgency about it. But now the time had come.

He guided his car into the motel parking lot and

brought it to rest under a dead street lamp. The time was 4:45, still too early for any activity around the motel. The windows were unlighted, the drapes shut.

Canister in hand, he crossed the parking lot to the door of room 14. It would be locked, naturally—he didn't even bother testing the knob. He had no need to get inside the room.

He cast a long, cautious look around, then crouched near the air conditioner.

It was a large unit installed under the window, and it was off now. He didn't know if Tess had left it off when she'd gone to sleep, or if it had clicked off automatically during the coolest part of the night. But this March was unseasonably warm, with near-record highs forecast for Saturday. She would turn it on eventually.

He put on his gloves and the mask from the lab. Averting his face, he opened the canister and dribbled a few drops of its contents into the AC unit's air-intake duct. When the air conditioner started running, the liquid would be aerosolized and dispersed as a mist throughout the room.

"No more postcards, Tess," he whispered behind the mask. "I'm sending you a message of a different kind."

Now he was home in his private room, his special sanctuary, staring at a wall covered with a collage of newspaper clippings, photos, and yellowed archival documents. One of the smallest items in the display was the one he most cherished—a black-and-white photo of his mother that he'd found in her high school yearbook. She had attended a small, private, fancy school for girls, a school catering to debutantes and heiresses. His mother had been both, until the first fruits of her germinating insanity had gotten her disinherited.

He had tracked down the yearbook in the school library and ripped out the crucial page, using exactly the same ruse Jack Nicholson had employed in *Chinatown*, a phony sneeze to cover the sound of tearing paper. Now she was on his wall of memories, or perhaps he should call it his wailing wall, a place to mourn the dead. Only in this case, it was his own death he came to mourn.

His mother had been just nineteen, a graduating senior, when the photo was taken. Melinda Davenport, later to be Mrs. Harrison Beckett. A pretty girl, austere and fine-featured and smooth-skinned. Looking at her, no one could guess that less than ten years later, in 1968, she would go insane.

After his mother had stopped living with them, his dad had warned him that someday she might try to get him to go with her, and that it would be dangerous to go. But when she'd visited him at recess, she hadn't seemed dangerous. And he hated school, which was boring, and he hated recess even more, because he was never picked for any games. So when she'd asked if he wanted to go to the rodeo, he'd said yes.

But there hadn't been any rodeo. There had been only miles of blurry back roads and the crazed repetition of a single song on an eight-track player, and she had hummed along with it in a furious nasal monotone.

"Na na na na na na na, na na na na na na naaa . . ."

By the time they reached the Howard Johnson's in Alcomita, New Mexico, he hated her. He knew this one thing with certainty. He didn't like to be scared, and she was scaring him very badly. If he'd had a gun, he would have shot her—*bang*, dead—and she wouldn't have scared him anymore. When her back was turned, he even pretended to have a gun, and he pantomimed pulling the trigger and making his mother go away.

Bang.

Dead.

Sometime in late morning, while a policeman talked through a bullhorn outside and the crazy song played on the portable phonograph, his mother filled the bathtub.

"You're dirty," she said. "You need to be clean. You're a very dirty boy, and you've caused me a lot of trouble."

He didn't think he had caused any trouble. He had been quiet and good. But he did not protest, because he liked baths.

"Can I play with my submarine?" he asked. The submarine was a plastic model he had taken to school for show-and-tell and had brought with him in the car.

She didn't answer, just went on filling the tub.

When the bath was ready, he slipped out of his day-old clothes and eased into the hot water, taking his submarine with him. Outside, the policeman was saying something, but over the blare of the record player he couldn't hear it. When the music started to bother him, he submerged, holding his breath, moving the toy sub underwater and imagining nautical adventures.

Needing air, he surfaced, and his mother was there.

She stood over the tub, and her face . . . her face was strange. It was not his mother's face at all. There was no love in her eyes, not even any recognition. She looked at him as if he were a stranger.

"Mommy?" he whispered.

She did not move, did not blink.

"Wipe out," she said, and the gun bucked in her hand.

Mobius blinked, reliving it—the impact, the sudden inexplicable numbness. He touched his chest. Through the thin fabric of his shirt, he could feel the lump of scar tissue in the shape of a starfish, where the .38-

caliber round had entered, and where the long ribbons of blood had come out.

His gaze switched from his mother's photo to the central item in the collage—the entire front page, both above and below the fold, of the Albuquerque *Tribune*'s September 21, 1968, edition. A huge headline stretched over the multicolumn story.

"WIPE-OUT" IN ALCOMITA HOJO'S

A tense, hours-long standoff at the Howard Johnson's motor inn in Alcomita came to an abrupt and tragic end at 12:20 P.M. when sheriff's deputies heard two shots discharged inside the room where alleged kidnapper and former mental patient Melinda Ellen Beckett was holding her eight-year-old son . . .

Melinda Beckett had lost custody of the boy after her third hospitalization for mental illness. She was recently separated from her husband, Mr. Harrison Beckett, who had been raising their son alone. Mrs. Beckett is said to have become obsessed with violent, paranoid thoughts, and had twice been placed in restraints while institutionalized.

Sheriff's deputies report that throughout the standoff Mrs. Beckett played the song "Wipe Out," an early 1960s hit for the Surfaris, on a portable phonograph. Deputies also found an eight-track tape containing the song in the dashboard tape player of Mrs. Beckett's 1964 Buick Grand Sport.

Harrison Beckett, who arrived at the scene only minutes after the twin shootings, is described as being in a state of shock and is currently under medical care. . . .

He would never leave medical care. Harrison Beckett was still in a hospital somewhere—Mobius had long since lost track of his father's whereabouts, as the Wyoming bureaucracy shuttled him from one institution to another. He was an incurable patient, one who—in the quaint parlance of 1968—had suffered a "nervous breakdown." Quite simply, he had lost all contact with the outside world on that day in New Mexico.

Two parents, both crippled by mental illness. It was almost enough to make him doubt his own sanity.

The other items on his wall were less sensational. There was his birth certificate, obtained from a Casper, Wyoming, hospital. Some of the medical records compiled during his long recuperation from the gunshot, the months of physical and psychological therapy. A snapshot of his triumphant release from the hospital at the age of nine. Nurses and doctors were all gathered, grinning at the camera, and in the middle of this crowd stood a wan little boy with a pinched face and cool, untrusting eyes. He remembered exactly what he had been thinking as the photo was snapped.

Bang. Dead.

It was too late to make his mother dead for what she had done to him. The psychologists had worked long and hard to make him understand this. And he did understand. But what the psychologists didn't realize was that there was a whole world of other people out there, and he hated them all. He hated the doctors who had brought him back to life. He hated the deputies who had cornered his mother and provoked her. He hated the social workers who had put her in a mental hospital in the first place. And the new family that had adopted him—he hated them too, hated their frozen smiles and evasive eyes and the way they touched him like glass.

He hated the entire world, and he wished he could

make it all go away with one pull of a trigger, one clap of his hands.

He wished he had a way to do it. A weapon to kill them all.

And now, perhaps, he did.

He was cleaning out his pockets, disposing of evidence, when he realized he was missing something.

The tape player.

Maybe it had fallen out in the car. He went into the garage and checked under the driver's seat. Not there.

Then he understood.

When Scott Maple had knocked him off balance, the player must have slipped out of his pocket. In the clatter of breaking glass he'd never heard it drop.

He had left it in the lab. The player itself was of no importance, a mass-produced item that could never be traced to him. But the tape inside . . . it was just possible that they could find him though the tape. . . .

No way. He was just getting paranoid.

Anyway, the incident at the chemistry lab would not be connected with the serial killings. And the tape player and the cassette inside would never be recovered in any identifiable form.

He had made a small slip, uncharacteristic of him, but everything was fine.

He was in no danger. Of course he wasn't.

Of course.

18

The fire was out by the time Dodge reached the Life Sciences Center at the northeast corner of the university campus. An engine from Fire Station 37 idled on the curving street under an elm tree's branches. Parked around the engine were three LAPD squad cars, light bars cycling blue and red in the pinkish light of dawn.

Dodge parked his unmarked Caprice behind the nearest patrol unit and strolled toward the knot of firefighters gathered with the cops near the front door of Life Sciences. The firefighters looked tired, and the cops looked bored. That was nothing new. Cops at a crime scene always looked bored.

If this was a crime scene. There was, as yet, no evidence that a crime had been committed. With any luck, it would stay that way. Dodge didn't need another fucking homicide on his plate.

Spears of light from the sun breaking the horizon jabbed his eyes as he crossed the greensward, his shoes collecting dew. On the fringe of the crowd, he ran into a fireman he recognized as the chief of station 37. He was wearing his heavy canvas turnout coat, the high collar snapped shut. Only the tips of his ears were visible, and they were blistered from the heat.

There was the usual exchange of bullshit hellos and

how-you-doin's, and then Dodge asked him what had gone down here.

"Fucking mess," the captain said. "Oh-four-fifty, we respond to an alarm. I lead in the company—two vehicles, wagon and pumper. The blaze is a worker, basement level of the building fully involved, no way we can get inside. It's strictly surround and drown. We pump in maybe ten thousand gallons. Use foam too, when the wind dies down. Finally some of us suit up in our BAs"—breathing apparatus—"and get in. Hosemen lay down lines, rest of us search for casualties. Visibility zero. Gotta feel our way through. I pretty much stumble over the victim. Deceased."

"You apply CPR?"

"Wouldn't have helped. This guy was a goner. Anyway, by then I'm drawing a vacuum on my facepiece, so I get the hell out of there."

"Where's the DB now?" Dead body.

"Still inside. Figured there was no point in moving it, disrupting the scene any more than necessary."

"You thinking arson? Is that why you wanted to keep the scene intact?"

"Don't know what to think. We got an arson unit coming over, but they're hung up on other cases right now."

"Busy night for the firebugs."

"They're all busy nights."

"Okay, I got the picture. Take care of yourself." Dodge started to walk away.

"Hey, Jim, one more thing. There's some pooled water from our hoses down there, though luckily there are floor drains in the lab, and once we unclogged 'em, the water mostly ran off. Still, you'll want waterproof boots. Got any with you?"

"Yeah, right along with my fly-fishing gear and my pup tent. Who do I look like, Eddie fucking Bauer?"

"You can borrow a pair out of the wagon."

Dodge thanked him again, then waded into the crowd and buttonholed the nearest uniform. "Who's the first officer?"

"Painter." The cop pointed toward a woman in blue.

Dodge didn't know her. Since he knew all the veteran West LA cops, this one was probably a recent transfer from another division. He looked her over. Wide hips, skin so shiny black it was almost purple. Reminded him more of a goddamn welfare whore than an officer of the law.

He took Painter aside, introduced himself, and got out his notepad as she ran down the details. She reiterated much of what Dodge already knew before getting to the vic.

"Male or female?" Dodge asked.

"Male. That's about all we can tell so far."

"No idea who he was? Student, teacher, janitor, night watchman . . . ?"

"His clothes were vaporized and so was any DL or other ID he was carrying. Can't tell what the hell he looked like. They may have to go by dental records."

"That bad, huh?"

"That bad." She added, "Some kids said it might be a student named, uh, Scott Maple."

"What makes them say so?"

"He's a grad student, apparently worked down there at all hours on some big project with a deadline."

"Oh? What's in the basement anyway?"

"Chemistry lab."

"I see." Like any cop, Dodge paid attention when the subject of labs came up. A lot of crime revolved around labs.

"You thinking crank?" Officer Painter asked.

"Could be. Or some designer drug."

"Pretty unusual to cook up something like that in a university chem lab, don't you think?"

Dodge shook his head. "When I went to college, we got some big-name rock groups to play on campus. Nobody could figure out how we induced them to show up. I mean, this was a little shit college in the middle of nowhere."

"Yeah?"

"Yeah." He was warming up to Painter a little bit. He liked people who showed an interest in his stories. "So I looked into it. Turned out some enterprising grad students in the chemistry department were paying the bands in LSD."

Painter seemed unconvinced. "Think that kind of thing still goes on? I mean, it was a long time ago."

His momentary enthusiasm for Painter's companionship vanished. "Right, it was the fucking dinosaur age." He didn't like the insinuation that he was old, especially coming from some fat bitch who'd probably been giving blow jobs to the high school football squad a couple of years ago. "So what the fuck else have you got?" he asked stiffly.

Painter seemed unaware of his disappointment in her, or maybe she just didn't give a shit. "We're trying to track down this Maple. His dorm mates haven't seen him."

"He got a girlfriend? Boyfriend? Anything?"

"Girlfriend. We're looking for her. Not sure if she's on campus this weekend. School's out for the holiday, you know."

"Oh, is this a holiday weekend? I had my head so far up my ass, I didn't notice."

She ticked a cool glare at him. "Just pointing it out. ME's not here yet; neither is SID. Not that there'll be much for SID to look at down there."

SID was the Scientific Investigation Division, the forensics experts. Dodge had to admit that Painter was right. No trace evidence would survive the fire—which might be why the blaze had been set in the first place.

"Any reason we should be thinking arson?" he asked.

"Lot of flammable chemicals spilled everywhere. Beakers and stuff, you know. Place went up like a torch. Could've been intentional, I don't know."

"You have no opinion?"

"It's not my job to have an opinion."

She sounded tired. Probably she thought she was tired. She was wrong. Let her spend the next fifteen years wearing a badge, taking shit from every asshole on the street, making no money, pissing her life away. Then she would know how it felt to be tired.

He thanked her for the recap, then got two pairs of the waterproof boots and hung around, waiting for his partner to show. By now the sun was jostling the treetops at the far end of the quadrangle. There was a line of rust-colored smog on the horizon, as usual, but the sky overhead was turning blue. Of course its clarity was an illusion. The goddamn smog was everywhere, but up close, you couldn't see it. Dodge thought there might be some sort of metaphor buried in that observation, but he didn't bother to dig it out.

Bradley arrived a few minutes later, at 6:15. Dodge filled him in, and then the two of them pulled on their boots and walked into Life Sciences. It was an old building constructed of solid brick, with hardwood floors slightly bowed from decades of hard use. Skylights in the atrium let in the sun. Dust glinted in the air, mingling with flecks of floating ash.

The door to the stairwell was across from the elevators. A sagging length of crime-scene tape was strung across the doorway. They ducked under it and took out their flashlights, beaming them down the metal stairs into the dimness below.

Dodge caught the smell at once. He felt his stomach clench like a fist. The odor was sickening, like a barbecue gone bad.

"Whew," Bradley said. This was as close to an expletive as Dodge's partner ever used. He was a family man, Al Bradley—or had been, till Cheryl sued him for divorce and took the kids to Seattle to live with their new daddy, a real estate salesman named Bob. Dodge thought it would do Al some good to cut loose with a nice stream of profanity now and then, but the guy was a straight arrow.

"Breathe through your mouth," Dodge advised, trying to sound cool, as if the stench didn't bother him.

Bradley nodded. "Always do. I'm a mouth-breather by nature. You never noticed?"

They went down the stairs, noting the black tracks of firefighters' boots stamped on each steel tread. Any other shoe prints—those of an intruder, say—would have been obliterated.

At the bottom of the staircase, they followed the boot prints and the smell to a ruined space that had been Organic Chemistry Lab II.

The laboratory was a single large room arrayed with the charred, skeletal remnants of wooden counters. The countertops had blistered over, the wood cracking and bumping up like alligator scales. Three-legged metal stools lay here and there, the cushioned seats incinerated.

Although a basement, the lab was not windowless. A row of narrow, horizontal windows ran along the top of the room at ground level. Daylight entered, diffusing in the thick, sooty air, barely penetrating the murk.

Dodge passed the beam of his flashlight over the

rubble, revealing wet mounds of debris and pools of bubbling flame retardant sprayed by extinguishers. As the fire captain had said, there were puddles of water here and there, amid piles of waterlogged ashes, but most of the thousands of gallons of water had disappeared through large drainage grates recessed in the corners of the lab.

Glassware was all over the floor. Dodge remembered Painter mentioning *beakers and stuff*. There were plenty of beakers and flasks and vials and test tubes and every other sort of glass container. A few were intact, but most had been either shattered or melted, and in some parts of the room, mounds of fallen glassware had actually fused into surreal volcanic cones.

"What a mess," Bradley muttered. His flashlight swung up toward the ceiling, where fluorescent lighting panels hung down on strands of electrical wire, the plastic covers warped. He aimed the beam at the far end of the room, illuminating rows of cabinets hollowed out by flame.

The smell was really bad now. All the windows had been smashed, either by the firefighters or by the thermal impact of the fire itself, but there was little breeze entering the room. The air was stagnant, choking.

At least there was no doubt where the body lay. The stink drew them directly to it. It was sprawled near the back of the lab, between two counters, partially buried in ceiling tiles that had popped loose and rained down on the floor.

Dodge and Bradley knelt by the corpse. Enough was left of the pubic area to confirm that it was a man. Dodge brushed away the foam tiles and exposed a charred, crinkly face. The hair was gone—all of it, even the eyebrows. Eyes like poached eggs swam in their sockets, all the color boiled out of them.

The sight didn't bother him. He'd seen gangbangers decapitated by shotgun blasts. He'd seen horrendous stabbings and mutilations. He was inured to the insults that could be directed at the human body. But the smell was something else.

"Maybe after this," Bradley told him, "you'll lay off the pastrami burritos." Pastrami burritos were Dodge's current poison of choice. They were sold out of a fast-food cart on Santa Monica Boulevard by a Filipino entrepreneur.

"No way," Dodge said. "I need my fix. Anyway, those burritos don't smell anything like this."

"They smell worse."

Dodge studied the corpse. The victim's clothes had been entirely burned away. He lay in a pugilistic posture, legs bent at the knees, arms pulled up as if sparring.

"Think he died defending himself?" Bradley asked.

Dodge said no. "The muscles contract because of the heat. Probably postmortem."

"You sure? Those look like wound channels on his arms."

"Splits in his skin. Heat contraction again. Like a fucking frankfurter on a grill. Gets hot, splits its seams."

Dodge started humming the Oscar Mayer song. Bradley told him to knock it off. "It's not funny. This is somebody's kid."

"Somebody's crankhead. Come on, Al, we both know what went down here. Asshole's got a key to the lab, sneaks in late on a weekend night to cook up some meth. Maybe GHB or something more exotic. Uses this 'special project' of his for cover. Tonight his luck runs out. Either he fucks up the recipe and the lab catches fire, or his competition whacks him and torches the place."

"That's all speculation," Bradley said. "I say he was clean."

"You have such touching faith in human nature."

"No. I just have two kids of my own." Bradley brushed away a few more ceiling tiles, then recoiled. "God."

He had exposed the victim's chest, where skin and muscle had been burned away altogether, leaving a gap through which the heart and lungs, relatively undamaged, were visible.

"Quite a view, huh?" Dodge smiled. He was getting used to the smell. "It's like those models they use in science class—the transparent guy with all his guts showing through."

"You're just chock-full of analogies this morning." Bradley swallowed. "What's weird is that his internals look pretty much intact. I mean, outside he's a toasted marshmallow, and inside he's still in one piece."

Dodge nodded. "That's normal. Body fluids prevent the inner organs from reaching the same temperature as the skin."

"How do you know all this?"

"Experience," Dodge said shortly. He didn't bother explaining that one of his first homicide cases had involved a teenager who'd set his parents' mobile home on fire, with them inside. They hadn't let him get a tattoo. He'd been a little upset about it.

"And your experience tells you this is a crime scene?" Bradley asked.

Dodge hesitated. He knew the kid had been cooking meth. But it would be easier to call it an accident and let it go. Easier on the school, the kids' parents, and most of all, himself.

But there was the media angle. College brat supplements his folks' handouts by turning school property into meth house. Blows up his worthless ass—or gets his ass blown up by pissed-off street rivals who don't like competition.

That was a story. Myron Levine would pay decent bucks for it, because the college was in Westwood—and Westwood was "affluent."

"Yeah," Dodge said, calculating what he could squeeze out of Levine for inside details on this case, "it's a crime scene."

Bradley looked away. "Hope you're wrong."

"Why? What difference does it make?"

"Maybe just because . . . well, because this would be a real bad way for an innocent kid to die."

Dodge couldn't argue with that. But what Bradley didn't understand, even after eighteen years on the street, was that nobody was innocent. Everybody was into something. Everybody was corrupt, tainted, dirty. Some were honest about it, and some put on an act—but no one was clean, ever.

The vic, whether Scott Maple or someone else, had been involved in something ugly. No matter how Dodge looked at it, this case was a whodunit.

And even if it ended up making him some money, it was going to fuck up his weekend, that was for goddamn sure.

19

The low buzzing of her cell phone startled Tess out of a deep sleep. She looked at the bedside clock—the digital readout said it was 6:47 A.M.—then fumbled for the phone, kept in her purse on the nightstand. She dropped it, had to grope for it under the bed, and finally managed to answer.

"McCallum," she said.

"What the hell's going on with you? I had to let your damn phone ring fifteen times." It was the unmistakable, slightly nasal, ever-welcome voice of the Nose.

"I'm a sound sleeper," she told Michaelson.

"Then you might want to consider turning up the goddamned volume on your phone."

"I wasn't expecting any calls."

"You weren't expecting any calls. Perfect. Then I guess you weren't expecting another dead body. But guess what? We've got one."

She sat up. "Where?"

"MiraMist Hotel, Santa Monica. Be there ASAP if you don't want to get shipped back to Denver on the next flight."

She really disliked this man. "I'll be there," she said tightly.

"That's big of you. Oh, and, McCallum? You ever make me wait more than five rings to get through to you again, I'll have your ass."

Click. He was gone.

She had fallen asleep fully dressed and had no time to change. Quickly she ran a toothbrush over her teeth and gums to get rid of the morning taste, then placed a DO NOT DISTURB sign on her door. There was a chance she would have time to come back for a quick shower later this morning, and she didn't want the maid busy in the room. She could live with an unmade bed, anyway.

Before leaving, she switched on the air conditioner, setting the thermostat to seventy-two degrees. The room was getting stuffy, and the day was already warm.

Tess met Andrus in the lobby of the MiraMist. "Sorry," the AD said, "you can't go up there just yet."

"Why not?" She had rushed in from the Valley, violating every municipal traffic law at least twice. The last thing she'd expected was a delay in visiting the crime scene.

"Michaelson called you too soon. He should have waited."

"Waited for what? Where is he, anyway?"

"Still on his way over. Look, grab some breakfast, relax for a while—"

"Relax? I'm not in the mood to relax. One of these rooms is a crime scene, and I want to look at it."

"Not yet. It's . . . off-limits." Andrus said it with a light flutter of his eyelids that told her he was concealing something.

She drew him aside, into a shadowed alcove. "What's up, Gerry?"

Using his first name was a signal. It meant they could talk as friends, not bureaucrats. But he merely looked away.

"Just be patient, Tess. Things are taking a little longer upstairs than expected."

"What things? You mean somebody's already up there?"

"Another investigative team is working the room."

"*Another* team? This is a RAVENKILL crime scene."

"It's more than that."

"More? Come on, Gerry, I have a right to know what's going on. I'm part of the task force."

"You're part of it because I pulled rank to violate bureau policy and bring you here. Don't make me rethink that decision."

There was steel in his eyes, as chilly as the steel temples of his eyeglasses. Tess took a step back.

"You can't take me off this investigation."

"I wouldn't want to." His voice was noncommittal.

"No, I'm saying you *can't*."

"Your personal feelings—"

"My personal feelings are not the issue. He sent me a new postcard, remember? He's been in contact with me. Has he made contact with anyone else?"

The question was unnecessary. She took Andrus's silence as her answer.

"Exactly. Which is why you need me working this case. So don't try to threaten me, and don't act like you've done me a favor bringing me to LA. Violating bureau policy . . . We're dealing with a multiple lust murderer, and bureau policy is to catch him, and that's why I'm here."

Andrus stared past her, his jaw working silently, and Tess wondered if she'd pushed too hard. Everything she'd said was true—but there was some truth on his side, as well. Under normal circumstances she would not have been part of this detail. Andrus had expended some of his carefully hoarded political capital to get her to LA. The fact that he'd done it out of self-interest, in the knowledge that a resolution of the case would reflect well on his leadership of the LA office, didn't mitigate the debt she owed him.

"Things are complicated, Tess," he said finally. "I'm not at liberty to go into all the ins and outs. Let's just say that I *do* need you on the task force—you're right about that—but I need the cooperation of other elements within the bureau, as well."

"What elements?"

He shook his head and smiled. "Loose lips . . . You know how that goes."

"They sink ships. Old wartime slogan. But this is a crime scene, Gerry. Not a war zone."

When he looked at her, she saw something flicker in his ash-gray eyes. "You sure about that?" Andrus asked.

20

Tess wasted an hour in the lobby, stealing doughnuts from a spread laid out by the Santa Monica PD. Nobody would tell her anything, and after a while she eased up on her paranoia enough to decide that nobody knew anything worth telling. All she could learn was that the hotel room had been entered by the local SWAT team, who'd found a woman dead and no sign of her killer. How the room had been identified in the first place, why the police department's SWAT guys had been brought in for what should have been a federal bust—these were questions without answers. The SWAT squad had been isolated for debriefing, the incident commander wasn't around, and the street cops guarding the lobby had nothing to say.

She slipped into the rear office behind the registration desk and found clear indications that the office had been used as a temporary command post. Coffee mugs and chocolate bars were scattered around, extra phones had been jacked into the walls, folding tables and chairs were set up in available corners. The nature of the work done here was a mystery. All wastebaskets had been emptied. Any computer gear had been removed. But under a desk, she found a wadded scrap of paper that had been overlooked, covered with scribbled writing. Most of it was indecipherable, but one string of words, circled and recircled by an insistent hand, stood out from the rest.

$$tox \ (aer) \sim .01 \ mg/kg$$

Tox must mean toxic. *Aer* probably stood for aerial or—no, aerosol.

Aerosol toxicity? A gas?

Had to be. A gas with a toxicity of approximately point zero one milligrams per kilogram.

Lethal stuff. The tiniest droplet would be deadly.

Tess stared at the piece of paper for a long moment.

Another investigative team, Andrus had said. A team dealing with hazardous substances?

If there was a hazmat squad upstairs, and if they were keeping their presence secret, then they wouldn't use the main elevator when they left. They would take the freight elevator and exit through a rear door.

Tess left the office and headed to the back of the hotel, passing several ballrooms named after local flora—the Bird-of-Paradise, the Oleander, the Bougainvillea. She went through an unlocked door marked HOTEL STAFF ONLY, into a hallway decidedly shabbier than those intended for public use. Corrugated cartons were piled against cinder-block walls. Bare fluorescent tubes flickered overhead.

She found the freight elevator and waited to see if anybody came down.

Andrus had been secretive and uptight about whatever was going on. And last night, when she'd overheard him on the phone in his office, he'd sounded agitated, stressed.

Damn it, Tennant, you can't afford to screw this up.

Tennant.

She took out her cell phone and called the main

switchboard at FBI headquarters in DC, asking to be connected with Special Agent Tennant. The call was transferred to Tennant's office, but she got only his voice mail. She terminated the call without leaving a message and speed-dialed the Denver field office. With the one-hour time difference, it was 8:30 in Denver—early, but not too early for Lori to be in.

Lori Woods was her closest friend in the bureau. She was not an agent but one of the twenty thousand civilian employees who received no media attention or publicity, never had TV shows built around fictionalized versions of themselves, never received any special commendation or acknowledgment, yet kept the whole nationwide enterprise running.

"Tess," Lori said when she came on the line, "how are things going in LA?"

How are you handling it? was what she meant. Tess wasn't sure she knew the answer to that question. "Things are pretty crazy," she said. "There's been another killing."

"Oh, damn."

"I'm about to enter the crime scene."

"That won't be easy."

Tess wanted to say something glib like, *It's what they pay me for.* But she couldn't fool Lori, so all she said was, "I'm not looking forward to it. In the meantime, I have a favor to ask."

"Ask away."

"I'm away from the office now. Can you look through the personnel database and tell me about a special agent name of Tennant, who works out of Ninth Street? I have a feeling he's somebody I should have heard of."

"He is. I mean, I've heard of him, and I'm only a lowly civilian."

"They also serve who only file and type. Who is he?"

"Grizzled veteran. Been here forever. Since the Hoover days. Must be pushing sixty by now."

"If he's sixty, he's past retirement age," Tess said.

"I heard they made a special exception for him. Postponed his mandatory retirement date."

"So he's got pull?"

"He's got balls," Lori said. "Some people say he's got a little something extra, too."

"Such as?"

"Such as inside knowledge of the bureau's various, um, indiscretions." Lori had lowered her voice.

"You're saying he's blackmailing the higher-ups?"

"No, nothing that crude. It's not like he knows anything personal. What he knows is the agency dirt. You know, the botched operations, the money that went down various rat holes without appropriate congressional oversight. You hang around this place for thirty-plus years, you learn where the bodies are buried."

"And he's holding that over their heads to extend his career?"

"It may not be so overt. I think they're just worried that he'll be harder to control if they cashier him. And of course he doesn't want to turn in his badge. He's one of those guys who eat, sleep, and breathe the bureau. No wife, no kids. He's married to the FBI."

"Okay, I get the picture. Now who the heck is he?"

"Didn't I tell you? He's chief of DTS."

Tess let that sink in. "I see," she said finally.

"He's been over there for a couple of years. Transferred out of Philly, where he was the SAC."

"A couple of years," Tess echoed. She knew why she hadn't stayed abreast of Tennant's assignment. In the past two years, since her return from bereavement leave, she had merely gone through the motions of her job. Anything outside her immediate purview had been ignored.

"Now you tell me something," Lori said. "Why do you want to know?"

"Because he's here. He's in LA."

"Well, I guess that's not too surprising. DTS gets around. But he can't have anything to do with your case."

"No," Tess said. "No, of course not. I was just curious, that's all. I couldn't place the name."

Lori sounded suspicious. "There something you're not telling me, kiddo?"

Tess tried to laugh off the question. "I wouldn't dare. Look, I've got to go. What's the weather like, anyway?"

"Cool and rainy. Clearing tomorrow."

"Sunny here."

"Sure it is. It's LA."

Tess promised to talk to her soon and ended the call.

DTS, she thought. Domestic Terrorism Section.

And a hazmat team. Man-lethal doses.

Terrorists and toxic substances. A scary combination. But she couldn't quite see where Mobius fit in. She—

The freight elevator hummed. It was coming.

She slipped into an unlocked janitorial supply closet, leaving the door an inch ajar.

The elevator doors slid open. Out came a group of men covered from neck to ankles in yellow Nomex jumpsuits. They wore heavy black gloves and boots, and carried helmets under their arms.

Hazmat suits. Tess had seen them before, at chemical spills and industrial fires.

Following them was another man, this one in a blue

business suit incongruously overlaid with a SWAT flak jacket and an oxygen canister. He carried a ballistic helmet and a gas mask under one arm.

"You're a hundred percent certain?" he was asking.

Tess studied him. Iron-haired, squat and muscular and thick-necked. She pegged him as Special Agent Tennant of DTS.

One of the hazmat guys tapped a piece of gear he was toting, which Tess recognized as a portable chemical detector, known to experts as a sniffer. "The APD is sensitive to one part per million. If anything was there, we'd have picked it up."

"Okay. You head over to City Hall East. I'll meet you there. The briefing starts at eleven hundred, sharp."

Tess wanted to hear more, but the men had already moved out of earshot. A moment later she heard an exit door clang shut. They were gone.

She left the closet and retraced her route to the lobby. Andrus was looking for her.

"There you are. You disappeared on us. I thought I might have to call out the bloodhounds."

"You could have paged me."

"True. I suppose I thought you might need some time alone before going upstairs."

"I was using the rest room."

"Well, you can go upstairs anytime you want."

Do I need a hazmat suit? she almost asked. But she preferred not to let Andrus know what she had found out, at least not quite yet. Not that she didn't trust him, but . . . well, actually she didn't trust him. He had been withholding information from her, and she didn't know why. Andrus was a good manager, and he kept the standard bureaucratic ass-covering office politics to a minimum, but he'd never been what might be called a stand-up guy.

"Who else is up there?" she asked.

"Michaelson. A couple of techs."

"Gaines wasn't invited? How about DiFranco, Collins, anybody else?"

"We don't need a hundred people tramping through the room."

"Maybe you just don't want a hundred people to know what's in the room."

He winced. "Tess, I would share everything with you if I could."

She wasn't sure she believed this. She didn't know what to believe right now.

"I know, Gerry," she said with her best fake smile. "I understand."

She didn't understand, of course. Not yet.

But before long, she promised herself, she would.

21

Tess knew exactly what to expect even before she stepped into room 1625. The details of Mobius's crime scenes never varied. Even the brand of duct tape was always the same.

What she couldn't anticipate was her reaction. That was what scared her, what set her heart pumping hard as she left the elevator and walked down the hall.

She had not been to a room like this since the night of February 12. She wasn't sure what it would do to her. Crazily she feared she would throw up or faint or run out screaming.

The door to the room was open. A Santa Monica patrol officer stood guard. Michaelson was inside, along with a crime-scene photographer and an evidence technician from the field division's crime lab, unpacking his gear as he prepared to bag and tag, dust, and vacuum.

Tess showed the cop her creds, then crossed the threshold. During her bureau-mandated bereavement counseling, she had learned several techniques for managing stress. Among these was a breathing exercise—a slow intake of breath, a pause, and an even slower exhalation. The method helped her sometimes. She tried it now.

Breathe in . . .

The corpse on the bed, wrists taped to the headboard, head lolling, eyes wide, mouth hidden behind a strip of tape slapped over her lips, a semicircular wound across the throat, a spillway of dark brown blood descending like a bib.

Hold the breath . . .

The woman was naked, her legs twisted in a pose of writhing. Her complexion was smooth and pale. Even in death, her eyes were oddly bright. She looked determined, somehow. There was a silent, still intensity to her face that made Tess think of that term soldiers used—the thousand-yard stare.

Breathe out . . .

Patches of purple lividity mottled the exposed portions of her back, where the blood, no longer circulating, had settled heavily. She had lain there for perhaps seven hours, more or less; the medical examiner would give a more precise estimate. Most likely she had died around two o'clock, later than Mobius's other kills. Tess thought of William Hayde, detained at the field office until after midnight. He might have had enough time to drive over here—it was only a ten-minute trip from Westwood—then slip on a disguise and pick up this woman.

It was unlikely, though. She was probably just getting desperate.

Breathe in . . .

The woman's clothes were scattered on the bed in what appeared to be evidence of hectic lovemaking. Tess scanned the sheets for a semen stain but saw none. There would be no semen in the vaginal canal, either. Mobius practiced safe sex.

Hold the breath . . .

The sheet under the woman was dark with sweat—

the residue of sex and, later, fear. Her sweat, not his. He would have been on top throughout the encounter. He needed to be dominant, needed to be in control.

A tremor worked its way through her. She fought it off. She would not yield to some idiot reaction of her body. She would be stronger than her emotions.

Breathe out . . .

She couldn't look at the woman anymore. The corpse, the staring eyes, the bloody neck—it was too much like Paul. She turned away and focused her attention elsewhere.

A minibar. She took a quick inventory of its contents. Nothing appeared to be missing.

Notepad of hotel stationery on an occasional table. No writing on any of the pages.

What else? Drapes drawn shut over a balcony door. Armchair. Table strewn with magazines of local interest. Bureau and desk chair. Small suitcase, its contents scattered.

"Her bag, I assume," she said to Michaelson.

The Nose sniffed at her as if deciding whether she was worthy of an answer. "Yes," he said finally, without looking at her.

"When did she check in?"

"Didn't."

"What?"

He expelled a loud sigh, an audible expression of his impatience with her stupidity. "It's not her room," he said.

"So whose is it?"

"His. *He* checked in."

"Mobius took this room?"

"That's correct, Agent McCallum. He signed for it under the name Donald Stevenson, using a credit card he'd recently obtained for that identity. If you'd been in the lobby when the AD briefed me ten minutes ago, you'd know all this. But I suppose you were off applying lip gloss or something."

Tess didn't wear lip gloss. "When did Mobius check in?"

"Yesterday morning."

"Why?"

"What do you mean, why? So he would have a place to do this." Michaelson jerked a thumb at the dead woman on the bed. "Why the hell do you think?"

She wouldn't be put off that easily. "It doesn't make sense. If he came here, he was planning to pick up a woman at the hotel bar. Odds are, any woman he met there would be a guest of the hotel. She would have a room of her own."

"Unless she was a hooker."

"This place doesn't strike me as a hangout for hookers."

"All hotels are hangouts for hookers. And a hooker would use the john's room. He had to be prepared for that."

"I suppose." It added up, but she wasn't entirely convinced.

"Anyway," the Nose added, "this lady wasn't checked in at the hotel."

"Well, she wasn't a prostitute. Not if she had a suitcase with her. Where's her ID?"

"Gone. Her purse was here, but the other squad took it."

"Without sharing?"

"I don't think their mothers taught them to share."

"That doesn't bother you?"

"Sure, it bothers me. It also bothers me that we're wasting time talking about it when we have a crime scene to work."

Tess wasn't interested in the scene. She was interested in Tennant and his DTS squad. "We're not going to learn anything from this room," she said. "He hasn't left us any leads. He never does."

"With that kind of attitude"—the Nose was turning his back on her—"it's no wonder you've been spinning your wheels in Denver."

"What does that mean?"

He shrugged, not bothering to face her. "After Black Tiger you were on the fast track, sweetheart. Denver should have been a stepping-stone to LA or New York, then to Ninth Street. Instead you got stuck there. Now I know why."

"Do you?"

"You've lost your edge. No surprise. Happens to the best."

"You don't know a damn thing."

"You let RAVENKILL ruin you. Losing Voorhees was a tough break, I admit. But you should've handled it. We get paid to handle tough breaks. Some of us earn our pay. Some of us don't."

She burned with fury. "You asshole."

"Sticks and stones," he said with casual insolence. "Face it, darling. You flunked the test. You got kicked off the island."

"You call me sweetheart or darling again, and I'll bring you up on charges."

"Sexual harassment law. The last refuge of the token female."

"You are on such thin ice."

"Save it. Just shut up and stay out of my way. I have a case to run."

Tess stood there trembling with anger. After a long moment she forced herself to look away from Michaelson, toward the woman on the bed.

Blood on the sheets. The faux crucifixion, the paschal lamb of Easter weekend. The innocent sacrifice.

The woman had died in a hotel room that was not even her own. She'd had a valise with her, and she'd been sitting at a hotel bar late at night—yet she wasn't a guest of the hotel.

The pieces didn't fit.

Unless she'd been unable to check in. No money? A traveler would always have credit cards. But maybe she had been afraid that a credit card transaction would be traced.

The other squad had taken her purse. Tennant's squad. Counterterrorist operatives.

Of course.

Tess moved for the door.

"Going someplace?" Michaelson asked.

"I need to get some air."

She thought she heard him chuckle, amused at what he presumed to be her weakness. She didn't care.

Quickly she descended to the lobby. She found Andrus on the phone in the rear office that had been used as a command post earlier. As she entered, he said, "I'll be there," and ended the call. He glanced at her. "Any trouble dealing with the crime scene?"

"It's not the scene I'm having trouble dealing with." She sat down opposite him.

"I'd like to think that insubordinate tone was not meant for me," Andrus said.

"Would you? I'd like to think that if the head of Domestic Terrorism was at a RAVENKILL murder site ahead of me, along with a hazmat team, you would decide to tell me about it. So I guess we're both wrong, aren't we, Gerry?"

His face paled, whether in dismay or anger she wasn't sure and didn't care. She was past thinking of bureaucratic protocol.

"I saw Tennant," she went on. "And I saw a squad of hazardous materials experts. And I think I know why they were here."

"Do you?" Andrus said.

"That woman upstairs was involved in some sort of terrorist activity. DTS tracked her to this hotel and set up a command post in this room. Then they sent in SWAT to conduct an arrest. They found her dead. For some reason they expected to find a biohazard of some sort—in her suitcase, I assume. But the room was clean, which means either there never was any biohazard, or it's gone. I'm guessing the latter."

"Are you? Why?"

"The worried look on your face."

Andrus shook his head slowly. "What do you want from me, Tess?"

"I want you to stop holding out. Share the wealth. I shouldn't have to skulk around in corridors and spy on my own colleagues. And I shouldn't be forced to make guesses when you and Tennant could tell me—"

"Don't link me to Tennant," Andrus interrupted. "We're not a team. Hell, you heard my end of the conversation with him last night."

"It was none of my business last night. Now it is."

"Okay, I concede the point. It is your business. And if you'd just been patient and not gone sneaking off on your own—"

"You would've told me? Prove it. Tell me now. Tell me everything."

"I don't know much more than you've already guessed." He held up a hand to ward off her objection. "I don't, Tess. Scout's honor. But Tennant has assured me he'll reveal everything, no more secrets."

"At the briefing?" she said.

"You even know about that? Jesus."

"I know it's at City Hall East and it starts at eleven o'clock. Sharp. I know you'll be at it, because you have to be. And I know you're taking me along."

The AD frowned. "I can pass on whatever I learn."

"I want to be there, Gerry."

"No one from the RAVENKILL task force is invited."

"Why not? That makes no sense. It's crazy."

"Tennant has his reasons. It's his show, not mine."

"I don't give a damn whose show it is. Get me in."

He heard the threat in her voice. "Or . . . ?"

She stood up. "Or I'll investigate on my own. And whatever I come up with, I'll share with the local authorities."

"The locals aren't primary. This is a federal case."

She leaned on the back of her chair and met his eyes. "It's *my* case."

Andrus held her stare for a moment, then laughed. "Oh, what the hell. I should've known better than to work around you. All right, consider yourself invited."

Tess took his hand. "Thanks, Gerry. And I'm sorry if I'm pushing too hard. I don't mean to make your life difficult."

He laughed again. "Yes, you do."

22

During the long trip into downtown LA, Andrus was silent. He sat with Tess in the backseat of a sedan driven by an agent who was both chauffeur and bodyguard. Andrus had his laptop computer open before him and seemed to be scrolling through a document, but Tess noticed that his gaze often unfocused and became distant.

She had never seen him afraid, and she wasn't sure if she was seeing it now. But something had him preoccupied, at least. And she was beginning to see the outlines of what it was.

As the freeway traffic blurred past, she broke the silence to ask, "Are we meeting in the mayor's office?"

"No. ATSAC."

"At-what?"

"The ATSAC command center. Short for Automated Traffic Signal and Control." Andrus still hadn't looked up from his computer. "All the traffic lights throughout LA are linked together in a network that's supervised from a central command facility. Computers correct the timing of stoplights at intersections to adjust to changing traffic flow."

"Cool. What does traffic management have to do with Mobius?"

"There's more than traffic management involved." He said nothing further.

The driver dropped them off at City Hall East, one of several buildings that made up the sprawling Civic Center that stretched across nine city blocks. Andrus led her to an elevator on the parking level, where a guard stood post.

"Going down," Andrus said.

The guard checked Andrus's credentials and Tess's also. Satisfied, he handed Andrus a card key. "Here's your ticket in, sir. And the downstairs access code is four-seven-two-four."

Andrus swiped the card through an electronic reader. The elevator doors slid open. He and Tess stepped inside, and Andrus pressed the down arrow. Tess felt the start of their descent.

"ATSAC is underground?" she asked.

"Five floors down."

"Sounds more like NORAD than a traffic operations center."

"It's a little of both. Remember Y2K? The city wanted a command center in case the millennium really did start with a bang. The mayor at the time, Riordan, decided to upgrade the existing ATSAC facility. Basically he created a high-tech bunker."

"How so?"

"It's earthquake resistant and supposedly can withstand a nuclear blast. It's got multiply redundant communications systems—including copper-wire and fiber-optic links to the command stations of the Sheriff's Department and LAFD. It's fully self-contained and self-sufficient. There's a dormitory, a kitchen, emergency food supplies to serve fifty people for two years. Backup diesel generators to take up the load in case of a power interruption."

"Impressive, in a *Dr. Strangelove* sort of way."

The elevator stopped. Tess exited with Andrus into a windowless corridor ending in a heavy metal door that reminded Tess of the door to a bank vault.

"Other cities did the same," Andrus said. "Even though Y2K was a nonevent, the command center has remained operational. You never know when it might be needed for the next earthquake, riot . . ."

"Or terrorist attack."

"Precisely. In New York, the city's counterterrorist command center was above ground—in the World Trade Center, to be exact. We saw how well that worked out."

Andrus inserted the card key in another reader, and the bank-vault door slid open.

"Just like *Star Trek*," Andrus said.

"Or *Get Smart*."

They walked through, and the door closed behind them. There was a second door just ahead. The space between the two of them, Tess realized, was an airlock corridor—what biohazard experts called a gray zone. The two doors would never be open simultaneously. The gray zone allowed for decontamination before passing from the outside world into the secure interior of the bunker.

"It's sealed off from outside contamination," she said. "But the ventilation system must bring in air from above ground."

"Sure—but the air passes through multiple filters to screen out biological and chemical toxins. Whatever's outside can't get in."

"So basically this is the safest place in town."

"That's the idea, Tess."

Andrus punched the access code into a numeric keypad mounted near the second door, which opened with a beep. Together they entered the main space of the

ATSAC facility, a large circular room arrayed with computer workstations, each with its own red-upholstered swivel chair. The workstations were modular desks fitted together to form two concentric semicircles, facing a video wall that served as a luminous, multicolored moving background for half the room.

Tess estimated that there were forty flat-panel display screens mounted on the curving wall, each showing a mixture of live video, scrolling data, and computer-generated traffic grids and maps. Some screens were quartered into four images; others showed only a single scene. The views were of major surface-street traffic junctures, including the intersection of Wilshire Boulevard and Veteran Avenue, where the Federal Building, home of the FBI's LA office, was located. Tess had heard that it was the busiest intersection in the city.

She looked around. The facility extended beyond this central room into glass-walled offices to her left and right, and corridors branching into darkness. This was a sizable complex. And it was buried five stories under City Hall, accessible only by a secret elevator. She wondered how many Angelenos even knew it existed. The government, she imagined, had not been eager to spread the word.

The soft hum of equipment mingled with the burr of recirculated air. She had never been inside a NASA facility, but she imagined that it would be like this. The noise and grit of the city seemed far away.

Thirty or forty people were already assembled inside, a few seated among the rows of swivel chairs, but most standing and conferring in small, restless groups. Andrus went through the meet-and-greet routine with many of them, while Tess hung back. She knew nobody here. But of course she was an outsider—a stranger to this city, and an uninvited presence in this room.

At eleven o'clock precisely, everyone took a seat. Tess saw that a few people, Tennant among them, had special chairs facing the workstations.

Andrus sat beside Tess in the row of chairs farthest from the video wall. She was surprised he wasn't up front, and said as much in a whisper.

Andrus just smiled. "This isn't my show," he said.

A woman seated at the front of the room stood up and spoke into a microphone, introducing herself as Sylvia Florez, manager of the Los Angeles Office of Emergency Management. Her voice ticked like a metronome, rapid and precise, as she reviewed the major players present for the briefing—the mayor, members of the city council, the chief of police, the county sheriff. Then there was a quick rundown of the other participants seated at the workstations.

From the city of Los Angeles, representatives from the Department of Public Works, the Department of Transportation, and the Information Technology Agency. From the LAPD, the heads of the Emergency Preparedness Division and the Hazardous Materials/Environmental Crimes Unit. From the City Fire Department, the assistant chief of the Bureau of Emergency Services, as well as the battalion chief, who served as Antiterrorism Coordinator. Two representatives from the county fire department's Office of Emergency Management. Two representatives from the Sheriff's Department Emergency Operations Bureau. An agent of the Governor's Office of Emergency Management—Southern Region. Somebody from the Terrorism Working Group, and somebody else from the Terrorism Early Warning Group, which was apparently a different entity.

There were more people mentioned, including Tennant and Andrus, but Tess wasn't listening anymore. She got the point. The crisis managers were all on board.

"Now I'll introduce Special Agent Jack Tennant of the FBI, who will present the details of the anticipated threat."

Tennant replaced Florez at the microphone. He addressed the crowd with an air of brusque impatience that made a sharp contrast to Florez's polished performance.

"I guess you all want to know what the hell we're dealing with. All right. It's VX."

There was a rustle in many seats. Tess frowned. She had heard this term but couldn't place it.

"Most of you know, but for those who don't, VX is a nerve agent. A highly toxic nerve agent. The most powerful nerve agent ever developed. And it's here in LA."

Tess wasn't surprised, not really. She had known it would be something like this. Part of her was even a little relieved. A chemical weapon was bad, but a biological weapon could be worse. Unlike smallpox or plague, chemicals weren't contagious. There was a limit to the death toll.

Which would be no consolation at all for those numbered in that toll, or for their families.

"We'll have an expert up here in a minute to give you a complete overview of VX," Tennant said, "but for now, I want you to understand just what 'highly toxic' means. It means deadly. It means that one drop of this fucking—sorry—one drop of this stuff, absorbed into your bloodstream, will kill you in ten minutes.

"VX interferes with the brain's signals to the vital

organs. Specifically, it blocks the action of a certain enzyme, the name of which I can't pronounce, and leads to a buildup of something called acetylcholine in the central nervous system. This buildup stimulates the organs to hyperactivity. Your whole body goes haywire, and bang, you're gone. Just like that."

He snapped his fingers, then paused to look out over the audience and see if his words had made the desired impression. His gaze drifted toward the back of the room. He seemed to recognize Tess. She thought she caught a hint of surprised displeasure in his glance. Then he was speaking again.

"The toxicity of VX is zero point zero one milligrams per kilogram, meaning that if you weigh eighty kilos—that's about a hundred eighty pounds—it'll take only zero point eight milligrams of VX to stop your heart.

"In liquid form, VX is thick and viscid, with the density and color of motor oil. Normally, however, it's dispersed as an aerosolized mist of fine droplets, like you'd get out of a spray can. As a mist, it can enter your body through your skin, eyes, nose, and mouth. Inhalation is the most dangerous route because of the high vascularity of the lungs. Once it's in your lungs, the stuff can be very quickly distributed throughout your bloodstream. Onset of symptoms normally occurs within one minute of exposure.

"The mist is odorless and invisible. It can be all around you, and you won't know it until you experience the initial symptoms of exposure: runny nose, sweating, upset stomach, headache. Like I say, this all starts happening within one minute or so. Move fast, get away from the source of exposure, and the symptoms will subside. Breathe in more of the stuff, and you'll progress to localized fasciculations or tremors, shortness of breath—then to myoclonic jerks, meaning big muscular twitches like you'd have in a seizure. This leads to muscle fatigue, then flaccid paralysis, where your muscles go limp and become useless. By that time you're suffering from apnea, severe respiratory distress, because your respiratory muscles are paralyzed. And then—well, then you're dead.

"That's the bottom line. Continued exposure means death."

He's trying to scare us, Tess realized. *And he's doing a darn good job.*

"VX can be introduced into a building's HVAC system or released into the wind in a crowded public place. If it's an outdoor release, then a lot depends on the speed and direction of prevailing winds. VX is heavier and denser than air and will tend to pancake, flattening out like a low-lying cloud and hugging the ground. Those at street level are more likely to be affected than those at higher elevations, like, say, office workers in skyscrapers. If the stuff is released indoors, the casualty count will be determined by how quickly it spreads through the building before an evacuation begins.

"In either case, our worst-case scenario . . . Well, let's put it this way. In the late 1960s, a release of VX in a place called Skull Valley killed six thousand sheep. In a crowded urban environment, we could be talking human fatalities on the order of ten thousand."

Tennant looked hard at his audience and let them think about that.

"Ten thousand dead," he repeated. "That's what we're looking at."

23

Tennant said a few more words, none of them very reassuring, then invited Dr. Robert Gant to the microphone to fill in the audience on the chemical itself.

The doctor was the head of a countywide network of emergency physicians drilled as first responders to a chem-bio attack—"bugs and gas terrorism," as he called it. He spoke quickly and fluently, discoursing on the chemical properties of VX. Tess caught the words "an organophosphate compound related to pesticides like parathion," but she wasn't really listening. Her attention was fixed on Tennant as he made his way through the room.

Toward Andrus. And her.

"I hope the air filtration system in here is as good as they say," she whispered to the AD.

Andrus blinked. "Why?"

"Because the shit is about to hit the fan."

Then Tennant was at her side, leaning over her chair and looking right past her, at Andrus. "What's she doing here?" he hissed.

Great. Another guy who talked about her in the third person. The Nose must be giving lessons.

"She's on the RAVENKILL task force," Andrus began in a low, conciliatory tone.

Tennant wasn't interested in conciliation. "I know she's on the goddamned task force. She's Tess McCallum. Black Tiger, all that shit. She was in Denver chasing Mobius, and now she's in LA. And I want to know why the fuck she's sitting next to you in this room."

"Because I invited her."

"Yeah, I figured that out. Damn it, I thought we agreed no task force members were going to be brought in."

"I brought myself in," Tess said, but both men ignored her.

At the microphone, in front of the wall of video images, Dr. Gant was reminding the audience of the Tokyo subway attacks in 1995. Sarin gas had been used that time. VX was more toxic than sarin. It was, in fact, the most toxic of all nerve agents.

"I do have some authority here," Andrus said coolly. "If I wish to call in Agent McCallum or anyone else, I don't require your permission."

"When you're in this building, you require my permission to breathe," Tennant said.

"Besides which," the AD went on as if there had been no interruption, "Agent McCallum knew most of what's going on anyway."

For the first time Tennant favored her with a glance. "Knew? How?"

Tess met his eyes, unperturbed. Tennant might intimidate some people at the bureau, but not her. "You and your hazmat team weren't as low-profile as you thought."

Tennant took this in with a scowl. "Who else knows?"

"Nobody," Tess said. "I didn't share it with the others."

"That's something, anyway."

"Although I probably should have," she added, just to piss him off.

Dr. Gant was reporting that VX had been stockpiled by the U.S., Russia, Iran, Iraq, Syria, and North Korea, and could be manufactured by any industrial power. It was bought and sold on the international black market and was known to be in the hands of terrorist organizations.

"I don't get it," Tess said to Tennant. "Why wouldn't you want our squad in on this deal? We know Mobius. I know him better than anybody. I've been after him for nearly three years."

"That's exactly why."

"Meaning what?"

"We don't have three years, Agent McCallum. We may not have three days. Your methods, and those of the other members of your squad, have failed. I can't afford failure in my operation. I'm not going to import failure or build on it or incorporate it into my plans."

She got hot. "You're implying we haven't caught him because we've screwed up."

"Right."

"There's another possibility. Maybe he just hasn't allowed himself to be caught."

"Criminals make mistakes, Agent McCallum. All criminals."

"Not Mobius. Not yet. He has a script, and he sticks to it. But maybe not this time."

"What's different now?"

"The VX wasn't in the script. It's an unplanned development. It means he has to improvise. He may slip up. He can be caught."

"When he is, we'll call you and let you know."

"I'm not leaving this case."

Tennant simmered for a moment, then dismissed

her with a shrug. "Fine. Stay involved. Feel useful. Be a contributing member of our effort." He moved off, then added over his shoulder, "Just keep the fuck out of my way."

Tess watched him as he returned to the front of the room.

"I don't like that guy," she murmured.

"Really?" Andrus smiled. "I find him rather charming."

Dr. Gant concluded his remarks, and Tennant went back to the microphone. He motioned to an ATSAC technician, who replaced the central image on the video wall with an aerial shot of a military base.

"Beginning in the mid-1950s, the U.S. government was a major manufacturer of VX and other chemical weapons. By treaty, these weapons are now scheduled to be destroyed. Pending their elimination, they have been stored in a handful of Army depots, including this seventeen-thousand-acre facility in Umatilla, Oregon. Officially the incineration of these weapons is ongoing, with their complete eradication expected by 2005.

"Unofficially, matters are different. Needless to say, what I'm about to tell you is highly classified and must not go beyond this room. The international ramifications of making this information public would be severe. But the fact is that after the September 11 atrocities, there was a reevaluation of U.S. military policy in this area. In the context of a new global war against terrorism, no weapon—no class of weapons— can any longer be ruled out. Trouble is, existing stockpiles of VX are aging and unreliable.

"Accordingly, last year the government secretly contracted with a private chemical laboratory to resume production of VX.

"The laboratory is located in Hermiston, Oregon, only a few miles from Umatilla, where a quantity of older VX remains in storage inside specially constructed warehouses called igloos."

Another video image, captioned UMATILLA K-BLOCK, showed rows of earth-covered, rounded buildings inside a double cyclone fence topped with barbed wire.

"The plan is to use these igloos to store new stockpiles of VX as they are manufactured. The first delivery of VX to the Umatilla depot had been scheduled for next month. Approximately fifty tons of the agent were to be moved via convoy from the lab to the Army base. Because the movement of VX was expected to be a clandestine operation, the convoy would have been small and only lightly guarded.

"One month ago, foreign intelligence sources informed our office of unusual activity among black-market arms dealers. It appeared someone was offering to reveal details of the convoy operation in exchange for a seven-figure cash transfer to an offshore account. In other words, someone familiar with the VX shipment was willing to set up the convoy for an ambush, thus allowing a substantial quantity of nerve agent to fall into the wrong hands.

"Subsequent investigation identified the likely suspect as Amanda Pierce." A photo of Pierce, possibly from her driver's license or an ID card, appeared on the video wall. "Pierce was an officer in the Defense Intelligence Agency before entering the private sector as a security consultant. She was hired by the Hermiston lab as chief security officer for the manufacture and transfer of VX. She was the only person possessing both detailed knowledge of the security procedures and the necessary sophistication to contact arms brokers working abroad. Pierce tested normal on psychological evaluations at the time of her DIA service, but through interviews with former friends and associates we discovered a more complex personality profile with pronounced sociopathic elements. She was evidently one of those people who can fake normal on standardized tests.

"Two days ago, on Thursday evening, Pierce drove out of the Hermiston area, heading south. Because she had scheduled Friday as a vacation day, we'd anticipated that she would take advantage of the holiday weekend to make her move. We also knew from our foreign intel sources that the liaison with her unknown contact was to take place in Los Angeles. Thus we were in position to follow her as she drove into California. She stopped for the night at a motel in Salem, Oregon, then continued her drive the next day, arriving in the Los Angeles metro area on Friday night.

"Unfortunately, after entering LA, Pierce executed a variety of countersurveillance maneuvers. It was at this point that she broke containment. In simpler language, we lost her."

"*You* lost her?" one of the city councilmen said from his seat next to the mayor.

"Yes, sir. I did. It was my fault exclusively. I take full responsibility." He added, "I fucked up."

Tess almost had to admire him for that. He had not survived three decades in the bureau by playing cover-your-ass politics, at any rate.

There was silence for a moment, and then Tennant went on.

"Pierce was not reacquired until early this morning, by which time she was dead. Evidently she had some very bad luck. She appears to have allowed herself to be picked up by a locally active serial killer who previously operated in Denver, killing four people there. He uses the name Mobius. He took her to his hotel room, which he'd charged to a phony credit card. He had sex with her, and he killed her—his usual MO. Then he left, and now he's in the wind.

"So Pierce is dead, another notch in Mobius's knife. Which we might say was just as well—even that he did the world a favor this time—except for one thing.

"In order for Pierce to establish her bona fides and seal the deal, she was supposed to hand over a sample of the VX produced at the Oregon lab. The lab had earlier confirmed to us that seven hundred and ten ccs, or twenty-four ounces, of the nerve agent were unaccounted for. It's a safe assumption that Pierce smuggled out this quantity of VX, probably in its original packaging—a metal canister approximately ten inches long and two inches in diameter. The total package—cylinder and contents—would weigh two pounds. When she traveled to LA, she would have brought it with her, most likely in her suitcase."

"You could have intercepted this woman at any time," the mayor interrupted to ask, "isn't that correct?"

"Yes, sir. We were holding off until she met with her contact. We wanted to collar them both."

"But you didn't, and now she's dead, and the VX . . . ?"

"Is gone."

"Taken by this man Mobius?"

"We think so, yes."

"A serial killer."

"Yes."

"A serial killer who's now armed with a weapon of mass destruction. A weapon that can kill ten thousand people."

"That's it in a nutshell, sir."

The county sheriff put in a word. "Have you considered the possibility that her contact killed her and made it look like the work of this Mobius just to throw us off?"

Tennant hesitated. For the first time he was stumped.

"It was Mobius," Tess said from the back of the room. Heads turned. "I've worked the case for years. The signature of the crime scene is distinctive. There are details that couldn't be copycatted, because they were never made public."

"Details like what?" a councilman challenged.

She could have answered: *Like the fact that the carotid arteries were not cut . . . that the victim's wrists were taped to the headboard . . . that duct tape was applied to her mouth . . .*

But she said only, "Details that have to remain undisclosed for the sake of the investigation."

"That's not an answer."

"It's as much of one as you're going to get."

Suddenly everybody was talking at once. The room seemed hotter and more crowded than it had been a moment earlier. People were talking back now, unwilling to yield the floor any longer. Tess had seen this behavior in every briefing she'd attended. Powerful people would not stay quiet for long.

"Folks," Tennant yelled over the clamor, "we need some order here. Chief Florez has to discuss the details of the counterterror procedures that are already under way."

The room quieted down as Sylvia Florez outlined the emergency plans.

"In the event of a mass-casualty situation, an emergency broadcasting system alert will notify area hospitals storing antidotes to biochemical weapons. Additional meds are being flown in from federal stockpiles. Medical strike teams will be mobilized to set up decontamination showers and other mobile facilities. We estimate that one hundred twenty nurses and fifteen doctors can process and decontaminate up to one thousand victims per hour.

"The efforts of the forty-nine thousand first responders in LA County will be coordinated with those of the Department of Public Services, the Departmental Operations Center, and Emergency Network Los Angeles.

"The LAPD's antiterrorism division has been mobilized. The department's response plans for a terrorist threat, available on the LAPD intranet, call for heavy deployment of LAPD undercover and uniformed units, concentrating on likely targets—sports venues, federal buildings, amusement parks, and so on.

"In compliance with Presidential Decision Directive Thirty-nine, federal assistance has been requested. National Guard units trained in WMD crisis management and U.S. Army chemical defense units are now on alert. Another available resource is the U.S. Marine Corps Chemical-Biological Incident Response Force—three hundred seventy-five men trained in NBC incident containment.

"Health and Human Services, the Federal Emergency Management Agency, and the EPA have been notified. As you've seen, the FBI is on the case."

Someone muttered audibly, "And doing a bang-up job."

Tess sucked in a hard breath. She didn't like having the bureau dumped on. But the fact remained that the FBI had lost Amanda Pierce—and now the FBI had to find Mobius and stop him before it was too late.

When the presentation was over, Florez asked for questions. Tess raised her hand, but Florez wasn't looking toward the back of the room and Tennant ignored her. Finally she stood without being recognized.

"When do we go public with this?"

"Never," Tennant said.

Tess wouldn't accept that answer. "It's Saturday. People will be going out to ball games, concerts, all sorts of crowded places. You already said that sports arenas are possible targets. So are theaters and shopping malls. People need to know."

"So they can panic?"

"So they can take precautions."

"What precautions, exactly, can the general public take against a psychopathic serial killer with a terrorist weapon?"

"Maybe we need a curfew."

The mayor waved off the idea. "There will be no curfew. We're not throwing this city into chaos."

"I don't think there'll be chaos," Tess persisted. "We've had government alerts periodically since the World Trade Center attack."

"And most of those alerts," Tennant said, "have been false alarms based on unsubstantiated information."

"This one isn't."

"We don't know that, Agent McCallum. Suppose Mobius doesn't even know what the hell he's got. Then he hears about it on the TV news. Then we've given him the information he needs. We're aiding and abetting."

"He won't need our help. He's smart enough—"

"I know, I know, he's an evil genius who never makes mistakes. So let's say we do it your way. We hold a press conference at two o'clock. Guess what the situation is as of two-oh-five. Every freeway is jammed bumper-to-bumper with people trying to hightail it the hell out of town."

"That's ridiculous. If the information is presented the right way—"

"The right way? What precisely is the right way to

tell ten million people that a nutcase is running around with enough nerve gas to depopulate an entire neighborhood? You'll have mass panic, mass evacuation, breakdown of order, looting, riots, the whole nine yards."

"People are better than that," Tess said. "They've proven it in the past. Give them a chance, and they'll prove it again. And they deserve to be told."

"Well, thank you, Agent McCallum, for airing your uplifting view of human nature. We can all benefit from your wisdom and perspective. But just in case you happen to be wrong, there will not be any public announcement."

The mayor seconded this, as did all the city council members.

Tess sat down. "What do you think, Gerry?" she asked Andrus in a low voice. "Am I crazy?"

"Probably." But he said it with a smile.

"So you wouldn't announce it?"

"No. I wouldn't."

"Suppose you had a wife or a son—"

"I'd tell them."

"So they get to know, and other people don't?"

"Life isn't fair, Tess." Andrus sighed. "I thought you already knew that."

She did. But she just kept learning it all over again.

24

Tess was walking on the palisades, the high bluffs that towered over the Pacific Coast Highway and the beach beyond. The salt air blew through her hair and caressed her cheeks. The sun was high in the sky, bright but cool, a California sun.

She wasn't sure how far she had walked. Looking back, she saw the MiraMist in the far distance, its tiered balconies gleaming. A mile away, she guessed.

After the ATSAC briefing, she had lined up with the others to receive packets of pyridostigmine bromide—"a single thirty-milligram pill every eight hours," Dr. Gant said, "starting now." The medicine was a prophylactic that would enhance the effectiveness of antidotes to VX, if and when they were used.

The antidote kits were passed out next. Gant spent some time demonstrating how to unclip and use the two self-injector syringes. "Carry this pouch with you at all times," he said. Tess thought he was being a little melodramatic. Even so, she had put the kit inside her purse, which she intended to keep on her person until Mobius was caught.

After that, she had found herself excluded from the activity around her. She was not part of any squad or task force. Tennant didn't want her there, and Andrus was preoccupied with a hundred logistical and bureaucratic priorities.

No one was willing to talk to her, anyway. She was the crazy bitch who wanted to open up the investigation to media scrutiny and start a panic and get all the incumbent politicians recalled in a special election. She was persona non grata.

So she'd left. Andrus's driver had chauffeured her back to the MiraMist, where her car was parked. She'd thought about revisiting the crime scene, but there was nothing for her to do up there.

So she had gone for a walk along the bluffs, wondering what to do next. She thought about informing Michaelson of the ATSAC meeting. It was an act of insubordination, but at least it would piss off Tennant. Unfortunately, she disliked Michaelson even more than she disliked Tennant. Besides, there was no wiggle room in her orders—Michaelson and the rest of the RAVENKILL task force were to be kept in the dark. They were out of it.

Effectively, so was she. She knew what was going on, but she'd been frozen out.

"Then go it alone," she murmured to herself.

She had threatened Andrus that she would investigate on her own. Big words, but what sort of investigating could she do without resources in an unfamiliar city?

She stopped at a railing and gazed at the blue mist of the ocean's horizon.

An unfamiliar city. No Rockies here, a sheer granite wall rising out of the mile-high plateau. No crisp winter mornings when new snow crunched underfoot and the only colors were the achingly pure blue of the sky and the flit of red as a cardinal hunted for seed. No summer rodeos, no autumn hayrides.

She didn't know this town.

But she did know *him*.

Mobius. Her nemesis. The man who had taunted her, hounded her, taken over her life.

In the surveillance room she'd bragged that she had some insight into Mobius's mind-set, that she knew what he was like when he was being himself.

Now was the time to prove it.

Mobius had taken the VX from Amanda Pierce's suitcase. How had he known about it? Had Amanda told him? Had he tortured the truth out of her?

Unlikely. A room with thin walls in a crowded hotel was not a place for torture. And Amanda Pierce, even in death, had not looked cowed or broken. Tess remembered the glare fixed on her face, the anger in her dead eyes.

Mobius must have taken the canister of VX merely on a hunch. Perhaps he'd felt its liquid contents sloshing inside. Perhaps he'd guessed that Amanda Pierce was not an ordinary tourist.

But there was no way for him to guess what the liquid was. He would need to find out. How?

Taste it, sniff it? If so, he was dead. But he would not be so stupid. Mobius might be insane, but—

Mobius.

That name. A reference, it was thought, to the Möbius strip. Something that a person trained in math or science would know about.

She had been going about this all wrong. She should not ask what a serial killer would do. She should ask what a scientist would do.

Faced with an unknown substance, a scientist would have it analyzed.

A sailboat drifted past, but Tess didn't see it.

After a long time she turned away from the railing

and headed back toward the MiraMist and her car. She knew what she had to do.

There might be no need to run, but she found herself running anyway, as she retraced her route along the bluffs.

25

The body lay on a steel table under a fluorescent light. Dodge looked at the skin, charred and blackened, and thought about a roast duck he'd ordered in Chinatown. There was the same crinkly quality, the same translucent sheen.

"Something's up today," Winston said as she prepped the X-ray machine.

Rachel Winston was a brisk, careful woman who eschewed the crude humor indulged in by most of her colleagues at the Los Angeles County Morgue. She was good-looking in a severe, ice-princess sort of way, and still young enough that her tits were more horizontal than vertical. Dodge had her pegged as a dyke, because he'd asked her out and she'd rebuffed him.

Fuck her, anyway. She probably got off on dead bodies.

"Yeah?" Dodge said. "Like what?"

"Lot of activity around City Hall. Cars going in and out. Looks very official. Started around ten-thirty this morning." She glanced at him. "You don't have any inside info?"

"Not a clue," he said, though now that she mentioned it, the West LA station had seemed unusually active when he'd stopped there at one-thirty, an hour ago, and on the drive to downtown LA he'd noticed a surprising number of patrol units on the streets.

"Well, the toilers in the trenches are always the last to know." Winston nodded at her assistant, a pathology technician with cornrowed hair. "Guess we're just about ready."

They were standing together in the morgue's radiography room, conveniently down the hall from where the dead bodies were stored. In the movies, the dead were always filed away in cabinets, but in actuality they were more likely to be stacked on gurneys or piled up in corners, awaiting inspection. There was a lot of death in LA County, and the cabinets were all full.

Another thing about the movies—the morgue technicians always wore surgical masks. So did the cops, when they were played by somebody like Brad Pitt or Robert De Niro. But this was real life, and nobody wore a fucking mask. They would think you were a wuss if you wore a mask. You just stood there breathing whatever germs and shit were there to be breathed, and you were stoic about it.

Dodge had visited the morgue many times, because it was often necessary for at least one detective working a case to observe an autopsy. Today he had drawn the detail while Al Bradley had gone back to Reseda. Truth was, he didn't mind. He still thought there was a story here, one that might be worth another two grand from Myron Levine.

Besides, he had no problem with taking a trip to the morgue. Sort of liked it, in a way. The place impressed him—all these pathologists working with quick efficiency, unpacking their lifeless patients, taking samples of fluids and organs, dictating comments into microphones suspended overhead. The comments would be typed up into transcripts attached to the official reports, the vials of fluid and plastic containers of heart and lung tissue would be sent to the lab for analysis, and the lab reports would go into the file as well.

It was fucking incredible, really, how the county of Los Angeles had succeeded in making the autopsy an assembly-line process—dissection on a mass scale, an army of doctors and lab technicians all working together to reduce body after body to its raw components, while reducing the fact of death itself to a sheaf of paperwork.

Every time he came here, he had the same thought: *This is how it ends. This is all there is.*

He didn't give a shit about religion and all that metaphysical crap. Death was a pile of flesh on a sheet of steel with gutters to carry off the sluice of blood. Nothing else. Just that.

Today, though, he wasn't going to witness an actual autopsy. There was always a backlog of corpses in the morgue. An autopsy was almost never scheduled until at least twenty-four hours after the deceased had been found. All that was happening now was a postmortem radiology session. Winston was going to shoot X rays of the victim's teeth, then compare them with the antemortem dental records of Scott Maple, who remained missing and unaccounted for.

Had the dead man been a South Central gang-banger—or, for that matter, a South Central honor student—there wouldn't have been any rush to identify his remains. But when the victim was presumed to be a lily-white college student in lily-white Westwood—an affluent kid with affluent parents attending an affluent school in an affluent neighborhood—well, pull out all the goddamn stops, fast-track this case, get it cleared.

"We'll do a full set of radiographs," Winston said

as she pried open the corpse's mouth with a wedging instrument. "Put on your aprons and gloves."

Dodge and the assistant complied. You weren't a wuss for wearing a lead apron in the X-ray room. There were your nuts to worry about. Radiation caused impotence or sterility or something.

"Guess there's no doubt how the guy died, anyhow," he said, just for the sake of conversation.

"There's always doubt." Winston sounded weary.

"I don't know, Doc." He knew Winston hated being called Doc. "Looks to me like the cause of death was proximity to an open flame."

"He's burned, all right. Full thickness burns throughout the epidermis and dermis. But that damage could be postmortem. We'll need to see his trachea. If there's soot in the airway below the vocal cords, then he lived long enough to inhale smoke."

The X-ray machine made a prolonged humming sound as the first bite-wing was shot. The image was displayed in black and white on a video screen in the workstation.

"That's the most likely finding," Winston went on. "Plenty of toxins in a chemistry lab. Hydrogen chloride, hydrogen cyanide, benzene, ammonia, sulfur dioxide, you name it. Or just plain old carbon dioxide— the blood samples will tell us his carboxyhemoglobin level, and if it's over fifty percent, we've got a winner."

"You enjoy your work too fucking much, Doc." The f-word just slipped out. He normally didn't curse around female colleagues if there was any chance he could get them into bed, and he hadn't entirely given up on Winston. She might not be a dyke. Maybe he'd just asked her out on the wrong day of the month. PMS made women crazy.

"I'm simply aware of all the possibilities," Winston said, unruffled. "Smoke inhalation is only one of them.

Thermal trauma to the larynx is another. It can cause spasms that bring on suffocation. Or there's vagal inhibition, which produces reflex cardiac death—"

"Okay, okay."

She shrugged. "I don't like making assumptions."

"Yeah, I get that impression." He tried a little wit. "Maybe you should have your own TV series. *Winston, ME.*"

She actually smiled, a rare thing. "I've heard worse ideas." To her assistant: "Okay, take the other bitewing."

The radiograph machine hummed again. It was something called an MDIS—Mobile Digital Imaging System. The rotating arm of the device could be moved manually to shoot the subject from various angles.

"We're lucky his damn teeth didn't burn up," Dodge said, for no particular reason.

"Teeth burn only at temperatures exceeding one thousand degrees Fahrenheit. Fillings last even longer. They can survive temperatures of up to sixteen hundred degrees."

"Learn something new every day on this job." He didn't mean to sound sarcastic, but he did anyway. He tried to compensate by adopting a friendlier tone. "You ever see one this bad?"

"I've seen everything. This one is nasty, though." Winston looked over the body with professional detachment. "Third-degree burns over more than seventy percent of the anterior body surface. Tissue desiccation and avascularization, skin blackening and contraction, probable artifactual fractures of the carpi and metatarsals—"

"Fractures?"

"Postmortem. Caused by the shortening of the ligaments attributable to thermal injury. The small bones crack under the strain."

"But no sign of foul play?"

She smiled again. "I thought you said the cause of death was obvious."

"Like you, Doc, I don't make assumptions."

"A wise policy. So far, I don't see anything to suggest that John Doe was a victim of anything other than bad luck or his own stupidity. But I could be wrong."

"You are," a voice said from behind them.

Dodge and Winston both turned. A woman in a gray suit and a string tie stood in the doorway of the room. It took Dodge a moment to remember where he'd seen her.

The elevator in the Federal Building. Special Agent Tess McCallum, the lady fed who'd brushed him off.

Now here she was, stepping right back into his life. *Interesting.*

26

Tess had spent the past two hours following a zigzag path that had led her, without knowing it, closer and closer to this room in the morgue.

Her first stop after leaving the MiraMist had been the Santa Monica Police Department, where she'd cornered the watch commander in his office, flashed her FBI creds, and asked about any crimes reported within the last twelve hours that involved chemicals, chemical supply companies, or labs—break-ins, burglaries, anything. She was particularly interested in the theft or unauthorized use of equipment meant for analyzing unknown substances.

The watch commander had nothing. He seemed relieved when she left. She supposed she was acting a little feverish. She was on the hunt, and it felt good. She felt . . . hell, she felt *alive*, and that had been a rare feeling for her in the past two years.

Her next stop was the LAPD's West Los Angeles divisional station on Butler Avenue. Another watch commander, another office. Same question. This time she got results.

Since midnight there had been three incidents within LA city limits that met her criteria. One was the theft of chemicals—but no equipment—from a San

Pedro warehouse. The second was a break-in at a North Hollywood laboratory, which sounded promising until Tess learned that it was a photographic lab and the burglar, a teenager, had been caught in the act, thanks to a silent alarm.

That left the most serious incident, a fire in a basement chem lab on a university campus. Tess wasn't sure what to make of the fire. If Mobius had entered the lab to use or steal some equipment, why torch the place? Then she was told that an unidentified corpse, possibly a student, had been found in the debris. And things started to make sense.

From the Butler Avenue station she went into Westwood, visiting Fire Station 37. Most of the crew who had worked the blaze had gone off duty—platoon change was at seven A.M.—but she found one fireman working a double shift, filling in for a buddy with weekend plans. He hadn't discovered the body himself, but he'd seen it. No, he hadn't seen any sign of foul play, but the remains had been in bad condition. Arson? The fire department had sent a team from the arson unit to check it out, but he and his crew had left before the squad arrived. They had seen only the two LAPD detectives working the scene.

Tess knew the detectives' names from the report— Alan Bradley and James Dodge. The names seemed familiar, but she wasn't sure why.

She drove to the crime scene but found it guarded by campus security guards who would not let her go inside even after they looked at her badge. This was a local crime. The feds had no jurisdiction here.

Quartz lights were positioned near the outside windows, and Prosser pumps sucked out standing water through thick hoses. The guards told her that some people from the city fire department's arson unit were at work in the laboratory. Eventually one of the guards condescended to see if the chief investigator would talk with her.

He came up wearing heavy canvas fatigues, knee-high rubber boots, and thick gloves, with a crowbar clutched in one hand and a camera hanging by a strap around his neck. His face was sooty and streaked with sweat, and he looked more like a coal miner than an investigator of any kind.

The investigator said his team had been working the site for three hours and had at least another hour to go. They had determined the site of origin in the middle of the room and were checking nearby electrical appliances and connections for signs of an overload. Most fires originated with electrical faults. "But even if we find a problem with the wiring, it doesn't prove much. A fire this hot will burn the insulation right off the wires and cause a short circuit."

"It was a hot, fast fire, then?"

"With the fuel load in that room? You better believe it."

"So you can't say it was arson?"

"Can't say much of anything yet. Normally what we look for is evidence of an accelerant at the origin point. And we have it—deep char, serious spalling of the concrete floor, burn-through of the counters in that area."

"So you know an accelerant was used," Tess said.

"Yeah, but the thing is, the whole lab was full of accelerants. Half the chemicals stored there were flammable—acetone, methylated spirits, solvents. And if it was arson, you've got to figure the arsonist used the stuff that was available. I took samples of the floor—"

"A concrete floor? You ripped it up?"

"No, it was spalled—that means chipped. So I could just sweep up the chips. And I put down some fuller's earth, let it absorb whatever was on the surface, and collected the dirt for analysis. Did that in undamaged parts of the room, too, for control samples. It's a science, you see. There's a procedure—"

"Okay, okay. Sorry to interrupt."

"Anyway, even if the lab finds accelerants in the samples, which I expect they will, it won't prove much."

"How *can* you prove it?"

"Not sure we can. It could have been arson, but it also could have been an experiment that went wrong and caused an explosion that spread as a fire. Or spontaneous combustion of chemical-soaked rags. Or a faulty electrical circuit . . ."

"What do you think it was? What does your gut tell you?"

"My gut tells me somebody set that fire. But my gut has been wrong before. Maybe the autopsy will tell us more."

"Where's the body?"

"County morgue. Where else?"

So here she was, at 3:15 P.M., stepping through the doorway of the radiology room and realizing why the names Bradley and Dodge had seemed familiar.

The two cops in cheap suits. Dodge was the obnoxious one.

And naturally, he was the one who was here.

27

"I'm wrong?" Winston said, giving the visitor a chilly reception. "Would you care to explain just how you know?"

Agent McCallum was unfazed. She approached the table, allowing Dodge a good look at her. He liked what he saw. In the elevator she had been distracted, nervous. Now she was focused and intense, a cat waiting to pounce.

"Because I know how this young man died," McCallum said. "And who killed him." She looked his way and nodded in recognition. "Hello, Detective Dodge."

He tried out a warm smile. "Hey, Special Agent."

She turned to Winston. "Tess McCallum, FBI." Her ID folder came out, but Winston didn't bother to look. "I'm part of a task force tracking a serial killer. I think he killed this man."

"Well, that's an interesting theory." Winston was acting territorial. She didn't appreciate this McCallum barging in and telling her she'd missed something.

"Look at his neck," McCallum said. "There should be a transverse knife wound above the Adam's apple."

Normally a slashed neck would be difficult to overlook, but the cracked, creased, crisped flesh hid any other damage. Winston studied the neck for a long moment.

"I see it," she said. "Incision begins near the left carotid. Travels across the anterior cervix just above the cricoid cartilage in a semicircular track, and terminates immediately before the right carotid."

"Ear to ear," Dodge said. "But he missed the arteries."

McCallum shook her head. "He didn't miss. He never cuts the carotids. He wants his victims to bleed to death slowly."

"So he's a nasty boy."

She gave Dodge an unfriendly glance. "Very much so."

He returned her glare with equanimity, wondering if Agent McCallum liked her boys nasty.

Winston had taken out a scalpel with a ruled edge and was measuring the cut. "Approximate width of the wound channel . . ."

"Three millimeters," McCallum said. "Four where it's deepest."

"That appears to be correct. How did you know?"

"He always uses the same knife."

"How many times has he done this?"

"Four times in Denver. This is his third in LA."

"So he moved to the coast," Dodge said.

Winston didn't seem surprised. "They all wind up here eventually. All the freaks."

"It's called diversity." Dodge was smiling. "It's what makes this city great."

Both women ignored him. He was pretty sure they were pissed off. That was okay. He liked getting a rise out of women.

"So what's this guy's MO?" he asked McCallum. "He goes busting into chem labs, wasting students?"

"No. He kills women. This homicide doesn't fit his usual pattern."

"Then how'd you happen to connect it to him?"

McCallum didn't answer. Instead she said, "He probably didn't plan on finding anyone in the lab. It was just luck, that's all. Good luck for him . . ."

"And bad luck for John Doe," Dodge said.

McCallum wasn't listening. She was working it out, thinking aloud. "He made the boy help him, then killed him because he couldn't leave a witness. Set the fire to conceal the crime. He would have known that an autopsy would reveal the cause of death, but he wanted to buy time, keep us in the dark for a few extra hours. That means he's planning to act soon. Tonight, maybe. Almost certainly tonight . . ."

"Act how?" Dodge asked, getting a little ticked off at Tess McCallum. When she still didn't answer, he pushed harder. "No offense, Special Agent, but it's time for the information to start flowing both ways."

She looked at him as if remembering that he existed. "You recover anything from the crime scene?"

"Like a piece of paper with a bloody fingerprint on it? Or the killer's business card? Sorry."

"We need to take a look."

"I already looked. So did my partner. So did the LAFD's arson unit."

"Nobody was looking for things that could be connected with Mobius."

Winston said, "Mobius?"

McCallum seemed irritated with herself, as if she'd said too much. "Never mind. It's just . . . a nickname." She turned to Dodge. "We need to go back there, check it out."

Dodge shrugged. "Who am I to question the wisdom and authority of a representative of the federal government?"

"Mind if we take my car?"

"We'll have to. Left mine at the campus. My partner drove me over here."

"Let's go, then."

Dodge didn't intend to be ordered around. He lingered, talking to Winston. "Think there'll be any problem with the ID?"

"Not once I get the antemortem data. His family dentist is in Palo Alto. So far we haven't gotten the records."

"But once we do?"

"Then it's no problem. There's a lot here to work with. Tooth wear, enamel hypoplasia, fillings in two incisors, porcelain crown on one of the molars. Lot of dental work for a twenty-two-year-old. Kid must've consumed a lot of Popsicles."

"So you can make a comparison?"

"Yes, Detective. I may not be an odontologist, but I can compare X rays easily enough."

Odontologist was a fancy word for *dentist*. Dodge had looked it up once. There were forensic odontologists who specialized in identifying remains from dental work, but they were used only as consultants, called in when the regular MEs were out of their depth.

"Okay," he said. "When you get the records, give me a ring pronto, okay? I need to know if this is Scott Maple. His folks are probably a little curious too."

"As soon as they arrive, I'll be on it," Winston said, but she was still looking at Agent McCallum, maybe hoping for more of an explanation.

If so, she was disappointed. McCallum walked out the door. Dodge followed, taking his time about it, just to get her steamed.

It worked. "Will you put a move on, please?" McCallum snapped.

"Sounds like this Mobius character has been active for a while. Another few minutes won't make much of a difference."

"It could make *all* the difference. He's on a tight schedule, I think. He's planning something, and he intends for it to go down soon."

"And what's this big thing he's got planned?"

She didn't answer, but Dodge found himself walking faster anyway. He was thinking of the activity around City Hall, the extra squad cars on the streets. He had a feeling that whoever this Mobius was, he was the reason for all the excitement. Which meant this was something big. Something Myron Levine would fucking kill to have as an exclusive.

Maybe this weekend wasn't turning out so bad, after all.

He waited until they were on the Santa Monica Freeway, McCallum at the wheel of her bureau sedan, Dodge in the passenger seat. Then he asked, "Care to fill me in?"

She frowned and looked at him. He knew she was measuring him as a potential partner, trying to judge if he was someone she could count on. He also knew that she would have to trust him, because time was tight and she had no choice.

"Can you keep a secret?" she asked.

28

At four o'clock they arrived at the Life Sciences Center. By then Tess had summarized the situation.

"And you're serious about this?" Dodge asked as they got out of her car, parked behind his.

She found the question bizarre and somehow offensive. "Is there anything funny about it?"

"It's just a little hard to believe. I mean, no offense, but this is a fairly long chain of reasoning and some of the links look a little rusty."

"Which links?"

"Well, the chem lab connection, for one thing. A knife wound isn't exactly an uncommon finding at the morgue. There are all kinds of reasons a kid might've been stabbed—drugs being the most obvious."

"Fair enough. But look at it this way. Mobius disappears from the hotel sometime after midnight. The fire starts a few hours later, less than four miles away. Mobius uses a knife that leaves a three-millimeter wound channel. The victim dies as a result of an injury inflicted by the same kind of knife. A chemical agent is taken from the hotel room. The victim is working alone in a chemistry lab, the perfect place for analyzing unknown substances. Time line, location, weapon, even motive—it all fits. If there's no connection, then it's one hell of a coincidence."

She expected him to put up further resistance, but he surprised her by nodding. "Okay, Special Agent. So what will he do now?"

"He?"

"Mobius."

"How should I know?"

"You seem to have guessed his tactics pretty well so far. Connecting him to the lab fire—that was sharp, Special Agent."

"It was obvious."

"Not to your colleagues, evidently. At least, I haven't heard from this antiterrorist expert. What was his name again? Tennant?"

"True. You haven't, have you?"

"Not a peep."

"Which means I know something Tennant doesn't know."

"Sounds like leverage. Though I doubt that you need it. You bureau folk don't play petty political games like us underpaid municipal workers."

She smiled. "Of course not."

The arson unit was gone, as were the campus security guards. All that protected the Life Sciences Center was a length of crime-scene tape around its perimeter, some hastily attached boards on the basement windows, and the lock on the door.

Tess went to find a guard with a key. She returned with a man in tow just as Dodge was putting away his cell phone. "Called Winston," he said. "No dental X rays yet. But I'm betting the deceased is Scott Maple."

"If he is, are you the one who'll tell his parents?"

"My partner will get to do the honors. He's good at that kind of thing. He's a compassionate guy."

And you're not, Tess reflected. She was glad Mr.

and Mrs. Maple wouldn't be hearing the news from Detective Dodge.

The guard unlocked the door. Before entering, Tess examined the lock. "I'll bet he got in this way."

"Can he pick locks?" Dodge asked.

She thought of the house in the Denver suburbs, the door swinging open under her hand.

"Yes," she said with a catch in her voice. "Yes, he can do that."

Dodge was looking at her strangely. She ignored him. Together they descended to the basement lab.

The boarded-up windows shut out the daylight. Tess took out a flashlight, and Dodge did the same.

"We should have boots," he said. "And gloves."

"I have plastic evidence-handling gloves."

"I meant heavy gloves to protect our hands from all this crap. And boots to keep our feet dry."

But most of the water had drained off or been pumped out. The concrete floor was slick, but there was only a thin film of water, not enough to penetrate their shoes.

The two flashlight beams explored the darkness, roving over heaps of debris and blackened wood and smashed, melted glass.

"Where did they find him?" Tess asked. "Did they tell you?"

"They didn't have to tell us. We saw for ourselves. The body was never moved."

"Firefighters didn't carry it out?"

"There was no point. It was a lost cause." He signaled with his flash. "Over there. That's the spot."

They approached the center of the room, moving carefully around sharp obstacles and sodden ashes.

"He was partially protected by some of this insulation that fell from the ceiling," Dodge said. "Otherwise the remains would have been in even worse shape."

Tess poked around for a minute or two, but the area had already been thoroughly picked over by the arson investigators. She had a thought.

"Just because he died here doesn't mean he and Mobius spent most of their time in this part of the lab. Mobius night have lured him or dragged him to the middle of the room, so he could start the fire where the body lay."

Dodge shrugged. "Maybe. But if they were somewhere else in the lab, how are we going to know?"

"Mobius wanted to identify an unknown substance. How do you do that?"

Her question was rhetorical, but Dodge surprised her with an answer. "Mass spectrometer, maybe. Or a gas chromatograph." He smiled at her raised eyebrow. "I've spent a little time in the police lab."

"You see anything here resembling that equipment?"

Dodge beamed his flash into the far corners of the lab. "There's a bunch of burned-out computers over there. Nowadays all this gear is hooked up to computers."

"Worth a look." She doubted the arson unit had spent much time in that part of the room. There might be something to find.

"I don't mean to come across as either obstinate or slow-witted," Dodge said, "but what exactly is it we're looking for?"

"Anything that doesn't belong here. Anything Mobius may have left behind."

"Does he ordinarily f— uh, make mistakes like that?"

"No. But I'm hoping he's gotten careless."

She produced two pairs of rubber gloves, handing one pair to Dodge. "Put these on. They'll protect your hands a little."

They worked in silence for a few minutes, each picking through a separate pile of rubble under the glare of a flashlight.

"So tell me about Black Tiger."

Tess was startled. "How'd you know about that?"

He shrugged. "Things get around. . . ."

This was no answer, but evidently it was all she was going to get. "I don't want to talk about it," she said.

"An officer of the law who doesn't like to tell war stories? It's unheard-of. Come on, spill."

"Well . . ." It seemed easier to tell the tale than to put up a fight about it. "I was stationed in Miami, new in the bureau, back in the early nineties. Every kind of bad guy was operating down there. We had animal smugglers—guys who would bring in endangered species from Latin America for sale to private collectors on the black market. Mercenaries selling war surplus stuff to revolutionaries or counterrevolutionaries. Kidnappers who snatched tourists in Mexico and demanded ransom from their relatives. We had expatriate Cubans training in the Everglades for the next Bay of Pigs operation. You get the idea."

"Sounds colorful."

"It was, actually." She'd almost forgotten the excitement of those days. "I'd joined the bureau for adventure, and in Miami you get all the adventure you can stand."

"So . . . the case."

"Yes, well, in addition to the cast of characters I just described, we also had the drug trade. There were major interdiction efforts going on. DEA and Customs handled border control, but there was always plenty for the bureau to do. One of the major players we had our eye on was a guy called Black Tiger."

"Scary moniker."

She smiled, warming to her memories. "You know

how he got it? He liked black tiger shrimp. No joke. He hung out at this sort of pseudo-Cajun place in South Beach, eating platefuls of the stuff. He was a tall, lanky guy with a gut like a bowling ball hanging out over his pants. He told me he worked out for two hours a day, but if he did, he wasn't doing ab crunches, that's for sure."

"He told you?"

She shrugged. "One of several conversations we had."

"How'd that happen?"

"I was part of a surveillance detail watching him in that Cajun dive. It was pretty routine. I was sitting alone at the bar keeping an eye on him in a mirror. I don't know if I was too obvious or if he had some kind of sixth sense, but he seemed to realize I was looking at him. So he leaves his table and comes over to me, offers to buy me a drink. I play hard to get, mainly because I'm so flustered I don't know what to say. But I think he liked me better for being stand-offish. He was used to having women fawn all over him. He saw me as a challenge."

"Sounds like my kind of guy."

She ignored him. "We talked. Afterward there was an emergency meeting of the squad. Big discussion. Do they let me go back to the restaurant and pursue the relationship, or do they take me off the case right now?"

"You wanted to continue."

"Damn straight, I did. This was a golden opportunity to get close to this guy, learn about his operation." And she had been young, eager. Another thing she'd nearly forgotten.

"It's not every day you have a chance to date a drug lord," Dodge said.

"He wasn't a drug lord. His end of the business was

money laundering. He cleaned the cash for the cartels and took a hefty percentage of the proceeds."

"Hence his ability to finance his shrimp habit."

"He financed more than that. He had an estate on Key Biscayne, a house in Boca, a penthouse condo in South Beach. Limo, couple of sports cars, not to mention personal bodyguards and assistants, half the cops in Miami on his payroll . . ." She remembered that she was talking to a cop. "Uh, sorry."

"No offense taken. I've heard there might even be a few corrupt cops in the LAPD."

She finished her inventory of Black Tiger's assets. "Onshore and offshore holding companies and shell companies. A porno movie production company. An orange grove. Some real estate near Walt Disney World. And a yacht."

"This guy sounds like quite a catch. Why didn't you marry him?"

"I'm allergic to shrimp. Anyway, the upshot of our squad's emergency meeting was that I would be allowed to reinitiate contact, but if it looked like I was getting in too deep, I would be pulled out."

"What constitutes 'too deep'?"

"A, uh, bedroom situation. Or a threat to my safety. Of the two, I think the bedroom worried me more."

"What were you trying to find out?"

"His contacts in the drug trade. We knew he did business with the cartels, but we didn't know who he was meeting or where or when. We had his phones bugged, his mail intercepted and opened, his homes under surveillance, his movements watched—but we never caught him with anybody who could be linked to drug trafficking."

"Until you came along and busted him."

"How'd you know?"

"Nobody tells stories about cases that didn't clear."

She couldn't argue with that. "Well, you're right. I figured it out on our third date. You know what clued me in? At the shrimp restaurant he always looked at the menu."

She waited for Dodge to catch on, but he said only, "I don't get it."

"He ordered the same thing every night—black tiger shrimp. So why read the menu?"

"Because there's more to it than the catch of the day?"

She nodded. "The menu he got was a communication from the other bad guys, giving him account numbers and other instructions. Black Tiger might not have been much to look at, but he had a photographic memory. He would glance over the information and memorize it all. When he paid his bill, he wrote his answer. The restaurant's owner was the middleman who passed the messages back and forth."

"And you worked all this out just by dining with this gentleman?"

"I'm very perceptive. Also I was strongly motivated to solve the case before things got hot and heavy."

"Were you in on the collar?"

"I was in on the kill."

She looked off into the shadows in the far corner of the room. This was the part of the story she didn't enjoy.

"I couldn't get away from him that night. He wanted to show me his latest toy—a plane he'd bought, a Cessna. He drove me to the airfield. I thought I had backup behind me. I knew they wouldn't let him take me on the plane. Trouble was, while I was figuring him out, he'd figured me out. I don't know how, but he'd made me. And he'd had his people create a traffic accident to block the road and cut off my pursuit. I was alone out there, and all of a sudden he wants me aboard the plane and he's not so friendly anymore."

"How many of them were there? I mean, I have to assume he hadn't arranged a one-on-one encounter."

"Three. Black Tiger, his driver, and the pilot."

"You were carrying . . . ?"

"Sig Sauer nine in a thigh holster under my skirt. But no way could I get to it with all of them watching me."

"Tight situation."

"I just knew I couldn't get on the plane. Do that, and I'm dead. I put up enough resistance so one of them tries to push me on board. That gives me an excuse to stumble and fall, and when I hit the tarmac I draw the nine-millimeter and roll under the plane and empty the clip at them."

"A regular Jane Wayne," Dodge said.

Tess wasn't sure she appreciated the comment. "It was just instinct. And I can't honestly say I knew what I was shooting at. I found out later they were all wearing vests, but I was low enough to catch them where they were vulnerable—knees, groins."

"Ouch."

"The driver and pilot went down wounded and basically gave up. Black Tiger had more fight in him. He has his piece out, and he's trying to cap me under the plane, and I really think only the landing gear saved me—deflected the rounds or messed up his aim. Anyway, I . . . I got him with my last cartridge."

"A kill shot?"

"In the neck. Not intentional—I couldn't even see the bastard. It was luck or divine providence or something."

"You believe in that? Divine providence?"

She shut her eyes, remembering Paul. "I think I used to."

"Well, that's a hell of a war story, Special Agent. I'm surprised the feebs—pardon me, I'm surprised the *feds* haven't made you their poster child for recruitment."

"They sort of did. For a while, at least. I've heard they still teach the case at the academy."

He seemed to catch her tone of voice. "And you're unhappy about that?"

"It's just . . . It all happened really fast. It was ten seconds, probably less. It shouldn't be such a big thing. It shouldn't— Hey, wait a minute."

She had found something.

It was a small metal object, rectangular, its exterior badly oxidized by the heat of the fire and the subsequent dousing of the flames. When she turned it over, she saw a row of small buttons.

"Could be part of the computer gear," Dodge said. "Zip drive or CD burner or something."

"No. It's a tape recorder."

"Maybe the vic was listening to some tunes."

"Probably." She opened the compartment containing the tape and saw a cassette inside. "But I'd like to be sure."

The cassette appeared to be intact. The player's metal casing had protected it from damage. There was no label on the cassette. It seemed to be a blank tape that the owner had recorded himself. She wanted a closer look. Maybe something was written on the other side.

The eject button wouldn't work. Without touching the cassette, she pried it loose with a ballpoint pen from her purse, then held it by the corners. No label on side two, no indication of the tape's contents. This struck Tess as odd. Normally when people dubbed a CD or a batch of MP3 downloads onto a cassette, they would label the tape so they knew what they had.

The cassette was made of clear plastic, the spools of tape visible inside. She peered at it closely.

"It wasn't Scott Maple who brought this here," she whispered. "It was Mobius."

Dodge frowned. "Where'd you get that idea?"

"Look at the tape. See how it's twisted? A single twist in the ribbon."

"Tapes get snarled sometimes."

"This was done deliberately. The twist was put in to make the double-sided tape into a continuous loop." She looked at him. "A Möbius strip. That's what it's called."

There was nothing else in the lab, or at least nothing they could find. They emerged blinking into the daylight of late afternoon.

"What now?" Dodge asked.

"I call my AD about this." Tess tapped the two plastic evidence bags into which she'd inserted the tape player and cassette.

"You're not even slightly curious about what's on the tape."

"I'm curious. But I don't carry a Sony Walkman around with me, and the machine we recovered is inoperable."

"There's a cassette player in my car."

Tess hesitated only a moment. She knew it was a violation of procedure to play the tape before the forensics technicians had a look at it. She also knew that the sun would set soon, that Mobius might well be planning to strike tonight, and that time was of the essence.

"Let's do it," she said.

Dodge slid into the driver's seat and started the engine, and Tess sat on the passenger side and carefully removed the tape from its bag. With a gloved hand she inserted it into the dashboard tape deck. The tape began to play automatically in the middle of a song.

No lyrics. Just guitar chords, drums. A fast, hectic beat.

"Recognize it?" Tess asked.

"No. Maybe. It's almost familiar."

The song ended, then began again—an endless repetition courtesy of the Möbius strip. At the start of the song there was a peal of tittering laughter and a falsetto voice simpering, "Wipe out."

"I know it now," Dodge said. "Shit, that goddamn song always did creep me out."

"It's called 'Wipe Out,' I assume?"

He nodded as the song played on. "Surf music from the early sixties. Some Beach Boys wanna-bes, as I recall. I don't remember the name of the group. Why the hell would Mobius be carrying this around?"

"I guess it's his theme song."

"But what's it mean?"

"That," Tess said, "is the million-dollar question."

They sat in the car as the song played again and again over the dashboard speakers.

Standing next to Dodge's car, Tess used her cell phone to call the AD. Andrus answered on the fourth ring. She told him what she'd found.

"All right," he said. "We'll have to see if the tape is playable—"

"It is."

"You listened to it? Without letting the lab have a look at it first? What if there was a fingerprint on the play button and you destroyed it?"

"The exterior of the player is oxidized. No fingerprints. Anyway, Detective Dodge and I—"

"Who?"

"LAPD homicide detective. He's assisting me. We played the tape, and it's a song—"

"Right, fine. We'll talk about it, but not over the phone. I'm dispatching Larkin to pick up the evidence. He'll deliver it to me, and I'll hand carry it to the lab. I'm also sending a crime-scene squad to the campus. I want you to stay there and watch the site until they arrive."

"I can get a security guard to do that."

"I want *you* to do it. That's an order."

"Gotcha." She was a little peeved to have to waste time hanging around, but there was no point in arguing.

"And, Tess?" he added. "Don't touch that tape player again."

Andrus clicked off. Tess stuck the phone back into her purse, fuming.

"You look unhappy," Dodge observed with a smile.

"My boss is an asshole sometimes."

"Whose boss isn't?" The smile lingered, incongruous on his hard, cynical face. "So after we're done here, you want to get together, go over what we've learned?"

She didn't quite understand. "Go over it?"

"At my place, say. I've got a house in the Hollywood Hills. Great view of the city."

Well, she got it now. It was their little dialogue in the elevator all over again.

"I think I'm going to be busy tonight. There's kind of a crisis, in case you hadn't noticed."

"This is LA. There's always a crisis. Anyhow, we've done our part. We're entitled to some downtime."

"Sorry. I'm pretty sure I'll be otherwise engaged."

The smile on his face flicked off, as simply as if he had flipped a switch. "Okay, then," he said in a tone that would have been more appropriate to *Fuck you.*

"I've gotta get going. Write this up. Paperwork, you know."

She disliked him, but she didn't want to be rude. "Thanks for your help," she said feebly.

"Protect and serve, that's my motto." He was already getting back into his car.

"Detective?"

He stopped, possibly wondering if she'd changed her mind.

"Keep quiet about this, all right? It can't get out to the media."

Dodge smiled again—a smile that was subtly different from before, in a way she couldn't quite define.

"I hear you, Agent McCallum." He zipped his lips with a forefinger. "Mum's the word."

29

"I don't mean to be rude, but today's not a good day for you to be jerking my chain," Myron Levine said as he slid into a banquette at Lucy J's.

Dodge gave him a cool smile. "That's uncalled for, Myron. My feelings are hurt. I'm getting all weepy." He let the smile go away. "Since when have I ever fucked with you?"

"You're fucking with me right now. Right this very minute. And I'm on a tight schedule. I'm on the air live at six o'clock. I don't have time for any crap."

"Then I'll get right to the point. I got something major. And it's gonna cost you."

"I'm all tapped out—"

"You want to sling bullshit, or you want to talk straight? It's your call. You're the one in such a goddamn hurry."

Levine looked away. Dodge knew the guy was a coward. He talked big, but it was an act, as phony as his bad toupee or the lifts he wore to look taller. He was a scared little man, and one of the things he was scared of was Dodge himself.

"What kind of money are you looking for?" Levine asked after a short pause.

"Ten thousand."

Levine's eyebrows shot up like two moths singed by a flame. "That's ridiculous. That's totally out of the question."

"It's a bargain. It's the sale of the motherfucking century."

Something about Dodge's coolness seemed to communicate a sense of sobriety to Levine. He calmed visibly. He became almost thoughtful. "What is it, more about Grandy?"

Dodge waved this away. "Fuck Grandy. When this gets out, nobody's gonna give two shits about police brutality. Even the fucking spooks won't care. They'll be too busy getting the hell out of town like everybody else."

Levine tried not to look interested, but as a poker player, he frankly sucked, and Dodge knew he had the reporter's complete attention.

"Why will anybody be leaving town?" Levine tried for humor. "Stage-three smog alert?"

"More like DEFCON One in a fucking war."

Levine blinked. "War? What is it, the goddamn Arabs again?"

"It's better than that. Imagine if I were to tell you that we have a weapon of mass destruction floating around in this city, only it's not in the hands of your run-of-the-mill little-dicked camel jockey. This time it's in the possession of a bona fide serial killer. What would you say about that?"

The question was rhetorical. Dodge knew exactly what Levine would say—namely, nothing at all. The man just stared.

"That's right, my friend," Dodge went on. "This city is in some serious shit. And I know the details."

"You shitting me?"

Dodge gave him a bored look.

"Okay, okay, you're not bullshitting, sorry, I just mean that this is, I mean, this is . . ."

Awful. Terrifying. Unthinkable. There were lots of words he could have used.

"This is *fantastic*! I mean, this is fucking incredible. If it pans out," he added cautiously.

"It'll pan out." Dodge waited, saying nothing more.

"So give," Levine said finally.

"What's it worth to you?" Another rhetorical question.

"*If* it pans out, like you claim . . . you'll get the ten grand."

Dodge smiled. "That's what I like about you, Myron. In the end, you're always willing to be reasonable."

When he was done with Levine, Dodge sat alone and had himself a slice of Lucy J's pie. He was going to grow a goddamned potbelly if he kept celebrating like this, but what the fuck. He had reason to celebrate. He'd obtained three grand in cash, with an IOU for the rest. He knew Levine was good for it. Gutless little troll didn't have the balls to double-cross him, and besides, he couldn't afford to shut off such a valuable pipeline of information—especially after today.

Anyway, Levine had gotten a bargain. Fucking story was worth twenty grand easy, maybe twenty-five. But Dodge had known that Levine would never go that high without tedious negotiations. That process would take time, and Dodge couldn't wait. Some other media outlet might get hold of the story.

There were a dozen—hell, a hundred—places that might spring a leak. Even in Tess McCallum's rushed synopsis of events, it had been obvious that just about every local government operation was involved in this case. Not everybody knew the whole story, but enough people knew bits and pieces. It would all come out before long, whether it was Levine who got the tip or some other jackass at a rival station or a newspaper.

And, honest to God, the story really ought to come out. The public, bless their precious constitutional rights, was entitled to know. And he, Jim Dodge, was just a public-spirited citizen. Sure he was. And pigs could fly to the fucking moon.

He swallowed his last forkful of pie and left his payment, adding a smaller tip than usual because the waitress with the Jennifer Lopez ass wasn't on duty today. Which was too bad, because with money in his pocket and a song in his heart, he was looking to get laid tonight.

When Special Agent McCallum had walked back into his life, he'd thought he might have been offered a second chance to find out if she was a natural redhead. But he'd decided McCallum was butch, or desexed or a nun or something. She hadn't responded to his manly charms or his pheromones or whatever women responded to.

Well, fuck her and the horse she rode in on. The way he had it figured, the news leak would prompt an FBI internal investigation. And who was likely to get nailed for talking out of school? Little Miss McCallum, who had a prior connection with Myron Levine in Denver. She would take the rap, and Dodge would walk away clean.

Tough break, Tess. Serves you right for giving me the cold shoulder.

30

Tess sat alone in a squad room of the Westwood field office, staring at a computer monitor as she studied the results of another database search.

She had waited at the Life Sciences Center for nearly two hours. First Larkin had arrived to ferry the tape player, sealed in its plastic bag, to the AD. A long time later the forensics team had finally showed up. Tess had left them at their work and driven the short distance to the field office.

In the hallway she'd run into the Nose, the last person she wanted to see.

"Hard on the case, McCallum?" Michaelson had asked.

She said something noncommittal. He studied her shrewdly.

"You don't have to be evasive with me. I know what's going on."

Tennant brought you in? she almost asked, but of course no one had brought him in. He was fishing for information.

"Going on?" she said innocently.

"The other squad. You know."

Yes, she thought. *I do know. And you don't.*

"The other squad's not talking to me." The lie came

easily to her. "If they've opened up to you, I'd like to hear about it."

He stood there, frustrated, evidently pondering several possible comebacks before settling on "Never mind."

She watched him walk away. His shoulders, she noticed, seemed to be sagging a little. He was out of the loop, and he knew it. She would have felt sorry for him if he wasn't such a jerk.

She'd found an empty squad room, commandeered a computer, and set to work.

"Wipe Out" was the song title. It had to mean something to Mobius. Maybe she could find out what. But it wouldn't be easy.

The idea that there was a vast searchable computerized archive of crimes and criminals, and that anyone with a badge could type a few keywords into a search box and obtain instant results, was unfortunately a myth. The reality was that most law enforcement databases were useful only for a fingerprint search, in which case the FBI's NCIC system was the best bet, or a search by the suspect's name. There was no nationwide archive at all, merely a variety of more or less inclusive databases run by states and counties, accessible only by dedicated terminals within courthouses and halls of records.

Tess, of course, had neither a fingerprint nor a suspect's name. She had the name of a song that might or might not be connected to a crime Mobius had committed early in his career—perhaps in his youth, even before he *was* Mobius.

The only official database that might be of help was VICAP, short for Violent Criminal Apprehension Program. VICAP listed crimes by modus operandi, including any signatures—distinctive peculiarities of the crime scene, such as notes or messages left by the

perpetrator. But when she typed in the Boolean search
term "wipeout OR wipe out," she got no hits.

This meant she would have to try other databases not
specifically designed for law enforcement. LexisNexis, a
repository of newspaper articles, was her first stop.
Her initial search yielded a number of hits, too many
to peruse. When she narrowed the search to eliminate
irrelevant articles, she came up dry.

The same thing happened when she visited the
major Web search engines. There were thousands of
Web pages containing the term "wipeout" or "wipe
out," but nothing that seemed relevant to her needs.

So what now? She had to conduct a more focused
search, and she had to cover the entire Web.

Most people didn't realize it, but even the most
popular search engines scratched only the surface of
the vast pool of material available on-line. There were
millions—actually billions—of Web pages that had
never been collected and indexed by any standard
search engine. This mass of material was sometimes
known as "the deep Web."

There were ways of accessing the deep Web. Just
as it was possible to send a robot probe into ocean
trenches, exploring realms off-limits to human beings,
so it was possible to launch a software robot—a bot,
in computerese—into the deep Web. A bot was a program that searched for specific keywords in specific
contexts. The search could be as narrow or as broad
as the user desired. It could take a long time—hours,
even—because the bot was simply set free to follow
link after link, collecting any data that matched the
search criteria, crawling automatically and unsuper-
vised through myriad uncharted Web pages.

Tess had downloaded a bot program in Denver for
use on a case last year. It had spidered across the Web
for twenty hours before finally returning the hit she

needed, a site unlisted in any of the brand-name search engines. She decided to try it again.

Since this wasn't her own computer, she had to find the shareware site where she had obtained the bot, then download the software and install it. This took only ten minutes, thanks to a high-speed connection. Next she set the search parameters, trying to include only pages in which "wipe out" was mentioned in conjunction with criminal activity. If she set the parameters too wide, she would haul up a mass of junk she could never sift through. Too narrow, and she might miss what she was looking for.

Before initiating the search, she instructed the program to place any Web links that it found in an online storage service she used, rather than on the desktop's hard drive. That way she could access the search results from her laptop or any other computer.

When she was ready, she launched the bot. Nothing to do now but wait, maybe get some coffee or something to eat. It occurred to her with a touch of surprise that she had eaten absolutely nothing all day, and it was now nearly seven o'clock. She was about to go in search of a vending machine when the squad room door opened and Andrus walked in.

"Gerry," she said with a smile. "You get the evidence from Larkin okay?"

"I got it," he said, but he looked strangely unsettled, and there was a coldness in his tone she hadn't heard before.

She frowned. "There a problem?"

"Problem?" He took a chair near her desk and swiveled restlessly. "No problem. What could possibly be a problem?"

Sarcasm was a blunt instrument in his hands. He rarely wielded it.

She shut off the monitor on her computer, leaving

the machine at work without a display, and pushed her chair away from her desk. She looked at him, saying nothing. Whatever was on his mind, he would give voice to it soon enough.

"You always have to do things your way," he said, "don't you, Tess?"

This was so unexpected, so incomprehensible, that she had no answer.

"No one else can be right if they disagree with you. It's your judgment and only yours that counts. Why is that? Is it because you're so much smarter than all the rest of us, or do you just think you're the only one whose intentions are sufficiently pure?"

"I . . . I don't know what—"

"You've always had this, I don't know, cowboy streak in you. Black Tiger, for instance. Sometimes I think you actually wanted to go *mano a mano* with that scumbag. You wanted to be Wyatt Earp at the OK Corral. And last night when you said you were looking for a chance to take down Mobius—you weren't kidding, were you? You want to be judge, jury, and executioner. You want to make all the rules."

"Gerry—"

"You basically blackmailed me into including you in the EOC briefing. Said you'd investigate on your own if I didn't go along. You forced my hand, made me tangle with Tennant—and my relations with him were none too friendly to begin with. And after all that, you still weren't satisfied. You had to start free-lancing. You had to go behind my back, behind everybody's back. Thanks a lot, Tess. Thanks for fucking me over, big time."

"Gerry, I honestly have no idea what you're talking about."

"Don't you? Okay then, I'll explain." He leaned

forward, the chair creaking on its casters. "A half hour ago the mayor of Los Angeles got a call from the news director at KPTI-TV, Channel Eight. The station's getting set to run with an exclusive report on, quote, 'a city under siege. Deadly nerve gas in the hands of a psychotic serial killer.' Does the mayor have any comment?"

"So it got out," Tess said softly, still not seeing what this had to do with her.

"Yes, it got out. And yes, the mayor did have a comment. He spent fifteen minutes begging the station to kill the story. Mayors don't like to beg, Tess. They like it even less when they beg and come away empty-handed. The story is set to run as a special report in about half an hour. Be sure to tune in. You can admire your handiwork."

"*My* handiwork?" Suddenly things were coming together.

"We told you we didn't want the story out there. You put it out anyway. Tell the people—that's your mantra, right? The people need to know the truth, they can handle it, they won't panic. Well, maybe they will, maybe they won't. Thanks to you, now we'll all get to find out."

"You think I leaked the story . . . ?"

"Oh, gosh. Did I give you that impression?" Sarcasm again. "Well, possibly the thought had occurred to me, seeing as how you made that eloquent plea for the public's right to know at the EOC briefing."

"For God's sake, Gerry—just because of that? Because I made a suggestion?"

"No, not just because of that. KPTI knows things they had to have gotten from you."

"What things?"

"The fire in the chemistry lab. And its connection to this case. You were the only one working that angle."

"In case you've forgotten, that's because I'm the one who made the connection in the first place."

Andrus ignored her. "And then you spilled it to a reporter, along with the rest of the story, so it wouldn't be hushed up. So you could get your way."

"This is crazy. I've only been in town twelve days. How would I have any contacts with the local media?"

"Does the name Myron Levine mean anything to you?"

She almost said no, then realized the name was familiar. "TV guy, used to work out of Denver," she said slowly.

"He interviewed you there, as I recall."

"Not exactly. He tried to. I wasn't interested."

"Not interested in going on the record, anyway. Off the record—who knows?"

"What are you saying?"

"I'm saying, Tess, that Levine is in LA now, and he's the one with the story, and you knew him in Denver, and it doesn't take a genius to put two and two together."

"I didn't talk to Levine. I didn't even know he was here. And besides, I'm not the only person who knew about the lab."

"Who else knew? Besides me, I mean."

"The cop I was working with." She'd disliked him from the moment she saw him in his cheap suit. "Detective Dodge, West LA. That's who my money's on."

"Well, that's great, Tess. But *my* money is on you."

"Gerry, you *know* me. . . ."

"Exactly. I know you. I know that you and Paul Voorhees were more than partners and more than friends. I know what his death did to you. And I know you've never been the same. This case—it's so personal for you, so raw and painful, you've lost all perspective. You think it's just about you and Mobius.

You think it's not a team effort. But it is. And I can't afford you on the team anymore."

She let a moment pass in the squad room, the silence occupied only by the hum of her computer's hard drive as the bot continued its search.

"No, Gerry," she whispered.

"I shouldn't have brought you back in. It was an error on my part."

"It wasn't."

"I'm sending you back to Denver."

"Please."

He stood. "End of discussion."

"Gerry—"

"I'll protect you as best I can. I haven't mentioned your name to the mayor or to anyone else. Officially I have no idea where the leak originated."

"It was Dodge, God damn it."

"If there's an investigation, I'm sure we'll look at Detective Dodge and any other possible source. And if my suspicions about you are proved wrong, you'll have my sincere apology."

"I don't want to leave this case."

"Should have thought about that before you sabotaged it." He moved toward the doorway. "Get out of here, Tess. If you're not gone in five minutes, I'll have you removed."

He left, and she was alone.

The door opened again, and she had time to think Andrus was coming back to inflict one more blow. But it wasn't Andrus. It was the Nose.

"Couldn't help overhearing the last part of your conversation," he said with a cool, sickly smile.

"It's none of your business." She got up and slung her purse over her shoulder.

"Probably not. Nothing seems to be my business these days."

She ignored him, but when she tried to leave, he blocked the exit. His smile was gone, and there was pure malice on his face.

"You'll talk to the media but not your own colleagues. Is that the way it is?"

"I didn't talk to the media."

"Save it."

"I was under orders not to share any information with you or the other RAVENKILL investigators."

"And you always follow orders. Isn't that right?"

"In this case I did. I wasn't eager to share with you anyway."

"No? Why not?"

"Because you're an asshole."

She took advantage of his surprise to slip past him into the hall, but he wasn't through with her. He grabbed her by the arm.

"You're finished, McCallum."

She shook him off and walked away. He called after her, his voice higher and more nasal than usual.

"You think your career was stuck in neutral before this? Just wait."

She kept walking, not looking back.

"By the time we're through with you, you'll be lucky to get a post at a resident agency in the fucking Ozarks."

Michaelson's voice rose to cover more distance as she continued down the hall. She thought of a sheep bleating.

"You're done. It's over for you. *It's over.*"

31

Had to be Dodge. Had to be.

The thought repeated itself, loud and insistent, as Tess sped north on the San Diego Freeway, toward the Valley and her motel.

She wanted to talk to the son of a bitch. Well, not exactly. What she wanted was to wring his neck. But talking would be a start.

She wondered if he was still on duty, or if she could get his home phone number from the watch commander—

Home phone number.

She was still wearing yesterday's clothes. Reaching into her jacket pocket, she found the snitch card Dodge had given her in the elevator last night.

At Ventura Boulevard she exited the freeway. Idling at a stoplight, she took out her cell phone and dialed the number on the card.

Three rings, and an answer. Dodge.

"You piece of shit," she said.

It wasn't how she had intended to begin. She'd meant to be diplomatic, clever.

"Not exactly the greeting I was hoping for." Dodge seemed unfazed. "Is this Agent McCallum?"

"You know it is." The traffic light cycled to green,

and she started driving again. "Damn it, I never should've trusted you."

"Something wrong?"

"Shut the hell up. You know exactly what I'm talking about."

"Afraid I don't, Tess."

"You *talked*. You leaked to the media, to Myron Levine of Channel . . . I don't know."

"Channel Eight. That's where Levine works."

"So you admit it?"

"Admit what?"

"Don't insult my intelligence. You went to Levine as soon as you left the campus, didn't you?"

"Let me get this straight. You're saying the story has come out, and Levine of Channel Eight has it?"

"Yes. That's what I'm saying."

"Did it ever occur to you that in an operation this size, there's bound to be a leak—maybe a dozen leaks? Anybody could've talked."

"Not about the chem lab. The fire. Scott Maple. No one else knew about that. No one but you and me."

"And Winston."

"What?"

"Rachel Winston, the pathologist. She's been known to cozy up to the media—or at least that's the rumor."

Tess blinked. She hadn't thought of Winston. "Dr. Winston didn't know the details," she said slowly.

"She knew Scott Maple died of a cut throat in an arson fire. And she knew about Mobius. You mentioned him—remember?"

That was true. But the name itself would have meant nothing to Winston. The killer's nickname had never been made public or shared with anyone outside the task force.

Still, Winston could have a contact inside the bureau—someone to help her put the pieces together.

Or she might have talked to another pathologist, perhaps the one who'd conducted the autopsy on Angie Callahan, Mobius's first victim in LA."

"You're reaching," she said to herself.

Dodge assumed the comment was directed at him. "No, I'm not. Winston knew enough to get Levine's attention. And who knows what other sources Levine might have?"

"Like you, for instance."

"I'm clean, Tess. Really. I take it you're getting blamed for this?"

"How'd you know?"

"You wouldn't be so upset otherwise. Well, they're hanging a bad rap on you—and you're hanging a bad rap on me."

Maybe she was. She doubted it. She still disliked Dodge. But what he was saying was at least possible.

"Look," he went on, "why don't we talk about it in person? I'm home now. Won't be going out again unless I catch a call. Come on over, I'll fix some dinner, and we'll discuss it."

Distantly she wondered if this was yet another attempt at a come-on. She dismissed the thought. Dodge was a pig, but nobody was *that* much of a pig.

Anyway, she needed to talk to him face-to-face. Study his eyes, his body language. That was the only way to know if he was lying.

"All right," she said. "I'll stop at my motel first, watch the news—there's supposed to be a special report coming on. Afterward, I'll stop by."

"Sounds good." He recited his address, and she scribbled it on the back of the snitch card. "It's in the Hollywood Hills just off Mulholland. Small place, but a view of the city that'll knock you out. You like linguini?"

She had eaten nothing all day. "I do," she said reluctantly, while her stomach seconded the remark with a gurgle.

"I'll see you in a while. Don't worry, Tess. We'll work this all out. By the time we're through, you'll be off the hook—and Winston will be hung out to dry."

We'll see, she answered silently as she clicked off the phone.

On her way to the motel, Tess picked up a meal at a fast-food place, using the drive-through window. She wasn't fond of microwaved burgers and greasy fries, but her stomach insisted on immediate satisfaction.

The motel room was stuffy, and because she'd left the DO NOT DISTURB sign in place, it had never been cleaned. She checked the air conditioner and dialed the fan to full speed. Time to get some air moving in here.

The motel chain called the room a suite, which simply meant that the bedroom area was separated from the living area by a partial wall. There was a rudimentary kitchen, as well, but she hadn't taken the time to stock the fridge or even to fill the ice-cube trays.

She carried the brown bag and large diet soda into the living area, set down her chow on a coffee table before the sofa, then noticed that her nose was runny. Allergic reaction or something. She used one of the grease-spotted paper napkins to wipe her nose, then found the remote control and turned on Channel 8.

The special report was already in progress. A garish logo—BREAKING NEWS: TERROR ALERT—ran along the bottom of the screen. The news anchor was doing a recap of the story at her desk.

". . . to repeat, KPTI sources tell us that federal, county, and municipal authorities tonight are searching for a canister of deadly nerve gas smuggled into Los Angeles by a suspected terrorist and now believed to be in the hands of a serial killer. This incredible story was first reported by our own Myron Levine in an exclusive. . . ."

So it was really out. She'd been hoping irrationally for some last-minute miracle, a hold on the story that would at least provide time for an official announcement.

Andrus didn't understand her concerns at all. Yes, she had believed that the public should be told, but not by a breathless newscaster breaking into Saturday-night programming to deliver a scare story. She'd wanted it done right—a sober statement presented by elected officials in a reasoned, thoughtful manner.

From the start, a leak had been inevitable. The news should have been put out in a way that would minimize panic.

Using the remote, she shuffled through the other channels. A second network affiliate had already picked up the story, the anchor reading an AP wire service bulletin that apparently summarized the KPTI report. Nothing had come on the other stations yet, but she knew it was only a matter of minutes.

Her stomach rolled, reminding her that she still had not touched her meal. She unwrapped the cheeseburger and hungrily tore off a bite.

When she clicked back to Channel 8, she saw Myron Levine doing a live stand-up outside Parker Center, the downtown headquarters of the LAPD. City Hall East, with its underground command center, would have been more appropriate, but Levine might not even know about that.

". . . serial killer nicknamed Mobius, who was in Denver two years ago when this reporter was himself stationed in that city. Mobius, known to the media as the Pickup Artist, was responsible for a series of slayings . . ."

So he knew the name Mobius—the name she'd let

slip in Rachel Winston's presence. Could Dodge possibly be telling the truth? She had no absolute proof he was behind the leak, just a strong suspicion reinforced by an equally strong dislike of the man.

She ate more of the burger, then paused, feeling a momentary shiver of light-headedness. Going without food all day had been a bad idea. She wasn't feeling so great all of a sudden. But it would pass.

She took a swig of soda, hoping the cold slush of carbonated water would revive her. For a moment it seemed to work. Then distantly she felt a headache coming on.

Levine was probably the reason. Just looking at him, flushed with the triumph of his breaking story, was enough to make her sick. The guy was a weasel, always had been, climbing the career ladder with reckless indifference to journalistic ethics.

Hell, even if she *had* decided to leak the story, she wouldn't have given it to that jerk—

A bubble of gas worked its way out of her throat with an audible burp.

God, what was going on with her tonight? She'd gone without sustenance for longer periods than this. Maybe she was coming down with the flu.

The flu . . .

A low warning thought rose almost to the level of conscious awareness, but before she could focus on it, the KPTI report shifted from Levine to a camera crew doing man-in-the-street interviews at Third Street Promenade in Santa Monica.

"You've gotta be kidding me. . . ."

"How do we know what's really going on? The government never levels with us. . . ."

"You're saying there's a serial killer that's got hold of the stuff . . . ?"

"Is this for real? Are you serious?"

"I'm just . . . it's scary . . . everything's scary these days, and just when you think it can't get any worse . . ."

"I think I'd like to move to a small town someplace and stock up on supplies and just hunker down, you know. . . ."

"I can't talk to you; I'm looking for my kids. . . . Marci! Terri! Where *are* you? We have to *go* . . . !"

Tess shook her head. "Thank you, Channel Eight," she muttered. "That's very helpful. That's just—"

She wanted to say *terrific,* but her throat was suddenly dry, and the word died in a croak.

Weird—and now she was conscious of a sick feeling in her stomach, a liquid queasiness that became a dry, pasty taste in the back of her mouth.

More soda. That was what she needed. Too bad there wasn't some nice Bacardi in it.

She picked up the big paper cup and raised it to her mouth, and her fingers splayed and the cup dropped on the table, spilling its contents.

What the hell?

Myron Levine was back on-screen, but Tess wasn't listening anymore.

As she stared at her right hand, another shudder twisted through the tendons and ligaments. Her fingers shook briefly.

And the thought that had almost surfaced earlier flashed with full clarity in her brain.

It can be all around you—Tennant's voice came back to her—*and you won't know it until you experience the initial symptoms of exposure: runny nose, sweating, upset stomach, headache. . . .*

VX.

She had been exposed.

She looked around wildly, her environment suddenly hostile, as she tried to understand how Mobius had done it. But *how* didn't matter at this moment. She had to get out. That was what Tennant had said—in the event of exposure, evacuate the area immediately.

The door to outside was only ten feet away. She got up, grabbing her purse off the coffee table, took two steps away from the sofa, and her knees buckled and she collapsed on the floor.

She knew what was happening. The nerve agent attacked the central nervous system. It caused flulike symptoms initially, then fasciculations, then convulsions and paralysis.

Finally, asphyxiation as the lungs stopped drawing air.

She struggled to rise, but she couldn't make her legs work. They were shivering all over with what Dr. Gant had called generalized fasciculations, a fancy way of saying that her muscular activity had been converted into a series of tics and flutters.

The most basic control she possessed, her control over her own body, was lost.

At the ATSAC briefing, both Gant and Tennant had stressed that a VX victim had to escape the contaminated area immediately, but neither of them had mentioned that she would be unable to use her legs.

Could she crawl? Maybe, if she dragged herself forward using just her arms . . . but if she couldn't stand, she would never be able to get the door open.

Anyway, she didn't have time for a slow, arduous crawl across two yards of carpet. Already her breathing was coming harder than before. Shortness of breath—dyspnea—another symptom mentioned by Dr. Gant when he was handing out . . .

Handing out the antidote kits.

She'd received one, too—a MARK I Nerve Agent Antidote Kit—the same thing combat soldiers were issued when they were headed into a hostile zone where chemical weapons might be used.

Gant had explained it all, as an official-looking crew passed out the pouches. Each kit consisted of two auto injectors, crayonlike devices that could be yanked free of their plastic holder and pressed against the outer thigh. A needle would deliver a standard dose of medication intramuscularly. The first injector contained two milligrams of atropine sulfate, which would improve respiration. The second device held six hundred milligrams of pralidoxime chloride, an antidote to VX, which would break the chemical bond between the nerve agent and the enzymes in the blood.

And she had it in her purse, which lay on the beige carpet beside her.

If she could reach it.

Her right arm was no good. It had stiffened up with a painful muscular contraction. She thought of rigor mortis and pushed the idea away. Death was not the imagery she needed in her head just now.

Try with the left arm. Teeth gritted, she willed her arm toward the strap. It was almost within her grasp. But her fingers wouldn't obey her, wouldn't close over the strap. They were fluttering, useless.

The effects of the nerve agent were spreading fast, covering more and more of her body. Soon the muscles of her rib cage would fail, and she would suffocate, smothered by her own body.

She didn't want to die that way. Fear gave her strength. Clumsily she hooked her hand over the strap and dragged it toward her.

She had the purse. But it was shut. She had to undo the clasp. Couldn't do it. No motor coordination. In desperation she slammed the heel of her hand against the purse. Again. Again.

The clasp popped open. *Okay, now get the kit out. Come on.* She could do it; she was almost there. . . .

She found the pouch inside the purse and scooped it out in a shaking hand.

With effort she ripped the first injection device free of its plastic clip.

The jerking and twitching of her legs had died away, replaced by a heavy sense of muscular fatigue and a numb, limp paralysis. This was a bad sign, a later stage in the progression of neurological attack. But at least it made it possible for her to inject herself cleanly.

Twisting at the hips, she pushed the green tip of the injector hard against her thigh, and the needle punched through the fabric of her pants leg and penetrated the muscle. She held it in place, counting to ten.

Popped it free. Cast it aside.

One down. One to go. The atropine was only the preliminary treatment. The second injection was the antidote itself.

She reached into the pouch again, and suddenly the shaking of her left hand became a generalized agitation of both arms, and she was rolling on the floor, arms crossed over her chest as if straitjacketed, then pounding the floor with her elbows, her hands.

The seizure passed, and she lay still, stunned by her exertions

But breathing. Still breathing. The atropine had kept her lungs working, at least.

Get the antidote into her system, and she might actually survive.

She rolled onto her side and reached for the pouch. Her left arm was heavy, fatigued, but not yet paralyzed. Movement was difficult, not impossible.

Snap the injector free. . . .

She was trying, but she had no strength. Her fingers could not exert enough pressure to break the injection device out of its clip. She couldn't do it. Couldn't—

Another tremor swept through her, jerking her sideways. The room darkened.

She wavered on the edge of unconsciousness, then came slowly back.

And found the injector, liberated from its clip, held loosely in her hand. The jerk of her arm had broken it free. All she had to do was stick the needle in her thigh. . . .

But her arm wouldn't move.

The last wave of seizure activity had stolen all her muscular strength. The extreme muscle fatigue Dr. Gant had called flaccid paralysis, which already had overtaken her legs, had now taken possession of her upper body as well.

The injector began to slip from her fingers. If she dropped it, she would never be able to pick it up. With an effort of will, she managed to hold on.

There was no hope of injecting the drug into her thigh—it was a million miles away. But another injection site would do. Deep muscle was what she needed. The muscle tissue of her breast and underarm was close enough that she could reach it simply by bending her arm at the elbow.

It was a slow process, though not painful—she felt no specific pain anywhere, only the numbness of utter exhaustion. An inch at a time she advanced the injector. She could see it clearly, could even read the words printed on the side of the tube—PRALIDOXIME CHLORIDE INJECTOR.

Now the injector was pressing against the muscle just behind her right breast. But she couldn't fire it, couldn't push hard enough to pop the needle through the protective tip.

She had enough strength left for one final exertion. She pushed herself up with one arm and thudded down on her side, and the weight of her body compressed the injector between its target and the floor.

She felt a sudden burning pain under her arm, and she knew the needle had plunged through her shirt and into her muscles, releasing its ampoule of medicine.

For a long moment she just lay there, certain that the injection had come too late. She felt no improvement. Her lungs were barely functioning. Every breath was a struggle.

You're not going to make it, she thought as her awareness flickered on the verge of a blackout.

Time crawled past. A minute or more. The TV still babbled; the air conditioner still hummed.

And she was breathing just a little easier.

Her lungs were starting to work again. She was weak and wheezy, but it seemed the antidote had kicked in.

All right, then. Time to summon help.

Her cell phone was in her purse, and it was already turned on—she left it on all the time to take incoming calls.

She willed her hand toward the purse, reached inside, and dug out the phone.

Got it.

All she had to do was dial 9, then 1 . . .

Her fingers stabbed at the keypad, missing their mark. The keys were too small, her hand still too shaky.

There was another way: press redial. It was only one button to hit, and it was bigger than the other keys.

On her fourth or fifth try, she succeeded. The phone's LCD screen lit up with the words SENDING CALL.

Who was the last person she'd talked to? Andrus when she was at the chem lab? No, it was Dodge, of course. She'd called him from her car, minutes ago.

She hadn't thought she'd ever be happy to hear Detective Dodge's voice again, but she would be thrilled to hear it now.

But he wasn't answering.

Three rings.

Four.

No pickup on the other end.

But this was his cell phone number, the one he gave to informants. He would always answer the cell phone.

Except tonight.

Six rings by now. Seven. Eight.

She lay on her side, fighting for breath, praying for Dodge to answer.

32

Dodge thought he might get lucky after all.

It had seemed like the longest of long shots, but Tess McCallum seemed to have bought the industrial-size bag of bullshit he was selling. He'd thought federal agents were supposed to be worldly-wise and cynical, but McCallum was a babe in the fucking woods.

By the end of the night he would have pinned the blame on Winston, and McCallum would be abjectly apologetic for all the nasty things she'd said about him.

Was there any way she could make it up to him?

Dodge smiled.

He could think of a way. A few dozen ways.

He turned into the driveway of his house, a bungalow dating from the 1930s, perched at the edge of a hillside. He hadn't lied about the view. From the front of the house he could see the full expanse of LA, from the dark rim of desert on the east to the infinite Pacific on the west. If there was any poetry in his soul, it was aroused by that view, at night, under a swollen moon.

Adjacent to the bungalow was a carport. He parked inside, killing his lights and motor.

As he got out of the car, he was thinking of Tess

McCallum and what he might be able to do with her in a very short time. Guilt was a powerful emotion, or so he had been told—he had never been much prone to guilt himself—and he intended to have McCallum feeling very fucking guilty before long.

Thing was, he didn't even care that much about her personally. There were women in his little black book who had her beat in the looks department. But he'd never bagged a federal agent. He wanted a taste of that certified U.S. Prime pussy. It was the kind of memory he could take with him into his old age.

Smiling, he stepped out of the carport, then heard a footstep behind him.

He pivoted, his hand sliding inside his jacket to unholster his Smith .38, and there was a flicker of motion on the margin of his sight, and crashing pain and the million lights of the city exploding before his eyes, weakness in his knees, numbness and confusion and roaring darkness, and he fell on his face and twitched and lay still.

33

After twenty unanswered rings Tess gave up on Dodge. If she was going to get out of this, she would have to do it some other way.

And she would get out. She had to. Mobius had taken everything else from her, but he would not take her life.

She tried to think, figure out what to do, a plan of action. There was poison in the air. How was it reaching her?

The air conditioner. That was how he'd done it, the son of a bitch. He had sabotaged the air conditioner. Put VX inside it, so the outflow ducts would spew it into the room.

With every inhalation she was breathing in more death. It would overcome the antidote, weaken her all over again, paralyze her, kill her right here on the floor.

She had to stop the AC. Switch it off. The unit was mounted below the window, trailing a heavy-duty power cord plugged into the wall.

No way she could reach the cord to yank it out. The distance was only two yards, but she still had no strength, no motor coordination, no way to get there.

Closer to her was another wall outlet, unused, almost near enough to touch. It might be on the same circuit as the AC.

Cause a power surge, get the circuit breaker to trip, and the AC might shut down.

She looked at the cell phone in her hand. Had an idea.

But to give it a try, she had to get nearer to the outlet.

She ground her palms into the carpet and dragged herself forward. Sweat leaked into her eyes. Her heart pounded a furious rhythm in her ears.

She was not very religious anymore—Paul's death had badly disillusioned her about such things—but she found herself bargaining with God, making a deal.

Just let me get out of this, she thought, *and I'll make it up to you. I'll catch Mobius. I'll stop him. That's got to be worth something. A couple hundred Hail Marys, at least.*

She thrust herself forward another inch, using her arms and a contortion of her hips, dragging her useless legs, while the air conditioner chugged, and the fan blades whirred, and the air moved around her.

Don't breathe, she ordered herself. *Once the AC is off, you can take a breath, but until then don't breathe.*

The outlet was within reach now. Slowly she extended her arm, the cell phone outthrust in her trembling hand, and jammed the phone's antenna at the outlet.

She missed contact with the holes. Tried again. No good. A third try—

The antenna plunged into one of the holes, and the phone sizzled with an influx of voltage, strong enough to lift her off the floor and shock her backward. Her fingers splayed, the phone fell in a shower of sparks— and half the lights in the room went out.

*   *   *

She lay on her side, stunned by the jolt. Somewhere behind her, Myron Levine was still talking, and a vari-colored play of light from the television bubbled over the walls and ceiling.

The TV was on a different circuit. But the air conditioner?

She listened.

There was no sound but her hoarse breathing and Levine's drone.

The AC was off.

No more VX would enter the room. She'd accomplished that much.

All she could do now was wait and see if the symptoms passed . . . or worsened.

She lay still. Her hands were numb and boneless. Her legs were sprawled on the carpet in limp disarray. She was panting, straining for breath. The muscles sheathing her rib cage still worked, but for how long?

For a few minutes she was almost sure her symptoms were continuing to worsen, in which case she had been wrong, deluded, and there was no hope. God, it appeared, had rejected the terms of her offer.

Then her chest shuddered, heaved, and she pulled a stream of air down her throat.

She could breathe. Really breathe.

Evidently God had been open to a deal, after all.

Slowly she curled into a fetal pose and lay there, clutching her knees, wondering what to do next.

She couldn't say. She knew only one thing with certainty. She had promised God that she would stop Mobius. And she intended to keep her end of the bargain.

34

Dodge came around slowly, conscious at first of the ache in his head, then of the awkward position of his arms, suspended above his shoulders. He thought of the suspect he'd once seen handcuffed to the bars of a holding cell, and for a confused minute he thought he'd been found out by his fellow officers. They'd gotten him for the leaks to the media, and this was his punishment—to be fucking crucified.

Then he remembered the footstep behind him in the carport, and he knew it was worse than that.

His eyes opened. He was in the bedroom of his house, lying in the bed with his arms tied—no, taped—to the bronze headboard. His mouth . . . there was something on his mouth—more tape, gluing his lips together.

Mobius.

This was his MO. McCallum had told him about it.

But Mobius killed women. . . .

Not always. There was McCallum's partner in Denver.

Shit. He blinked, looking around.

The room was dark, the curtains shut, the glow of an outside spotlight trickling through. Dodge thought it must be around eight-thirty, maybe as late as nine. There was a chance that a call would come in for him. He and Bradley were still catching calls, and when he didn't answer, Bradley or the watch commander would get worried and send a unit to check out his house. The patrol cops would see signs of a struggle in the carport, would come in with their guns drawn and blow this crazy asshole Mobius away.

Sure. It would happen just like that.

Dodge had heard enough bullshit from suspects and witnesses, not to mention from other cops, to know when he was slinging the bull himself. There wasn't going to be any last-minute rescue. In the carport he'd had one shot at walking away from this situation with all his parts, and it had gone wrong and now he was fucked and it was over. Just that simple.

Movement in the dimness. The man who must be Mobius, pacing. He wore a dark windbreaker and latex gloves. His face was barely visible, a shadow among shadows.

"Sorry I hit you so hard," the man said.

Dodge didn't remember getting hit. The footstep he remembered. The sudden sense of danger. After that—nothing. Concussion, he figured. Amnesia. Common in head injuries. The least of his fucking problems.

"I knew you'd be armed," Mobius went on in a quiet, conversational tone. "So I had to subdue you immediately. It was the same with Paul Voorhees. Only *he* never woke up. He was lucky. Luckier than you." Mobius took a step closer. "Are you afraid? Afraid of dying?"

Dodge wouldn't have answered even if he could. The answer was fucking obvious. Yeah, he was scared. He was propped up in bed, his pants wet, a sick feeling at the back of his throat, his heart working double time, his body quivering all over—and this cocksucker had the balls to ask if he was scared.

"You shouldn't be. Dying is nothing. I died when I was eight years old. I'm dead now. So are you. We're all dead, all of us, though we try to pretend we don't know."

Dodge worked his mouth under the tape, as if he could gnaw through it and then sink his chops into Mobius himself. This was great, just fucking great. Not only was he going to get offed by this piece of shit, but he would have to listen to a goddamn philosophy lecture first.

But Mobius seemed to have said his piece. He moved around the bed, and in the chancy ambient light Dodge saw the glint of a knife.

He cuts their throats. That's how he does it.

Fear flashed through him like a punch of nausea, and he released it the only way he could, by shaking his arms wildly, tugging at the duct tape, and when it didn't break, he thrashed his legs, kicking like a petulant kid, and distantly he felt his bowels loosen and he knew he had crapped himself.

God *damn* it, he didn't want to die.

He exhausted his strength and lay quivering on the tangled sheets. Mobius just watched him from the shadows. The guy didn't look very big. Tall, maybe, but not pumped up the way ex-cons usually were. One on one, Dodge could take him, no problem.

Come on, shithead, untape me and we'll see which one of us is the alpha dog.

He tried to force out the challenge past the tape on his mouth, but all that emerged was a grunt, low and plaintive and humiliating.

It sounded like a plea. He hated that sound. He'd

made many men plead, men he'd stomped and pounded, men whose fingers he'd broken and whose ribs he'd bruised, and although he enjoyed it when they begged for mercy, he was always secretly embarrassed for them, dismayed by their show of weakness.

Now he was the one being weak. He shouldn't let things play out that way. He should be tough, go down in defiance, not give an inch.

Should, but couldn't. He was forty-four. He wasn't ready for this. It was too soon. He had plans. He had the money he was making on the side, his retirement money, and what he meant to use it for—the islands, every day spent beachcombing, every night a visit to a different island bar to bag a different island girl. Sun and sand and sex—decades of it—fuck, he was only *forty-four*.

"Are you ready, Detective? I don't like to start until the subject is ready."

Bite me, you faggot asshole.

"Usually I see a kind of resignation. It makes things easier."

Dodge wouldn't make it easy. He was not through living. He would not let this scumbag take his future away.

"Of course, some people simply lack the proper temperament."

Eat shit. Dodge wished he could scream it at him.

He'd never really believed he would die. Never believed in a point of termination. Not for him. Other people died. He was forever. Other people left the world, but he . . . he *was* the world.

Dodge shook his arms once more against the duct tape. The headboard rattled, banging on the wall. The mattress creaked.

"There, there," Mobius said. "There, there."

Everything blurred. Dodge thought Mobius had done something to his eyes. Then he realized he was crying.

They would find him—someone would find him—and he would be dead in his own shit and piss, with dried tears on his face, and people would make remarks and get a laugh, and then he would go under Winston's knife—his second trip to the morgue this weekend. . . .

A gloved hand on his face. Pushing up his chin. He fought to twist free of the hand. Couldn't.

In the other hand—the knife.

Let me out of this, let me out. . . .

Like it was a bad dream and he could wake up. Like it was a TV show and he could change the channel.

"There, there," Mobius said, and the knife flicked—a hot wire of pain in his neck, then something warm and wet, which was blood.

35

When Tess could move again, she got to her feet and staggered to the door and flung it open, leaning against the door frame to inhale the warm, dry breeze.

She didn't know how long she stood there, letting the uncontaminated air refresh her body and dilute the toxins in her blood.

The sluggishness left her muscles, and the flulike symptoms that had been her first warning signs finally abated. She was still exhausted and shaky, sore where her arms and legs had seized up in convulsions, and her heart was running too fast and too hard, but she knew she was past the worst of it. She would be okay.

Looking down, she was surprised to see that her purse was in her hand. She must have picked it up without conscious thought. The cell phone was gone, of course, as was the antidote kit, but she still had her gun, her FBI credentials, and her car keys. She wondered if she ought to drive herself to a hospital for observation, or use the phone in the manager's office to call the police, or—

Thinking of a phone call reminded her of using redial on her cell phone, trying to reach Dodge . . . and getting no answer.

It was his cell phone number, the one he handed out to informers. He would have answered it—if he could.

"He's in trouble."

Her own voice startled her, coming raspy and thick. She'd been working with Dodge. If Mobius had been following her or watching the arson site, he might have seen them together. Having targeted one of them, he might also have set his sights on the other.

Dodge had told her his address. It wasn't far. She could be at his place in ten minutes.

She shook off the lingering effects of the gas, then closed and locked the door of room 14 so nobody would venture inside. Her bureau car was parked only a couple of yards away. She felt steadier on her feet as she walked to it, and when she started the engine and pulled out of the lot, the sense of purpose revived her further.

Speeding down Ventura Boulevard, she lowered all the car windows and shut off the air conditioner and the vents. She thought it would be a long time before she used the AC again.

The night air felt good, rushing in on her face, and by the time she headed up Coldwater Canyon Avenue into the Hollywood Hills, she was feeling almost strong again.

That was good. The night had just begun—it was only 9:25—and she would need to be strong for whatever was to come.

Tess parked down the street from Dodge's house, on a turnout where her car was half hidden by eucalyptus trees. She'd driven the last quarter of a mile with her headlights off, in case anyone was watching from the windows.

The Beretta felt reassuringly solid in her hand as she left the car and prowled past hedges of oleander to the driveway. At the end of the drive was a carport, with Dodge's car inside.

No other vehicles were in sight. If Mobius had come, he'd either left already or parked elsewhere.

Dodge's house was old, small, single-story. It stood on a small, untidy lot against a stand of trees. From the front stoop, the lights of the LA basin would be visible. That was the view Dodge had bragged about.

No lights were on. The curtains were shut, and the place looked empty, but it couldn't be, not if the car was here.

For a moment she wished she hadn't fried her phone back at the motel. She would have liked to call for backup, especially since the queasiness and blurred vision brought on by the nerve agent hadn't entirely dissipated. Maybe she should've stopped at a pay phone along the way.

Too late now. She was on her own.

Both the front and rear doors were probably locked. Most likely she would have to force a window. But she decided to try the front door first.

Quickly down the slate path, the stones uneven from the seismic shifting of the earth in the decades since the bungalow was built. Up the two front steps to the door, then crouching low, huddling for cover in case she'd been spotted. A wave of dizziness quivered through her, another aftereffect of the gas.

Silently she grasped the doorknob, and it turned—

Turning freely under her hand . . .

The door opening . . .

Briefly she was disoriented in space and time, and she was entering the house she and Paul had shared, hearing the hiss of running water in the kitchen.

She almost called Paul's name, as if he might be here.

Then reality snapped back, and this was LA, and it was Dodge she was looking for, and Paul was two years dead.

Probably it was a mistake to go in alone. Probably she was walking into an ambush or another gas chamber like room 14.

She entered anyway, moving fast through the doorway, then stepping to one side and hunching down as her vision adjusted to the space around her.

Living room. Very small. Reflective surface of a TV set, and the faint greenish glow of a VCR's clock underneath. A low shape that was a sofa, and the sharper rectangles of end tables.

The room was empty. She was almost sure of it. If anyone was here—anyone alive—she would find him elsewhere.

She listened to the house. A creak from somewhere in the rear. Wood settling? Scrape of a tree limb against the roof? Or a footstep on a floorboard?

Another creak.

Footsteps. Back of the house.

She crossed the living room, treading silently, and peered through an open doorway into a dining area. Beyond it lay the kitchen and a hallway. The kitchen was barely larger than a closet, and she could see its complete interior from where she stood. No one there. And no water running either—

Water running in the sink . . .

Hissing through the pipes . . .

Pile of dinner dishes . . .

She fought off the memories and the new attack of vertigo that came with them. Her stomach twisted. A greasy, sick feeling rose in her throat, and she thought she might vomit. With effort she forced down the sickness.

Then she headed into the hallway.

The bedroom would be down there.

Mobius's execution site.

Halfway down the hall, a bathroom provided the

only illumination in this part of the house—the fifteen-watt glow of a nightlight. She detoured into the bathroom, whisked open the shower curtain.

No one was hiding there. But from down the hall came another creak—different in quality from the first two—then a soft click.

She thought of the sound a pistol's slide might make as it was racked back.

Mobius had never used a gun, but she drew no comfort from that fact.

If he was out there and armed, she would have to face him. To stay in the bathroom was suicide. He could draw a bead on her from the darkness of the hall, and she would have nowhere to hide or run.

Before exiting, she jerked the nightlight out of the wall outlet, darkening the hall. Then she pivoted through the doorway and jumped to the far side of the corridor. She braced herself against the wall and waited.

No shots were fired.

Still, she'd heard someone. She was certain she had.

Slowly she approached what must be the bedroom, the last door in the hall other than the door to the backyard. Mobius could be just inside the doorway, waiting for her to enter.

Her left hand still carried the nightlight. She pitched it into the darkness of the bedroom.

As it dropped with a clatter, she ducked into the room and took cover behind the open door.

Her diversionary tactic hadn't drawn any fire. Either Mobius was cool under pressure, or he wasn't here at all.

She sidled along the wall, staying low, and felt a light switch poke her between the shoulder blades. The switch might control an overhead light or a lamp on a bureau or bedside table.

She needed light. Darkness had given her an edge as long as her intrusion had been undetected. Now it worked against her, giving her enemy too many places to hide.

She flicked the switch, then swept the room with her gaze as a lamp on a table came on.

The bed and what was on it registered instantly, but she refused to take it in until she had looked into the closet and behind the bureau.

Then another glance into the hall.

Mobius wasn't here.

But he had been.

She turned back to the bed where Dodge lay in his cheap suit, fully dressed, wearing even his shoes, his wrists duct-taped to the headboard, mouth sealed against a cry, throat opened in a gout of drying blood.

His eyes stared, empty.

She touched his neck, impelled by her training to check the carotid artery for a pulse, but of course there was no pulse. The blood had stopped flowing. It was already becoming tacky and dark.

But not very tacky. Not yet.

And Dodge's skin was warm, his eyes moist with their last tears.

He had died only minutes ago.

The noises she'd heard. That third creak, that soft click.

It had been the creak of the back door opening. The click of the latch sliding into place as the door eased shut.

Mobius had escaped out the back while she was searching the bathroom.

He couldn't have gone far.

She ran out the back door, the gun leading her, and scanned the shadowy trees. A spotlight mounted on the rear wall threw a pale glow over the grass.

Moving through the trees, she found herself at the edge of a steep hillside sloping down into a canyon. She looked down, and there he was, limned in starlight, a tall, masculine figure slip-sliding through the chaparral brush fifty yards away.

She didn't know if her voice had come back until she heard herself shout, "Stop, FBI!"

Her cry echoed and reechoed across the canyon, scaring a bevy of birds into reckless flight. The man on the hillside didn't even slow down.

She pointed her gun at him, but he was far away and there was too much darkness and ground cover and her arm was still shaky from the effects of the VX. She knew she would miss, so she conserved ammunition, slipping the gun into the waistband of her slacks as she scrambled down the slope.

She expected him to continue descending into the canyon, but he surprised her, veering to his right, where a second hillside intersected with the first. He crossed over to that slope and began climbing toward the ridge. His movements were assured, confident, and she realized he must be retracing the route he'd taken when he arrived. He had parked somewhere in the maze of cul-de-sacs off Mulholland, then crossed the hills and sneaked onto Dodge's property from the rear.

She was yards behind him, hampered by the lingering weakness of her muscles and her unfamiliarity with the terrain. She couldn't catch up to him, not in time.

But, damn it, he was practically in her sights. She could *see* him, *see* Mobius, or at least his faint silhouette, his progress marked on the far hillside by a shifting wake of brush.

She yanked the Beretta free of her waistband and fired off a round, aiming high, leading the target.

Whip-crack of the bullet in the air, thud of impact

on sandstone, but the figure didn't stop moving, wasn't hit.

From the rising plume of dust, she judged that the shot had been wide of its mark by a yard. She adjusted, fired again.

This time the figure stopped—she thought she'd nailed him—no, he'd only frozen momentarily when the shot landed close.

She'd come within a foot of him. Next time . . .

A scrub oak beside her swayed as a bullet made a soft *thwack* in its branches.

He was shooting back.

She threw herself behind the tree, using its slender trunk as cover. Another shot went off, kicking up dirt and gravel near where she'd lain a moment earlier.

The bastard was armed, and a good shot too—better than she was.

When she glanced out from behind the oak, she saw him disappearing into a copse of eucalyptus trees halfway to the ridge.

The trees provided perfect cover. She had no chance of hitting him now. Her best opportunity was to get back to her car, try to cut him off before he could drive away.

She ran uphill, bending almost double at the waist to form a smaller target in case he decided to pick her off from the safety of the trees. She wondered how it would feel to be shot in the back, or if he was a good enough marksman to place the round directly in her skull—no warning, no awareness, no time even to hear the gun's report—just a shattering impact and lights out.

But she didn't get shot, and now she was scrambling into Dodge's backyard, clear of the hillside, safe.

She kept running, her heart working hard, breath coming in explosive gasps. If there was any VX left in her system, she must be sweating it out, purifying herself.

Fast around the side of the house to the front, then down the street to the turnout where she'd parked—brief, frantic fumbling in her purse for her car keys, and then she was at the wheel, cranking the engine, flooring the gas as she slammed the gear selector into reverse and backed into the street. She popped the lever forward, putting the car into drive, and sped east on Mulholland, in the direction Mobius had been going.

Side street ahead. Car pulling out. Blue coupe. Moving fast.

Him.

It had to be him.

He must have made it to his vehicle just when she'd reached hers.

She gunned the motor, the bureau car bouncing on the road, spraying dirt as she swerved into the shoulder on tight curves. She flicked on her high beams. The fleeing car bobbed in and out of the light. Camaro or Firebird, California plate.

Another rough curve, her tires wailing as she fought with the steering wheel to prevent a skid, and then the road straightened out and so did she, and she was closer to Mobius's car.

The license plate. *Read it.*

Two-two-three . . .

He put on a burst of speed, racing out of the range of her high beams, challenging her to keep up. She floored the gas pedal. The sedan shook, bounding over ruts and potholes, each impact nearly banging her head on the ceiling. She realized she wasn't wearing a seat belt.

Closing in again.

Two-two-three-XK . . .

He swerved left, and it took her a split second to understand that he was taking a hairpin curve in the road.

She spun the wheel, too late.

The road switched hard to the left, and then there was no road, only a tangle of brambly weeds that scraped the hood and windshield, clawing at her through the open windows as she stood with both feet on the brake pedal.

The car shuddered to a stop a hundred feet off the road, on a gentle downward slope that became a precipice not more than fifty yards farther ahead.

There was no hurry now. Mobius was gone in the night. She took her time easing the sedan into reverse, backing and filling until she found the tracks made by her own tires and was able to slowly climb the hill and regain the road. Layers of foliage brushed the car, clinging briefly and pulling free, leaving twigs and briers and leaves behind. Her hair was full of the stuff.

Once on the road, she made a U-turn. The sedan was making a variety of unsettling noises, several warning lights were glowing on the dash, and the left front tire seemed to be going flat. Even so, she made it back to Dodge's house.

A brief stagger brought her to his front door, still open as she'd left it.

She entered, turned on the lights, found a phone. She had Andrus's number on speed-dial on her fried cell phone, but she couldn't remember it offhand, so she called the field office's switchboard. Larkin answered.

"It's McCallum," she said. "I just had a run-in with Mobius."

"You're kidding me."

She ignored this. "And I got his plate number."

"Tess, if this is some kind of gag—"

"It's no joke, Peter. I'm goddamn serious. I need you to run a trace on Mobius's license plate. *Right now*."

She recited the plate number, which she'd memorized just before losing the coupe on the switchback curve.

"I'm putting it through," Larkin said. "Christ, what the hell happened?"

"He killed a cop. Tried to kill me. I didn't get a look at him, but I know what he's driving. Blue Camaro or Firebird, late model. Of course, the plate could've been taken off another vehicle—"

"It wasn't."

"Results came back?"

"They sure did, and the plate goes with a late-model Firebird belonging to . . . God damn it."

"What?"

"Looks like we all screwed up."

"What does that mean?"

"We had him in our hands, and we let him walk. Let him walk right out."

She sank down slowly on her knees, still holding the telephone handset. "Who is it?" she whispered. But she already knew—even though it couldn't be.

She'd looked into his eyes, right into his eyes, and there had been nothing.

Nothing at all.

He couldn't have fooled her so completely. Couldn't have.

But he had.

"It's Hayde," Larkin was saying. "Our friend from the interrogation last night—Mr. William Hayde."

PART THREE

PART THREE

36

Mobius, underground.

He felt curiously at home here, in the subterranean deeps, one hundred feet below the city pavement. He liked the sense of entombment, of burial. He had died once, sinking into the bloody water, a shout of bubbles pouring from his mouth, and he had never really returned to life. It was appropriate that in his simulacrum of living he should find himself interred.

He waited, doing his best to attract no attention. Surveillance cameras were mounted around the station, and later the tapes were sure to be scrutinized, even digitally enhanced. The platform was brightly lit by banks of overhead lights, and he had to assume that the video would be of good quality.

To conceal his features, he was wearing a baseball cap and an oversize bomber jacket with the flaps turned up. On tape he would be a meaningless, unidentifiable smudge.

He glanced around at the other people gathered on the subway platform of the Hollywood/Highland station, waiting for the next northbound Metro Red Line train. Ridership was high on a Saturday night, and on the return trip—the run south into Hollywood from Universal City—there would be even more people, families returning from movies, couples finishing their dates.

There would be many people to kill on the south-bound train.

"We're putting out an alert," Larkin said. "Trouble is, he could be anywhere."

"Maybe not." Tess was thinking hard. "Michaelson told you to check Hayde's background. Did you?"

"Sure. He told us the truth. Used to live in Colo-rado Springs. Moved here to—"

"Work on the Metro."

"Shit."

"It's an ideal environment for a chemical attack. Sealed off from the outside, lots of people, public access . . ."

"I'll tell LAPD to focus on the Metro stations. Call you back."

Larkin ended the call, and Tess stood there with the phone in her hand, still thinking.

She was right about this. She was certain of it. Not only was the Metro a logical target, but it was some-thing Hayde was familiar with, something that had a personal association for him.

And for Mobius, she knew, it was always personal.

At 10:15 the train pulled into the station, six heavy-rail cars bearing the logo of a red M. Each car was seventy-five feet long and had a maximum capacity of 169 riders. One thousand passengers, more or less. It was crowded now, and on the return leg it would be full.

Mobius boarded with the others, choosing the cen-tral car, grabbing one of the few empty seats. He sat there with a paper bag on his lap, looking like any ordinary man.

The train started moving, and the dim walls of the Red Line tunnel blurred past. Other parts of the subway system had been drilled through loose sediment, but the segment from Hollywood to the San Fernando Valley penetrated solid rock.

In the seventeen-mile network of subway tunnels, the Hollywood/Highland station was the westernmost point on the south side of the Hollywood Hills. From that station, the Metro Red Line proceeded northwest through the mountains toward its next stop, Universal City, a trip of a little more than two miles that would be covered in about four minutes.

The train accelerated, hitting its top speed of seventy miles per hour. Mobius and his fellow passengers were deep under the mountains now. At certain points in the trip the train would be nine hundred feet below the surface.

Nine hundred feet was not quite deep enough for Hell, but for the riders on the southbound train, it would be close enough.

Casually he reached into the brown paper bag and removed the device.

It would attract no attention even if someone looked his way. He had wrapped it in aluminum foil to resemble a sandwich. He made a brief show of starting to open it, then allowed it to drop on the floor under his seat.

Was anyone watching him? No.

He reached for the package. Instead of retrieving it, he pressed it to the underside of the seat, securing it with loose strands of duct tape he had left in place for that purpose.

Duct tape was such useful stuff. It bound wrists, sealed lips, and affixed a package of death to its hidey-hole.

Before straightening, he rustled the paper sack as if

stuffing the package back inside. Anyone who had glanced at his little drama would have seen a man drop his sandwich on the floor, retrieve it, and shove it back into the bag in disgust.

Everything was set.

Minutes from now, after the train had reached its northernmost point and turned around to head south again, after it had picked up riders at North Hollywood and Universal City, after it had reentered this long stretch of tunnel under the Santa Monica Mountains—when the cars were crowded with distracted, tired, intoxicated people, people who were heading home early, frightened by the media reports, jamming the train to full capacity—then there would be an outbreak of chaos.

He could imagine it in clear detail—the screams, the bleeding arms and legs cut by flying glass.

And all the while, the invisible, odorless fumes of VX fanning out, entering the intake ducts of the air-circulation system, traveling throughout the train, until all six cars were filled with gas.

A fully loaded train meant roughly one thousand people.

The ones in the central car would be first to die. But others in the adjacent cars would follow.

Not all of them, of course. Some would be far enough away to escape the worst of the fumes. They would inhale a nonlethal dose of the gas and escape onto the platform of the next station in time to rid their bodies of toxins.

Unless the train stopped in the tunnel, under the mountains.

That was possible. The trains were designed to cease operation automatically during an earthquake. There might be other emergency protocols, including one for a terrorist attack, that would initiate a shutdown of power.

He hoped so.

Because if the train did stop somewhere deep in the heart of the mountains, then no one—*no one*—would survive.

Mobius smiled, a calm, almost beatific smile that felt rare and beautiful on his lips.

It was all coming together. Everything was falling into place.

Tess bent over the corpse of Detective Jim Dodge, going through his pockets, feeling like a grave robber.

Well, there was no time for the respect ordinarily afforded the property of the dead. She needed a vehicle, and her bureau sedan was too badly damaged to be dependable. In Dodge's pants pocket she found his car keys. She needed a cell phone also, and her own had been sacrificed back at the motel. She took Dodge's phone out of his jacket.

She tried not to look at him. She wanted to believe he'd been unconscious the whole time. But she knew he hadn't been. He'd died with his eyes open, and the duct tape binding his wrists to the headboard had been creased and twisted by the straining of his arms.

A phone rang—not the cell phone, but a landline. She answered and heard Larkin's voice. "Found the car."

"So soon?"

"You were right about the Metro. LAPD found the Camaro illegally parked outside the Hollywood/Highland station."

"You have to stop the trains. Get the passengers off."

"I know that, Tess. We're on it."

"It has to happen *now*. He has nerve agent; he can take out an entire train—"

"Tess. Chill. We're on it. You're not the only brain in this outfit. Subway operators are under orders from the dispatchers to stop at the next station and empty the trains. Everybody out. All Red Line traffic shut down, all sixteen stations evacuated. LAPD's coordinating it with the ROC—Rail Operations Center, the Metro's command post."

"Any idea which train he took?"

"There's a couple that departed Hollywood/Highland at the right time. Could've gone east toward the center of town, or north into the Valley."

"The Valley," she said instantly. "He'll want as long a stretch of uninterrupted travel as possible."

"In that case, he's pulling into the Universal City station right now. And some friendly folks in blue are waiting for him. They've got Hayde's DL picture, and they'll be on the lookout."

"Then we've got him?" Tess could hardly believe it. "We've got Mobius?"

"If he's on that train," Larkin said, "he's fucked."

The platform of the Universal City station slid into view. Mobius was already on his feet and heading for the exit.

The train stopped, the doors eased open, and his breath caught in his throat.

They had caught him. Somehow they had tracked him here.

Two LAPD police officers waited directly outside the train.

Only two. He might have a chance to fight back.

He tensed his body, then heard the loudspeaker reverberating through the station, and he knew he was safe for the moment.

"This is an emergency," a recorded voice was saying in waves of amplified distortion. "Exit the station immediately."

Other cops were shouting above the loudspeaker's repetitive message, telling the passengers that extra MTA buses were being requisitioned to get them where they needed to go. "Head to street level and you'll be taken care of," the cops were saying.

He'd made it past the first hurdle, but there would be police at the main exit, checking every passenger. They might identify him. He couldn't take the risk.

But he also couldn't stand around on the platform, drawing attention to himself.

Things were getting unexpectedly complicated. But he would handle it.

Nothing worried him any longer. Not even Tess McCallum would be a problem now. She might have seen his license plate during the chase—but it didn't matter.

He couldn't be stopped. He had the power. A power he would unleash—soon—and with it, kill them all.

37

Tess hadn't known what to expect as far as traffic was concerned. Of course she'd insisted at the ATSAC briefing that the city could cope with news of a crisis, but maybe she'd been wrong.

Or maybe not.

Because amazingly the freeways and the surface streets were clear. If anything, there was less traffic than usual for a Saturday night, and the drivers who were out here showed no signs of panic. They braked at stop signs and traffic lights, they signaled before changing lanes, they drove within the speed limit—or at least didn't exceed the limit any more than on any other night.

At first she thought maybe they just hadn't heard. They could have been at a party or a movie, insulated from the news. But idling at a red light, she clearly heard the radio from the minivan beside her, a news-caster's voice talking about the threat of chemical attack. There was no anxiety in the newscaster's tone or in the expression of the woman driving the van.

Down the street she saw a crowd of people gathered around a big-screen television in a bar. As she passed the plate-glass windows, she saw the image of Myron

Levine switch to a basketball game. Someone had changed the channel.

There were more LAPD units on the street—black-and-white patrol cars, and detectives' cruisers in the same color scheme, but lacking rooftop emergency lights. Plenty of cops, but nothing much for them to do. The streets were quiet. She passed a woman carrying a bag of groceries from a corner convenience store, a man walking his dog, kids skateboarding in a parking lot. There was no fear here.

When she shot onto the Ventura Freeway, speeding east to Universal City, she saw only a light stream of traffic moving at a steady pace.

She had been more right than she knew. The news hadn't panicked the city. Its citizens were stronger, calmer, saner than the political leaders had been willing to admit. A degree of risk was part of the package of urban life—of all life these days.

If Mobius had hoped to terrify the city, he'd misjudged matters. Although, she had to add, if he succeeded in pulling off an attack, if the theoretical risk became real and tangible, the city's sea walls against panic still might crumble.

Well, it was up to her and Andrus and Tennant and all the others to make sure that didn't happen.

She parked near the Universal City Metro station, at a red-painted curb below a stern NO PARKING sign.

Let Dodge get a ticket. He wouldn't be paying it.

Crowds milled around outside the station, apparently waiting for MTA buses to take them to their destinations. Some passengers were still filing through the doors, each one briefly stopped by uniformed police officers on a pretext of directing them to the waiting area. Tess knew they were actually checking each face and comparing it with William Hayde's driver's license photo.

Even here she saw no panic, not even any unruliness or complaining. Word of an emergency situation had spread throughout the trainload of riders, and they were responding calmly and reasonably—more calmly, in fact, than the bulk of the attendees at the ATSAC meeting.

Tess approached one of the patrol officers and showed her bureau creds.

"Sorry," the cop said. "No one gets in without Stage One clearance."

"Stage what?"

"Stage One," a voice said from behind her. She turned and saw Jack Tennant. "It's a new wrinkle the Emergency Management honchos dreamed up. Basically you need one of these."

He fingered a laminated card hanging from a strap around his neck. The cop glanced at it and gestured to let him go through.

Tess thought Tennant was going to abandon her, but instead he jerked a thumb in her direction and said, "She's on my dance card."

The cop let her pass.

She accompanied Tennant to the lower level of the station, past a few stragglers ascending from the platform. Every face that slipped by received her close scrutiny. But Hayde's face was not among them.

"Thanks for getting me in," she told Tennant.

He shrugged. "I hear he went after you."

She nodded. "I guess you weren't the only one who wanted me off the case." This was a cheap dig, but she felt entitled.

"I was wrong about that."

This surprised her. "Were you?"

"Never should've kept you off the task force. Tell

you the truth, it wasn't because I doubted your competence." He looked away, then seemed to realize this was cowardly and turned to meet her gaze. "In the LAX fiasco, one of my agents nearly got killed. A female agent."

"You weren't trying to protect me because I'm a woman?"

He smiled. "What can I say? I'm a male chauvinist. At least I own up to it. How'd he try to take you out?"

"VX in the air conditioner of my motel room. I don't suppose there's any chance he used it all up."

"No way. He wouldn't have needed more than a few drops. It was sort of a test run."

Tess thought it was a test she'd nearly flunked.

Tennant was looking her over. "Have you received medical attention?"

"Only the antidotes I self-injected."

"You should be at a trauma center, under observation."

"I'm fine."

"You don't know that. Those the same clothes you were wearing during the attack?"

"Yes." They were, in fact, the same clothes she'd been wearing for the past thirty-six hours.

"You should've changed. Droplets of nerve agent can get trapped between your clothes and skin. You could be outgassing right now."

"Sounds more like a problem you'd encounter after a quick meal at Taco Bell."

"I'm serious."

"I think I'm okay. I got pretty thoroughly aired out over the last hour."

"If you feel any symptoms, report it immediately."

The evacuated train was sitting at the station platform, six cars, fully lighted, completely empty. There was something eerie about seeing it there, as if it were the last train still running in a depopulated world. Mobius's kind of world. A world of the dead.

"I'm checking out the train," Tennant said.

"Not alone."

"My guys aren't here yet."

"I'm here. Let's go." She saw Tennant hesitate and added, "You really don't have to protect me. Even though I'm a woman."

38

At the entrance to the subway train, Tennant asked Tess if she was carrying a cell phone or a pager. "Cell," she said. She had Dodge's phone in her purse.

"Turn it off."

"Okay. Why?"

"We don't need any extra radio signals in there." He didn't explain further.

Tess killed the phone, then followed Tennant into the first car. She'd never ridden the LA subway, and she was surprised to find the car clean and bright, almost untouched by the etched graffiti—scratchitti, she believed it was called—that infested most public transit systems. The seats were upholstered in red, presumably color-coded to the Red Line. In the hasty evacuation, a few newspapers had been left behind, along with someone's vinyl jacket. Tennant lifted the jacket, checking for a package underneath, but there was none.

"If he intended to disseminate VX," Tess said, "he would have tried to get it into the AC." Which was still on, she noted uneasily. She hoped she wasn't breathing in more of the stuff. It was doubtful she could survive a second exposure in such a short time frame.

"That's probably true." Tennant was methodically checking underneath the seats with a flashlight. Tess got out her own flash and did the same. "But there's no easy way to access the AC vents—not without being seen by the other riders. My guess is, he planted a bomb."

"Nothing in his profile or past behavior suggests a proficiency with explosives."

"Maybe he's learning on the job."

They reached the end of the first car and crossed into the second, then continued their methodical search of the seats, the floors, and every cubbyhole and niche.

"By the way," Tennant remarked, "you're clear on that news leak thing."

She looked up, startled. "What?"

"It wasn't you. Well, you already knew that—but now the AD knows it too."

"I'm not following."

"It's like this. When I heard about the leak, I called up an old friend of mine in the LAPD. Got to know him when I was stationed here back in the eighties. He's with Internal Affairs now."

They moved into the central car.

"My friend told me IAD has been taking a long look at that detective you paired up with—Dodge. Dodge doesn't know it, but they've got him down for passing confidential information to the media. Specifically, to this Levine guy at Channel Eight."

"So it *was* him," Tess muttered.

"Yeah. And IAD's closing in. This Dodge guy's about to be in a whole lot of trouble."

"Not anymore. He's dead."

It was Tennant's turn to look up in surprise. "Courtesy of Mobius?"

"Exactly."

"Well, then I guess his problems are over. And so are yours, as far as the leak situation is concerned."

"You say you already told Andrus?"

"Called him as soon as I knew."

"How long ago?"

"Hour, maybe."

"Would've been nice if he'd gotten in touch with me."

"He's a cold fish, that guy. I don't— Whoops, here we go."

He was crouching by a seat. Tess knelt beside him and saw a squarish package wrapped in aluminum foil, taped to the seat bottom.

Duct-taped. Of course.

She stared at it, aware that she was looking at a bomb of some sort, probably not very powerful, but carrying a deadly payload of nerve agent.

"He planted it during the northbound run." Her thoughts came in a rush, her brain pressed into high gear. "Would've wanted it to go off when the train was southbound. Ideally, under the mountains. That would be the longest stretch of uninterrupted tunnel."

"Train's been sitting at this station for a good ten minutes," Tennant said. "Bomb might go off at any second. Safest thing is to get out of here, let it blow."

"Then we lose the evidence."

"We don't need evidence to identify him."

"But we may need it to get a conviction."

"Shit." Tennant looked at the package.

"Can you disarm one of these things?"

"Maybe. I did a little munitions work in Vietnam. All right, get out and let me handle it."

"No way."

"It's not a two-person job."

"Yes, it is. I'll hold the flashlight. You need both hands free."

"If it blows—"

"We get splashed, and we die. That's a good reason to hurry up and get started, don't you think?"

Tennant put down his flashlight, and Tess aimed hers at the package. Carefully Tennant peeled away the tinfoil, uncovering a gradated glass cylinder—a test tube—stoppered at one end, filled with amber liquid.

"VX," Tess said, for no good reason.

Taped to the test tube was a wad of puttylike explosive. A wire extending from the charge was soldered into the guts of a small, battery-operated traveler's alarm clock.

"Standard electrically initiated explosive device," Tennant said. "Alarm acts as a triggering switch, sends a current through the ignition wire—and blows the test tube to bits."

"Scattering VX everywhere."

"You got it."

In the movies a bomb's timer helpfully displayed the minutes and seconds remaining until detonation. Here the clock's digital display merely showed the current time, 10:41. The alarm could be set for 10:42 or 11:00 or any time at all. There was no way to know.

It felt to Tess as if an hour had passed already, and Tennant still hadn't gone to work on the device. "What are you waiting for?" she asked in a voice she hoped was steady.

"Fancy bombs can have a tilt switch or even a radio receiver for remote detonation."

"Great." She was liking this less and less. At least now she understood why Tennant had wanted her cell phone turned off.

"I doubt Mobius would be that goddamn clever. The guy's a serial killer, not a Special Forces op."

"Is that what you were? In Vietnam?"

"Just a grunt." He spent an endless stretch of time

studying the test tube. "I don't see any funny business. We—"

As Tess watched, the clock's LED readout changed to 10:42. They both froze, waiting.

Nothing happened.

"Better get this thing defused," Tennant said. "We might not be so lucky a minute from now."

Gently he took hold of the ignition wire and tried to ease it free of the explosive charge.

"Won't move. Glued down or something. Got any tools on you?"

"Tools?"

"Wire cutters, needle-nose pliers, anything like that?"

She was going to ask him why she would possibly be carrying needle-nose pliers around, when she remembered the nail clipper in her purse. She dug it out. "Will this work?"

"It'll have to."

He snagged the wire between the clipper's tiny jaws, then worked it back and forth.

"Almost got it."

Click.

The wire was cut.

And the alarm went off.

The sudden loud buzzing noise startled Tess so badly she nearly dropped the flashlight. Tennant, she noticed, didn't even flinch.

"Made it by a good two or three seconds," he said with satisfaction. "No problem."

Tess wasn't sure she saw it that way, but she was alive, anyway. And there was one other good thing.

"He's shot his wad," she said. "Used up the nerve agent. Right?"

Tennant shook his head. "Unfortunately, no. From what I can tell, there's only about two hundred ccs of

VX in this tube. Meaning there's still five hundred ccs left unaccounted for."

Tess sagged against a handrail. "So he's doling it out a little at a time. Working up to his big strike."

"Looks that way." Tennant frowned. "And if taking out a trainload of passengers is his idea of a warm-up act, I don't want to see the main event."

39

Tess was still trembling a little as she disembarked from the train, leaving Tennant to remove the disarmed bomb and search for any secondary devices.

By now the station was crowded with uniformed cops, federal agents, and assorted emergency personnel. The loudspeaker finally had fallen silent, but the confusion of voices was nearly as loud.

Amid the hubbub she saw Andrus, Michaelson, and another man engaged in intense discussion near the platform. She wondered what Michaelson was doing here, but the answer was obvious—once the news had gone public, it would have been pointless to keep him off the task force any longer, and probably impossible, as well.

She approached at a fast clip, catching pieces of their conversation.

". . . couldn't get out," Andrus said. "The police are checking everyone who exits."

"Well, he's not in here." That was the unknown man, who had the stiff, flustered looked of a bureaucrat in over his head. "The hiding places . . ."

". . . sure?"

". . . all searched. Lavatories, supply closets . . . reviewing the tapes at the ROC office now."

"Maybe McCallum was wrong." Michaelson, of course. "Maybe he was never on this train."

"He was on it," Tess said. They all turned to her as she stepped up to the group. "Tennant and I just found the package he left."

"Package?" the bureaucrat said. The laminated card hanging around his neck read DOBBMAN, MTA.

"A bomb. A nerve-agent bomb. Don't worry; Tennant defused it." She gave them a rundown of events.

"Well, in any case, he's not here," Dobbman of the MTA said. "He didn't exit the station, and he's not still inside."

Andrus asked him if there was any way to get off the train between stops.

"Impossible. The doors can be opened only by the operator. They're never opened while the train is in motion."

"So what the hell happened to him?" Michaelson asked. "Did he just disappear like a goddamn ghost?"

"He's not a ghost," Tess said. "But maybe there's another way for him to dematerialize. Let's say, in all the confusion of evacuating the riders, Mobius separates from the crowd and slips off the platform—into the dark."

The three men looked at her, then shifted their gazes toward the train, the track, and the tunnels beyond.

"You think he's in there?" Andrus said, as if testing the idea by speaking it aloud.

"That's crap," Michaelson blurted. "He wouldn't go someplace where he's cornered."

"Who says he's cornered?" Tess looked at the MTA rep. "There must be ways to get in and out of those tunnels."

Dobbman nodded. "Of course there's access. Maintenance exits, air vents, storm drains. But he wouldn't know how to find them."

"Yes, he would. He's a civil engineer, and he worked on the Red Line. He's seen the blueprints."

There was a long moment before anyone spoke.

"All right," Andrus said finally, "let's take a look."

The tunnel was wide and dark, with rounded walls lined in concrete and plastic to prevent any seepage from methane gas pockets in the rock. Faint echoes of dripping noises echoed in the distance.

There were two tunnels bored through the mountains, one for northbound train traffic, the other for return trips. Each tunnel, Dobbman of the MTA had reported, was roughly twenty-three feet in diameter and more than twelve thousand feet long. Trains were powered by an electrified third rail, producing 750 volts, that lay adjacent to the tracks. He had warned them to stay clear of it.

Tess intended to heed that advice. She kept her distance from the tracks as she advanced into the darkness, leaving the lights of the platform behind. Andrus and Michaelson flanked her, with four LAPD officers arrayed in pairs to the front and rear. They were headed north. Another search team had gone in the opposite direction.

She should have felt safe, surrounded by armed professionals and carrying a gun herself, but all she could think of was Mobius popping up out of the shadows to splash her with liquid death.

She had survived the nerve-agent attack in her motel room, then the shoot-out in the hills. Already tonight, Mobius had failed twice to kill her.

Third time's the charm?

"What's she doing here anyway?"

The question, as startling as a slap, came from Michaelson.

"It's come to my attention," Andrus said, "that there's a more likely suspect in the news leak."

"You can say his name," Tess put in. "It doesn't matter now. He's dead. Mobius—I mean, Hayde— killed him." To Michaelson she said, "It was Detective Dodge, the cop I was working with."

Michaelson wouldn't let it go. He looked at Andrus. "You're sure he was the leaker?"

"We know he'd passed other things to the same reporter. Internal Affairs was after him."

"That doesn't prove he was peddling the info this time. It still could've been McCallum."

Still talking about her in the third person. She was really getting tired of that.

"Dodge had an ongoing relationship with Myron Levine," Tess said as calmly as possible. "And Dodge knew everything I knew."

"How convenient for you."

"What are you saying? That I'm trying to pin the blame on a dead man?"

"Who knows what you might try when your career's on the line?"

"God, you're such a prick."

He ignored her, as usual. "As far as I'm concerned, McCallum remains an unreliable member of this investigative team."

She wouldn't let this pass. "Sometimes I think I'm the *only* member of the team who's doing any actual investigating. In case you've forgotten, I got you Hayde's license plate and directed you to the Metro. I practically handed you Mobius on a platter—"

"You did?" The Nose glared past her, refusing to meet her eyes. "Then where is he, McCallum? If you've handed him to us, why don't we have him?"

Andrus held up a stern hand. "*Enough.* Agent McCallum is back on the case. Period. And for the record, Tess," he added, "I apologize for jumping to conclusions. I made a mistake. I'm sorry."

The Nose made a low sound signifying disapproval and turned away.

When Tess looked back, the Metro train had receded into the distance. Its headlights cast only a dim glow. The lights of the station platform were entirely gone, hidden behind the curving wall of concrete and rock.

"How far are we planning to go, anyway?" Michaelson asked.

Tess thought the Nose was in an awful hurry to give up the chase. Probably didn't like being in the dark. She hoped he wet his pants.

"Until we find some indication he's been here," Andrus said. "Shoe prints or something."

"Not a sign of him so far," Tess said. She'd been expecting the tunnel to be strewn with litter from tunnel workers—gum wrappers, cigarette butts, soda cans—but it was surprisingly clean. Other than some scattered papers blown off the platform by the draft of passing trains, the circle of her flashlight beam had picked up nothing but the train tracks, the dangerous third rail, and the small metallic heads of the automatic sprinklers installed between the tracks.

They walked on. Now the train was lost to sight, and only their flashlights provided illumination. It was like exploring a cave, but a curiously artificial cave of unchanging dimensions, a cave that stretched forever into the darkness.

Still no indication that anyone had passed this way. Maybe no one had. She could have been wrong.

Andrus got on the radio to the other search team. They had found nothing. The tunnel's dirt floor south of the parked train seemed undisturbed.

"We're wasting our time," Michaelson groused.

Andrus looked at Tess. "How about it? Keep going or turn back?"

"Since when is it my call?"

"Since you're the one who came up with this idea."

"Fair enough." She let the pale oval of her flashlight beam drift over the walls. "If he's in here, he could be a mile away by now. Or he might have exited via a maintenance access tunnel. I guess we should head back."

It felt like the right choice. But she wished she could be sure.

Tess and the others were retracing their steps, nearing the platform, when Michaelson said, "Hold on."

He beamed his flashlight into the gully between the rails. Among the sprinkler heads, its beam picked out something small and shiny, something that could not have lain there long without being caked in grit.

He and Tess and Andrus gathered around the find, while the patrol cops watched the shadows, wary of a surprise attack.

Three flashlight beams centered on the object. It was a cuff link—silver border, black pearl inset.

Hayde's cuff link. The one that had winked at Tess so insistently during his interrogation.

"Recognize it?" Michaelson said.

"Yes," Tess answered. "It's his. He *did* come this way."

They looked toward the darkness at their backs.

"So unless he's found a way out," Andrus said, "he's in there somewhere."

"Like a fucking spider in his hole." The voice belonged to Tennant, emerging from the train a few yards away.

"Spiders have webs," Michaelson said, "not holes."

"I was referring to the trapdoor spider. One of the

only deadly breeds in North America." He glanced at Tess and shared a smile with her.

"No secondary devices?" she asked.

"None. But the one he installed would've been enough to take out half the passengers—maybe more."

"And he's still got plenty of VX left."

"But he won't use it." Tennant stared down the tunnel. "My boys from DC just arrived. We'll go in and get him."

"SWAT can do that," Andrus said.

"When they get here, they can help. We're going first."

"You'll need hazmat suits."

"Nah." Tennant patted his vest. "Just big noisy guns."

"Guns won't help you if he gets close enough to douse you with that stuff."

"He won't get that close." Tennant's face was hard. "Count on it."

Tess believed him.

40

Tess was surprised how quickly things were wrapped up at the station.

It was agreed that Tennant and his men would work their way deeper into the tunnel in the direction Hayde had gone. SWAT teams from the FBI and LAPD would enter the tunnel at other access points, then seal off all known means of egress. The tunnel continued in an essentially straight line to the North Hollywood station—NoHo, to the locals—and that station, as well as the Universal City depot, was now under police lockdown. There were no stations after that. NoHo was the end of the line.

Somewhere under the earth, between Universal City and NoHo, Hayde would be found. Then the only question was how he would choose to handle this final crisis. He could surrender or fight. If he fought, he would use whatever he had left of the VX. In the confined space of the tunnel, with limited access to outside air, he would have an ideal environment in which to release the nerve agent.

Unless, of course, he was already out of the tunnels. He could have escaped via a maintenance passageway, stolen a car and gone . . . anywhere.

And if he was out there, roaming loose, he might not be found or stopped in time.

This was the thought that flicked at her, rough as a lizard's tongue, as she took the entrance ramp of the Santa Monica Freeway, heading for the ATSAC command center, where the crisis managers were again gathering.

The cell phone in her handbag buzzed. She answered it out of habit: "McCallum."

"Who is this?" a female voice asked.

Tess remembered that the phone had belonged to Dodge. "Sorry," she said. "This is FBI Agent Tess McCallum. I'm an associate of Detective Dodge—"

"Of course. Agent McCallum. I met you in Radiology. This is Rachel Winston."

The pathologist. "Hello, Doctor."

"You screening Jim's calls?"

"Something like that." She changed the subject. "Working late?"

"Emergency hours—because of the, uh, well, the emergency. You know, you could've shared more info with me."

"I was under orders to keep quiet."

"Well, it's all over the media now. Anyway, I finally got that information Dodge was looking for. Maybe you can pass it on to him?"

"Will do," Tess said, hoping Winston didn't pick up on the catch in her voice.

"The antemortem X rays from Scott Maple's dentist came through. I've just had a chance to make a comparison, and I can say definitively that the body from the chem lab is not that of Mr. Maple."

"Wait a minute. Is *not*?"

"No question about it. You can have a forensic dentist double-check the results, if you want, but I guarantee my conclusion will hold up. There are no significant similarities between the teeth on Scott Maple's films and the teeth I radiographed this afternoon."

"So it's someone else," Tess said half to herself.

"Must be. Look, I've got to run, but—"

"Could it be someone older?"

"Excuse me?"

"In the X-ray room you said there was a lot of dental work for a twenty-two-year-old. Maybe that's because the victim was older than twenty-two."

"Good point. My guess is, we're dealing with someone in his late thirties at a minimum."

Tess thanked the doctor and clicked off.

Then she stared at the blur of the freeway, trying to make sense out of things.

Scott Maple hadn't died in the fire.

So who had?

41

Into the bowels of the city once more.

The elevator dropped Tess five floors below City Hall. A card key, left for her on Andrus's orders, let her into the air-lock corridor, and a new four-digit code gave her access to the main space of the ATSAC center.

Again she saw the semicircular arrays of computer workstations, the rows of swivel chairs occupied by city officials, the wall of video images. But now the screens showed nothing but intersections in the San Fernando Valley along the route of the Red Line. The central screen displayed the Universal City station, where additional LAPD units and rescue ambulances had gathered, along with unmarked vans that might contain chem-bio protective gear.

And there were at least two satellite live-remote vans. Word of the evacuation had reached the media. Tess checked her watch. Midnight. The local newscasts must be staying on late.

In time with this thought, one of the screens switched from a traffic shot to a local station's video feed. The volume was muted, but Tess could see the words SPECIAL REPORT: SUBWAY EVACUATION. A field reporter was doing a live stand-up in Universal City.

The newscast cut to a photo of William Hayde. It looked like the ID photo given to the police. Someone in law enforcement had passed it to the media— maybe with an okay from the higher-ups, maybe not.

Tess stared at Hayde's face. The cool insouciance of his half-hidden smile. The lift of one eyebrow.

A killer's face?

No one else paid attention to the news show. Everyone was talking at once, and the volume of their combined voices kept rising as each speaker competed to be heard over the rest.

Tess picked out Sylvia Florez of Emergency Management arguing hotly with the mayor and someone from the Terrorism Working Group—or was it the Terrorism Early Warning Group? She saw Dr. Gant pounding the flat of his hand on a table as two LAPD representatives shook their heads angrily.

She pushed into the crowd and found Andrus exchanging words with a pair of officials from the city fire department. Remarkably, Andrus had taken off his jacket—the first time she had ever seen it removed. To relax his habitual formality to that extent, he must be really peeved—or really scared.

"Not your jurisdiction," one of the LAFD guys was saying, and Andrus snapped back, "We're federal. Everything's our jurisdiction."

A turf war. She was reminded that the AD was, in the end, a bureaucrat, not a street agent. He fought desk battles. She found herself wishing Tennant were here.

"Gerry," she said, getting close enough to speak into his ear.

Andrus turned away from the fire department people, evidently fed up with the discussion. "What?" he barked, transferring his frustration to her.

"I have some news."

"So talk."

Before she could begin, the Nose was beside her. "Mind if I join you, or are you still operating on a need-to-know basis?"

Tess shrugged. Michaelson was a jerk, but he was now part of the team.

"Got a phone call from the morgue," she said, addressing both men, her voice raised over the commotion around her. "The body in the fire isn't who we thought it was. In fact, it may not be a student at all. It may be someone older."

"So it's a night watchman," Michaelson said. "A janitor, whatever. Who cares?"

"What if it's Hayde?"

"Hayde is Mobius. You told us so. Remember?"

"I told you what car Mobius was driving. When the plate number came back as Hayde's, we assumed he was the guy. But what if Mobius wants us to assume that?"

"Oh, for Christ's sake," Michaelson said.

She was beginning to regret allowing him into the conversation. But Andrus, at least, looked thoughtful. "It's not impossible," he said slowly.

Thank you, Gerry, she thought.

"He could be playing us," Tess said, wondering if her theory made any sense and if she even believed it herself. "He could have set up Hayde in order to throw us off."

"That would presuppose his knowing that Hayde was pulled in last night," Andrus said.

"Maybe he *does* know."

"How?"

"Say he was watching the building."

"Doubtful. He was getting ready to strike at the MiraMist."

"He struck later. Didn't arrive at the hotel until after we were through with Hayde."

Andrus frowned. "Still seems unlikely. How would he even know who Hayde was?"

"There's another possibility." Tess hated to say it, but both men were looking at her, and she had no choice. "He may be operating from the inside."

"*Fuck* this," Michaelson blurted. "You're fucking crazy, McCallum. Gerry, she's out of her goddamn mind."

"Just shut up and listen to me."

"Do you have any evidence the dead body is Hayde?"

"Not yet—"

"Then why the hell are you wasting our time?"

She looked at Andrus, and his shoulders lifted. "Have to say I'm with Dick on this one." Calling him Dick was a little jab at Michaelson. Everyone knew he hated that name. "The body could be anyone. A professor, a burglar . . ."

"Come on, Gerry."

"I'll tell you what. When we get hold of Hayde's medical and dental files, we'll have the morgue make a comparison. But for the moment, let's not jump off any cliffs, shall we?"

She frowned but nodded. Maybe she had allowed herself to get overexcited.

Or maybe there was another avenue of investigation she could pursue.

"Okay," she said. "Just keep it in mind. Mobius is smart. He's always one step ahead."

"One step ahead of you, anyway," the Nose observed.

God, she'd love to punch that guy. Instead she elbowed her way through the crowd, into a hallway. She thought about entering one of the glass-walled offices that ringed half the main room, but she preferred more privacy. She continued to the end of the hall, past a kitchen and lavatory, and found a rear office with an open door.

The office was small and tidy, most of its space taken up by a metal desk, one of the ubiquitous swivel chairs, and a file cabinet. A fluorescent panel glared down from the low ceiling. On the desk was a computer, and at a glance she identified a high-speed modem.

When she had initiated the bot search, she'd arranged to have any hits moved to her on-line storage service as they came in. She could access those results from any computer on the Net.

She sat at the computer and brought it out of suspend mode. The Windows desktop appeared on the screen.

No password required. She was good to go.

Activating the Web browser, she navigated to the storage service and logged on. The bot had dumped a list of URLs—Web page addresses—into the main folder.

Somewhere in that list, there might be an explanation of Mobius's taste in music, and with it, a link to William Hayde—or to someone else.

Who else, though? That was the unanswered question. It would almost have to be someone on the task force, someone who knew that Hayde had been picked up as a suspect.

She clicked on the first URL in the list and found a review of the song "Wipe Out," which had attracted the search bot's attention because the reviewer enthused about the song's "killer guitar riffs."

The next Web page was somebody's on-line diary, which mentioned "Wipe Out" as a favorite song in one entry and a "cool movie about serial killers" a month later.

Maybe she hadn't sufficiently narrowed the search

parameters. She might be stuck with a bunch of garbage here.

As she opened the next file, her mind returned to the possibility of a mole on the task force. If there was a mole, he might not be the original Mobius. He could be copycatting the Denver crimes. Being an investigator, he would know all the details of the killings, even the signature elements that hadn't been publicized.

Maybe. But she didn't buy it. It felt wrong. She'd stood inside the room where Amanda Pierce had been murdered. She'd been in Dodge's bedroom. She could sense Mobius in those killing zones. She could *smell* him there.

Unless she was going crazy. She'd been battling posttraumatic stress disorder for two years. Maybe it was a battle she had finally lost.

The third Web page was a dead end, as were the fourth, fifth, and sixth. The bot had dredged up the detritus of the Web—fan fiction, chat room transcripts, message board threads. She was beginning to think she was wasting her time.

Suppose there was a mole on the task force, and he was the real Mobius, the original. In that case she'd been working side by side with him. Not just here but in Denver also . . .

But nobody on the task force had been stationed in Denver. Most of them had been in LA for at least the past three years. A few had come from other offices. Michaelson, for instance—

She paused in the act of opening another URL.

Michaelson.

He was relatively new to LA. She was sure of it. But how did she know? She'd never talked to him about his past or about anything else of a personal nature. Still, she could almost remember . . .

Before this, I was stationed in Salt Lake City. Pretty

hot there in the summer, and colder than hell all winter long.

The interrogation. He'd been talking to Hayde.

That was where she'd heard it.

Salt Lake City wasn't Denver. But it was within an eight-hour drive via I-80 and I-25. Hop on a plane, and he could have made it in no time.

No. That was crazy.

She was allowing her dislike of Michaelson to influence her judgment.

On the other hand, she disliked him only because he'd been hostile to her from the start.

Ignoring her. Never meeting her eyes.

Because he was afraid of what she might see? She'd looked into Hayde's eyes and seen nothing.

What would she see in Michaelson's eyes?

She tried to push these thoughts away. She had no evidence to go on. She had to deal in facts, not speculation.

The next half dozen Web pages yielded nothing. She kept opening them, but she no longer expected success.

Michaelson . . .

She couldn't keep her mind off that subject. Michaelson had been the one who found Hayde's cuff link in the Metro tunnel. And he'd found it as the searchers were retracing their steps. Had he planted it as they started their search, then conveniently discovered it on their return?

The cuff link had convinced everyone that Mobius had escaped into the tunnels. Suppose he hadn't. Suppose he'd slipped into a rest room or another hiding place inside the station, then emerged when police officers and FBI agents arrived. No one would have questioned how he'd gotten in. No one would have guessed that he'd been there the whole time.

She was on the fifteenth URL now. A garage band called Killer Elite, whose repertoire included "Wipe Out." Another blind alley. But it might not matter anymore.

Not if Michaelson was her man.

The stupid things he'd said to her at the crime scene—the hostile, sexist remarks—were they evidence of a deep-seated hatred of women? Mobius's hatred?

As she'd said earlier, there would have been time for Hayde to get to the MiraMist and pick up Amanda Pierce after leaving the Federal Building. But the same was true of Michaelson. He could have driven into Santa Monica and met Pierce at the bar.

She was on the third-to-last Web page now. Still nothing of interest.

So add it all up. Michaelson had been in Salt Lake City in the appropriate time frame. He displayed hostility toward her and toward women in general. He avoided eye contact. He could have been present at the Universal City station from the time when the train arrived. He was the one who'd found the cuff link.

And just a few minutes ago, when she'd raised the possibility that Hayde was a red herring, Michaelson had practically gone apeshit.

Proof? No. But—

Wait.

She had opened the second-to-last URL. This one was different from the others. Not a diary or a record review. Evidently a public library in New Mexico had gone to the trouble of electronically scanning old newspapers into digital files and posting them on the Web.

What she had opened was the front page of the

September 21, 1968, edition of the Albuquerque *Tribune*, datelined Alcomita, New Mexico.

The headline read: "WIPE OUT" IN ALCOMITA HOJO'S.

She skimmed the article. A woman, Melinda Beckett, had abducted her eight-year-old son and driven him from Casper, Wyoming, to New Mexico. A standoff with sheriff's deputies had ended with Melinda's suicide—and with the attempted murder of her son.

Her eight-year-old son . . . in 1968 . . .

The boy would be in his early forties now.

The right age for Mobius.

And for Michaelson.

She read further. Deputies said the woman had been playing the song "Wipe Out" over and over on a portable phonograph. An eight-track tape containing the song had been found in her car.

"Wipe Out." Violent death. Insanity. A traumatized boy.

It was coming together.

But was the boy Michaelson? Or was he Hayde?

The article gave no further information. Details about the child apparently had been withheld to protect his privacy.

She opened the last URL and found that it was part of the same Web site. A later edition of the *Tribune*, containing a follow-up to the "Wipe Out" case.

The boy, near death, had been revived in the ambulance on the way to the hospital. After extensive surgery and therapy, he was said to be okay. His name still wasn't given.

But there was a photo.

It showed the boy as he'd looked on the day of the standoff, when he was carried into the hospital on a stretcher. His face was turned toward the photographer, and the strong southwestern sun lit the planes of his cheeks and brought out the sharpness of his staring eyes.

His eyes . . .

In three decades, everything about that boy had changed—except his eyes.

They were eyes she had seen before.

Not William Hayde's eyes.

And not Michaelson's, either.

She turned, half rising from her chair, knowing only that she had to get help, she was in danger—they were all in danger—and then he was there, filling the doorway, the knife in his hand.

He looked at the computer screen, then at Tess, and he smiled.

"Wipe out," Andrus said.

42

The knife came at her fast. She threw herself away from the desk and hit the floor, rolling. Her gun—she needed her gun—

In her purse.

On the desk.

Out of reach.

She thought about shouting for help, but Andrus had already kicked the door shut, and she knew her voice would never carry far enough to be heard in the main room over the bedlam of conversation.

Andrus was closing in.

She kicked out with both legs, connecting with the desk chair to send it rolling on its casters. The chair banged into Andrus's knees. He pushed it aside, and by then she was on her feet. She grabbed for her purse, but he was too quick, almost intercepting her hand with his knife, and she had to retreat. She backed away as he advanced. The office was small, and the only exit was the door behind him, the door he had closed.

No way out.

"Gerry . . ." She could try to reason with him.

Didn't work. The knife sprang at her again. She dodged sideways, evading the blow, but now she was trapped in a corner, with the file cabinet on one side and a blank wall on the other, Andrus drawing near.

He was tall. She had never realized how tall. In all the time they'd worked together in Denver . . .

Denver.

He'd been right there during the Mobius killings. And when he'd left town, the killings had stopped.

She should have seen it. Somehow she should have known.

The knife again. Circling toward her. She yanked out the top drawer of the file cabinet, blocking Andrus's reach. He banged his wrist on the metal drawer and jerked his hand back, then jabbed at her underneath the drawer. She was quick; the strike just missed, the knife blurring past her midsection and driving into the wall. It was caught there, imbedded in the drywall that separated this office from the one next door.

She dived to the floor and snap-rolled past Andrus, or tried to, but he grabbed her by the hair. Sizzles of pain shot through her scalp as he wrenched her backward, and then she was staring up at him as he struggled to work the knife free of the wall, and she knew that once it was loose, he would run the blade across her throat.

His gun rode in his waistband holster, just above her. She grabbed at it, tried to wrest it loose. He released her hair and snatched her wrist, and she sprang upright, jerking him off balance as she threw her body sideways across the desk, slamming his elbow on the desktop, freeing her wrist from his grip, and now the purse was within reach and she closed her fingers over the strap.

He struck her face with the flat of his hand, a powerful blow that nearly knocked her unconscious, but somehow she held on to the purse and now her hand was inside, groping for the gun.

She curled her forefinger over the trigger and squeezed once, blowing a hole in the handbag.

The gunshot was curiously muffled. The purse had acted as a silencer, absorbing the noise. The dull crack of the gun's report was a sound in a dream, and only the hard recoil made it real.

Andrus spun. She thought he'd been hit. No, he was pivoting away from her, diving behind the desk, and she knew he would draw his own gun, and in these close quarters the two of them might easily kill each other.

She took cover by the file cabinet, not an ideal position but the only one available.

Then Andrus was up and he fired twice, not aiming. She ducked as plaster showered her. Then the door was open, and Andrus was gone.

He'd fled into the hall. Maybe he was on his way back to the main room, hoping to take out some of the crowd—

Take out some of the crowd.

She looked at the computer on the desk, still displaying the newspaper story of a traumatized boy who had Gerald Andrus's eyes.

And she knew.

Mobius had never been interested in the murder of random strangers. He had planted VX on the subway merely to implicate Hayde and give himself cover.

The deaths that mattered to him, the ones that counted, were always traceable to the defining incident in his life, the standoff in 1968, and the way it had ended—with his mother shooting him, then killing herself.

He hated her for what she'd done. Hated all women.

Sought to dominate them, to bring them pain, and finally to take their lives.

But not just women. His mother hadn't acted alone. In his mind, at least, she'd been driven to her final acts of violence—she'd been trapped, cornered—left with no escape except death.

They had done that. The sheriff's deputies. Men with guns and badges. Officers of the law. Upholders of authority.

He must hate them, too.

All of them.

And now he had a command center crowded with them—windowless, airtight, five stories underground. A full complement of the top law enforcement officers in the city, along with the politicians they reported to.

A crowd of men with guns and badges, men he hated, men he intended to kill.

He hadn't used most of the VX. He'd been saving it.

For them.

For now.

43

She had to warn them. No one had come this way, so presumably Andrus's gunshots had gone unheard in the main room. As for Andrus himself—he was probably on his way out of the command center, leaving his victims to die when the VX was released . . . if it hadn't been released already.

Tess opened the office door, risked a glance into the corridor.

Gunshot.

There was no sound this time, only a spray of drywall fragments inches from her head.

She ducked back inside, slammed and locked the door.

A silencer. He'd fitted his Beretta with a silencer.

And he'd been waiting for her—she wasn't sure where—another office or an intersecting hallway. He intended to make sure she didn't get out to warn the others.

In the subway he'd planted a vial of VX attached to a bomb. Probably he'd done the same thing here. He could have easily smuggled in the package, left it in the main room.

When the bomb went off and the vial burst, everyone within range would be sprayed with deadly droplets. No one was wearing any protective gear. Penetration of the skin, the eyes, the nostrils would be instantaneous—and fatal.

With only a few drops of VX dribbled into her motel room air conditioner, he had nearly killed her. Now he would release a hundred times as much—in a windowless subterranean chamber. Even those victims who weren't splashed in the explosion would have trouble getting out before the fumes, rapidly circulating, began to do their work.

And all of this would happen at any minute. As soon as the bomb's timer went off.

She had to clear the station. There must be a way.

By now Andrus might have left. He couldn't hang around until the explosion, not if he wanted to survive.

She risked another look into the hall. Across the way, the door to another room hung open. Through the doorway she saw cardboard boxes, piles of equipment. Some sort of storage area.

Had the door been open when she'd come down the hall? Or had Andrus opened it, and was he hiding inside?

She glanced in both directions. To her left, a blank wall—dead end. To her right, several more doors, all closed, with the continuing hubbub of the main room audible in the distance, around the corner.

She had to risk leaving cover, even though in the corridor she would be exposed, vulnerable to Andrus if he was hidden anywhere along its length.

She lifted her gun, took a breath, and moved into the hall with one quick step, crossing to the far side and hugging the wall.

No sound but the distant voices.

No movement.

Except . . .

A crack of light, widening, in a doorway down the hall.

Someone was behind that door, easing it open, preparing to shoot.

On blind reflex she leaped into the storeroom, then shut and locked the door behind her.

Andrus hadn't left.

And now she was trapped in here.

She looked around the room. Cartons, cleaning supplies, a rack of hazmat suits and helmets, six in all . . .

And the control panel for the public-address system. A microphone, a bank of illuminated push buttons, a pair of amplifier cabinets.

She scanned the panel, saw something labeled a voice-storage module with a list of prerecorded announcements pasted below. Announcement One was titled ALERT & EVAC.

She powered on the amplifiers, activated the first announcement, and a female voice, deeper than her own, blared over the speaker in the ceiling and the other speakers throughout the complex.

"This is an alert. The premises are not secure. Evacuate immediately. This is an alert. The premises . . ."

Behind her, the door shuddered.

Andrus, shooting at the lock.

Tess ducked behind the PA console, and the door flew open.

She fired three rounds at the doorway before realizing that no one was there.

He'd shot off the lock, flung the door wide—and taken cover.

The recording continued. From the main room came shouts of authoritative voices telling the command center's occupants to exit single-file, no delays, everybody out.

She shouldn't leave the storeroom, not without knowing where he was, but she was tired of this cat-and-mouse game, so she burst into the hall, gun raised, ready to kill or be killed.

No one was there.

Andrus had left the area.

So what to do?

Make a run for it, she decided, join the crowd fleeing out the door. Leave Andrus down here, if he chose to hide and die. The VX fumes would get him—and if not, he would be trapped, caught in another stand-off, like the one that had started it all in 1968.

She started down the hall, checking every door she passed, aware that Andrus could be concealed behind any one of them. The PA system bleated its insistent message all around her.

Turning the corner, she saw the main room straight ahead. Already it had mostly emptied out. The two LAPD representatives—the ones whose voices she'd heard—were hustling stragglers through the doorway.

And on a chair in the middle of the room, neatly draped without a crease—Andrus's jacket.

That was where he'd left the bomb. Under his jacket, on the chair.

She opened her mouth to cry out, tell the policemen to grab the jacket and fling it away—

And the room exploded.

44

Noise, light, a shattering blast, and Tess pivoted and dived around the corner before she could be spattered with debris.

Her ears chimed. Bluish lights shimmered across her field of vision.

This bomb had been more powerful than the one in the subway. Mobius—Andrus—wasn't fooling around here.

She struggled to her feet and dared a look back.

The main room was hidden in a cloud of smoke and dust and shining droplets that made rainbows in the air. The droplets were VX, and they were everywhere in the room.

She peered toward the exit. Had the last evacuees made it out? She couldn't tell. The haze of debris was too thick.

All she could make out were a few overturned chairs and smashed computer consoles, and ragged pieces of Andrus's jacket fluttering in the breeze from the air-conditioning.

The air-conditioning . . . which even now was drawing in the mist of VX, to circulate it throughout the complex.

The filters were designed to screen out toxins only

from outside. Against a nerve agent already inside the command center, the filters would be useless.

She couldn't exit through the main room. To go in there would mean instant death.

But there was no other way out.

She was stuck in here, and all she could do was wait until the AC system brought the gas to her. It wouldn't take long.

Her best bet was to take refuge in the rear of the facility, as far from the main room as possible.

She retreated down the hall to the last two doorways, the office and the storeroom. The office, she supposed, was a better refuge. It had a phone and a computer—maybe she could get in touch with the outside world. There was nothing in the storeroom except the PA system, still repeating its idiot spiel, and some boxes and gear and—

The hazmat suits.

A rack of them. She'd seen them when she'd entered, though she had barely registered their existence at the time.

She darted into the storeroom, and yes, there they were, five orange suits and matching helmets.

Five . . .

There had been six before.

Then she understood.

Andrus had forced open the door in order to draw her out. He hadn't wanted to engage her in a firefight. He had wanted—needed—access to the suits.

While she'd gone down the hall and nearly walked right into the explosion, he'd been suiting up. Now he was in a mobile self-contained environment, breathing filtered air, protected from exposure. He was safe even in this toxic atmosphere.

And she could be, too.

She grabbed a suit from the rack and spread it out

on the floor, then prepared to step into it. To do so, she would have to put down her gun. For a minute or two she would be completely vulnerable. If Andrus crept up, he could take her out before she had any chance to react.

Couldn't be helped. She had to get into the suit or the fumes would kill her.

She set the gun down, then slipped her feet inside the baggy socks built into the suit. She pulled the suit up around her armpits, then worked her arms into the sleeves until her hands had filled out the heavy-duty rubber gloves attached by gaskets. A row of yellow rubber boots lay underneath the suits. She slipped into the nearest pair.

The suit wasn't heavy, but it was large—at least one size too big for her—and awkward to handle, and she found herself struggling with the thick folds of neoprene rubber. A seam, similar to the closure of a Ziploc bag, ran up the suit from the midsection to the chin. She pressed the flaps together, sealing the front of the suit.

Now only her head was exposed. She removed a helmet from the shelf above the rack. It was not a hard plastic shell like an astronaut's helmet, but rather a loose tent of cloth with a flexible face mask in front, and when she dropped it over her head she felt as if she were enclosed in a bubble. Another Ziploc seal secured the bubble helmet to the suit, and now she was fully protected.

A rush of claustrophobia drained her strength, and for a moment she had a suicidal impulse to remove the helmet. She fought off the fear.

The air trapped in the suit would go stale in only a few minutes. She groped for the battery-operated air pack at the back of the suit and turned it on.

The electric blower came to life, and the suit puffed

up with an inflow of air. Filters in the built-in air circulation system would screen out VX and any other toxin. At least, that was the theory.

The suit, inflated, had swelled to twice its original size. Instead of hanging off her, it was now as hard and smooth as an exoskeleton. She must look like the Michelin Man. The thought almost made her smile, but the smile died when she noticed a fine mist clouding the room.

The VX had made its way through the complex's air-conditioning vents. The storage room was filling with it. If she'd been a minute slower in donning the suit, she would be dying right now.

45

She picked up her gun, holding it awkwardly in her gloved hand. Carefully she tried inserting her forefinger between the trigger and the trigger guard. Couldn't do it. The glove, swollen with air, made it impossible to get a grip on the trigger. She was unable to shoot.

Of course, Andrus couldn't use his gun either.

Over the roar of the blower, the PA continued its announcement. She turned to the control panel and shut it off.

"Hi, Tess."

Andrus's voice, close to her ear. He was right behind her. She tried to pivot, but the clumsy suit made any quick motion impossible. Slowly she turned in a graceless pirouette, an oversize ballerina in a puffy suit. She expected to come face-to-face with Andrus and see the lifted muzzle of his gun.

But he wasn't there. The room was empty except for her.

"Hope I didn't startle you."

His voice, as close as ever. She realized it was coming from inside her suit.

The bubble helmet was equipped with a radio set—microphone and speaker. He was addressing her over the air, from the transceiver in his own suit.

"I don't startle that easily," she lied.

"Don't you? Funny. I could have sworn I heard you gasp. But I could be wrong. After all, I also thought you'd be dead by now."

He'd assumed she'd been killed in the explosion. That was why he hadn't lingered by the storeroom to get the drop on her.

But silencing the PA system had been a giveaway that she was still alive. And he must know where she was—at the control panel.

She had to get out of here before he came this way. Shuffling in her rubber boots, she moved toward the door.

"You've spoiled things, Tess." He was trying to sound cool, faintly amused, but she heard the undertone of raw anger in his voice. "My careful plans have been shot to hell—and all because of you."

"Sorry."

"You're not. But I'll make you sorry. You're not getting out of this. You're going to die down here."

"It's your own future I'd be concerned about, if I were you."

Out in the hall now. Moving in the suit was hard work—like wading through thick silt or operating under the higher gravity of an alien planet. Her faceplate had fogged up with sweat. She rubbed her face against the visor to clear it.

"Not at all," Andrus said. "I intend to come out of this just fine. An hour from now, I'll be safe . . . and free."

She glanced inside the office across the corridor. Andrus wasn't there. The office looked eerily normal, a place of business like any other, except for the knife—Mobius's knife, a knife that had slit throats—still stuck in the wall.

She hesitated, then took a step inside the office.

"How will you manage that trick?" she asked.

"Before long, a hazmat team will enter this installation. I'll blend in with them, leave with them. Easy enough—these suits all look alike."

"They'll be looking for you."

"Eventually—but at first they'll assume I was killed in the blast. They'll mourn for their beloved assistant director, I'm sure. But they'll forget one thing."

"What's that?"

"It's Easter, Tess—and I am the resurrection and the life."

Brave words, Andrus thought.

He could put up a front of bravado with Tess. But he couldn't hide the truth from himself.

He was, to put it indelicately, fucked.

Oh, he hadn't been lying to Tess. He still intended to survive this debacle. He would escape with his life and with the money he'd hidden in a secret bank account when he began moonlighting as Mobius three years ago.

Then there would be a new life under a new name. He had a variety of false IDs similar to the Donald Stevenson persona that had served him so well at the MiraMist.

But he would not have his triumph. He had meant to decapitate this city. He had meant to commit a crime that would elevate him to legendary heights.

She had ruined it for him. She had made a mockery of his comeback, the grand finale of his criminal career.

"That's a hell of a plan, Gerry." Tess's voice crackled over the headset in his hazmat suit. "You must have worked it out pretty quickly after you got hold of the VX."

"I worked it out beforehand. Remember how you

told Tennant that Mobius would start to make mistakes because the VX wasn't in the script? You were wrong, Tess, dead wrong. The VX *was* the script."

"You planned all this?"

"Yes, indeed. In the current climate of terrorist and counterterrorist activity, I knew it was only a matter of time until I obtained the kind of weapon I needed. I've been doing research for months. Don't you recall my lecture on this command center? I knew a lot about the place, didn't I? That's because I always knew this would be ground zero. I had to know the installation's layout—and its vulnerabilities."

"Wait a minute. You're saying that when you picked up Amanda Pierce—"

"I already knew who she was and what she was carrying. Come on, Tess, honestly now. What are the odds of a serial killer meeting up, purely by accident, with a woman toting a canister of nerve agent?"

"Coincidences happen."

"Maybe so. But chance, said Pasteur, favors the prepared mind. And—if I might add an aphorism of my own—the prepared mind leaves nothing to chance."

46

Tess had reached the end of the corridor.

"So you arranged to meet Pierce?" she asked.

"Of course. I'd been briefed on the case. I knew Pierce was carrying a sample of a toxic agent used in chem-bio warfare. I wasn't told what kind. I was hoping for anthrax, actually. I could have had a lot of fun with anthrax."

"You have a peculiar idea of fun."

She halted just inside the main room, surveying the destruction. Half of the workstations had been knocked over, the computer terminals smashed. Swivel chairs lay upended everywhere. The beige carpet was spotted with VX droplets.

At Universal City, she had thought of the evacuated subway train as the essence of Mobius's world, but this was his true world, this hell of rubble and poison mist, deep underground, sealed off from light and air.

He must be somewhere in this room. He couldn't afford to leave the exit unguarded. But the clouds of VX and pulverized debris stirred up by the air-conditioning limited her visibility. He could be hidden behind one of the long semicircular arrays of workstations or concealed behind a pile of overturned chairs. He could be two steps away from her, veiled by smoke and fog.

"Whatever it was she'd gotten hold of," Andrus said, "I wanted it. I waited until she was en route to LA—and then I called her."

"*You* called her?"

"Why not? I was able to learn her cell phone number without raising any suspicions. That's an advantage of being on the fast track to a senior post. People are eager to do you favors. I knew that her phone was encrypted, and that if I contacted her on the road, there was little chance of Tennant listening in."

It was difficult to scope out the room. She could barely turn her head inside the bubble helmet, and the rippling plastic of the face mask warped her vision with shifting lines of distortion.

"And you told her . . . ?" Tess prompted.

"That I was the person she would meet in LA. That our meeting place had been changed. That she should wait in the MiraMist, at the hotel bar."

"You got her to go right to you."

"Clever of me, don't you think?" Andrus sounded obscenely pleased with himself.

No, she was wrong to think of him as Andrus. For Andrus, she might have some human feeling.

He was Mobius. He was the killer who'd taken Paul from her.

"Oh," he added, "and I warned her that she was under surveillance. The evasive action she took the next day, the way she lost Tennant's team—it was all thanks to my timely heads-up. I couldn't have Tennant interrupt our little tête-à-tête, after all."

"Suppose she hadn't lost her pursuit."

"Then I would have aborted the mission. But she came through for me. I picked her up, I fucked her— she enjoyed it, I think—and then, well, you saw what I did then."

"Yes. I saw."

The flickering video wall threw varicolored strobo-scopic light over half the room. One of the fluorescent panels overhead had been knocked out; another siz-zled at half its normal brightness. The room felt like what it was—a cellar—dark and vaporous and claustro-phobic.

Tess shuffled forward, sliding on her rubber boots, trying to avoid broken glass from computer monitors. A tear in her suit would allow the nerve agent to quickly seep inside and mingle with her air supply.

"By the way," he said, "I was still in the hotel room, sitting on the bed with the late Amanda Pierce, when you reached me on my cell phone to tell me about my latest postcard. I was playing with dead Amanda's hair as I talked to you."

Her stomach clenched, but she knew he was only trying to get to her, and she wouldn't let him. "What was the deal with those postcards, anyhow?"

"Just my nutty sense of humor, Tess. I'm a party animal at heart."

"You went to a lot of trouble to get my attention."

"Maybe you remind me of my mother."

"Do I?"

He laughed, the sound harsh and raucous over her headset. "No. Nothing's that simple. I don't have a mother complex. You know what I think of all that psychological mumbo jumbo."

"You always said you had no faith in profiling. You trusted your gut instinct."

"Exactly. And you thought I had no instincts. See how wrong you were? I know more about the dark side of human nature than you could ever imagine."

"You know more about insanity, that's for sure."

She advanced farther into the room. The smoke was thicker here. She was moving through billows of gray-ish haze, lost inside a darkening cloud.

"Wrong again," he said. "I'm the sanest person you'll ever meet. I've always known exactly what I wanted and how to get it."

"Is that why you joined the bureau? To get an insider's perspective on law enforcement, learn what you were up against?"

"You have such a quick, bright mind, Tess. I admire that in a victim. Originally I'd planned a career in the sciences. That's where the name Mobius came from, by the way. The Möbius strip, an endless loop, coiling back on itself—the perfect symbol of my life."

"You're a poet, Gerry."

"Every killer is a poet, because every murder is a work of art. Another aphorism of mine. Anyway, I changed my plans and decided to follow in the footsteps of my adoptive father. You know, I'm sure, that dear old Dad was one of J. Edgar's top G-men."

"Did you hate him?"

"Hoover? Never met the man."

"Your father, I mean. Did you hate your father?"

"I hate everyone," he answered without emotion.

"But him, especially? Because he was in law enforcement? And law enforcement killed your mother, nearly killed you?"

"Once again I stand in awe of your perspicacity."

She moved between the two rows of workstations, not far from the video wall. The exit wasn't far away, but she knew she couldn't reach it without encountering Mobius first.

"So you established yourself in the bureau, and then when you started killing in Denver, you could supervise the investigation. You had everything you wanted. And then you stopped. You were inactive for two years."

"Learned I was going to be transferred out of Denver. Needed to put my alter ego on ice. I couldn't

have Mobius following me around—it might look
suspicious."

"Must've been hell for you, holding yourself back
like that."

"I have remarkable self-discipline. Besides, I was
biding my time, waiting to move on to bigger things.
When the Amanda Pierce case crossed my desk, I
knew I'd found it. I reactivated Mobius for the
occasion."

Spears of light from the video wall stabbed at her
through the fog. Bits of torn paper floated around her
like confetti, glittering in a spectrum of colors.

"You could've used a new MO," she said.

"I wanted to be Mobius."

"Why?"

"For you, Tess. To bring you to LA. You were an
item of unfinished business for me."

Another twist of her stomach. "You killed Angie
Callahan just to bring me here?"

"As I've been telling you, it was all part of the
script."

Angie Callahan, a woman she'd never known, had
died for her. A sacrifice on an altar. Mobius's gift in
her name.

Paul had died in her place. Now Angie Callahan
had died to summon her to LA. She wasn't responsible for either death—or was she?

The fog was deeper now, or maybe it was the fog
in her mind. . . .

Her eyes blurred, and she nearly stumbled over a
broken swivel chair in her path.

"How about Hayde?" she asked, struggling for com-
posure. "Was he in your script, too?"

"Actually, no. I did a little improvising where he
was concerned. He was so ideal for my purposes, I
just couldn't resist. When Larkin told me that Hayde

had worked on the Metro system, I knew he was the perfect fall guy. I could release part of the VX in the subway, and Hayde would be the obvious suspect. He would divert any possible suspicion from me."

She almost moved on, then took a closer look at the upturned chair. It must have been where Andrus had draped his jacket, dead center in the blast. The bomb had blown it apart—casters scattered, seat cushion shredded. The backrest had been separated from the chair, leaving only a vertical bar attached to the seat.

The bar was held in place by a single loosened bolt. Wielded as a blunt instrument, it would make a serviceable weapon at medium range. She had already taken one precaution, but she needed every possible edge.

Closing her gloves around the metal bar, she pried at it. Her face mask began steaming up again.

"When did you kill Hayde?" she asked. "Before or after you picked up Pierce?"

"Before. I lingered outside the Federal Building, followed Hayde and Michaelson when the interrogation was concluded. Michaelson drove Hayde back to his car on Melrose, and then Hayde drove home. I killed him as he was unlocking the gate to his condominium building. It was late. There was no one around. I have to say I took no pleasure in the act. It was just business."

"I doubt Hayde thought of it that way."

"Tess, haven't you learned not to trouble yourself about what other people think? At any rate, I put his body in my car, and later I transferred it to the chem lab."

"To substitute for Scott Maple. What did you do with him?"

"So many questions. It's your inquisitive nature that

makes you such a world-class investigator. Really, you surprised me at Dodge's house. I didn't think you would survive the trap I'd laid in your motel room—and I certainly didn't expect you to anticipate my next move."

"Or see you driving Hayde's car," she said. She had almost succeeded in wrenching the metal bar free. "Which you parked at the Metro station, so the police would find it there."

"And therefore link the attack to Hayde that much more quickly. I assumed no one would look for the car until after the subway had been gassed. You out-thought me, I'm afraid. As a result, the train was evacuated before the bomb could explode. I ought to be peeved at you for that. You didn't let me have any fun tonight."

"You got off at the Universal City station, didn't you?"

"Of course. There was no trouble. The cops who boarded the train were looking for Hayde, not me. Still, I didn't dare exit the station. As the AD of the bureau's LA office, I'm known to quite a few of our boys in blue. One of them might have recognized me. So I slipped into the shadows until you and the other law enforcement types arrived."

"You never hid in the tunnels."

"No, but I did plant one of Hayde's cuff links when we were searching. Michaelson found it on the way back. Another diversion—I wanted Tennant and his men sidelined."

With a final twist of her shoulders, she separated the bar from its mounting. The effort exhausted her. She straightened up, unsteady in the clumsy suit.

"You know, Gerry, just because your life started out badly, you didn't have to hurt other people."

"Thank you for that moral from today's *After*

School Special. But you're mistaken. I had to do exactly what I did. Not that I'm complaining. How many people in this soft and aimless society of ours can honestly say they have a purpose in life?"

"Well, you failed in your purpose. Your big scheme is a bust. You've got nothing to show for it."

"On the contrary, I have one thing to show for it." She heard the volume of his breathing ratcheted up another notch as his voice rose in a snarl. "I have *you.*"

She caught a flash of orange on the edge of her field of vision, and she turned—slowly, so slowly in the bulky suit—turned as Mobius lunged at her from his hiding place behind an upended workstation.

She swung the bar at him, hoping to split open his face mask, but the swing missed, and then he was on her, his inflated suit colliding with hers, the two of them staggering backward in drunken slow motion.

She raised the bar again. He ripped it out of her hands and jabbed it at her chest. The blow felt distant, transmitted to her body by vibrations as the suit shivered all over like the skin of a pudding.

He drew back for another blow. She pushed over a desk between them, blocking his advance.

"I did make one rather serious error," he said. "Paul Voorhees. I was going after you, of course. I knew you lived in that house. But you and Paul were so discreet about your office romance, I had no idea he was spending his nights there. When I saw a bureau car in the driveway, I assumed it was yours. As the kids say today—my bad."

"As the kids also say—fuck you."

The video wall was behind her, a waterfall of streaming images. There was no place for her to go. She couldn't outrun him—couldn't run at all in the suit.

"I'll tell you a secret, Tess. You think Paul was

unconscious the whole time. But he wasn't. He came to, at the end. He watched me cut his throat."

He stepped over the obstacle of the desk, his movements cautious, like an astronaut in old footage of a moon mission.

"Paul tried to call your name. And do you know what I told him?"

He produced a simpering little laugh like the giggly falsetto in his theme song.

"I told him I'd already taken care of you."

His face was dimly visible behind the bubble helmet's visor. Steam and sweat had coated the clear plastic and seemed to be coating the lenses of his steel-rimmed glasses, as well.

"I told him you were already dead."

But through the mist of his face mask, she could see him well enough to read his expression.

He was smiling.

"You should have seen the tears in his eyes, Tess. You should have seen Paul cry. . . ."

She made a noise, probably a scream, or maybe the scream was only in her mind, and she flung herself at him, even while a detached, observing part of herself knew that this was precisely what he wanted her to do.

She landed a gloved fist on his helmet, creasing the visor, and then the metal bar caught her in the side of her head and knocked her down. She fell on her back, her upper body propped against the wall below the Niagara of soundless video. She couldn't rise, not with the thick legs and arms of the suit inhibiting her movement, trapping her like an upturned tortoise trapped by its shell.

"Women really are emotional creatures," Mobius said. "Your buttons are so easily pushed."

She drew up her legs as far as possible, reached along her side with her right hand.

"I only wish"—he straddled her, leaning down, the shaft of steel huge in his hands—"I had my knife. That's the way I wanted to end this."

Tess looked up at him as her right hand closed into a fist.

"You want your knife?"

She slid it free—the knife inside her boot, the knife she'd wrenched out of the office wall and concealed on her person for use at close range.

"Then *take* it," she said, and with one long vertical sweep she slit open the left side of his hazmat suit from hip to armpit.

The suit deflated instantly. A moment later his face mask was smeared with a new layer of droplets.

Not sweat, this time.

VX.

47

Mobius felt the suit collapse around him, saw the mist swirling before his visor—inside the helmet, sharing his air, entering his respiratory system and the pores of his skin and the corners of his eyes.

And he was dead.

He knew it.

A dead man.

But this was nothing new. He had died when he was eight years old, and although the first-aid squad and the doctors claimed to have brought him back to life, he knew better.

There had been no life for him since then. There had been only patient planning nursed by truculent hatred, a secret campaign against the living, a nocturnal war fought on many fronts, with murdered women as the markers of territory seized.

But not life. He'd always known that—and hadn't cared.

But he did care now. Not about dying. About *losing*.

He squinted past the fog of his face mask and saw the knife in Tess's gloved hand, his own knife, and he saw how to salvage victory, even at the end.

It was a knife sharpened on women's throats.

Now let it cut one more.

He dropped the metal bar, twisted sideways, and grabbed her hand, clamping his gloved fingers on hers.

"You don't win," he said.

He pushed her arm slowly backward, toward the seam joining her helmet to her suit.

One cut, one gouge or slice, and whether he opened her neck or not, she would be dead just the same. Dead from the same toxins that were speeding into his bloodstream with every pump of his heart.

She braced her left hand against his arm, fighting to hold him off. Valiant try, but he was stronger. Stronger than she imagined. Stronger than any of them had ever guessed. They had snickered at him, the company man, the supervisor, with his stiff, tidy formality and his spotless eyeglasses and crisp, measured words. He was a martinet and a toady, a politician, not a real agent at all. Capable enough when behind a desk, but helpless in the field.

That was how they'd seen him—while at night he was Mobius, the dark riddle their best brains couldn't solve.

They had always underestimated him. He was not an ordinary man. He was a thing of will.

And with his last will, he would drive the blade into Tess McCallum's neck and take her with him into the dark.

"You're dead, Tess." He grunted, forcing the knife closer. "Dead like me."

Her body strained as she grappled with him. The blade touched the folds of neoprene rubber at the base of her helmet.

He pushed forward with the full weight of his upper body, forcing the knife closer. . . .

His visor brushed hers. Tess's face was inches from his own, separated from his by two layers of clear plastic. Her eyes were big with fear and desperation. She couldn't hold him off, and she knew it.

He was almost there. Time for one last effort.

A killing thrust.

Now.

He rammed the knife home, hard enough to puncture the thick rubber and the throat behind it—

But nothing happened.

His hand, his arm, hadn't moved.

Wouldn't move.

Tess shoved him back. He couldn't fight her. He was suddenly weak, his body useless.

He fell off her like a heap of bedding and lay helpless on the floor.

A shiver scurried through him, making his teeth clack loudly, and a spasm of pain roared up his lower back. Abruptly he twisted around, bent at an impossible angle by a muscular contraction that just as abruptly released, leaving him limp and dazed, until the muscles of his abdomen clutched tight, compressing him into a fetal ball of pain, a moaning thing inside the loose folds of his suit. New pain galvanized his rib cage, his thighs, his shoulders, whipsawing him from side to side. Something spattered his face mask as he shook his head—mucus, runnels of phlegm escaping from his nose, his mouth—he was *leaking*, his insides streaming out of him in a river of snot and drool. His glasses were grimed with the stuff, he couldn't see, he was blind inside his helmet, and all he could hear was the idiot roar of the air blower and a series of guttural noises that seemed to be coming from him.

New waves of convulsions ravaged him. He was tossed by tides of pain, and then finally the tides receded and left him beached and winded, arms and legs too heavy to move, face coated with a wet, gluey caul, eyes clogged, ears deafened, alone in a void and sinking, sinking into the soapy water of the bathtub.

When he looked up, he saw his mother standing over him, the gun in her hand.

He opened his mouth to ask why she'd hurt him, but the question faded away, unasked.

Tess watched Andrus die.

He was Andrus again. Not Mobius. Not now.

He had nearly succeeded in knifing her when the muscle spasms and convulsions started. The VX, invading his system in massive quantities, had manhandled him with ruthless ferocity, and all she could do was drag herself safely away from his thrashing limbs, then watch.

She knew he was in pain, and part of her was almost sorry about it, but the greater part was sorry for Angie Callahan and Paul Voorhees and Scott Maple and William Hayde and all the others.

Finally he stopped moving. His faceplate was slimed with nasal secretions, but she could still see his face, pressed against the plastic, big-eyed and agape.

"Wipe out," Tess whispered, and then she struggled to her feet in the bloated orange suit and made her way out of the room.

48

Tess had never been to Andrus's house.

That this was true of the house in LA came as no surprise. What seemed odd, when she thought about it, was that in all the time she'd worked with him in Denver, she had never once visited his house there.

Now she knew why he had invited no one to his home. He kept too many secrets there.

The media were already outside the house in the predawn darkness. She saw Myron Levine doing a live stand-up in the glare of a portable arc lamp. Levine saw her as she walked up the front steps and tried making eye contact, but she turned quickly away. She had nothing to say to him.

Her FBI creds got her past the uniformed cop at the door. Inside, forensics experts from the LAPD's Scientific Investigation Division were at work, bagging and tagging. Cops and federal agents stood around everywhere, contaminating the scene. Radios crackled and cell phones chirped. A TV was on, showing one of the newscasts. Levine again—she just couldn't get away from that guy.

"Find anything interesting?" she asked the first familiar face, which belonged to Larkin.

"Oh, it's *all* interesting. Hey, are you all right?"

"I'm fine. They got to me in the air-lock corridor outside ATSAC. Decontaminated my hazmat suit, then made me take the longest shower in history to be sure there was no VX on me."

"So you're okay?"

"The suit held up fine. They checked it for leaks. Not a one."

"No, I mean—*you're* okay?"

She got it. "Me, the human being? Well, it's the first time I've ever killed a longtime colleague and personal friend."

"How do you, uh, feel about that?"

"Pretty good, actually." She smiled at him. "Pretty damn good."

Larkin shook his head thoughtfully. "You know, I wasted a lot of brownnosing on Andrus."

"Think of it as practice for the next AD."

"True. I *have* honed my skills. So I guess it's not a total loss."

She couldn't tell if he was joking. She wasn't sure she wanted to know.

The house was a leased bungalow in Van Nuys, a nondescript district of the San Fernando Valley. The living room and dining area were decorated in such generic good taste that Tess suspected the rental had come fully furnished. But something was missing.

"A dog," she said.

Larkin glanced at her.

"Andrus said he had a dog. A terrier. Always talked about how he had to go home and feed it."

"He lied. No dog here. No dog food in the pantry, no water dish, no poo-poo in the backyard."

"Why would he make up a dog?"

"To sound normal." Larkin shrugged. "You know, domestic. But normal he definitely was not. Come on, I'll show you."

Larkin led her past the master bedroom and a small study—rooms like the others, tidy and uncluttered and empty of personality.

"By the way," he said, "I just got word the mayor wants to meet with you, bestow his thanks for saving his ass—and everybody else's."

"The mayor? I should've changed."

"There may be a press conference later. You're a superstar, Tess."

"You'll have to start brownnosing *me* now."

"I already am. Didn't you notice?"

"I did, actually."

It looked like this was Black Tiger all over again—only bigger. Maybe she would put her celebrity status to better use this time. She was tired of idling in neutral. She was ready—well, ready to start living again.

A nice feeling. If only other people hadn't had to die to make it possible.

This reminded her of a loose end in the case. "Did you find the body?" she asked as they entered a rear hall.

"What body?"

"Scott Maple—the grad student from the chemistry lab."

"We found something better than a body. We found *him*."

"Alive?"

"Luckiest young man in LA."

Larkin opened a door to a stairwell that descended into a narrow basement.

"Vegetable cellar or some damn thing," Larkin said. "That's where Andrus kept him."

Tess stood at the top of the stairs and beamed her flashlight into the dark. She saw stone walls, a wooden chair, a worktable strewn with coiled wire and batteries and a roll of Mobius's ubiquitous duct tape.

"He would've killed the kid," Larkin said, "except for something Maple mentioned in the lab. He said he was doing bomb calorimetry. You know what that is?"

"Put a sample inside a sealed container, then blow it up in a bucket of water. Difference of the water temperature before and after tells you how many calories were released by the blast, which equals the calorie content of the sample."

Larkin was impressed. "Very good. Anyway, I guess Andrus figured anyone who knew how to assemble a bomb calorimeter—"

"Could assemble a bomb," she finished. She remembered thinking that Mobius had never demonstrated any knowledge of explosives. "He knew a small bomb was the most efficient way to disperse the VX, but he wasn't sure he could build one without blowing himself up."

"So he drafted young Mr. Maple. Forced him out of the chem lab and into the trunk of Andrus's car at knifepoint. Drove him here and kept him down in the cellar for the past twenty-four hours or so. Padlocked the cellar door whenever he went out. Maple shouted for help, but no one could hear him from outside."

"How's he doing now?"

"He'll spend some time in the hospital. Dehydration, exhaustion, some contusions and cuts from his run-ins with Andrus—or from beating his fists against the door. But he'll be okay."

"Thank God for that." Tess took another long look into the cellar, then switched off her flashlight. "Why do you suppose Andrus kept him alive after the two bombs had been made?"

Larkin shrugged. "Insurance policy, in case he needed another bomb, maybe."

"I don't think so. I think he might have wanted someone left alive who could explain what happened.

He wanted his story to be told. He wanted newspaper clippings."

"Hey," Larkin said, "that reminds me."

He escorted her to the guest bedroom at the far end of the hall.

The rest of the house betrayed no hint of individuality. But this room was different. It had been Mobius's sanctuary.

One wall was covered with a collage of photos ringing the front page of the Albuquerque *Tribune*, the same page Tess had seen in the on-line collection.

She stared at the yellowed sheet of newspaper, then at the faded photographs. Gerald Beckett at various ages, with his birth parents. Later, with his adoptive parents, Mr. and Mrs. Andrus.

Her gaze returned to the newspaper headline: "WIPE OUT" IN ALCOMITA HOJO'S.

"He knew the song might lead to him," she said.

"What song?" Larkin asked. " 'Bad Moon Rising'?"

"What?"

"That was the song on the tape."

"No. It was a surf rock tune from the early sixties. 'Wipe Out.' The same song his mother— Wait a minute. What did you do with the tape after you picked it up from me?"

"Delivered it—" He stopped.

"To Andrus," she finished.

"Shit."

"He switched tapes. Once he had it in his possession, he substituted another recording—one that couldn't be linked to his past." She almost smiled. " 'Bad Moon Rising.' He probably figured Gaines would have a profiling field day with that one. I'm surprised he didn't pick 'Helter-Skelter.' "

"You think it's funny?"

"Almost. In a way." Then she remembered Dodge, and

her smile left her. "No. It's not funny. I told him that Dodge and I had heard the tape. We were the only people who knew its actual contents. That's why he went to Dodge's house."

"His personal residence? Cops have unlisted addresses."

"And Andrus had access to the bureau's computer system—which includes a database of everybody's address, listed or unlisted."

"Point taken. So he, uh, got rid of Dodge."

"And tried to get rid of me. He wanted me off the case before I could talk to anyone. The leak to the media was just an excuse. He had to get me out of the field office—and back in my motel room."

"Which was sabotaged."

"Yes. Although I suspect he did that earlier. He'd brought me to LA just to kill me. He didn't need any additional incentives."

Larkin let out a puff of breath. "Let's face it. He was the boss from hell."

"Maybe that's where he is now."

He gave her a quizzical look. "You believe in that stuff?"

"It would be nice to think there's some ultimate justice."

"He's dead. Isn't that justice enough?"

She thought of Paul, what he had been, what she had lost.

"No," she said. "Not nearly."

The mayor was waiting. Tess left Larkin in the room that had been Mobius's inner sanctum and returned to the front of the house.

"Well, look who's here. The hero of the hour."

The maddening nasal voice could belong to only one person.

She turned and saw the Nose detach himself from a crowd of agents.

"Hero of the next fifteen minutes, anyway," she said.

"Don't be modest. Use it for all it's worth."

"I intend to."

"You know, McCallum"—for once, Michaelson met her gaze—"I had to help get the brass and the politicos out of that room and through the air lock. But when I saw that you weren't with us, I was going to come back for you."

She said nothing. He took her silence as skepticism.

"Really. I was. But then the goddamn bomb went off, and we had to shut the door and get to ground level because the gas was all over. We had no protective gear." He gave a little laugh. "And you think this is all a line of bullshit, don't you?"

"Actually, I don't. I believe you." She smiled. "I don't think you respect me enough to lie to me."

"Oh, I respect you. I just don't like you. No, on second thought, I guess I don't respect you, either. But that'll just be our secret."

He was about to walk away, but she decided to tell him something. "You know what, Dick?" He hated being called Dick. "For a few minutes, I was almost convinced *you* were Mobius."

"Were you?"

"A lot of things pointed to it. But, of course, I should've known I was wrong. I'd seen the artist's sketches of Mobius in his various disguises. He was a man with bland, totally unmemorable features." She showed him a kindly smile. "And let's face it, Dick— there are some features *you* just can't hide."

The Nose blinked, then understood. His hand went unconsciously to his proboscis.

"You'd better hope we never work together again, McCallum," he growled.

"Believe me," she said, "I do."

She could have left then, but Levine and the rest of the reporters were still outside, and she felt suddenly too tired to fend them off. She retreated out a side door and leaned against a eucalyptus tree in the yard, screened from the media by a high fence overgrown with oleander.

The stars were fading. There was a glow in the east. A new day.

The side door eased open, and Larkin poked his head out.

"Tess? The mayor . . ."

"In a minute."

He left her alone. She thought about the story in the *Tribune*, the eight-year-old boy whose mother had gone crazy. She thought about the laboratory in Oregon under government contract to make chemical poison.

There seemed to be no connection between those two things, yet they had come together like the words and music of a song. An old song, as old as history. Insanity breeding insanity, the stockpiled weapons of war replaced by new and deadlier armaments, terror giving birth to new terror. An endless cycle, a loop circling from one generation to the next, returning always to the same point. A Möbius strip.

Sow the wind, harvest the whirlwind. And no one learned, ever.

Yet it was morning, and the sun was rising, and it was Easter.

That had to count for something.

Tess stood unmoving for a long time and watched the brightening sky.

Author's Note

As always, readers are invited to drop by my Web site at http://michaelprescott.freeservers.com.

The characters and plot of *Next Victim* are purely fictional, but the facilities, agencies, and procedures described are based on fact. The underground ATSAC command center in downtown Los Angeles does exist, but the installation is off-limits and highly secret. My depiction of it is based on the few available details, embellished by my research into similar installations elsewhere.

VX nerve agent is real, as are the antidote kits used against it and the emergency procedures initiated in the event of a chemical attack. Large stockpiles of VX remain in existence at several military bases, including the Umatilla depot in northeast Oregon. Officially the U.S. government no longer manufactures VX and will have disposed of its remaining inventory by 2005. A secret program to make new reserves of VX is my fictional invention—though perhaps not a wholly implausible one, given the realities of war in the twenty-first century.

I began writing this book before the terrorist attacks of September 11 and completed it afterward. By the time I finished, the story was more timely and less far-fetched than I'd ever wanted it to be. Throughout this process, I received valuable and generous assistance from my editor, Doug Grad, and my agent, Jane Dystel. Special thanks to them—and to everyone else who offered me advice and help, as well as encouragement and reassurance in these difficult times.

Michael Prescott is the author of four previous novels of suspense, including two *New York Times* bestsellers. He is currently working on his next novel.

You can contact Michael Prescott at his Web site: www.michaelprescott.freeservers.com